SAOIRSE BERGER'S BOOKISH LENS IN LA LA LAND

Nicole Schubert

Earnest Parc Press

For my mom and dad
and all the other beautiful creators of magic
+ the assistant editors

Author's Note:

I used to be an apprentice film editor. One studio I worked at had an editing building with a second-story walking bridge that led to a screening theater building with a tiny bathroom and sink where I cleaned the coffee pot every morning. This editing building inspires where Saoirse works, even though it may not be the same setup anymore. Likewise all spots around L.A. are inspired by real and imagined locations.

Also, here are a few editing and bookish terms to bring you into Saoirse's world.

Editing terms to know:
Cutting room = editing room
Cutting = editing
Shoot/shooting = to film/filming, whether action or still photography
Shot = something filmed, whether action or still
Footage = filmed action, cut together or not
NG = not good
CU = close up camera angle
BG = background
POV = point of view
PA = production assistant
Show = old school Hollywood term for feature film (*What show are you on?* ...instead of *What movie are you working on right now?*)
The lot = studio grounds
Temp dub = temporary audio mix of music, dialogue, sound effects for work-in-progress screenings
Stage = sound stage for audio mix to a giant movie-theater-size screen
On location = filming out of town

Bookish terms to know:
Bookish = relating to books/reading
Bookstagrammer = someone that posts about books on IG/Insta
Booktuber = someone with a video channel about books
#bookstagram = hashtag for bookish IG posts
TBR = books **to be r**ead featured in video or post
Book haul = recently acquired books featured in video or other posting
Book crate = bookish goodies—books, candles, swag—mailed in cute package like wine or cheese club
Reading slump = reading burnout

This diary belongs to: Saoirse* Delphine Berger

Jan 31, 18th Birthday Eve

18th Birthday Hoorays: For Successful Launch into Adulthood & Happiness as TRUE HONEST SELF... and bc I need LOVE too!

1. Keep head up and be positive so you're ready when door opens and you can jump through.
2. Go to college in fall even if you applied to all the wrong ones.
3. Keep up BLGirl until fall/college (IG AND booktube) with Sadie, even if in reading slump.
4. Be happy for Deva, River and Sadie for finding love, even if you have none.
5. Take action to get noticed by right person (Leo!) w/happy smiles and doing cute, fun things at work.
6. Beware of hyper-romantic fantasy mind and falling for stupid hotties when bored.
7. Trim ends of hair regularly.
8. Always think independently/outside box to stay out of sheep herd in shiny sparkly fabulousness.
9. Be nice to fam and never show annoyance with them no matter what, even when super irritated.
10. Support Mom with her cheese endeavor.
11. Never tamper with Stupid Jake's gaming superstation (he's 12!) but do call him stupid names in here, like Mr. Griffin/aka Family Guy and Stupid Jake, to lessen irritation.
12. Redecorate living room bc Mom's too busy w/cheese, even tho she used to be a set designer and wowed Dad w/bold choice of sofa on student film they met on.
13. Pretend you don't know how stupid Dad looks in his cowboy boots and bald head.

14. Be proud you stood up to Aunt Lauren and are doing gap year PA job with Unc Unc instead of her.
15. Write diary pages daily to clear out overthinking headspace and reign in romantic stupidity.
16. Do not call self names. Or pick at eyebrows when nervous. Or obsess over aubergine nose.
17. Act normal around Leo Landis no matter how hot he is to nurture normal friendship and normal deep connection on soul creative-purpose level. Do NOT go by his cutting room incessantly to say hi. DO flirt but in professional friend-like creative way. Sexy, talented, older/mature (23), inspiring, cinema genius he may be but long-distance relationship w/Yale gf going on 6 months. He's not breaking up w/her! Even if super friendly! DO NOT THINK THIS IS SOMETHING AND YOU FINALLY FOUND TRUE LOVE!
18. Be on high alert so when opportunity for action and love arrives, you will notice. Hooray, Saoirse*!

*That's Saoirse, Diary, as in SEER-SHUH, like Saoirse Ronan in Lady Jane (love that movie!), tho she says SIR-SHUH, which is wrong, per the Irish, which I'm not.

Friday, February 1 (birthday 18)

18 Hoorays status. Pages read: 0. Nervous eyebrow pulling: at least five, ugh! The outside right part is totally gone. Hate self. No control. Why do I do this??? Photos taken: five gazillion. Posted: 2 (t. good control, no overposting, BookishLens fans happy, deleted the rest).

Santa Monica, my room over garage, 5:00 p.m. I know I shouldn't care, but I do. Not one relevant person has said *Happy Birthday*, just Mom and Dad. Dad called from Vancouver on location and sang with crew (badly but sweet). Mom left note: *Happy BDay! My girl is 18! I love you so much! And am so proud! See you at Aunt Lauren's tonight. Will celebrate you! She has a surprise and is making your favorite raspberry cheesecake. xox*

Gross. I love that cheesecake. Why is Mom so happy? Could it really be this stupid fromage business? Why can't I be that happy?

Did see Leo today. Wishing he knew it was birthday and whisked me off for romantic-friend birthday celebration lunch. But that is fantasy. Reality consisted of failed normal-friend connection attempt combined with awkward bagel moment after.

First, saw him when walking slowly over bridge to other building to clean coffee pot. Have been alone in cutting room all week with nothing to do but answer phones. Everyone else is on mixing stage for Unc P's temp dub, which sounds great btw, and I'm sure the exec screening Monday will be amazing.

Leo was standing below bridge, facing parking lot, hands in pocket, looking deep in thought and in chartreuse blazer and bolo tie. So hot!

I yelled down, "Hey, Leo!"

No response.

Did it two more times.

A platinum-and-pink-haired girl on a bench pointed up at me.

"Someone's trying to say hi." Beautiful. Ponytail on top of head. High-waisted wide-legged pants. Fluttery blouse. All business. Oh my god, was it Isla? Gordon-Ferraro? His girlfriend?! Why was she here? She goes to Yale!

Leo looked up. I waved awkwardly. He waved without really looking and kept on *mmmhmm*-ing into the earbud mic, turning away. I swear I didn't see the earbuds. The other person must've been doing all the talking. Isla—(googled, it's her)—sat back on bench looking at phone. Neither of them had any clue about my cheerful enthusiasm and authentic desire to connect because I just know we would all be amazing friends. No, it was total humiliation of invisibility.

And how was I supposed to know he was on the phone?!

I went back to the cutting room to comfort my cheerful wanting-to-connect heart. Made coffee and dove into pre-stage-meeting bagels they left for my peon paid-intern ass. Just as I shoved in a giant cream-cheese-covered bite, Leo poked his head in.

Me mouthful panic.

"Hi." His eyes twinkled, amused by my bagel bouche. "Is Peter here?"

Finally, my moment to shine like a beacon of notice-me light. Instead bagel crumbled onto floor and blew out between us as I tried to explain, "...age. Chhhage!" I pointed westward in direction of the mixing stage, which is all the way over at Warner Hollywood and not even on the lot.

He laughed. "I'll call him. Thank you," like maybe he was charmed. And then I swear he paused and looked at me with super-charm intensity. Like super intense and charming. Like our eyes locked and he was amused by me and seeing me and liking me and noticing me more than usual for the first time! What did it mean? A step toward deeper friendship connection?

I smiled back through the bagel as he said, "Nice horse race," about the pink cutout-cardboard horses on the wall that I made for Jena (first assistant editor), and left.

It was wildly exciting. And he noticed the horse race! Of Jena's dating life! That I made! Which is cute and fun! And shows off said fun cuteness with fun-and-clever one-horse-per-guy unique standout adult creativity, cheering up cutting room and first assistant editor with humor and play re morbid reality of dating life with suitors represented by pink horses taking the lead or falling back constantly and constant search for top horse to actually reach winner's circle. Miserable. But fun. And he saw!

Though now feeling like circus-bagel clown, yearning for friendship and more of his big Texas-Montana charm and smile and bonding with his rapid-fire Tarantino-esque mind, talent and picturesque work, not to mention all the idle studio-lot editing-building chatter and sweet hellos we have as we pass in the hallway or as I pass by his open cutting-room door constantly. Which is why I love him in the first place—the sweet hellos, not me passing by the open door repeatedly throughout the day.

But HE HAS A GIRLFRIEND. Who is in town! GET OVER IT.

Must Hooray-focus on happiness of cutting room instead. Internship is super opportunity. As official adult, can appreciate super-talented and broodingly cool Unc P, even if married to equally talented and overbearing Aunt Lauren. He is an uncle who gave me a cool job (w/me impressing editor Mike and Jena in interview) next to cool directors, like starboy film-prodigy darling Leo. Unc understands me and appreciates that I graduated early and have a gap-year job that's helping me figure out my life. Even if being next to Leo sometimes feels like a negative feeding ridiculous fantasy mind. Ignore fantasy mind. He actually came by and noticed you and found you interesting after initiating with bridge hello. This is an excellent start THAT IS REALITY.

Ignore that he doesn't know it's your birthday. How could he? And other people do. Like Deva and River. And next Friday we'll celebrate at Deva's to launch me into adulthood with friendship encouragement and hoorays. Also, she'll sneak alcoholic bevies. We'll sip. And River will blast our trembling ears w/TMI about his love for Hot Steve. Am getting better at hiding mortification and hand sweating that occurs during River descriptions of intense passion. Maybe a sign of adulthood? Still, how am I the only one of us still single? Who's never had sex? Not that I'm t. ready for that. Or want that. Am I? Do I? What do I want? Would I sleep with LL? But still.

Reread the friggin' 18 Hoorays, SEEEER-SHUH! Forget Leo Landis fantasy! Find something positive!

5:50 p.m. K just checked IG. ClydeDogBoy comes through again. Why does he make me feel so normalized? Like all cells are lining up? Even if I've only known him a month. If messaging on IG counts.

This morning he wrote "Cool px" on my birthday morning shot of light on water of tulip stems.

Then he wrote his questions of the day in private message: *What's your take on love? How's your day so far?*

LOL anonymous weirdo. I seriously wonder who he is. But also am happy it's anonymous. Want to keep it so. Easy. No pressure. I like easy. Especially bc IRL feels t. pressurized.

My reply: *Love is beauty. Day weird. You?*

Yeah, day will probably continue to be weird. Sadie informed me Aunt Lauren's plotting for me to meet her new *project* tonight at birthday celebration: Hector Rojas, "Latino," per AL (but what if he wants to be LatinX? Grrr! The pressure to proper-speak is annoying, as is the fact that she labeled him in the first place), high school senior, artist. As I label him. Yes, I see that, Diary. He got picked by AL's nonprofit to paint a mural, together with two girl artists (Nia from Sadie's school & Ellie).

I know that sounds mean, "project," but I can't stand it. Nor do I have to like it. Or any of AL's benefactoring students into upper-middle-class-do-good bliss. Who is she helping here? And who needs her philanthropic madness that gives her life meaning? Shut up, Saoirse! They're happy. You're just jealous you're not making street art, even if you don't make street art. Crap. And leave Hector Rojas out of your annoyance with AL! He's in the art thing THAT YOU LOVE—Santa Monica Street Art Collective. He paints art on walls. She pays for it. It beautifies the city. You like beauty. You took photos of that beauty last month. The mural she paid for. Because you love it. And you met ClydeDogBoy because you took those photos!!!

Your EGO IS HUGE, RAGING LIKE A BANSHEE!

ClydeDogBoy wrote back: *Love is beauty is a kaleidoscope of joy.*
Some days are just weird. That's ok. My day good. Esp after
Clydesdale bath. He smells nice.
Clydesdale is his gigantic dog in all his posts, covering his face so
I don't know what DogBoy looks like. Like me, he never shows his
face. Here's what I do know about CDB that makes me assume he's
18 and a decent person and solid friend:

1. He loves his Bernese Mountain Dog and his Bernese loves him.
   How do I know? Clyde lounges on top of him, obscuring him in
   all px. And dogs know if someone's a good person.
2. He lives in L.A. with his mom and 'lil bro Mateo. Half the time
   they're with their dad. They seem happy and nice. He only posts
   his family and Clyde, not himself. But still.
3. He goes to some giant high school and is graduating this year per
   cool artsy photo of lockers through people in hall.
4. When at his dad's w/step mom and toddler twins, the Abuelita is
   there too and likes him, and he likes her. Another good sign.
5. He's a good big bro. See Mateo w/teasy captions. People only
   tease those they love.
6. The mom (Ofelia) is strict but w/humor. CDB posted her yelling
   at him and she replied w/a smile. She has big, black curly hair
   like mine. Also, they have a cat. She barely posts, just hippy
   spiritual quotes.
7. He's into art. See locker shot again. Also, someone paints Clyde
   on walls. Most of his page is Clyde art or actual Clyde. Plus, he
   shoots street art a lot, hence him finding me on #lastreetart and
   messaging me and us having IG art-love connection.

Seems real. I wrote back: *Clyde looks great today; glad he smells*
nice. You're right, weirdness will pass. Thx, Dog.
He wrote: *Well, happy day whatever it is. At your service with a*
BigDog high five. Go get 'em, Tiger.
See, this is why I love this weird friendship. Anonymous. Don't
feel judged. Esp by my outsides. I suppose he could think I'm Sadie if
he saw a BLGirl vid. But that seems unlikely. No 18-year-old

DogBoy is gonna be into BookTube and videos about books, even if Sadie is stunning and sweet and an amazing actress, covering up my self-butchered-eyebrowed camera shyness.

So, yeah, I like that me and DogBoy keep it light. No pressure to be someone else. Or be defined by how I look or where I go to school. Or don't go. Or where I'm going next year. Where am I going next year? Whatever.

Me: *Thx, BigDog. Off to bask in my own kaleidoscope of love. Enjoy the good-smelling fluff ball.*

That's what I wrote. It felt great, even if *fluff ball* was total dork. He doesn't seem to care.

6:30 p.m. Almost leaving for Aunt Lauren's. Sadie texted to be sure I'm coming. AL must've told her to. She reiterated about this Hector guy and how her mom thinks I'll love him. Ugh. And how it'd be "amazing and fortuitous" for me to use my "aesthetically pleasing and unforgiving photography and blogging acumen to photograph Hector's art once it's done." For her fundraising brochure.

Expecting misery. Why is AL doing this? Because me and this Hector person both like art? Because she feels sorry for me and thinks I need help w/love so I'm not alone? Which may be true. Because it makes her feel good to help? What if she asks me to do tricks, like when me and Sadie were eight and recited Rilke for her Friday night salon? And Mom thought it was *a bit showy* but secretly loved it. And Dad said nothing bc he's not a big convincer, even though he thought it was showy too and that Sadie and I shouldn't be treated like circus lions. Maybe that's why he's a 40-something balding film editor in cowboy boots. They give him confidence. Make him more assertive. Hey! How about a cowboy-western book series for BLGirl?!!! Yes! Genius! Let's do it!

Also must stop being so hard on Aunt Lauren. Sadie did poems too. And now look at her with her photographic memory and soon-to-be-Academy-Award-winning acting career. Maybe that's why we're having the party tonight. Yes! Sadie's film wrap! And Mom's delusional and thinks it's for me. I don't have to be the center of attention! Hooray! I hate being the center of attention. Feel better already.

18 Hoorays working. Keeping focused on the positive.

Back home after Svenssons', 10:00 p.m. Yuck. Maybe I'm just not a very nice person. Maybe the gods are punishing me for rejecting AL's help. She means well, and I don't know why I judge her so harshly.

Also, the only good thing going for me just blew up in my face.

Here's what happened:

Arrived 15 minutes late due to traffic between San Vincente and Sunset. AL didn't even say anything except, "Happy Birthday, gorgeous, brilliant Saoirse Delphine Berger, my favorite niece," when she opened the newly painted red door.

"Only niece. You painted the door."

"Best niece ever," she added, "Good feng shui," and grabbed me and kissed and hugged me, like a normal, loving aunt who adores you. And invites you an hour early because you're always late. Controlling? Yes. Okay? Also, yes. And it's nice that she always remembers my birthday. Plus, their house is comfy. They haven't let it go due to over-busy life like Mom starting new cheese biz who has stopped cleaning up around Stupid Jake's gaming console and says, "Let him reap the consequences of his mess—he'll clean it up eventually." Also, AL and UP are v. generous.

Sadie, with new adorable short haircut, stepped away from arranging flowers—tulips—and plates and dishes for people to help themselves (her usual Friday night job) and cheek-kissed me too. "Enjoy the two months of being older, Cous."

God, she's so beautiful. No makeup. Green eyes glistening. Adorable light-brown hair, only slightly curly, unlike mine, which'll never go anywhere near straight. And in a dress. Who wears dresses? Orange. Simple. She doesn't need decoration. I'm jealous and happy at the same time bc I get to adore her and look at her often. While I hide behind hipster-streetwear stupidity. Why? To look cool and not draw attention? To make self invisible but seen? Because I actually like it? Who knows!

Nick waved from the kitchen bar, munching on bread sticks. "Happy Birthday, Cous."

"Everybody should be here at eight," Aunt Lauren said as she straightened the strap of my overalls and snuck in, as if a totally innocent question, "How was the stage?" Far from innocent.

Sadie and Nick tensed. Clearly this was about AL getting intel about the movie/mixing stage that Unc wasn't telling her.

"Great," I said.

"Great," she smiled, not thrilled with the short answer but backing off, thank god! And tg for Unc P's privacy rule: No talking about the movie to anyone, even AL, even if she's the writer/producer. His office and the cutting room are his sacred spaces. I respect that. The rule goes for Mike and Jena too to protect UP from the nosey studio and press. Maybe if UP were more confident, he wouldn't need the rule. Or maybe it's because AL is so nosey. And meddling. In everything!

Mom says AL and UP's drama is why Sadie and Nick are turning out to be such good actors. And why AL and UP are so good at what they do. And why Dad is so calm and responsible—to balance out his sister. Our Berger side really is boring, while the Svenssons are exciting and welcoming. High highs, low lows.

AL changed the subject, "I made your favorite raspberry cheesecake and Sadie's chocolate mousse so we can celebrate both of your successes."

My birthday isn't really a success for me, more for my parents. Though me turning 18 and being awkward on the outside and into a lot of things and master of none and alone and not wanting to go to Columbia or maybe any other college bc I applied to all the wrong ones due to insane romantic book fantasy, thinking I wanted to be a writer, and panicking about it completely and belonging nowhere, may not be a success for them either. But I knew what she meant.

"And I invited someone I really want you to meet." AL beamed. I braced myself. "Hector Rojas, one of my new artists. He's at SAMO. You'll like him. And I was thinking we can start that website for the Collective and you can blog about the art. Since you're so good at writing."

Blerg.

Sadie laughed silently. That helped.

"He's really quite handsome and charming as well. And I think he's going places."

Nick groaned.

"What?" AL said.

Nick shook his head.

AL wasn't going to let it lie. "No, I heard that, Nick. Just say it."

"You have no idea what he wants. Maybe he paints for fun."

"Fair enough," AL acquiesced. It's nice that sometimes she admits she's wrong, even if briefly. "But seriously, Saoirse, I want you to collaborate with me on this. Columbia will love it. Or wherever you go. Or work. In the future."

Why did she care so much about my future? And what did it even matter in the grand scheme of the cosmos, spinning out like a magnetic, magical top, attracting things in, then exploding out into a big, fat, beautiful heart of a universe, hugging us with love and dimensions humans can't fathom? "Oh, right, yeah, I could see that," I said. Cowardly!

"And he's LatinX."

Nick groaned again and shoved an earbud in, disappearing into his music as he set the table.

"What?" AL said, bringing over plates, getting in his face. "It gives him a different perspective. Gives *us*, his audience, a different perspective."

"Since when are you into street art? Like *actually* into it rather than trying to *save the arts*?"

"I'm just saying, our country needs more artists like him right now and Nia and Ellie–women, in high school, giving us female perspective—and I think Saoirse could help them and this organization succeed."

Perennial politisation. Blerg.

"Mom, leave Saoirse out of it!" Sadie defended. "No one wants to talk about art at a party!"

"Everyone likes to talk about art, and I'm sure it can't hurt to meet him. Here, garlic and bread to start." Aunt Lauren makes the best roasted-garlic/olive oil spread. Super comforting. And for a minute, she let her causes go and I felt like I belonged there. They're my family. Aunt Lauren's my godmother and cares and loves me and somehow shows up just as much as Mom and Dad. Not that Mom and Dad aren't there for me, but AL is just in your face and opinionated while Mom tells me to figure stuff out on my own. Though sometimes she does try to get her way with passive-aggressive scowls.

Hence, the Svensson dichotomy: loving, warm, family AND totally controlling at the same time.

Then, the disaster…

Sadie's friends from school came for her first-ever film wrap. Indie film. Directed by a guy from AFI that AL mentors, Lars. Drama. UP and AL say Sadie's performance is amazing. I believe it.

AL's friends were there too, like every Friday. The salon. As well as AL's random invites, like Hector Rojas, to keep it interesting, which I usually love about her. But not this time and not that I'd ever admit it. Also, with Hector came his mom. His younger brother, Mateo. And big Bernese dog.

Yup, you guessed it: ClydeDogBoy. Why? How? Because I just had to go photograph Aunt Lauren's street art mural in spite of my better judgment, that's how! And not figure out that CDB *IS* Hector.

Here's how it went down: Me standing by Sadie and her mom's bestie, Taylor Rae Mayfield, the actress. Super cool. Talented. And always at Friday nights, so like family too. They were discussing how ridiculous it is that we feed cats grain-based food when they're pure carnivores, as if you'd ever feed a cheetah sliced bread.

Aunt Lauren brought her guests over. How I didn't see the dog when they walked in, I don't know. But in that moment, I imagined AL introducing me to Hector as his future bride and her Santa Monica Street Art Collective marketing machine: "She has a lot of time. She was homeschooled for half of 10th grade and went to a microschool that she loved, but who knows what that is, and then graduated a year early. Or something like that. We don't know. She's unique. Too smart for anyone's good. Like how is she ever going to find her peers? I'm hoping at Columbia. My alma mater. She's bound to get in if she stops scowling. But you'll like her."

That's what I imagined because I've heard her say all those things.

Here's what she actually said: "Here they are…my daughter, Sadie, and my niece, Saoirse, the one I was telling you about who's gonna help us promote your mural. Sadie and Saoirse, this is Hector. And his mom, Ofelia, and brother, Mateo."

"And Clyde," said Hector, with a solid, confident, deep voice as he looked at Sadie. Sadie! Not me—the one AL was fixing him up with, that he's been conversing with anonymously for weeks with witty repartee and banter and philosophy on IG—but Sadie!

He definitely has a great voice, my friend. MY friend!

Then, over came Clyde. To me. I patted his soft brown-and-black coat.

"Yes, Clyde," said Aunt Lauren. "He's gonna be on the mural."

Of course, he was.

My heart pounded, all over the place. Fear? Joy? I don't know. Probably both at first. Then, probably just fear and dread and hating that I was eclipsed by Sadie. Invisible. And it was my fault. Because I knew: I was wearing ugly overalls and Hector thought I, his anonymous IG friend, was Sadie.

Also, he was even better in person. Equally good to his words. Tall, lanky, probably just over six foot, red painter pants, plain white T-shirt, small tattoo on his wrist (a Mexican bird?), wild hair. The same hair that peeks out from behind Clyde on his posts. Light brown, loose curls. His eyes, piercing dark brown, confident. Poised smile, diplomatic, but with a spark that says, *I am definitely my own person and am curious to know if you're your own person too.* As if we have that in common. As if we belong to each other, anonymously. That was nice. And probably fantasy because I was reading into it. Because of talking to him for weeks. And my stupid fantasy mind, creating this deep-connection friend fantasy. Yes, friend! Unlike true-romance feelings for Leo Landis, I really wanted CDB to be my friend. And now this friendship will never be.

"Hi," said Hector, one side of his smile going up a notch. Sexy lips. Kindness. Was I reading into that too?

I shook his hand. Like an idiot.

"Saoirse's excellent at making things sing," Aunt Lauren boasted.

But he was already turning to Sadie.

"She and Sadie host a site about books," AL continued.

"BookTube channel," Sadie corrected and smiled, half shy, half flirting, at Hector. "Hi."

He smiled and fell in love.

"Sorry, channel," said Aunt Lauren. "And what's the other thing?"

"Bookstagram," I said and blood rushed to my cheeks. Crap. Awkward again. For a second, hoping maybe he wouldn't care about how pretty and confident and nice and successful Sadie is and how she's amazingly inviting and present and so is her family. Because he didn't notice me. At all.

Or take his eyes off Sadie for a second. "Yeah, BookishLensGirl, I think I know it," he teased and smiled as if they had a special secret. A friend secret meant for me. And then this other thing, like love and magic and excitement and joy and attraction, *not* meant for me. Never me. Only Sadie.

Which is when the ground slid out from under me.

And I pulled Sadie into the hall, excusing us.

"What are we doing?" Sadie asked.

"It's him."

"Who?"

"That guy I've been messaging."

"What guy?"

"On Instagram. I told you. Or maybe I didn't actually say it. You have to pretend to be me."

"I always pretend to be you. That's what we do." She smiled wryly.

"I know. But...I don't know."

"What's wrong? Something's weird."

"How so?"

"I don't know. You seem nervous. Like...you did something

wrong. Or have a secret. Or lied. Did you lie?"

"No, no lies. Just, nothing. We talk about nothing."

"Who?

"Me and Hector. But on Insta. I didn't know it was him. You can't see his face. And he goes by ClydeDogBoy. And he thinks I'm you. I mean, he must."

Yeah, he definitely saw her on BookTube. My heart sank.

"Now you look sad. I've never seen this many emotions on you. Do you like him?" she asked.

"Me? No! No. It's not like that. It's just. A friend. Which is, I guess, why it's such a bummer. I don't want to betray him."

"Why would you betray him?"

I wasn't sure, but it felt like that. Maybe bc he followed me first. Off my #lastreetart-hashtagged shot. And I followed him back. "It doesn't matter," I said. "You got this. You're perfect at being me."

"I am perfect at being you." She grinned. We laughed. I love my cousin. She's a good person. And we definitely have fun with our charade.

"So, what do you want me to do?" she asked. So pragmatic.

"Nothing. Just cover. Like usual. And pretend you know what he's talking about if he says something."

"Okay."

We went back and AL started w/the usual school thing, which makes me feel like a weirdo and I wanted to leave.

First, she introduced us to Hector's mom, Ofelia. Italian hair, like on IG. Put together. Strong handshake. Confident. Sense of humor. She was happy to meet me. "So do you go to Devan Academy, too? With Sadie?"

"Actually, I…" I was going to say: *graduated and doing gap year.* But Aunt Lauren interrupted, "No."

"Wildroads?" asked Ofelia.

"Not any more," Aunt Lauren continued. "Her brother Jake does, with our Nick. He's in 7th, and Nick's a sophomore, but you knew that." Apparently AL just got Mateo a scholarship to Wildroads for 6th grade, earning her another gold star for her do-gooder bliss.

"Yes," smiled Ofelia, then back to me, truly curious, "So where *do* you go?"

AL jumped in again, "She's had a unique path and education. Including Devan and Wildroads."

God. Couldn't she let it lie?

Which is when Taylor Rae jumped in on my behalf. "Progressive, she even graduated after junior year."

"Oh, that's just like..." Ofelia started to say.

But AL cut her off too. "She's just too smart."

And I was thinking, *Here we go.*

And sure enough, AL started in about my weird education and I wanted to disappear: *Independent-charter-hybrid thing, Devan and Wildroads in 9th but got bored. Homeschool. Then sweet little microschool Aporia Prep.*

And then, Sadie defended with, "Great microschool and the only place she actually learned anything. Apparently," to get back at AL because Sadie wanted to go to Aporia with me and River but AL wouldn't let her.

Hector laughed, totally charmed.

"Well, who knows what microschool means anyway," AL continued, perfectly played, "but yes, that was amazing for her. And she did all her units by end of eleventh, and some at SMC, so she graduated early."

"Fantastic," said Ofelia.

Why do all adults find this topic so interesting?

"And she's got a great little gig for her gap year," AL beamed, stealthily maneuvering into her comfort zone. "On Peter's film. Our film. As an intern. And next year, she'll go to Columbia or some other amazing school. Because she really is all that." Which is when AL hugged me, like she was proud of me.

I forced a smile, trying to be cheerful. "We'll see next month."

"Yes, it's a tough wait," Ofelia said. "Hector was in the same boat. But now he got early enrollment to Lewis & Clark."

Which is when Hector whistled like an explorer or some such thing to deflect his embarrassment when his mom hugged him, looking modest and even cuter.

Ofelia turned to me, as if sensing I was uncomfortable. "And, we know about homeschooling. We did it for a bit."

"Really?"

"Their father insisted they stop though," she said. "He's a teacher." Then shot Hector a look, like his dad and this topic were off limits.

"Well, it is really quite progressive," AL added. "And you worry about socialization, but she seems fine." As if I wasn't standing there!

"I think it's fantastic," said Ofelia. "More like the real world than this outdated education system. Did you know it was started by the Prussian army?" AL didn't know what to do with this unexpected information.

But Sadie did. "Exactly what it's like at Devan." Everyone looked at Sadie's smile, so sweet and innocent but then she went for the jugular. "Devan Academy for Girls, the supposed amazing private education but where no one actually cares what you think or if you have an original idea as long as you sit up and follow orders. Memorize the lesson before your teacher teaches it and get your competitive brown-nose hand up so you can beat out your friends for that plaid-clad A. Forget about teamwork or thinking differently or having an opinion or question."

Ouch.

But that's when the hair on the back of Hector's neck stood on end and he fell in love for real—with MY words about Devan and Sadie's gorgeous cherry-red lips that smiled as she spoke and her bright-green eyes that crinkled. Just like everyone else falls in love with BookishLens, our BookTube baby. My words, her smile. Crap.

"But you're going to a great college, hopefully," AL defended. "What's wrong with that?" And slipped in that it's probably Sarah Lawrence to impress Ofelia.

"Or Harvard," Sadie added. "But if I get in, it's not gonna be because of my crap grades or sucking up at Devan or Saoirse writing my essays." Which sucked the air out of the room because Sadie was right. If she gets in, it'll be because of her acting. "I mean, Devan was a total waste of time."

"For you," AL defended. "But not everyone is you or has your opportunity." Ouch.

"Yeah, but everyone has something," Sadie said, with passion, playing back my words again. "I mean, how are you supposed to figure out what you love or want if they don't let you be curious? Or give you choices or let you think for yourself?"

"Exactly," Hector agreed.

My heart sank.

Sadie blushed and smiled at me. "Exactly, like how are you supposed to know what ice cream you like if you never get to pick yourself?"

GAH! That part was hers. The rest was her photographic memory of all my texts to convince her to stick it out at Devan bc it was almost over and to laugh about it. She is brilliant like that. My mind. Her mouth. She can't think of anything to say and I can't say anything if someone is looking at me. Why?

And why was Hector so understanding? This was unusual. And hot. But he wasn't looking at me, he was looking at her. "So, what kind of ice cream do you like?"

A groan escaped Aunt Lauren's throat, which she covered up with an "excuse me," as if the cringe-throat-fart was a burp. She had no idea this set-up of Hector with me would end up being about Sadie.

Sadie shrugged. "Mint."

"From Rose Creamery?" Hector said, flirty and referencing my BLGirl post about ice cream that me and Mr. Griffin had on Main Street.

Sadie had no idea what he meant but faked it perfectly, "Exactly!"

"So you follow BookishLensGirl?" I said, trying to help.

"I do," Hector said and shot Sadie another look meant for me.

My heart sank. I tried to be upbeat, "Yeah, I saw that too. Good one, Sadie. Rose Creamery on Main. Love that place." I gave her a goofy thumbs up. She laughed and did it back.

"Well, good one to you too," inserted AL. "Saoirse manages BookishLensGirl."

"And produces," Sadie added. "And markets. Saoirse's amazing. I'm sure she'll rock the street-art thing."

Sadie smiled at me. And Hector was mesmerized by her.

And I felt truly awful. I was nothing. Idiot Wizard of Oz hiding behind stupid curtain not wanting to show face. "But really, it's all Sadie," I said, "BookishLensGirl," sweet, magical, fun and me hiding behind wizardess lie.

Hector moved closer to Sadie as if in a trance. They started talking, mostly him talking, nervous. Her beautiful, beaming.

Aunt Lauren watched, then turned to me and Ofelia with a forced smile. "So..."

And I felt awful.

And she went on about college and how the street-art publicity will help Hector get into college, even though Ofelia just said he's already in at Lewis & Clark, and she said she's hoping I'll go to Columbia, her alma mater, because "I know a writer when I see one, and she's a writer," even though I'm not, and more about how Sadie is likely going to Sarah Lawrence, "we hope."

So, yeah, from that point on, even after Mom and Mr. Griffin arrived and we played Pictionary, which I love, I existed in a sort of out-of-body, observant, floating-above-the-room place, feeling sad and jealous.

My heart melting into a puddle on the floor. Watching Hector love on Sadie and everyone else totally happy. And normal. Why couldn't I be happy and normal? Why did every good thing happen to everyone else? Sadie has a boyfriend! Even if he's at college and they're on hiatus. And now, she has ClydeDogBoy. My ClydeDogBoy. My friend.

And the only good thing that made me happy.

Saturday, February 2

Morning, my room, 10:10 a.m. Slightly better. Hector/ClydeDB IG messaged last night but have not responded: *Nice to meet you in person, Sadie.*

Then he liked 25 photos on BookishLens. He also commented— *Nice work, Sadie—o*n a post about my favorite book, *Franny and*

Zoey, with a shot of my feet from two years ago, before Sadie was even my BLGirl cover.

How could he like my words but not me? How could he not even notice me? Aubergine nose? Eyebrows? Invisibility due to understated streetwear? Lack of confidence in person? Maybe.

Still, I no longer want to be friends with a traitor.

Instead, will embrace adult behavior so can maintain semblance of self-respect. There are plenty of people who are not models or Sadie who have amazing boyfriends and are loved and found attractive inside and out.

And technically, I'm not gorgeous but I'm okay. And Leo Landis notices me. He sees my unique beauty. He thinks the awkwardness oozing out of my oversized pores is cute because the confidence races past. Actually, pores not so bad. Also, not sure about confidence. Do I have any at all? Yes!

And for sure, Hector is superficial art snob. Unable to see beauty radiating out from within, choosing external beauty above all. And if love = beauty, then he loves Sadie. Not my photos or words. Or soul.

Whatever. Just never going to reply.

Instead buying dress.

Sunday, February 3

My room, 3:10 p.m. Bought dress. Lime green with little yellow pear-pattern trim (super bargain at TJ Maxx!). And flowery Blowfish skater sneaks (also bargain at this secret treasure chest!). Perfect blend to venture out of neo-street-style comfort zone and perhaps invisibility into LL friendship with friendship dress flag.

Then, Leo will be my friend. He will like my mind. Our brains can kiss. Even if our bodies can't. Even if he has a girlfriend. It is an intellectual crush. Our brains can have sex. Would I have sex with him? Yes. Brain sex!!!

And yes, this dress is inspired by Sadie. Am squashing jealousy and taking highroad. I inspire her with my words and she inspires me to be naturally beautiful and different in a good way rather than my weird-normal natural, which is just way too weird.

Heart hurts.

So does overthinking head.

Action item: Wear dress tomorrow.

My room, 9:30 p.m. Nervous about wearing dress tomorrow. What if LL doesn't notice or like it? Even just as friend.

Have been obsessively re-stalking him and gf Isla Gordon-Ferraro all day and found new info since initial stalking two months ago when we first met in editing-building hall and then editing-room lunches. It doesn't look good. IGF is amazing, like maybe she-can't-possibly-really-exist amazing. She will eclipse me with big shadow. Even if she's not big physically, her personality is.

Isla: Actress. Writer. Director. Works with refugees. Mentors teens. Is only 20! Younger woman to him! Won award at Sundance for her short. Has TED Talk. Goes to Yale, history and economics. Has elegant, high-fashion, rave-glitter style. Totally unique. Crap.

Am unworthy. Esp after googling Isla and Leo together and seeing her with him on red carpets, like at his first feature, when he was only 21, and in interviews.

She's GORGEOUS. Has five sisters (new info) and is Scottish Italian. Her dad played bagpipes at her sister's wedding on South Uist. Super cute.

I can't compare. Am dust. Simpleton. Young. With BookTube channel that benefits no one.

Must go to most prestigious university if ever want to attract Leo Landis. Must be amazing. Maybe AL Columbia-mania a blessing after all. Or maybe can get Dad to wear kilt. With his boots.

Confused.

Must wear dress tomorrow no matter what.

Monday, February 4

Morning, screening room, 9:22 a.m. Leo noticed and liked my dress!!! Was walking to screening early to check w/projectionist and LL was walking over from his car. I yelled, "Hi, Leo!"

He waved and *actually* said, "Likin' the dress," in artsy-fashion-style-appreciation way. How did I know?!!! Mind meld!!!!!!

Me, heart racing: "Thanks."

"What're you up to?" he asked, looking at my hair like he liked it too. This was new.

"Screening," I said and got stupidly nervous, like not knowing what else to say. But I needed to say something interesting. Even though I wasn't interesting. Ridiculous. But at least he noticed me!

"Let me know how it goes," he said. "Good luck."

I smiled and nodded, and he walked off. That's it.

Heart still racing while waiting in screening room for exec. Am idiot in cute flirty dress.

Action item: Stay positive.

Home after work, 4:20 p.m. Flitty-flitty happy bo-bitty! Adulthood and life poss. beginning in spite of partial invisibility and personal humiliation during exec screening.

Going to lunch with Leo Wednesday!!! Our cutting room and their cutting room, like a date. Of cutting rooms. Not me and Leo, yet. But still. It will be perfect opportunity to establish and solidify friendship foundation in case he breaks up with IGF! In the future! Near or far! Also being realistic as this is JUST a work lunch between film directors and editors where I am simply part of the crew and not the reason for the lunch. Clearly not a date, yet, but...IT MAY BE THE START OF SOMETHING GOOD!

This lunch decision happened this afternoon after Unc P's screening for the studio exec. It's Unc's first cut and first screening on the big screen. I'm so proud of my Unc Unc.

He and Mike were t. nervous. I don't know why bc the cut is good, and Jena was annoyed with them for being nervous bc it meant more work for her when there didn't need to be. They kept asking her if she'd checked stuff, like the dinner/fight scene, where they did tons of cool work, which she did and adjusted SFX and rechecked it a gazillion times bc she's so meticulous, which is why she's so good at her job. Too good, in fact, bc she wants to be an editor but keeps getting assistant gigs, which pay amazing but then don't lead to editing. As first assistant, she's more like a glorified mom. Unc, Mike, me and everyone we deal with are the kids. She really needs to start networking. I'd tell her to network with LL but I'm doing that, though not for editing work, rather poss. camera work. And friendship.

I was the only one that stayed in the theater with the exec during the screening, in case he needed something or something happened. He wanted to see it on his own, and clearly, I don't count as an actual person, the lowly paid intern.

The exec's assistant Piper called Jena yesterday specifically to say the exec wanted to see the movie on his own, which made everyone more nervous. You couldn't tell about the nervousness though when Unc talked to the exec in the theater lobby before the screening. UP's great at making everyone feel comfortable and like he's got it all handled, which he does, even when he's nervous, which is why he's so good at his job. Mike's like that too but more quiet and hangs back and lets Unc do the talking.

"All right then, Saoirse'll be here if you need anything," Unc told the exec. "And we'll catch up when you're done."

"Great," said the exec. "I'm thrilled. We're all thrilled." And he gave Unc the most reassuring smile and handshake and went into the theater.

Mike told me to text the exec's reactions and left. I went into the movie-sized theater and sat last row on the left. It was dark and the opening sequence had started. I don't think the exec knew I was even there, even though he looked right at me when Unc introduced me. At least, he seemed to. Maybe he has a lazy eye. Or is blind. Or just hadn't noticed me enter the dark theater.

In any case, I was invisible and he started doing yoga in the aisle for the first half hour of the movie. He made huffing sounds during the sun salute and farted twice when he rolled his feet over his head.

Then he drank water and recorded into his phone: "Yoga stretch, thirty minutes. Four ounces water." Then he did more active exercise, starting with a low jog in place. During the dinner/fight scene, with all the cool music and SFX they mixed and Jena checked a gazillion times, he took two calls from Piper and rattled off one-word responses between deep-knee bends, like: "Yes, meeting, lunch, delete, forty thousand, Wednesday." He also called "Max" on speaker and, after the outgoing message, said, "Max. Yes, on for doubles Saturday at ten. Late." Thirty minutes later, he recorded, "Light cardio thirty minutes," into his phone and sat in a seat next to the aisle. He slouched low and put his feet up on the seat in front of him after taking off his loafers, rolling ankles and rubbing his head as he watched the film, occasionally grabbing his phone and texting as if he just thought of something.

I didn't text any of this to Unc or Mike, just *"Done. Went great!"* at the end.

I also said, "Bye, thank you," to the exec as he left, even though that was weird bc he's the one who should've thanked me, as if I was saying *'thank you for letting me into your life so I could watch you sweat and fart while you didn't pay attention at all to the sweat and nerves that went into the beautiful cinematic masterpiece you just glanced at occasionally for the past 102 minutes'*—yes, a bit long, but it's a first cut! Relax, people.

The exec looked right at me when I said the weird *thank you* and just kept walking without reacting, like he still couldn't see me. Maybe he does have a lazy eye or brain damage. That sounds mean but less mean than the alternative astounding-rudeness option. What a nob.

Actually, his name is Rudy Dirks, so it fits. Rude-y! Rude-y Dorks!

Rude-y did, however, send Unc an email that said, "*Good work!*" Thank god!

Unc and Mike were so happy and made so much noise in the hall that everyone came out of their cutting rooms and knew the screening went well, including Leo and his editor, Melanie. OMG!

Unc P asked if they wanted to go to lunch with us to celebrate. They couldn't today bc of a meeting with their exec (different person, a woman I think). Hence, Wednesday! Let me repeat that in case you didn't hear: We're all going to lunch Wednesday!!! So happy, on t. cloud of joy.

And I now have two days to become friend-risistable to LL as lunch is perfect chance for him to get to know me. And see me again!

Happy too for Unc and his movie because (a) it's actually really good (subjective, I know, but still) and (b) the exec did send the "*good work*" email even though he didn't pay attention. All around happy.

My room, 9:05 p.m. Just got message from CDB: *Hey! How's it going? Love today's shot!*

Which is super annoying. It's a shot of a giant-headed blue-alien creature getting out of a Mini Cooper in the studio parking lot. I saw him after the exec screening, clearly an actor in a sci-fi movie, probably back from lunch. Funny. Must've been difficult to drive with that head!

No one else got the humor so it's extra annoying that CDB did. Am still super irritated about Friday. Never writing to him again. Like how could he not even talk to me? After messaging me for four weeks? And now only messaging Sadie? On *my* BLGirl IG!

Also, how could he just so boldly like so many photos? Shamelessly putting it out there that he really likes her. Like fearless or something.

Still ignoring.

Sick of BookishLens anyway, so it won't be hard. Plus, sick of reading and never want to read again.

Have identified options:

1. Quit BLGirl entirely. Cons: Lose bookcrate $, time with Sadie and potential pathfinding in unexpected ways.
2. Feature books that are also movies and watch movies instead of reading. Pros: Could start w/western theme as inspired by Dad's cowboy boots. Gives me something to talk to Leo about as he is true cinemaphile and loves westerns...as friendship and exciting life begins!

3. #2 + redo books already read. It's a cheat but Sadie would make
    it work. Major pro: Speed! It takes five seconds to write fun new
    scripts for Sadie on already-read books.

Starting with #3! Western theme w/fake reading and book
regurgitation. Will do photo shoot of Dad's old cowboy boots now
and post, then do western book hall and series with Sadie later in
week.
Ignoring Hector's little likes and comments completely.

9:50 p.m. Me to Hector: *Yeah, it was hilarious when the alien
stepped out of the Mini Cooper on the lot. G'night.*
Idiot.

Tuesday, February 5

My room, 10:30 p.m. Leo lunch tomorrow! V. excited! Though am
keeping self adult-calm so can be fully prepared. Got new dress with
cherries on sky-blue palette. Rewatched *Pulp Fiction*, LL's favorite
movie, in case it comes up. He talks about it in almost every
interview and mentioned it to Unc P last time our cutting room had
lunch with their cutting room and I sat there like silent blue jay who
has everything to say but says nothing. Tomorrow owning
bluebirdness. Dress symbolic! Happy surprise.
Still nervous.
Will prevail with positivity even if invisibility occurs. Unless they
cancel. I hope they don't.
Hector/ClydeDB wrote: *Hey! How was your day?*
Ignored.

Wednesday, February 6

My room, morning, 6:30 a.m. Blue-jay-symbolic dress on. Letting cuteness sink into core to encapsulate confidence in spite of nerves for biggest day ever. Ignoring Hector note still. He does not care about my day. He cares about Sadie's, and mine is going to be amazing in spite of him.

Cutting room, 4 p.m. Anxious again. But this time flittering happiness that's making me so flittery I'm nervous. Perhaps joy and anxiety are two sides of same coin.

Because: lunch!!! Of two fabulous cutting rooms with two directors, two editors, one assistant...and one peon PA (me!), who shined! Noticed by Leo Landis!!! More than ever before!!! Perhaps even flirting!!!

Let me recap this joy of joys:

First, we drove in two separate cars to Thai in Larchmont—us w/UP and them w/Leo. Leo, Melanie, Unc, Mike, Jena, me.

They don't have an assistant bc Leo reedits everything himself. Melanie is editor + assistant, even tho she's already cut two indie features and one got picked up by Sony after Sundance. Mike says the studio indulges Leo bc he's a magical starboy. He thinks Melanie puts up w/it bc it's a great credit bc everything Leo touches turns to gold.

Maybe one day I'll turn to gold.

Like today!

I think Melanie hates me bc of the time Leo showed us a scene and I overreacted. It was their big opening. I loved it so much I jumped up and down and clapped and squealed, "OMG it's so good!" I couldn't help it. Idiot. Childlike. Overenthusiastic. Weirdo. I also blurted out that I LOVED the kids on the bikes, SO AMAZING & BEAUTIFUL! Which is when Leo said to Melanie, "See, we gotta do more of the bikes," which she hated and clenched her fists and fake agreed. And now she hates me too.

Whatever. Today, she was on the other side of Jena so I didn't have to deal. It was me, Jena, Melanie on one side, and LL, UP, Mike on the other.

Leo was directly across from me. Woo! Totally focused on Unc for the entire first half of lunch, larger than life with his big stories and energy, even if he's just 23. Unc is like that too. Though, Leo has great posture and is tall while Unc is more slouchy and relaxed and medium-sized.

Then, there was a lull and Leo noticed his barely touched Pad Thai and started to eat. He also noticed me. "So what's your story, Bagel Girl?"

Blood instantly rushed to my face. I choked on my food and started coughing. I had to stand up and walk away from the table.

"You okay, Berger?" Unc asked and brought me water.

I had a sip then sat back down.

Which is when Leo teased (good sign!), "Didn't know that was such a loaded question."

"It's not, I just...," again, tongue-tied, blushing.

"She's a YouTube star," Unc said to the rescue, "too coy for her own good with a quarter-million followers on Instagram and YouTube."

Embarrassment! Everyone looking.

"Wow, that's almost more than me," Leo joked. "I thought I was good with 30K-plus. What's it about?"

"Books," I said. OMG! More attention.

"And a smarty too," he said, "What's it called?" and pulled out his phone to look it up!

More blushing. "BookishLensGirl." God.

Unc and Mike laughed at my love-shy expense. Jena asked for more napkins.

Then, Leo found BLGirl on IG and followed and looked at everything and laughed too! "Cool boots. And the alien! I saw that guy. That was hilarious."

OMG, he noticed! The alien! The boots! I'm so glad about the boots! And the humor! That HE GETS!!!!

Then he went to BookTube. "Ah, and look who's here too," meaning Sadie, and showed Unc.

"The star," Unc said. "But you're lookin' at the mastermind. Berger does it all. Sadie just makes it shine."

And just like that, Unc broke *my* privacy rule: No telling on BLGirl! But who cares? Because now LL SEES ME!

So I mentioned the upcoming western theme and movies, thank god, bc it hooked him in. Bc he LOVES WESTERNS! And he said, "Awesome. Like what?" looking right into my eyes. So sexy! And hot. And listening. To me!

I quickly listed movies Dad and I watched (luckily!) bc I really didn't have a plan yet. "Uh...*Blazing Saddles*...*Butch Cassidy*, and um, *Hateful Eight*!" Memory on fire! Thank god for the last one esp because he said, "I love Hateful Eight," and followed us on BookTube! "Can't wait to see it," he said and smiled and leaned forward on his elbows to get a closer look at me, like it was just me and him at the table. Like in a magnetic Dr. Who tunnel. His piercing-green eyes shooting forces of life into me, like our brains and love for cinema were making out and no one else existed.

Then, Mike asked the waiter for the check, which pulled us out of the tunnel. And I said, playfully, "Just don't tell anyone it's me. It's a secret. Everyone thinks I'm Sadie," and blushed. Horribly.

Leo laughed, amused. And this time, more than just our brains wanted to touch. I think. Like the magnetic force existed in our entire reality. With everyone else there too.

Or was it just me? What about his gf?

My heart raced.

"You're secret's safe with me," he said and smiled. Flirting. Def. FLIRTING!

And I felt sexy. I mean, if this is what sexy feels like. For sure better than when Trey touched my boobs. Boob, I mean boob. In 10th. And then basically ignored me.

Yes, this was sexy. And I've been holding onto it all day.

What a relief.

Plus, three other things that happened:

1. On ride back, Jena pointed out that I don't need to worry about Leo telling anyone that BLGirl is scripted by me and not Sadie (so pragmatic!) bc he'll NEVER come in contact with anyone that cares. Which was slightly insensitive but made me REALIZE: It's okay (and amazing!) to own that I AM the Wizard of BLGirl Oz! It's REALITY! MY WORLD! Leo loves it!

2. Later in the day, Mike backhandedly gave me a confidence boost when he showed us a scene and I hesitated to give my note and he lit into me. Mike's been annoyed with my weird self-doubt for a while, and I guess he couldn't hold it in anymore and just yelled for me to: "Just say it! No one in this town's gonna wait for you! Even if you have something to say! Which you do! Because otherwise you wouldn't be here!" He meant it in a nice way, like tough-love advice. Which makes me REALIZE: I have something to SAY! And need to say it! And I did. And Mike said, "See! That's why we hired you. Plus, the great coffee," which was funny and made me feel wanted, and me and Jena laughed.

3. Unc Unc, Mike AND Jena noticed that LEO LIKES ME!!!!!!!!!!! AHHHHH! I'm sure it's because, as Dad says, whenever they're not cutting, they're all about gossip and drama, in a cute way, like noticing random editing-building love when it occurs. And Jena said, "What about Isla?" And Mike said, "I thought they broke up," and UP wasn't sure, "Yeah, maybe, maybe they did break up," bc he's space-y and couldn't remember. Which makes me REALIZE: I HAVE A CHANCE! I work with funny and cute gossipy filmmakers, that are smart and nice like little garden gnomes (tho not Jena, she's tall, lean and more like Glenda the Good Witch, tho in a more judgey way), and who NOTICE THINGS LIKE LOVE! So they can gossip about it when not working on their movie!

So, yeah, embarrassing, grateful adulthood happening. Practicing expressing. Not idiot-clapping and jumping and chirpy-bird cheering.

Heart beating so fast.

Also, took long way out of building after work to walk by Leo's cutting room. He wasn't there.

Will go by tomorrow.

To nourish this cinematic friendship. Not fantasy romance.

What a sexy friend I have.

SAOIRSE BERGER'S BOOKISH LENS IN LA LA LAND 31

My room, 10 p.m. Am on cloud nine as LL liked more posts, including birthday flower shot, acknowledging that BLGirl has led to surprising evolvement of awesome life path appearing and possible start of life! As per 18 Hoorays, you never know what it will lead to, even if sick of books. Will keep it up.

Excited about new video with Sadie too. Doing it tomorrow.

And ignoring that Stupid CDB liked post of Dad's boots.

LL did too and that's all that matters.

Writing script for tomorrow now. About westerns! To impress Leo!

Thursday, February 7

My room after recording BLGirl at UP's office, 11:00 p.m. We did it! Awesomeness of western movies and books TBR and watched by BLGirl fans! Can't wait for Leo to see video!

Recording went great. Sadie amazing and a mess and rock all at once. Plus, she agrees if Leo is broken up with Isla, he'd be great for me! OMG! It's happening!

Is it happening?

Yes!

And the BLGirl cousin-ship rocked the show tonight!

Let's recap to review what's up w/Sadie (and Leo goodness!):

First, we drove to UP's office and I told Sadie about our Leo lunch and my feelings for him and how her dad and Mike think Leo might be single but also seem unsure. She said that's typical bc they're gossips and she'll try to get intel at dinnertime bc her parents talk about Leo a lot (weird!). Apparently, AL maps her and UP's relationship onto Leo and Isla's, like if AL's mad at UP bc he's working too much and she feels left out (which she does!), she'll say she's surprised Isla puts up with Leo working so much since she's such a strong, independent woman on her own, making her own films. And why does Isla need to feel like Leo's more in love with his movie than her? Weird! And UP says that "just because he's into his work doesn't mean he loves it more!"

Which is a bummer for AL and UP. But hooray about Leo!

Sadie said her parents also talk about me at dinner (also weird!).
UP says he's so happy I'm there (yay!) and that I'm always surprising
them with great notes. Then AL says it's "just a nice little job for
now," but next year I'll be at Columbia studying writing bc "we had
such a nice time touring the campus" and "it feels so good to support
another writer."

I told Sadie I still don't see myself at Columbia, and Sadie asked
me to hold off telling AL, "please, not now, she's been really insecure
lately, and it's all she has in her fights with my dad." I agreed.

Sadie also said both UP and AL really like Leo and that he's a
good guy!

Then, we shot the video with western movies and *Little House*
books. I tried to find western/cowboy books but there aren't many,
and those I found, like *Shane*, I don't want to read.

So, we featured western movies that Unc Unc recommended and
the ones I blurted out to Leo, filming Sadie in front of Clint Eastwood
on Unc's poster of *The Good, The Bad and the Ugly*, holding the
Shane book (from library) and my entire *Little House on the Prairie*
collection. Thank god I still have those. Putting BLGirl on retro kick
and regurgitating books is excellent. Will probably remain in reading
slump forever. Giving self high-five for excellent and doable plan to
fool and, simultaneously, satisfy BLGirl fans. It also gives LL more
reason to notice and like me!

So, yeah, the recording went stellar, even with our silly glitches.
As usual, Sadie memorized and interpreted the script perfectly: "And
now our BookishLensGirl Top-Nine awesome westerns to watch, and
screenplays to read if so inclined and curious, in addition to *The
Good, The Bad and the Ugly*, including *Shane*, written by Jack
Schaefer, screenplay by A.B. Guthrie, Jr."

Sadie held up *Shane* with a smile and some hip-hop moves, while
the book "kissed" Clint, then continued: "In no particular order, we
have, one, *Shane*! Two, *High Noon*, screenplay by Carl Foreman,
based on a magazine story called *The Tin Star*. Three, *The
Magnificent Seven*, the 1960 film classic or 2016 version, both based

on the even-more-classic *Seven Samurai*, with multiple screenwriters, including revered Akira Kurosawa, that you can find on IMDB, which is a fabulous resource for films. Four, *Red River*, from a *Saturday Evening Post* story by Borden Chase, who's also the screenwriter with Charles Schnee. Five, *Butch Cassidy and the Sundance Kid*, by famed writer William Goldman, who also wrote *The Princess Bride*, which you may know and love, as do I. Six, *Blazing Saddles*, a comedy with five screenwriters, including Mel Brooks and Richard Pryor. Seven, *Unforgiven*, screenplay by David Webb Peoples. And eight, *The Hateful Eight*, based on a screenplay by Quentin Tarantino, who will be inspiring next month's reads of pulp fiction with his movie *Pulp Fiction* as we segue into screenplays and movies instead of pure prose."

Such a cheat!

Which is when Sadie gave me a weird look and we cut, which was fine because it's so easy to edit.

"There's only eight," she said.

"What?"

"Movies. You said top nine. Which is weird to begin with; I mean, where's ten?"

"No, it's nine with *The Good, The Bad and the Ugly*."

Which is when she gave me the "really?" look and I told her, "It doesn't matter."

"I feel like an idiot saying top nine when the last is number eight, even if the other one came before, because of the poster. But still. And we don't say the writers."

"Fine, we'll do it over with nine and repeat *The Good, The Bad and the Ugly* with screenwriters."

"And then finish with Laura Ingalls retro reviews?"

"For people that want to go back into this wonderful classic, yes."

"Why are we doing this?"

"I told you, my dad's life crisis. The cowboy boots. My obsession with Leo Landis's obsession with Quentin Tarantino. I don't know. I don't want to read anymore."

And as my love crisis came tumbling into the room, so did hers. Hers made itself known as a mere exhale. So strange for someone killing it onscreen. She just doesn't express her feelings IRL often, except when they squeeze out the sides, like the exhale. Which is how I knew this was serious. And then it got worse, like I've-never-seen-her-like-this-before worse.

"What's going on?"

She shook her head. "Nothing."

I waited.

"Paulie met someone."

"Oh, crap." Paulie and Sadie have been together since 8th grade. They did a trial separation when he went to Univ. of Michigan last August. Clearly, that's history now.

"Yeah," she said and exhaled again. "She's in his dorm."

This was dire. I had to say something. But I didn't know what. I exhaled too.

Her eyes filled with tears. I felt awful. It must've showed bc her face contorted, trying to hold in the tears, shaking her head. "And my mom's insane," she said like she was in pain, "more than usual." So I hugged her and she burst out crying with an explosion of snot and unexpected, unfettered emo into my shoulder. "Which just makes it worse," she wailed.

I let her cry until she pulled back and wiped her face on her dress like she didn't care. "Everything feels like it's coming apart," she said, with snot on her burnt-orange-and-red dress looking quite snail-trail shiny, and I thought I'd have to frame the camera up to avoid it if we finished filming tonight. "And she thinks my dad's cheating on her with some actor dude."

"What?!" This was new.

"Like movie cheating, not cheating cheating. Like they-want-to-make-a-movie-without-her cheating. And she's completely losing it. I don't know what to do."

Wow, yeah, this was worse than usual for Aunt Lauren.

I didn't know what to say. She looked broken and desperate. "I can't even tell her about Paulie now because she's so mad at my dad, and she'll just say it's because Paulie's a guy and that's just what they do, and look at my dad. And it's not even about her. Or him. Like she's a victim. Of nothing. All the time. It's not fair."

I exhaled again. Yup, that was Aunt Lauren.

"And it just makes it worse that she's so angry, because I love Paulie. And it's not his fault that he met someone better and more beautiful than me. I feel so ugly."

That's when it got more dire and I had to rally.

"Oh, Sadie, you're not ugly. You're like the only person that can pull off snot and look gorgeous, like...Sophia Loren...or whoever that is in that Italian movie you love. *8 1/2*?"

"Claudia Cardinale, *Once Upon a Time in the West*." She walked over and moved the fronds of a giant plant, and there was the movie poster, hidden by the door, which is why I missed it.

"Oh."

Sadie, through tears: "It's stylish and inspired *Once Upon a Time in Hollywood*, so I don't know why you wouldn't include it and make it ten."

"Right, good idea," I said and told her I hadn't noticed the poster behind the door.

"Plus, my mom loves it too and me. And my dad." The tears came back hard. "But right now, it's *Breathless*. I mean the girl, the reason I cut my hair. Even though mine's not that short."

I had no idea what she was talking about.

"Actually, *Loves of a Blonde* is more like it. She gets dumped. Mascara everywhere. That's what I'm like."

Sadie loves old Euro movies from the 60s. The style. And she likes to imitate the actresses.

"Hey, we should do a French and Czech New Wave thing next!" I said, way too enthusiastically given the circumstances. "And Italian!" But I reigned it in. "Sorry, I just like the movie idea."

She nodded. "It's a good idea." And wiped her tears and smiled for two seconds before her face contorted again. "Do you think he ever loved me?"

"Of course, he loved you. You guys were together since eighth grade!"

Which made her start to cry again. "I'm so ugly."

"No, no! Sadie, c'mon." I hugged her again. More snot, now on my shirt. "You're gorgeous, inside and out. Please don't do this. It's like a fact that you're beautiful. I mean, here, check it out. Remember, Hector?" Which is when maybe I reached too far. "He's all about you and how pretty you are. Look. *Nice to meet you in person, Sadie...*"

I showed her my messages, and she read them through her tears. "And all these likes. Look. Look. He really likes you. I can tell. He keeps trying to talk to you."

I showed her Hector's ClydeDogBoy page. The photos of Clyde made her laugh. "See," I said. Finally giving her some relief. Thank god.

She nodded. "That's nice. He's a nice guy." Then she got all teary again and made the scrunchy face with more nodding, and the pain started to come out, but then she worked really hard to reign it in and fight the tears and shook her head side to side as if that would keep it in, which it did, and then she dropped her chin and made a weird motor cry and took a deep breath in and exhaled and nodded and succeeded. Wow. Amazing. It was like watching a transformer or sculptor taking clay through a full range of emotions. Sadie is a true emo artist.

She took another deep breath and exhaled. "Okay, you're right. I have to be strong." She reassured herself and smiled through her remaining tears. "And I have us."

I nodded. "We have us," which was nice.

Then, we redid the video with *The Good, the Bad and the Ugly* as nine, adding screenwriters and changing it to Top Ten with *Once Upon a Time in the West* as ten, ending on the poster before going on to *Little House* reviews and doing it in one take. No mistakes. God, Sadie has an amazing memory. And smile. She just has it. She belongs to acting. And maybe she belongs in a relationship with Hector. That would be good for her. And maybe I'm okay with it. V. sad losing anonymous friendship tho. But he doesn't care anyway. Fake friend!

And I have LEO! With hope from cutting-room gossips' observations and nosiness.

"Thank you," Sadie said when we finished. "This really helps.

And maybe Leo Landis'll like the movie thing. I mean, *Hateful Eight*, right? Can't go wrong. And *Once Upon a Time in the West*."

Which made me feel good. And hopeful.

Plus, she added a line from the end of the movie that he might love: "I hope you come back someday," which Claudel says to Bronson with love and longing. And Sadie rocked it. Just like the Italian actress. Maybe better!

I told her she was right, "Leo is going to LOVE THIS!"

She told me I glowed when I talked about him.

I told her I was worried it was a fantasy. His girlfriend was just here. "Why would they break up?"

She said, "distance" and "maybe she has class, unlike Paulie, and broke up with him in person...if they're broken up. You have to think positive. You look so happy when you talk about him."

Which made me want to cry with joy. And believe her. I do believe her! Do I believe her? I guess we'll see. Because no one knows but him. And Isla Gordon-Ferraro.

Then Sadie said, "I just want to be hopeful for you because otherwise there is no hope." And then her face contorted and she started crying again and I hugged her and she sobbed into my neck, "I hope my parents stay together. They fight all the time. And it's so weird that they fight about Leo Landis."

I smoothed her hair and told I thought it was going to be okay. Which I don't know.

"That's what Paulie always says, that it's going to be okay." She sobbed more. And I held her. Then she wiped her face on her dress again and told me the BookishLensGirl episode is amazing, the best ever, and if LL doesn't notice and love me for it, he's an idiot.

If he's broken up with Isla.

What if he doesn't notice? What if he doesn't like it?

Sadie told me to trust my instinct about LL. And agreed if she ever sees Hector again she'd be open to new love too.

Action item: Add flashing number graphics to the countdown for clarity and post.

Go to bed.

Stay positive. He likes you.

That's what my instinct says.

Friday, February 8

Morning, my room, 7:49 a.m. ClydeDogBoy loves the western video. I hate ClydeDogBoy. But reigning it in for Sadie's sake. It's simple annoyance and I can deal. Plus, positive vibes = LEO LOVE! Embracing that!

7:51 a.m. And now CDB's asking Sadie out: *Hey! Loved the western-themed post! Did you see Hateful Eight is playing at the Aero?*
Really hate him now. Can't deal. Not responding. Not being anonymous wingperson. Even if it makes her happy.

7:54 a.m. Stupid ClydeDog also wrote in comments that he likes the poster in Unc Unc's office. And noticed in another video that I have a Polish poster of the movie *Blow Up* in my room. Which means he's stalking our account. Blowtard. How did he notice that? No one notices that. I really hate him.
Also letting it go. Bc I am adult!
Instead, funneling energy into positivity vortex to REMEMBER THAT THERE IS ROOM FOR LOVE FOR ALL, including me! Leo will notice new video! And he has MAGNETIC ENERGY FIELD THAT FITS MINE!
Wearing pear dress again.
That's all it takes.

Bathroom, next building over, cleaning coffee pot w/Ed Sheeran hope, 1:20 p.m. Holding steady. Must maintain cute and fun positivity re love to stave off Aunt Lauren's crazed behavior and own momentary self-doubting negativity to remain shining adult beacon of amazingness for Leo.
I am not Aunt Lauren. Even if she is my aunt. And just dumped all her paranoia on me. Shoo, AL's desperate paranoia about possible

movie-cheating Unc, shoo. He's not cheating. They'll figure it out so I don't have to. Her desperation is not mine, like when I momentarily feel desperate, which I'm not now feeling, anymore.

Bc Leo *IS INTO ME*! Friend or more! And I am not my family!

I am lovable, capable adult. Smart. Observant. Cute and fun. Also funny and good friend and niece and amazing peon PA. In adorable pear dress!!!!!

Invoking *What would Sheeran do?* tactic to embrace rock-god confidence with good actions and thoughts. Let's recap. Bc that's what Ed Sheeran would do if he were me. So he could move into and remain in positivity and continue flow towards Leo love. If he loved Leo like I do.

First, this morning: Saw Leo in car, sitting, looking sad or upset, eyes closed. Felt bad for him, like maybe he was sad about gf/ex Isla and needed a friend—like if he and Isla are broken up as everyone suspects, even with mere forgetful-gossiper intel.

I hovered near his car but out of view behind shrubbery so as not to look suspicious and worked up courage to say hi. Finally, he got out and I cutely emerged from shrubbery as if just then walking by as he shut his door. I waved and said, "Hey...," with adorable happy-positivity smile, "how's it..." But he cut me off, holding up finger and giving weird wide-eye signal, like he couldn't talk bc he was on phone, turning away without fully acknowledging me.

My heart sank. But the Sheeran in my head reminded me: *He's busy! On phone. It's about work and important other conversation. You did the right thing. You said, hi. Don't take it personally! He likes you!*

Yes, he does. It sunk in. All was good again.

But then AL flipped out and involved me. Which makes me feel awful. For her and me.

Let's continue to recap:

First, Unc P and Mike were already in serious work mode when I got in. UP told Jena, "no calls," and she relayed that to me, which is t. normal for a director going into new cut bc he needs to be in creative-bubble zone.

Then, AL called just after 9:30 a.m. I answered as am peon in hierarchical totem pole of film-editing room and it's my job. I report to first assistant Jena, who reports to editor Mike, who reports to director Unc. Unc is king of our world; we all work for him.

Stupidly, I put AL through anyway bc I got distracted looking at IG and didn't think it was that big of a deal. UP wasn't happy and said, "No more calls," again. Mike was annoyed with me, which annoyed Jena, who looked at me like *what is wrong with you?* "No more calls; Peter's not here." Gah! Why is there so much pressure about the stupid phone?!

Then, at 9:50 a.m., the phone rang again: *Lauren Berger Svensson.* I answered.

"Hey, Sweetie, is he there?"

Me: Loud exhale.

"He must've turned off his cell, and I really have to talk to him."

I looked into Jena's room but she was in Mike's room now. Our rooms are in a line: my peon PA room, open archway, Jena's middle-tier room, Mike's room. His door is directly across from the archway so I can stare straight at it. It was shut. Tight.

"They're cutting," I said.

"I really need to talk to him now."

Crap.

"Saoirse, just go get him. It's fine."

So, I did. Through archway, through Jena's room, knocked on Mike's door, stuck head in. Mike stopped the film. Three heads turned. "It's Lauren; she said it's urgent."

Unc: "I thought you weren't putting her through."

Me: "She, I…" Jena exasperated. I drooped. Unc groaned.

Mike: "C'mon, Berger, you got this," which made Jena more exasperated, like she wasn't doing her job in managing my every peon move.

Me: "What should I tell her?"

"Nevermind," Unc said and stormed into my room to take the call. "Lauren, hi…no, I'm not agitated…no, I'm working!...Yes! Fine! I told you that already. Yes, 6:15. I pick him up every week! Okay, bye."

It was all about them!

He walked past me, "No more calls, Saoirse, no matter what," and slammed Mike's door shut.

I went outside for a walk. The Sheeran in my head told me: *It doesn't matter.* If it were him, he'd blow it off, *do NOTHING and know they're being stupid about their relationship*, AL out of her mind.

I went back, passing Leo's door, which was closed. The phone rang again, 10:48: *Lauren Berger Svensson*. I didn't pick up, Jena monitoring. It rang again. I answered, "Cutting room."

"Hi, Sweetie, is he there?"

"No, he's out." C'mon, AL!

"Really, where?"

"I don't know. He just walked out." Lie.

"Oh, c'mon, I just talked to him half an hour ago, where would he go?"

I looked at Jena, then my shoes. I think that's a natural instinct when you lie. "I have no idea. Maybe he needed to think or something. In quiet. Can I take a message?"

"A message?! Saoirse! I know he's there! Put him on the phone!"

Crap. Mike came out to grab something from Jena's room. You could hear the movie in the background.

"What was that?"

"It's Mike; he's working."

"Without Peter?"

"Oh, shoot; gotta go. I'll let him know you called." I hung up. What a liar.

She called again twice. I didn't answer. Jena nodded like that was the right thing to do.

Finally.

Aunt Lauren texted me three times. I didn't respond.

Sheeran told me I did the right thing even though I couldn't breathe. I set a boundary. *AL will be okay. THIS IS ADULT.*

I needed a connection. A positive one. Sheeran told me: *You need a connection. A positive one. That's what I'd do. Make a connection.*

I knocked on Leo's door. No answer. I poked my head in anyway, even though his door was closed and I could hear them working. Leo was editing, engrossed. Melanie staring. Me with cutest happy smile: "Hi, how's it going?" Leo not looking up. Melanie, stink eye, *Can't you see he's working?* Me, embarrassed, holding up hand in wave, mouthing, *Oh, sorry!* and shutting door.

Crap. The Sheeran in my head said he would've done the same, putting self out there for positive connection, and surely, Leo noticed some of the happy cuteness and maybe even needed it today to cheer up, what with his furrowed brow and working so hard and sad in car earlier. *You can talk to him later. He's working on his passion project, and it has nothing to do with you!*

Which is the plan. To talk to him later instead. When the time is right.

Even though momentarily am feeling like teeny shrinking-to-invisibility antwoman wanting to stick head in hole and disappear bc Leo was engrossed in editing and Melanie tried to make me feel like crap for trying. Cow!

Went back to cutting room. Twenty minutes later, phone rang with jumble of numbers and: *Bermuda.* I answered, "Cutting room." A Brit voice spoke, far away and muffled, "Hi, could I please speak with Peter Svensson."

"He's not here right now. May I take a message?" *Good work, Berger!* Sheeran exclaimed.

The Brit continued, "Oh, right, too bad. We keep missing each other. J Boone calling. Finally, got a break from set and a signal." He laughed. Sounded friendly. "We'll keep trying. Thanks."

"Thanks, I'll give him the message."

And he was gone. I felt good. Adult-like.

Until lunchtime when Unc came out, happy with the work, and asked if there were any calls.

I told him about AL and J Boone. "He said you have his number."

"J Boone? Why didn't you put it through? We've been trying to reach each other for weeks!"

They were all pissed, like *What were you thinking?!* As if I was supposed to forget the rules and know who J Boone is! Actor.

Famous. Who Unc P is movie-cheating with because J's doing UP's next film and AL is jealous bc she's not. And it's urgent to get it going before J signs onto something else, which is why they so desperately need to talk. But I DIDN'T KNOW! It wasn't my fault!

I hated them in that moment. And all the stupid phone rules. And that Dad is on stupid location, bc If he wasn't, I would've seen J Boone's stupid big spy movie (just looked it up) and would've known he's like the next James Bond and he's important. Maybe. And that AL is way too jealous of UP when she doesn't have to be!

Now feeling awful again. Am idiot. Knowing Unc Unc will never think of me and Leo together as fabulous. Or see the love between us, because his opinion of me, his lovely niece, that he usually adores, is now: phone idiot.

Am trying.

While also devouring third donut from Jena treats (she always brings the best from Sidecar!), which Sheeran would never do so as not to eat poorly and pack on pounds. Or stones for him.

But *what would Sheeran do?*

The Sheeran in my head said: *Whoops! Not the end of the world now is it?* And laughed. Bc Sheeran is a positive chap focusing on positive LOVE! YES! Must get out of coffee-pot-cleaning bathroom and stop eating donuts with dignity. Somehow. How?

The Sheeran inside my head said: *You're trying too hard. Sit back. Bring in happy love energy like attraction beacon. Less is more. Attract!*

Bench outside cutting room, 5:40 p.m. Am attracting love while waiting for delivery for UP and Mike on bench. Sitting tall like bright positivity beacon in cute pear dress and writing in you, Diary, so insides start to feel like cute outsides. Usually it's the opposite.

It is working though. No longer feel annoyed. Though sort of like flattened soufflé after watching everyone spin out today. Exhausting. Plus, eating all those donuts and having sugar crash.

BUT Unc no longer hates me. He walked by after lunch and commented on the pink-cardboard horse race, noticing that Jena's newest Bumble date, Will, had taken the lead ahead of other suitors.

UP teased Jena, which she loved. He also said his assistant Beth reached J Boone and, "thank you for relaying that message," as if I'd done it all right! Jeez.

So yeah, maybe I attracted in that goodness. And tonight going to Deva's for birthday celebration. Sadie joining too, which is good as UP working late and AL could get crazed with paranoid jealousy and victimy self-sabotage, which would make Sadie's life miserable at home.

Also good that Sadie's coming so she doesn't slip back into small-exhaling sadness over how, for no explicable reason, she and Paulie are not each others' The One. Deva and River t. perfect at happiness and distraction and laughter.

Only wish ClydeDogBoy could go back to normal anonymous friendship so can tell him *day weird* and he would make me feel better and normal without even knowing any of the stupid details. But no, he wants to take Sadie to the Aero.

Oh, shoot, there's Leo...

Bench, 5:45 p.m. Have now attracted in hot love goodness by being cute, fun attraction beacon! Sheeran SO WISE! Less is more! Esp with patience and cuteness sitting tall in pear dress!

Here's how it went down: First turned sideways on bench when saw Leo approaching and hid face behind you, Diary, as was instantly nervous and shy. Saw LL go by out of corner of eye towards car. But then he came back. "Saoirse?"

I pretended I hadn't seen him, "Oh, hi," and felt happy light beacons shooting out from around all edges of my body.

"What's up?" he said, eyes brightening.

"Uh, just...writing in my diary," I said with stupid sing-songy voice, "waiting for a delivery," and gestured back at the cutting room and told myself not to care that I merely have a peon job and was talking in stupid sing-songy voice that signaled nervousness and blushing. He didn't care.

"That's cool. I used to have a journal. And then...I didn't," he said and smiled, warm and mildly humbled.

"Cool." I tried to be cool, though also blushing.

"And, um, apologies about before," he said, "It's uh...strange day. Work...life. You know?" shaking his head and exhaling like he was trying to figure it out or come to terms with something and wanted to connect. Like his day was weird too and his soufflé flattened. Then, he laughed it off with a headshake-exhale and shrugged, eyes twinkling, "Have a good one, BookishLensGirl," and turned to go but stopped. "Hey, lunch some time?"

What?

"Sure," I said, COMPLETELY CALM. "I'd love that," AS IF I WAS SUPER CONFIDENT AND HAD INTERESTING LUNCHES ON A REGULAR BASIS RATHER THAN NEVER.

Positivity working!

He smiled again and said, "Great," like he wanted to connect and I was some kind of oasis, then left.

Oh. My. God.

I am Sheeraning goddess!!!!!!!!!!!

Saturday, February 9

Deva's living room bday sleepover, blowup bed, under covers, 1 a.m. Buzzed. Trying not to move when writing so as not to wake up Sadie on same blowup bed.

Leo Landis has liked western video and bunch of other videos and photos since bench!

Want to tell him about Aero next Friday in case he wants to see *Hateful Eight* too. Not sure. Not as confident as at bench.

Also not as patient as have now just set Aero date for Sadie and Hector, anonymously, as BLGirl pretending to be Sadie as stupid anonymous wingperson just wanting to help bc it would make her so happy. Though now not sure that was right thing to do. Was overflowing with love earlier and Schnapps and looking at Sadie, sleeping-cutie beauty, and me with so much love tonight and happy bday celebration, with best friends, and gnocchi at Ugo and Deva's dad's actually-on-fire crème brulee and HBD song from everybody—

Deva's mom, dad, Lenore, River, Deva and Sadie—and playing Say Anything and Dictionary at backyard fire pit and yummy sneaky secret peach Schnapps and Deva and River talking about so much love, love, love and happiness and everyone helping Sadie with sad heart bc of Paulie and bringing her to peaceful heart, and Deva saying to follow true heart, plus overexcitement about Leo and positivity attraction at bench with lunch invite, which led me to set the Aero date. Bc Sadie needs love too.

Crap. I may have overreacted.

With heart too full. And overflowing. And having to act. Due to impatience.

Must reflect now to find true heart.

Also must pee. Going to pee.

Back. Now parched. Must get water.

Back. Hydrated. Now must pee again.

Back. What if Sadie doesn't want to go on Aero date with Hector? Her sleeping self says yes, look at her, peaceful. Also snoring. Yes, she will be happy! It will boost her confidence in love. Still panicky.

Rereading...

CDB message to BLGIrl/Sadie ignored for two days: *Hey! Loved the western-themed post! Did you see Hateful Eight is playing at the Aero?*

Me just now like impatient emo idiot who can't help self in spreading love for Sadie and maybe just wanting to text CDB a tiny little bit, my old friend: *Really? Cool!*

ClydeDogBoy/Hector: *Wanna go? It's next Friday.*

Me/BLGIrl, looking at Sadie sleeping and snoring: *Probably.*

Him: *Probably? Ha ha. K lemme know.*

Me: *Will do.*

Him: *What's your number? I'll text you the info.*

Me, again looking at Sadie sleeping, not wanting to wake her, like idiot, so sent my number so could respond, then: *Going to bed now. Thx. Later.*

Hector immediately texting my phone instead of IG: *G'nite.*

And now he has my number. And thinks it's Sadie! Ahhhh! Why?

Why did I do that?! Why do I keep writing him? Why did I give him *my* number? Why did I momentarily forget that he doesn't even know I exist and that all our messages before don't mean a thing? Why did I make it sound like Sadie wants to go to the movies with him? I have Leo! Two soufflé hearts connecting as one. Maybe that's why.

Also have true heart full of friend love glooping out like overheated key lime pie.

And want to share?

Bc Sadie needs love?

Yes! Love after Paulie. With my heart full of Leo bench moment kept secret all night with actual excitement for self while hearing about fabulous lives of fabulous Deva (and boyfriend Gus transferring from San Diego State to join her at UCLA) and River (taking second gap year after freshman year at Loyola with Hot Steve to backpack in Europe and New Zealand). See! It all works out!

And Deva helping Sadie when Sadie tried not to but cried about Paulie, and Deva made her feel better.

And my heart was full, even with me only having bench love so far.

And Deva told Sadie to cry and not hide from feelings bc Paulie was her first true love, and of course, it was super painful because it really meant something, and that's okay.

And I snuggled with Leo-hope secret in heart. And River told Sadie she'll be happy the breakup happened now so she'll be free at college next year, which Deva quickly shut down and told Sadie not to negate or ignore or push down true-heart feelings, which helped, because Deva always knows what to say, bc she has real adult parents that talk to her and Lenore like real adults and also she's disgustingly smart, which is why she's going to med school next year and is only 20.

Then Sadie started to feel better, and Deva said, "Sometimes you have to hit rock-bottom before things can open up and you can fly."

And I knew that maybe that's why Leo asked me to lunch today, because I hit a rock-bottom bc those around me are insane, resulting in flattened soufflé that made room for love flying in from other flattened-soufflé person (him).

That's when Deva told Sadie to follow her true-heart love feelings: *That's all there ever is. You can't pretend you don't feel love when you do. And it's important to acknowledge when you have a big love. Because it has value even if not reciprocated.* Something like that.

And Sadie felt even better. And it all worked out and now bravery exists in my soul to invite Leo to Aero like normal person who likes normal person and has cinematic friendship. There is hope. Life starting!

Though what if Sadie doesn't want to go to Aero?

Shhh, Saoirse, go to sleep. I mean, look at her, she's probably dreaming of Hector right now.

Home from Deva's, 2:20 p.m. True heart not feeling open and confident like last night. Schnapps fog gone. Friends gone. Everyone has love but me.

Let's recap and analyze to get past this *again*:

First, told Sadie about Aero date, placing phone nonchalantly in front of her on kitchen island as she drank tea and we devoured greasy eggs-and-bacon breakfast made by Deva's dad. "Hope this is okay. I felt Schnapps-compelled."

Deva's dad heard *Schnapps*, and Deva covered, putting on her sweetest smile, "We just took a little." Which isn't true bc we drank most of it. Actually, I did. They kept giving me shots since it was my birthday. I blame them.

Her dad (Naval) feigned upset about the Schnapps, which he procured in Heidelberg where Deva's mom was stationed and he studied engineering, and Deva's mom (Karla) pretended to care, but no one cared and they laughed, and Deva whispered that she'd order more and he'd never know.

Meanwhile, Sadie read the Hector texts and started blushing, like about to cry she was so happy. And River and Deva got in there too and checked out ClydeDogBoy and the messages with BLGirl/me and CDB liking the cowboy boots and videos and all the cute comments, and then River said, "All I see is a sheep dog," and Sadie showed them Hector's other page (him + art), while I said, "Bernese Mountain Dog," and River called Hector "lanky art boy hot," and my stomach sank, and River added, "He's funny too, which means he's smart!" and then sang, "Sadie's got a suitor," and she blushed again and said, "Maybe I like him."

I stopped breathing and Deva took my phone to look closer at the messages, bc she's, you know, like a stupid psychologist-anthropologist-MacGyver, and there were so many messages last month between me and CDB, and she said, "This is all you," to me, bc, of course, it was. Which is when my heart raced and Sadie got worried and said, "That's the problem, what if he doesn't like me in person?" which was weird bc everybody loves her in person and guys fall at her feet!

And River said, "No! He likes you in person. He just said he did, I saw it—*Nice to meet you, Sadie.*"

And Sadie looked at me like she needed help, and I said, "Exactly, he loves you in person! Like at your house! I mean, he didn't even notice me," and I felt stupid tears rising and did a weird pumpkin smile to hide them, trying to make it look like a Ferris-wheel sparkle, which only Deva noticed. And Sadie didn't bc she was just so relieved that Hector loves her in person and spontaneously hugged me.

And Deva said, "So you don't like him?" to me, and Sadie said, "She likes Leo Landis!"

"Who?" Deva said.

"I saw that name," River said and grabbed my phone while my heart took a dive. And he clicked through to Leo's page and yelled, "OMG! Hot! Like literally and film-director hot" and "I love that movie," re Leo and Isla at last year's Indie Spirit Awards with Leo's last film, which River held up for all to see. And Deva's parents got in there too, and Naval said, "Great movie," and Karla said, "I love the part about the revenge."

Which is when Deva looked at me, like *what the hell?* And I said, "He works down the hall," as if it was fine. And Deva said, "With a girlfriend?" And I drooped, and Sadie said, "No, it's okay, we think they broke up, or at least their relationship is shaky, at least that's what my dad says. And Mike."

"Who's Mike?" River asked, and I reminded him he's our editor, and he said, "Right, right, I knew that."

And Deva said, "Please don't do this to yourself," to me, "you always do this," referencing multiple big-fantasy crushes (not like this!), even though here I was helping Sadie and all I wanted was a little love too! And I said, "This is different," re Leo, "because we're friends," meaning me and Leo, "and that's enough, because he's just super interesting; I don't need more," which was untrue, and my heart started squeezing, pumpkin lips smiling, fake Ferris wheels spinning, bc *why can't I have love too?*

Which is when River found a celeb-gossip photo of Isla walking on Yale campus w/soccer-player guy smiling—"New Yali Love for Isla Gordon-Ferraro?"—and showed us, like *See, it's okay!*

And everyone laughed bc who believes that crap? And I could see that Isla and the soccer guy's hands weren't even touching. Even though I wanted them to!

But Sadie cheered me on, "Well, I think Saoirse should go out with him, if he's single."

And River cheered, "Me, too!" and Sadie said, "I'm gonna find out."

And for a second, I felt good, like there was hope and the gossip was funny and there was just a happy, warm feeling all around.

But also I was gonna cry, exhausted from Schnapps and late-night texting and setting up stupid dates and just wanting love too.

I guess, Deva felt bad for me and shook her head and hugged me—like *when will you learn, you silly hopeful-romantic friend? That I love anyway*—and kissed my hair like a funny, overly judgey, helpful wanna-be-Jungian-scientist-anthropologist-MacGyver friend, and said, "You'll figure it out...And we'll see what happens with Hector," like everything's okay and none of us should worry about anything.

I tried to believe her.

And hate Hector.

And we all agreed the Aero date is great for Sadie, so I can feel good about something. Like "a regular meet cute," I said in a kind of happy/sad voice. And Sadie hugged me, and I felt all her Paulie sadness flow away.

Sheeran would be proud.

He'd also tell me: *The attraction beacon is in your hands.*

Bass-turd.

4 p.m. Confirmed Aero date for Sadie and Hector for Friday, continuing cute, fun attraction-beacon-and-positivity altruism to bring in joy for all. Me/Sadie texted Hector: *Sounds great! Would love to go.*

Hector to me/Sadie: *Great! Should I pick you up?*

Me: *Can we meet there?*

Hector: *Sure.*

Me: *Awesome!*

Blerg.

Then I texted Sadie: *You're on for movie at Aero Friday. You're meeting him out front.*

Sadie: *Sweet! Thank you so much xoxoxox Hey, did you see Leo loved the video and a bunch of stuff?! Maybe he wants to go too. It can be a double date.*

Heart racing.

Breathing.

Barely.

Flattened soufflé of nerves. It's true. And now having low-level excitement of anticipation.

6:44 p.m. Drove to Surfrider beach in attempt to inflate soufflé and took shots of water and surfers and gulls and just sat there too. Felt better. Safe. Empowered. Loved. By the world! Maybe even worthy.

That gave me courage to message Leo on IG. Told him about QT retrospective at Aero. Tried to imply he should go. We should go. Yeah, I actually said it: *Was thinking of going. Lemme know if u want 2.*

Dork. Not spelling stuff out.

Embarrassed. Wanted to take it back but kept hope alive.

He responded right away: *Cool! Working all weekend tho. Thx.*
Again, flattened soufflé.
But then he added: *Still would love to have lunch this week though. If you're free.*
YES!!!!!
I messaged back: *Sure, let's do it.*
Simple. Direct. Nice!
He replied: *Great! Will get back when I'm free.*
My world has started.

9:19 p.m. Checked IG and saw Leo went out with friends tonight. He posted: "*They always got my back,*" with photos of him and his producer Chris and two other guys at a Downtown L.A. microbrewery, as if he needed them to have his back. Like something's going on. A breakup perhaps?

Felt slight FOMO wave, like what if he doesn't need me as a friend? But that was insane.

And now remembering bench. Like real adult. It's getting easier! And love.

Instinct and intuition working. Leo is going through something big.

Responded to Sadie re Leo double date: *He can't go. But we're going to lunch. Going to bed. G'nite.*

Sadie to me: *Lunch! That's great! Thanks again, Cous! I love you! Sweet dreams xox*

Me to Sadie: *Sweet dreams. Love you too xox*

Me to self: Hopeful, happy Leo dreams.

Action item: Go to bed.

11:30 p.m. Hector to me: *What's your take on happiness? How was your day anyway?*

Turning phone off.

Monday, February 11

Morning, my room before work. Looked at Hector's happiness question-of-the-day text again. Ignoring bc today is about hope. Remembering that Leo Landis asked me to lunch at bench and beach and was def. flirting. And loves his friends. Even though I wasn't at brewery to enjoy it with him. But good friends not jealous of good friends' friends. Happy good friend has other good friends that have his back. He will be my friend. That is completely possible and likely, even if he is with IGF forever.

Even if that goes against intuition.

Which says something big is going on with him!

Liked Leo's microbrewery friends post from last night.

Cutting room, 11:55 a.m. Leo's door closed all morning.
Unliked post.

12:02 p.m. Liked post.

2:05 p.m. Back from lunch. Went and took photos of movie posters in Unc's office to get out of head and off Leo's page. The posters he has are v. cool. Unc thinks it's cool that I think they're cool.

Aunt Lauren, however, came by and thought it was weird that I'd be that into the posters, like *You like those? Wouldn't you rather be doing something intellectual, like reading, or shooting something to help get you into Columbia, my alma mater?* Weird. Judgey. About art!

Or was this about her?

Ignoring bc I don't get it. Not letting her hijack my day with insecurity and jealousy of UP anymore.

Posted *Being There* movie poster with sunflower CU in foreground.

Which, *Btw, Aunt Lauren, IS an amazing work of literary fiction AND cinema!*

Mentioned *Being There* book in post too. Hector liked it

immediately. Took it back down.

3:20 p.m. Put *Being There* post back up so as not to be stupid idiot. I like it. Why wouldn't I post it? Thinking about doing series on Polish poster art from 80s, like my *Blow Up* one. Or maybe 70s.

Aunt Lauren walked by Mike's part of the cutting room three times without coming in and left.

Ten minutes later Unc Unc stormed into the hall and yelled into his phone, "Where are you? C'mon, Lauren, can you just stop this?" and left.

Tuesday, February 12

Work. Leo's door still closed.

Waiting patiently.

And impatiently.

Which is fine as long as I don't act.

Don't act, Saoirse.

Be still.

And calm.

Like an owl, only moving head.

Or hawk.

Or sleeping cat, drunk from heat on hot summer's day, not moving head at all, but only having happy dreams about chasing through reeds, catching mouse, or butterfly that he never catches, so mouse lives.

Wednesday, February 13

Work, 10:20 a.m. LL cutting-room door closed entirely for past two days. What if he's finishing his cut early? And I never see him again?

No, that is fantasy mind going berserk. Sheeran says: *Attraction beacon!*

Cutting room, 12:15 p.m. And it worked! Unc P was in Leo's room for an hour and then they just now went to lunch.

Actually, attraction beacon unlikely that powerful but it's amazing that this happened. I'm not sure why exactly, but I have a feeling it is. Like maybe UP and Leo can talk about love and breakups and movies and feel happy again and Leo can be ready for new love. Me!

Actually, that is full-on romantic insanity brewing.

But hopefully lunch will at least make Unc Unc feel better as he was v. sad and confused and frustrated in hall before going into Leo's room after hall phone call with Aunt Lauren, which I overheard when lurking outside Leo's room debating—"*knock, don't knock, knock?*"— and UP was telling Aunt Lauren, whispering loud, not seeing me, "No, I'm meeting J Boone at two! I told you five times! But I can go now, lunch now, you and me...just us, nice, come over here...what?...that is not real!...fine! Forget it. No lunch! I'll go with somebody else!" and hung up and shook his head like he didn't know what to do and noticed me, but not really noticing because he was in a fog, in his head, as he walked over and said, "Is he there?" meaning Leo.

And I said, "Yeah, I mean...maybe...he might be in there...I was just...," pretending not to be lurking, gesturing to phone, as if that's why I was there, "researching, for, um, Jena, and an address, to send the thing, but it sounds like he's in there," exaggerated listening at Leo's door, nodding.

UP noticed none of this, "Thanks," and just went in.

And now they went to lunch.

While I sit tall and cute in blue-jay dress at cutting-room desk attracting in good things for Leo and Unc Unc and me!

Also Columbia entering mental sphere (in spite of self) as means to catapult self into league with Yali Isla Gordon-Ferraro. Columbia = low-risk safety net to impress LL.

Too much time to think.

Stop thinking!

Also thinking about Hector happiness question, which am not supposed to think about.

12:55 p.m., work, about to go to lunch. Replied to Hector question to stop driving self crazy!

Me to Hector: *Happiness is hope. It's also truth and beauty. And connection.*

Wanted to say *belonging* instead of *connection* but sounds too needy.

Positively embraced refrain.

Rather than honesty.

It's fine!

In car in parking structure, post lunch, 2:14 p.m. Went and took shots of street art. Girl dreaming, blowing towards globe/earth with birds. From all angles. At Ogden and Genesee behind Melrose.

I like taking photos. Also checked out Heck's IG again against better judgment and his art is t. cool.

Secretly looked at art schools for five seconds. Stupid. Why would I do that?

Instead posted photo of gull from Surfrider Saturday and ignored culture-related shots. Need to feel like bird flying free over beach. That is my truth for today. While waiting for Leo to set lunch date.

Which I know he will.

4:30 p.m. ClydeDogBoy likes gull. ClydeDogBoy writes to me/Sadie on BLGirl IG message: *Happiness is beauty is a kaleidoscope of joy. And joy is all just love at its core. Love the seagull. He's feelin' it! So is the big dog. Day?*

Heart expands.

Mind goes into overdrive. Putting phone away. Hate CDB.

Must separate appreciation of Heck's art and how I feel about him as a non-seer of me and annoying, flawed person, while also able to leap the tall building of Sadie's heart and make her feel better.

Can LL please just come out of his room now that he's back from lunch?

Thursday, February 14

Valentine's Day!!!! At work, 2:30 p.m. Leo Landis has broken up with girlfriend. And we have a date Sunday. Oh. My. God.

This is how I know:

Yesterday, I texted Sadie: *Yes, I'll drop you off at* Aero, in attempt to act on positivity and promote goodness while sitting here like blue jay. She's super nervous about date.

I also told her about LL/Unc lunch (but not Unc Unc sadness part). This prompted her to get intel on Leo last night, if there was any. Which there was. And she called just now to tell me everything in perfect Sadie-drama reenactment fashion, like Emmy-worthy daytime TV:

Sadie to UP at dinner last night, nonchalantly to see if he'd bite: *So, I heard Seer's been hanging out with Leo Landis.*

Aunt Lauren: *What?!*

Unc: *Really? Great.*

Nick: *I could see that.*

Yay, Nick.

Sadie: *Well, you know, just friends or something.*

Aunt Lauren: *Good. He has a girlfriend.*

Sadie: *I said just friends.* Bc she was sussing it out, not bc she knew at that point.

UP: *I thought they broke up.*

AL: *What? Why? They were so cute together.*

Sadie: *Really?*

UP: *I don't know. Did they?* He asked that to AL, somehow needling.

Aunt Lauren: *How should I know? You're the one that goes to these lunches and meetings and doesn't tell me anything. Or take my calls.*

UP: *So now this is about us?*

AL: *It's always about us.*

She got up and put her dish in the sink. Hard. Loud. Upset.

UP to Sadie: *He's a good kid.*

AL: *So now you're defending him?*

UP: *From what? That's my opinion. Break up or no break up, he's a good kid.*

AL: *How do you not know if they broke up or not?*

UP: *I can't remember! They went back and forth.*

AL: *Because you never pay attention to anything! Unless it's about you!*

Then she left, down the hallway.

Unc P yelled after her: *Actually, they did break up! Because she wants space! He told me yesterday! At LUNCH! Before I met J BOONE! About our film!!!! And she broke up with him! Because he works so much! And so does she! So you don't have to worry! HE'S the one who's jealous! Because SHE's dating someone else! And I didn't say anything because it's none of our business! So maybe you can stop blaming Leo when you're mad at me! And just say it!*

Huh, *Just say it.* Kind of like what Mike said to me. But different.

And AMAZING! About LEO!

Sadie and I cheered.

Tho also a bummer about AL/ UP. I told her I was sorry, "I hope your mom's okay, and your dad," even though I was super grateful she got the intel. She felt the same about the intel, luckily, like there's no choice about her parents fighting but the news about Leo is great.

After the call, I thought I was going to have a heart attack. Then, the next thing I knew I was in the hall pacing in front of Leo's door like I was going to—*IDK!*—say Happy V-Day or something? My heart racing—*knock, don't knock, knock?*

Which is when he opened the door. Randomly. Bc he had to go to the bathroom. And I was just standing there.

I screamed.

"Hi," he said, amused by my terror.

My heart raced more, heart attack pending. "I was, uh, just, like, in my head, I don't even know, like, uh, writing a thing, in my head...heh heh." Trying to cover.

"That's cool," he said, still amused, looking at my eyebrows.

"Thanks," I said, calming down, looking at his smile, like OH MY GOD! How was this happening? Hoorays 18!!!! And somehow, bravely, cutely, brightly, happily, compelled by positive breakup news, I said, "Happy Valentine's!" Flirting!!!

"You too," he said, sexy flirting back. And cute! Then teasing, "I mean, where have you been? You haven't come by in days."

Haaaaa!

I laughed.

He said, "But can I...," gesturing down the hall, "get past?"

Oops! I stepped out of his way. He looked at my hair. "I'll stop by in a little bit...," sexy, flirting, then, "Gotta, you know...," gesturing down the hall, "Pee!"

And he bolted down the hall. And I came back here, and then, OMG, he came by later! And asked me to lunch! Normal single guy who likes single girl, standing in doorway on way out, courier bag over shoulder. "Hey, how's Sunday for lunch?"

Me hiding phone, secretly looking at #lastreetart, perhaps appearing intriguing. "Great."

"I gotta work but maybe you can help me. Look at some scenes?"

"Sure," I said, nonchalantly-intriguing single girl.

"Great! It's always easier to work when someone's around. How's noon?"

"Perfect."

"Perfect. Thank you. See you then," he said, smiling, leaving.

"Happy Valentine's!" I yelled after him.

He turned back. "Happy Valentine's," he said in low sexy voice, w/Dr. Who tunnel smile—not caring that I said *Happy Valentine's* twice in one day.

How do I stay normal?

I HAVE A DATE WITH LEO LANDIS, FRIENDS OR MORE!

Now texting Sadie that I might go into Aero movie tomorrow (in case LL randomly shows up). And so I can talk to him about it SUNDAY!

Bc I finally belong! With perspective on future. Like possibly film school wherever LL is living. Near his next set as we cohabitate. Even if just friends. Best friends. Housemates. Friend-partners. Bc he is my refuge. And he can teach me camera and I can be a cameraman. Camerawoman. Cameraperson. Director of photography! And film breathtaking cinematic wonders for talented filmmakers like LL!! As roommates. Or more!

I finally have something to look forward to.

Also texting Sadie to wear strawberry dress tomorrow not cute tops or jeans (she keeps sending photos!): *Wear the strawberry dress! It's super cute!*

10:12 p.m. Trying to calm down from overdrive of excitement re Sunday.

Looked through shots of street art and posted a few from the other day and wrote: *A kaleidoscope of angles, each with its own story.*

That helped.

And it's true. The same piece could have so many meanings.

Like I can look at Leo's closed cutting-room door from many angles. Was looking at it like he was keeping me out. But he was keeping him and his amazing filmmaking skills in, as confirmed by selfie just now: him and Melanie beaming with film in background, "Scene done!" So sweet. He loves his work. Dedicated to his craft!

Also, Dad is coming home tomorrow. For whole weekend. Finally. He makes me feel v. calm. So easy to deal with. No ulterior motives. Except the cowboy boots. I wonder if there's a motive besides fashion. Nevermind. He talks to me like normal human, and we play backgammon and do crossword and that's all that matters.

I wonder if Leo does the crossword.

Liked Leo's photo.

Action item: Go to bed.

Midnight. ClydeDogBoy/Hector liked my street art posts and texted me/Sadie: *Flat or bubbly?*

It woke me up. Annoy-ville. But replied so Sadie doesn't have to deal tomorrow.

I assumed he meant water and wrote back: *Flat. You?*

I was right. Hector: *Bubbly. Like me* ☺

Silly, cute person. Tho still hate him.

Me/Sadie: *Are you insinuating I lack effervescence? Because that's hardly the case. Underneath my calm exterior is a storm-surge of energy and ideas.* Lol. Super weird amount of confidence suddenly.

Heck: *Roger that. A calm, cool oasis/geyser of intent and surprising and refreshing photography angles and ideas.*

Aw.

Me: *Aw Heck, that is sweet. But are you comparing me to Old Faithful?*

Heck: *Affirmative. You are an old soul and faithful answerer of questions. See you tomorrow night!*

Heart racing bizarrely. Stop!

Me: *See ya, Aw Heck.*

Heck: *Aw Heck? ho ho affirmative.*

Sweet. Hilarious. And he noticed the angles in the shots. Who does that?

I will miss his daily bits.

Heart sad but acknowledging the cousinship is rocking love with Heck and Leo. And Heck is also friggin' blind.

In other news: Went downstairs earlier. Stole Mr. Griffin's headset. He chased me round house and outside. It was super fun. I let off steam. Then Mom came home. Her wrath almost made it not worth it. But it was.

Demoralizing re 18 Hoorays tho.

But also not so bad. Hee hee.

Ho ho.

Am in love.

Friday, February 15

Night, my room post movie/date. I probably should never see Hector in person again. Ever. It's just not a good idea. Too uncomfortable. Like every cell in my body stands at attention when I see him and my heart expands or something and then it sucks back in like a black hole, agitating, even in my arms.

Bc he likes Sadie more! And I feel so hurt! And rejected! Ahhhh! Why????? I don't even like him! But I do bc there's this stupid draw, like good and bad all at once. Like a magnet, exciting, repelling, attracting, sharing ideas, philosophy, creative imaginings, back and forth, all night long.

And then Sadie enters and I'm dust, like stepped over like he's doing a Texas two-step, dancing to spell of silent Sadie siren goddess winning ALL HIS LOVE. Blerg. I WANT LOVE TOO! I'm NOT JUST A FRIEND-BRAIN. Even tho I am!

So confusing. Why???

Okay, let's recap with pros and cons in extreme adult calmness and brevity so never have to think about it again:

Pros: Sadie happy. She has love thanks to idiotic Wizard of Oz (me), bravo queen of Cyrano deception. Plus, movie was amazing and am now set for Sunday Leo date with cool cinema acumen.

Cons: Stupid Hector!!! Making me so ARRRRRRR!!

So, yeah, basically, I ended up on their date and it was yucky for me.

We started at the Aero. I dropped her off, parked across street on Montana and waited in car till they were in.

Hector had on stupid red pants again so he was easy to spot. Plus, he's tall. His face lit up when he saw her. She lit up too. They talked outside Aero, kind of awkward, him talking mostly, hands dug deep in pockets of red jeans, Sadie nervous laughing, smiling, clutching phone. She looked cute in strawberry dress. They matched with red of strawberries and pants.

I waited 15 minutes after they went in, got popcorn and sat in back. They were in middle seats. Hector kept leaning over and talking to Sadie. She kept laughing. Happy. Gross.

Then, he went to the bathroom and noticed me. I pretended not to see him. "Hi!" he waved, "You her *out* if it goes bad?" Him teasing, funny, me totally awkward.

"I, uh, no…"

He was amused. "It's okay; I think we're good. But thank you."

Cute, flashy smile.

Thank me? Yeah, you should thank me. If it weren't for me, you wouldn't be here, like if you didn't love MY photos!

After the movie, Hector asked if I wanted to go to dinner "with us?" And Sadie said, "Yeah, join us!"

Us??? Two and half hours in and they're an "us?!"

So, I politely declined, but Sadie insisted, so I drove with them in his old red boxy 1970s BMW 2002 like a stupid fool to the Promenade for Hummus Bar, cafeteria style, which was a good choice. Love the hummus with pine nuts and fries. But that's about it, and the whole thing exploded in my face, and why did I ever go????

Basically, from second-one when we sat down, it was pretty much me and Heck talk, talk, talking about movies—*the* movie, like sparky, fiery talk, and all QT movies, bc I love them so much and so does he, apparently, even when we disagreed—with Sadie sitting cute and pretty and occasionally chiming in with cute and witty items, bc she's funny too, which started the Texas-two-step dance, stepping right over me, dancing with Sadie as if I wasn't there or was mere Socratic sawdust from awesome cinematic discussion. Like a real discussion, like how discussions are supposed to be, back and forth with disagreements too.

And then after Sweet Sadie, he'd turn back to the sawdust (me! terrible metaphor, but I felt like sawdust! and then I didn't! bc then I was magic dust too!!! like magic dust dancing between us!) and we got into it again, which was fine until he brought up the Tarantino violence, I mean, not in a cinematic way, but he thinks I should admit that it's not for everyone, which I didn't want to, and he argued that I had to accept the subjective angle, but I wanted to look at it objectively, like how objectively amazing Quentin Tarantino is as a filmmaker and the merit in the originality and humor, especially in *Pulp Fiction* and *Once Upon A Time in Hollywood*, bc the dialogue is just so smart! And fast! And the characters are hilarious. How does QT even think of these things? Like the whole Manson thing? It's just so satisfying to see something completely different and out there. And the music is fun. And the juxtaposition of the styles with humor. And the style overall! I'm so blown away.

Which made Heck's eyes sparkle from my enthusiasm bc he felt it too (I think), and then he toyed with me, bringing back up the "gratuitous violence and blood," head tilting, sparkly eyes shooting out fun interesting-convo lightning bolts, being contrary, to mix it up, to make the conversation SING! We were singing! Back and forth! Magic sawdust in Socratic tango wonder! Like in that song from *Pulp Fiction*, "Girl, You'll Be A Woman Soon," Thurman and Travolta dancing separately but together bc they're hearing the same song, at least that's what I was hearing in my head.

But then, Heck smiled at Sadie, and she shrugged, like she agreed with him about the violence, like it's not for everyone, like maybe she doesn't even like it but also does bc she can see the wonder in it too, and I should acknowledge that. Which made me fuming mad. Why did I get so mad? And why were they judging me for liking Quentin Tarantino so much? And why couldn't Heck just be excited about the novelty and my excitement? He likes novelty! I know this! He *IS* novel!

Which is when I began justifying it, saying how, "I guess I put things in pots and focus only on the good pots," and don't even notice the violence and blood, really, "I mean, I do, but the amazingness just makes it irrelevant," and seriously, "I don't like violence." It's not like that's a thing! And I just somehow couldn't give them the satisfaction of agreeing! Why???

Heck liked the pots metaphor and laughed, which was nice, bc I felt like I was being honest and true, but then he said, "You don't think you're giving him too much credit?" Just to be contrary! And funny, because he turned to Sadie and admitted that "it's subjective and objective, depending on how you look at it," like I'm doing objective, like QT is objectively good, and he's doing subjectivity of viewers, but he said it to HER NOT ME, playful, laughing, bc they're an *us*!

Which is when I lost it and yelled, "Fine! Maybe I'm just an idiot and too easy on the violence! Maybe I'm a bad person!" which had nothing to do with the argument, only me taking it personally, and I stood up, "I have to go to the bathroom," and stormed to the bathroom. And felt like an idiot baby, nowhere near adulthood. So I rallied and told myself in the mirror that I had to go back out there with dignity.

So I did, and maybe it was worse in my head than reality bc they didn't even notice when I came back with happy cuteness and said, "Sorry. Just a little too into it. I think we should change the subject."

Nice. Adult-ish.

I sat down.

While Heck playfully tried a bite of Sadie's baba ganoush, laughing together, lightning bolts of cuteness and laughter and joy between them while I was a Socratic third wheel, invisible, irrelevant, rejected, ignored, flattened wheel. Flat tire.

Too much of a weirdo.

I had to get out of there.

But he rallied with, "No worries. That's the fun of it. Embrace the shock value and enjoy the ride," which should've been great bc he was smiling at me, the flat tire, like he didn't care that I'm a flat tire. Or that I like QT. As if he's a weirdo too. And understands. And likes me and does care, in a way, but not completely. Bc ultimately he only cares about Sadie and her smile and her HAIR!!!!

I said I had to go and Sadie said, "Please stay just a bit longer."

So I did, and it got worse. Bc then Sadie told me, "You think too much," even tho Hector does too! Which is why we even had the stupid great conversation and BANTER! FUN! HAPPY! FINALLY!

And then Heck teased Sadie for being quiet and "demure" and gave her credit for the BLGirl photos (MY PHOTOS!)! "Probably the best artist in the room," and I said, "definitely" with more Cyrano lies, and she got embarrassed and shook her head, which came off as gorgeous humility, and he made her feel better with, "You know what I mean, best photography in all of L.A.," and nudged her playfully, smiling in that friend smile MEANT FOR ME! And I said, "Exactly, Sadie is a master of disguise, demurely hiding her talent," stabbing myself in my own heart like Travolta with the stupid EPIPEN!!!

Then they teased me about Leo. Sadie said, "She's obsessed with QT because of a guy," and Heck said, "Oh, a GUYYY," which should've felt great but made it WORSE bc of his idiotic eyes-and-smile combo, teasing, like magnetically flashing, and my heart squeezing, I DON'T KNOW WHY!

Then he asked his stupid questions of the day! GAH! And Sadie didn't answer so he teased, "C'mon! You answer these in like two seconds usually," and she asked why he asks them, and he said, "Because you have all the answers," meaning me!

Then he asked us what it is we love, like what we love to do most, and Sadie said, "act," and he said, "Not photography?" and she blushed, realizing her mistake, and he said he gets it bc he loves comedy and drumming more than art, which made Sadie laugh, "What?" And he teased her, "You just wait till I force you to listen to my drums. Blood may shoot out of your ears like a Tarantino movie."

And I laughed and cried inside all at once, and he asked, "And you?" meaning what do I love to do? And I was tongue-tied, so Sadie told him, "Writing and math," and he said, "Thank god, someone's doing something with their life," like they're doing interesting creative nothings TOGETHER while I'm BY MYSELF as a practical and boring overachieving humanity helper.

Sadie thought that was funny too and laughed. While I fake smiled, Tarantino blood squibs exploding inside my face, blood-squib tears rolling down inside my cheeks.

I stood up and said I really had to go and Sadie insisted we all drive together, so Heck dropped us off.

Sadie screamed with joy when we got in my car. I feigned excitement, which she interpreted as me thinking it didn't go well for her.

So she brought up Paulie again, like did he ever really love her? (*Yes!*) Or "was he just in love with the idea of me? Like I'm sure he did love me in some way, but why is it so easy for him to let go?"

Super annoying! I told her we don't know but should focus on what we do know, which is that Aw Heck had a good time tonight and so did she.

And she said, "What if it doesn't last?"

And I said, "Why wouldn't it last?"

"Because I'm not you."

"Why would you want to be me?"

"Because you're so confident?"

Which seemed impossible, "What?!" especially after my bathroom explosion. Which made us both laugh.

And then she said, "He is nice," about Hector, and "He likes you too," like she's happy me and Heck talked so much and had amazing magnetic-sparky conversation. Weird.

I said we should give Heck her number so she can text him directly and she said—*please, please, please*—could I just text him a bit longer. And told me she's meeting him Tuesday. ARGH!!!

But then, she said, "Thank you Saoirse D Berger, I love you," which was nice, and, "Oh, by the way, what's *Aw Heck*? He loves it."

Saturday, February 16

Night, 11:20 p.m. Today was a good day that could've been a bad day but wasn't thanks to DadSheeran. Yes, that is his new name. And thank god he's here, stupid cowboy boots and all. Bc his sister is insane! Someone, please, stop her.

Here's what happened:

I had work bc Unc Unc and Mike are recutting a scene. LL wasn't there so I was enjoying my normal boring peon tasks (coffee, bagel run, etc.) with excitement about tomorrow tucked in my heart.

Then, AL called at 10:50 a.m. exactly. I channeled Ed Sheeran and answered, "Cutting room."

She said, "Hi, honey, it's Aunt Lauren," but her voice sounded weird, like her—*I'm on a mission*—voice and—*I'm calling someone important because I really want them to do something for me and I have clout, like when I called the governor and got him to address public school policy down here.*

Gross.

She said she wanted me to get Jena on the line. "The three of us need to talk."

Crap.

I exhaled and looked at Jena, headphones on, working. "Jena?"

She looked up. She was going to hate this. I breathed deep. "She wants to talk to us."

Jena took off her headphones. "Who?"

"Lauren."

"Us?"

"Yes."

"Why?"

I don't know!

AL must've overheard and said something about women sticking together in this business.

"Something about women sticking together. In this business. And a pow-wow," I relayed to Jena.

Jena groaned and picked up the phone. "Hello?"

I summoned Ed Sheeran into my body. Sometimes fantasy mind has perks.

Aunt Lauren: "Jena! Hello! Thank you! Are you still there, Saoirse?"

Me: "Yup. Here."

AL: "Good, good, how are you both doing this morning?"

Jena: "Great."

Me, mimicking: "Great."

AL: "Excellent, what are you working on?"

Jena exhaled, perturbed. "Just adding a few sound effects and adjusting music for the train scene. And they're looking at the dinner."

"Well, good, that sounds productive," AL said, full of positivity and cheer, and clearly this had nothing to do with film or work. "So I just wanted to have a little girls' pow-wow, because we, as women in this industry, really need to stick together."

Jena shook her head, like *what a nightmare*, and I had a feeling this had nothing to do with women in the industry either. Why was Aunt Lauren doing this to us?

"I mean, this business is tough for anyone to succeed, and for women, it's even harder. We have to fight for our wins. We have to be amazing, over and over. And if we fight, we're called aggressive."

I groaned, and Jena laughed silently and mouthed, "Oh my god." Which made me giggle. Gah. We both laughed.

Aunt Lauren heard. "What?"

Me: "I said, *uh huh.*"

"Well, it really is important, especially in today's world. And every time we see a woman being kept on the outside, we need to work together to keep her in."

Oh, snap. This was about her and Uncle Peter! AGAIN!

Then she went on and on for five minutes, and Jena and I listened and looked at each other, like *oh my god*, until she said, "Okay?" and we "mm'hmmd," and she said, "Thank you. I knew I could count on you." And that was it.

But what about us? Didn't she for one minute think about us and the stupid hierarchy of this job, women or not? Ed Sheeran would be put to the same task: Don't put the calls through.

And it's NOT EVEN ABOUT THE JOB!!!

Jena said, "They need to keep their relationship out of our business," and went back to work.

Which bizarrely made me defensive of AL and UP all of a sudden, as my aunt and uncle, not the director/writer-producer of the movie I'm working on, and I wanted to yell: *This is why they're good! Because they're so friggin passionate! And bring it all to work! Lighten up, people! Let them have their emotions! That's what makes artists! That's what makes GREAT artists!!!*

But I didn't because I was also pissed at AL for doing this to us. It wasn't fair. Jena and I are pawns. And this was TMI. And all I want is for AL and UP to be my rock-solid aunt and uncle! How will I ever look her in the eye again?

Luckily, Dad. I mean, DadSheeran.

"Yup, that's her," he said, sitting in my orange beanbag chair, cowboy boots staring me in the face, larger than life because of the angle. If I took a photo of his boots right then, they'd look huge. Which I did and posted them. Too funny.

Dad loves hanging out up here in my room above the garage. He fits in. He loves to come up and see what I'm listening to, which is always nothing exciting so he pulls up his latest playlist. He's super up on music and cuts all the big battle scenes to loud punk. So weird. And cute.

"It's just how she operates," he said. He should know. He's her brother.

I told him I can't stand it, and he told me she's always been like that, "The more success, the more she spins out and overcompensates. Drives me crazy."

"Really?" Blerp. Sounds like someone else I know, with a large aubergine nose.

"Yup. And then it passes. Best thing to do is ignore her."

"Easy for you to say."

Then he told me this stupid story Mom came up with to help him deal with his sister. In the story, AL is a wildly determined creative person throwing a birthday party and wants to decorate with giant, beautiful balloons. But there's a shortage of balloons in the land so AL does the footwork and sends a well-crafted message to the Balloon Fairy. The Balloon Fairy gets the message and happily sends an airplane full of balloons to AL. But wildly creative AL is also wildly insecure and doesn't trust that anyone can do their job right, so when the plane full of balloons is trying to land, it can't be AL's running back and forth on the runway signaling the pilot where to land. The plane keeps flying back and forth over the landing strip, and she keeps getting in the way of the goodness.

Eventually, AL gets out of the way and it lands and everything works out. But only after all that worrying and waving and running back and forth while the pilot wastes gas and time flying overhead with no idea why she's on the runway, jacking up the panic on the ground and the confusion in the air.

Yup, that sounds like AL. Metaphorically. And we're the pilot that needs to be patient and calm and wait until she gets off the tarmac to land the plane.

But I'm not patient or calm!

Get off my college tarmac, Aunt Lauren! Stop telling me how to answer phones and where to go to school! I need to land my plane with confidence, where I want it and how, so my life can start!

Something like that.

It made me feel better. And it's a funny story too. Good work, Mom! Maybe MomSheeran is the real brains behind DadSheeran. Naw, maybe just when it comes to AL.

Then Dad said, "But, you're right. She shouldn't have done that to you guys today...girls..."

"Women!" we said in unison. And laughed.

And he said, "I'm sure everything will be okay with Uncle Peter too. Eventually."

I hope so.

"But we should definitely ignore it for now. Until they both get out of the way." Then he suggested we go watch polo up at Will Rogers. It's so random but he got it in his head and we went a few times before.

"And later, we'll play cards!" I love that we can just be in the moment. In spite of his boots. And I love our routine of playing cards. And backgammon too.

He blasted Beastie Boys in the car. Then we walked to the polo field and he asked how I'm doing. Another great thing about Dad is that he actually listens and cares. Mom cares too but I don't think she listens. She's too focused on figuring out her life and managing Jake.

Here's how it went down:

Me: "I'm okay, I just..."

Dad: "Don't like work?"

Me shrugging.

Him playfully pressing: "Sort of like work?"

I admitted I like it. Esp with Unc P and making money and learning about filmmaking.

Then he asked about BLGirl and I tried to sound excited. I told him it's doing great and we got a new bookcrate sponsor and an invite to YALL. "Woo!"

He saw right through that bc last year I was super excited about YALL (BookTuber heaven) and now I'm not. Flatlining instead. Why can't I be excited?

So he called me on it, and I yelled, "I'm sick of reading!"

And he was thrilled. "Ah! Truth."

So we laughed and I relaxed a bit. It *was* truth, but there was more and I felt tears coming and somehow Dad knew and asked if something else was going on.

I shook my head *no* but that's when the tears got rambunctious and I tried to stop them.

Why was I crying?

He pretended not to notice. "Any news from any of the schools?"

I told him no and croaked, "Still the same, responses come end of March and April," tears getting hotter.

"You don't sound excited about that either."

And then the tears exploded as I shook my head. Why? Why? And he hugged me. And I cried, "I don't know why I'm crying."

"Because you're eighteen?"

"No!" I yelled but laughing too bc it was so stupid. And maybe true.

"No longer my little bird. Now you're a big bird ready to fly the nest."

"That's so stupid, Dad." I laughed more. And tears came again. "I don't know where to fly."

"Well, you don't have to go anywhere."

"Yes I do. But what if I get there and it's the wrong nest and I don't belong? And Aunt Lauren's pushing so hard for Columbia. And what if she's right?"

"Oh, honey," he said, hugging me. "Ignore her. You don't need to rush. It'll all come together. You have so many talents."

"But what if I never figure out what I want? What if I waste it all?"

"You'll figure it out."

Then he said his usual about college being more than just classes bc he knew exactly what he wanted in high school and went straight to film school.

But I don't know anything.

"We all have our own timing," he said, "and you either figure it out or it comes to you when it wants to."

Which didn't really help, but I said, "Great. I guess, I'll just be sitting here waiting."

And he teased, "Just be sure to get off the runway."

Nice one, Dad. But it made me laugh bc I love him so much and maybe it was good to get it out.

And he hugged me again and told me he and Mom are always there for me while I wait to figure out my life. And it felt nice to hear even though I already knew it. And only have till May to decide. On college.

I'm just happy he's home.

Then we went to watch polo but it doesn't start till April and he didn't want to hike (in boots!) so we drove to In-N-Out by the airport and watched planes. He misses In-N-Out in Vancouver.

Tonight, we played Scrabble (not cards), and Jake had a meltdown bc he was losing, and Mom got super mad. It was hilarious. Jake also yelled at me when I called him *Mr. Griffin*, "It's Peter Griffin not *Mr. Griffin!*" So I called him a *baby* bc he doesn't know how to lose, and he stormed off. Dad was the peacemaker, and Jake came back and we started over. Then he complained again when losing and rubbed it in when winning, but finally we all ate ice cream and watched Dr. Who. Well, me, Jake and Dad watched Dr. Who and Mom worked on her cheese business on the dining room table, then came and sat and cuddled with Jake.

Everyone happy. I love my family. We live in the grey area.

Except that Dad's leaving tomorrow and gone another month before they wrap and he comes back to cut. So off we go into our own little lives. And mine is so uncertain.

Except that I'm meeting Leo tomorrow.

11:40 p.m. Was just finally falling asleep so I'll be awesome for tomorrow, when Aw Heck texted Sadie: *Fun last night. You up? Wanna talk?*

Crap. No. Ignoring.

11:52 p.m. Felt guilty so texted back: *Yes! Super fun. Was asleep. Can we talk Monday? Family day tomorrow. Weird but what we Svenssons do.*

Which is true—Sunday is Svensson family day. Though Bergers are family so sometimes Sadie and I hang.

Him: *Sure. How was your day?*

Gah! Why? Why? Go away!

Me: *Family weird. Day good. You?*

Him: *Ah, family! Another kaleidoscope. Of love and other emotions and ideas different from mine, at least that's how it is for me. And some the same. I usually wait until the pendulum swings. And pass the time with happy things. Today I took Clyde to the secret beach so he could run free and chase gulls. He was a happy camper.*

Wow, longest text ever.

Me: *Secret beach? Happy for happy Clyde. Everyone should run free sometimes. Or all the time. Yes on kaleidoscope. Could use patience while ducking the pendulum. G'nite, Dog.*

Stupidly forgetting how much I hate him.

Him: *Will take u 2 secret beach some time. G'nite. Sweet dreams.*

Aw, Aw Heck was being aw sweet. I copied and sent to Sadie. She texted back: *Thank you!*

Then more from him: *Forgot to say, looking at your shots. Will you take some for me? I want to do a thing for my friend Nia's mural downtown.*

Nope. Not me. I didn't respond.

Sunday, February 17

My room, 8:45 a.m. Anxious. Writing to calm down before biggest day of life.

Had breakfast with Dad. Mom distracted by phone. Jake still asleep. Dad and I read paper and talked and did crossword. Sunday's is SO HARD! Even together we can't do it. But we laugh and that's fun. I miss our routine. When he's here, we text each other words all day. But it's not the same when he's away bc we can't finish it together at night before bed so we don't do it at all. Today's an exception.

And now bringing Dad to airport. Going to cutting room after. What should I wear? Want to throw up. Too nervous! What if it shows? Especially since plucked one side of eyebrow too much. Looks like I'm in constantly inquisitive state. May wear baseball cap, pink *Lungfish* one, schwag from Mom. Would add coolness-uniqueness factor. Esp with new dress. It's plain green so will look casual. But happy and energized. Green is happy and energized color. Plus, hip from stand-out cap.

My car, studio parking lot, adjusting cap in mirror, 11:48 a.m. He's here. I'm parked next to his car. The rental. Range Rover. What a waste. Surely the studio got it for him. Heart pounding so loud. Afraid of heart attack. Imagining studio guard finding me. Ambulance. Leo running out. Me almost dead on stretcher. "What happened?" he says and kneels down, cupping my face in his hands, nuzzling nose to nose, dreamy in the eyes. "I love you, mi amore," he whispers because his mother spoke Italian and he loves spaghetti Westerns and Serge Leone and has hot Latin blood in his veins, now pulsing into mine.

I am insane.

My room, 7:30 p.m. Am like goddess. Warrior princess. Floating. Two inches above ground. Am inflated with love. And joy. If I die now, I will know what it's like to have lived and loved, expressed and created, laughed and cried and snorted with happiness, like literally shooting water and snot out of nose due to hilarity.

It was the best day ever, and I am overcome with bliss.

And Leo Landis has invited me to OSCAR PARTY!!!!!!! And QT might be there. And he got all nervous and humble, like QT is a god to him. And it was so cute. And I could relate bc that's how I felt earlier about him, so we were one in that moment. And I love how he is SO REAL in spite of being also so smart and talented!!!!!!!!!!!!!!!!!

So yes, we had a real day. And I felt present and in the moment the entire time. That never happens.

Here's what happened:

First, I finally got up the nerve to walk in. Used my key for the building. So quiet. Kind of cool. His door ajar. I heard voices from the screen. Looked in. He was working, intense. Watching, stopping, trying, changing. Again, watching the screen. Another change. *Good.* Going back to start of scene. He did this over and over until he watched it all the way through and said, "Perfect," out loud, and exhaled and sat back and stared for a moment like he was thinking.

I know it sounds dorky and boring, but trust me, it was like watching a Fellini masterpiece. Because he's so hot! Anything LL does is hot. And that's when I poked my head in and said, "Hello?"

He beamed. Leo Landis beamed at me. "Perfect timing. Let's have lunch."

I was disappointed; I won't lie. I wanted him to show me what he'd just done, like expecting it bc he said he wanted to share it with me. But then, he said he'd been there five hours already and was starving.

I apologized. I could've come earlier.

"No, no," he said. "I got so much done. And later I'll show you what I did. And you can tell me what you think." And he smiled. And flirted. And I felt better instantly. And said, "Okay," calmly, even tho I was so happy inside.

Then, we went to Farmers Market. He loves the blackened shrimp at Gumbo Pot. He pulled back my chair, which was v. sweet. He also opened my car door earlier so I could get in. I like him so much!

The woman at Gumbo Pot knows him and likes him. Everybody does.

He had the shrimp. I had the same, though I wasn't hungry and was worried my breath would stink like garlic. But his would too. I didn't notice if it did. I was too enamored.

And nervous.

Luckily, he talked endlessly, esp at first, so I didn't have to. So much energy! He told me about his family and growing up in Austin and then Montana. He has three older sisters. He says they always looked out for him and taught him "everything about women," which was a joke, "as if I know anything at all." His eyes crinkled with laughter. "I don't know anything at all about your sort," he teased. So hotly, sweetly funny and humble and modest and clearly knowing all about *my sort*! And he knows how to make every inch of my skin sparkle, like sparklers on 4th of July. Love those! Which is what he was doing right then.

Then he took a sip of lemonade and leaned forward on the table, and the Dr. Who tunnel of intense attraction happened again.

I got extra nervous with all the positivity coming at me, a ripple of sexy, bright, happy love that made the sparklers go nuts, like little Ferris wheels spinning with joy.

"So tell me about you, Saoirse Berger of BookishLensGirl."

Swoon. I mean, I swooned and blushed and went into a state of romantic panic, Ferris-wheel sparklers darting like fireflies all over the place, making me nervous because now I had to talk and I SO wanted him to like me.

So I talked fast, in a blur, and told him everything, like about starting BookishLens and how I always felt alone and kept switching schools because they were all so boring, till Aporia, which is why I always read books and started BLGirl bookstagram and how it took off and I had all these fans and they wanted me to do BookTube but I hate to be onscreen and never showed my face for three years, so when Sadie said she'd do it, it was easy. Like that, like a flood of information. And I kept talking more, not even really looking at him, like I was looking at the air or the inside of my head, and I went on about how BLGIrl works perfectly and I read the books and write about them, and Sadie is me on camera and people love her and us and it's amazing. And I was so nervous, and then I said, "And no one knows it's really me. And we even make money from sponsors, and yeah..."

Then I stopped and he was looking at my hair, like maybe not even listening, and I blushed like a beet, which I hate. Beets, that is. I threw up once eating raw beets. Stupid. Why did I even do that? It's like eating raw potatoes.

And Leo was staring and didn't seem to care about me being a speed-talking beet, like maybe he didn't hear a thing (and luckily, wasn't mindreading) and was mostly interested in my eyes and hair and how I got sauce on my cheek, which he wiped off.

Ha ha, happy cuteness wiping my cheek.

"So you're just working and doing that?" he said and checked out my hair more, or maybe I had something in my hair, or on the cute pink cap, which I was wearing backwards, so he could actually see the hair, or maybe he liked the cap!

"And applying to schools," I said, "for next year, since this is a gap year, because I graduated early, even though I'm eighteen," which was an embarrassing thing to say, even tho Isla is younger at 20! So I talked faster to make up for it, about all the places I applied to— UCLA, Berkeley, Columbia, NYU, Exeter, Edinburgh, bc of JK Rowling—as if it would help, and then I told him I wasn't even sure what I want to do and applied to the wrong major due to romantic-book fantasies about being a writer. "And, yeah..." Then I shrugged cutely and took a sip of lemonade and hoped it was okay that I ended on a downer.

"Impressive," he said, in spite of the downer, like he didn't even notice how boring and sad it was.

I was shocked, like, *What? Impressive? Me? Impressive like Isla Gordon-Ferraro?*

And he told me I was just "a serious girl," which he loves, but was also maybe more interested in the seriousness of the curls on my head than anything. "With a little bit of mischief with the YouTubing there. Also impressive, BookishLensGirl."

So he was listening! And definitely flirting! And the Ferris-wheel sparklers were back and spinning! Stomach jumping, not knowing what to say next.

So I asked him where he went to get the attention off me, even though I already knew.

He said he went to school in Montana and studied filmmaking and liked school because that's how he figured out he loves movies and then just went for it, making his own films, which is how he met his girlfriend, through the DP, of his first short, there, at school.

Girlfriend?

As if she still was. His girlfriend. Criminy. I panicked.

But then he said, "Ex, ex girlfriend," as if explaining, nodding,

"We broke up a few weeks ago. She goes to Yale. It just wasn't working." And then he shook his head and did a huge exhale.

While I cheered inside.

He said it was still raw and hoped it was okay that he was telling me all this.

I said of course it was.

And he thanked me for listening and said it helped to talk.

And I nodded like a normal, cute adult friend and wise owl who can sit still and be patient.

And he smiled and said I actually remind him of her.

What?

Which he wasn't sure was a good thing, but more like teasing and maybe flirting again, or just friend flirting, and said, "Makes me nervous to talk to you."

Funny! Cute! Humorous and hotly vulnerable, sexy elk, so secure in himself that he can say anything, able to love and lose, risk and fail, be honest and show his pain...and be open for new love with playful funniness...for me!

I melted.

But quickly pulled myself back into solid cuteness and normal adult form and laughed. "Well, I'm glad you're okay."

Then we finished eating and walked back to his car, continuing easy friend mode.

He asked what I actually want to study and I said I wasn't sure but maybe (totally idiotically nervously)..."I really like camera, so, maybe...DP? You know?" I really just wanted him to say, *Yeah, amazing. You're such a good photographer you'd make a great DP. And then I could hire you.*

Instead, he said there are definitely good film schools, like NYU. His DP went there, who's fantastic, and we'd see when we get back to the cutting room. "And you can tell me what you think." Hooray!

He also said, "Thanks for listening," as he started the car.

And I wondered if he meant: *Thanks, friend, for listening and talking about my ex that's messing with my heart,* or *Thanks, CUTE YOU, for listening but let's focus on now instead of the past because I really like you.*

Maybe both.

Back at the cutting room, he showed me the first half of his movie, and it's amazing.

It's about a mischievous brother and sister, 11 and 9, and their relationship. Set in Mexico City. The parents are out and they burglarize the neighbor apartment for fun, stealing fencing swords and helmets. Clever. Funny. The kids always outsmart the adults and get away with things.

I wanted to see the rest, and he said, "Next time," (hooray!) and asked what I thought. I told him the things I loved about his characters and their relationship and how it's a great metaphor for society and how I think the kids have something special together.

I must've talked for a long time bc when I looked up, he was staring. Like maybe mesmerized.

And my heart raced.

And he laughed...then said, "You really get it," with sparkly eyes, like he was happy, just like me, bc we see things the same way. Our brains making out, just like I anticipated!

And I wanted him to kiss me right then. And maybe he did too. But he has control, like a normal adult, focused on work, and said, "Now you can tell me what's not working," as if everything else, including me, was working just fine.

I had to regroup from the romantic insanity. So I did. And told him what I thought, which was that maybe the boy shouldn't help the girl steal eggs till the end and instead should sabotage her for fun. But she still gets away with it. Like me with Jake! I told him it's bc that's what he already has in other places "and it works so well."

And he said, "Any chance you're free next Sunday?" like he was totally into me. "For an Oscar party? Tarantino might be there. Not that I'm trying to name drop or anything," which he was, name-dropping that is, but in a funny making-fun-of-himself way.

Which is when I happy-panicked, Ferris wheels of joy spinning inside. OMG! "Uh, yeah, I mean, no, I'm not busy," I said, catching my breath, paralysis happening.

"I mean, you don't have to. It should be fun though. You okay?"

I broke the paralysis. "Yeah! Yes, wow, no, Tarantino. It's super exciting. I guess it just took me by surprise. He's amazing. I mean, like you." Oh, god.

He laughed. "Yeah, not even close. I'm even nervous about meeting him. You'll have to be my wingman."

And I was in love.

I *am* in love.

And am going into uncharted territory. Never before has something this good happened. Maybe this is my moment to shine. To start my life. To flow through without being insane or botching or overthinking.

"Great, I'd love to be your Tarantino wingman."

And girlfriend.

Monday, February 18

My room, 10:30 p.m. Focusing only on positive.

Let's start with me and Leo. He was distant today. Simple hand wave from cutting room. But I realize it's bc Melanie is there and he's focused on his film. He is, after all, I now know, very rational and down to earth and committed to his work. I wondered if he could be two people at once and just loves me bc I was so nice about his film, blown away by his cinematic mastery. And normalness. But I reigned that in.

Then I worried that maybe I was too excited. What if he retracts his Oscar-party offer? What if he lures Isla back with awesome Hollywood glitz? Or worse, what if he lures her back by just being himself and because she really loves him for him? And he still loves her for her?

I reigned that in too.

Then I thought, *Do I really love him for him?* YES!

Then I thought, *But does he love me for me? Could he love me for me? And am I good enough for him?* YES! Hopefully. Or will be! And AL Columbia-mania a blessing to solidify that with impressive education.

Hector texted: *Coffee tomorrow?*
I asked Sadie.
She said: *Yes! Tomorrow would be great! French cafe on Main? 4 o'clock?*
I set it up. Not even upset at either of them. Bc I HAVE LEO!
Sadie texted: *Thank you!*
I ignored his question of the day: *What's your take on rain?*

Tuesday, February 19

Night after Promenade/Pier with Deva, River, Sadie. Hector/Sadie coffee date went great today. She's smitten. Today was the first time she felt better about herself and Paulie. Hooray! Was like normal self. Funny and playful. Am bowing and curtsying in mind, taking at least partial credit for that goodness. In spite of Tarantino blood-squib tears.

That's the good part. The rest of the evening was not so good as friend unit and heart support at risk. Though also may be fine as could just be hyper-romantically paranoid.

Here's what happened:

First, Promenade. Deva wanted to hear about Sadie's success and buy this blazer for River that was his Christmas present. River's indecisive and perfectionistic and Deva has no clue about clothes so she wanted me to help. Which was fine, and fun, bc I love to shop. And look at colors. Mostly I like green. Like Leo's eyes!

The blazer we found, however, was cranberry, at Zara, with light-blue stitching, which makes it look like a pomegranate and River loves it. More hooray.

Sadie showed up and told us about her happy dates with Hector, including Friday, gross. This was outside the changing room as River came in and out with options for jeans to go with the blazer, which he bought himself since Deva only got him the blazer, and he was super happy.

Also, everyone was excited about Hector (but me), and

apparently, there was no mention about the rain question on the date today, which was good. He doesn't seem to bring those questions up with her alone in person. Also, Sadie/Heck made another date for Friday sans me (yay!). And he's helping her prep for her audition next week, which she's super nervous about and he made her feel like it's possible. Woo!

Sadie thinks it's fun to go back and forth with texts w/Heck, pretending to be each other. I fake agreed, and both Deva and River love the whole Cyrano thing and think it's fun to watch (like I'm a friggin' seal). Then we all agreed (me like ball and chain) that I should keep being Sadie and texting Hector a tiny bit longer to keep Sadie's spirits high and make it easy. Gross.

Then, Sadie decided we should go to the Pier, which was fine with everyone, even me, until she brought up Leo. "Hey, how was the date with Leo?"

And Deva said, "What?"

And River said, "Date?"

Which was when the problem arose because Deva was upset I hadn't told her. "Why didn't you tell me?" Like I was supposed to tell her!

Which made me defensive bc she's so judgey and I said I didn't know why, like maybe it was bc I hadn't had time, and she didn't believe me and looked hurt, like I was her best friend and why wouldn't I tell her? Bc she loves me and is always so helpful.

Which made me mad, and I said I just wanted to protect my little friggin' nugget of hope and joy, which is the truth, and let the seed grow stronger first on its own, like we're doing with Heck for Sadie, before we overanalyze it.

Which made her more hurt, and Sadie said, "I thought he broke up with her," meaning Leo and Isla.

And River said, "Really?! For sure?"

And I said, "Yes," and Deva got more upset bc I didn't tell her that either, so I said, "Really, I was just nervous to talk about it, because you know, I don't know, it's just so new. For me. To have someone."

Because really I just need you to believe that I can have love too!!!

And Deva said *fine* and that she just wants me to be okay because a lot of the time I don't seem okay because I always have crushes on unattainable people and nothing ever happens.

So I yelled, "I'm okay!" And she yelled that I'm never okay and now I have this new fake prince and new fake romance and what if I open my legs to this fake prince and the fake romance dives and she has to wipe me up. Like she always does!!!!

Which is when we really got into it.

And I yelled, "What?!"

And River cheered, "Legs! Yes! Legs!"

And I yelled again, "There are no legs! Only hearts! Also, he is not fake!"

"He's 23 and in rebound mode!" Deva yelled.

"I'm 18!"

"Exactly! So when he bails because he's 23 and young, and so are you, you're gonna take it personally and think it's your fault because you're not good enough or did something wrong, and we'll have to wipe you up from the floor." She really let me have it, maybe to offset her feeling momentarily hurt before.

Which made me feel hurt. "Why are you saying this?"

"Because you live in a book-induced fantasy land."

"So I can't have a life because I'm 18? And read? And you guys can? His girlfriend is only 20!"

"Need I say more?"

"Ex! His *ex* girlfriend."

"Do you really believe that?"

"What?"

"That it's a real breakup. And this relationship is gonna last?"

"You think we're a relationship?" I said, suddenly hopeful.

"Every time two people interact it's a relationship. But how you and he define it is a completely different story."

This made me a little nervous. "He's a serious person. He's not going to pretend. And me too. He likes that about me! You don't even know him!"

"I think we should give him a chance," Sadie said, thank god, even though she doesn't really know him either.

River finally looked up from his phone. "Remember when I was in love with Professor K? And we gave *him* a chance?"

"Oh, god," Deva groaned. "Please, don't talk about that."

"Who's Professor K?" Sadie asked.

"That Russian teacher he had," I said.

"Oh, right," said Sadie, remembering.

Deva shook her head disapprovingly, and I was relieved the focus was off me.

"And then I went with him to ComiCon and he hit on a girl," River said. "Still painful."

"River was the wingman," Deva explained to Sadie, "unselfishly and uselessly stupid."

"Wingman?" I croaked, maybe audibly, maybe not.

"Thank god for Steve," River said. And laughed.

I deflated. Maybe I am a moron.

"Oh, honey, one day you'll find your Steve and Leo will be dust," River said to comfort me.

I felt worse.

But then Sadie defended me, "She's a hopeful romantic. Let her be. She's following her heart. Like you said, Deva." Sadie hugged me. "And Leo is a good guy according to my dad."

Deva took this in.

"Really," Sadie confirmed with her big sweet, totally believable smile.

And Deva backed down. "Fine, I'm sorry, that took me off guard." And she told me to nurture my seed and let it grow, "And maybe he'll be a good stepping stone," meaning Leo, and she smiled like she was trying, but also kind of fake, bc I know she just said it bc she likes me and wants to help and wasn't really sure what to do but thought maybe there's hope for me in love if I get out of my way, or get lucky one day.

Stepping stone?

"Exactly!" Sadie agreed with Deva and suggested we ride the Ferris wheel. Her joy was contagious. And everyone felt better...

What did that mean, stepping stone?

...but me.

We walked to the line and River showed us his dad's new Tesla (AMAZING!) while I spun out.

By the time we were halfway through, I was imagining standing on a stepping stone in a cute little brook with Leo, happy, then Isla bounding over, stone by stone, him welcoming her onto our stone then bumping me off accidentally into the water to be with her. Him so relieved and kissing her cheek and looking at her hair like he looked at mine. Me invisible with cute sneakers in cold brook water.

My heart deflated. I was like a quail whose proud-in-love crown feather drooped after getting drenched in a rainstorm of disappointment.

Deva noticed (AGAIN!). "You okay?"

Why does she have to notice everything?!

And I said, "Sure," and she didn't believe me and I couldn't stand it and yelled, "Why do you always doubt me?"

And she yelled, "I wasn't doubting you! I was asking if you were okay!"

And we got into it again:

"You were doubting me!"

"Because you doubt yourself!"

"I'm not doubting myself!" I yelled, totally doubting myself.

"You're too sensitive. You can't help it. It's your worst and best quality."

"What does that even mean?"

"It's why people tease you."

"People tease me?"

"Because you ask all those weird questions. And post weird existential crap. Talking about ideas. No one even knows what you're talking about. I mean, I do, and that's why I love you, but no one else does. It's like you're in a fantasy world!"

Which totally depressed me. "They tease me behind my back?"

"Like Hector," Sadie cheerfully chimed in.

"Hector teases me?"

"No, the ideas part," she said.

"Behind my back?!"

"No, he doesn't tease you. I'm saying he's like that too, weird and talking about ideas all the time. I like it," Sadie said and smiled.

Which took me by surprise, because it was good and bad, like finally someone on my weirdo team but then I'm not allowed on the team.

ACK!

Then Sadie added, "And if you change your mind about the Oscar party, Hector's friend is having an Oscar party in some art loft downtown." As if Leo was getting back with Isla. Or I would change my mind. Or he would cancel!

I told her I didn't think I'd change my mind.

Which made her happy, and she said, "Good."

Which was surprising and made me realize everything will be okay.

And River gave me a hug and said he loves how weird I am and doesn't always understand me but it's okay and why he loves me, also bc I'm cute, like his little sister, and added, "Right, Deva?" because he wanted us all to get along and enjoy the stupid Ferris wheel.

Deva agreed but was still hurt so I apologized this time and we got on the Ferris wheel and Sadie told us Elaine showed up at the cafe today and that she loves how Heck makes everyone feel included.

Also she loves that he brought Clyde and drew caricatures of them on napkins. Which were AMAZING! Especially the one of Sadie, super hilarious and cute with sparkly, happy eyes and a bunch of thought bubbles over her head that said "joy" and "hope," "beauty" and "truth," and "connection."

And Deva leaned on me to get a better look. And my heart expanded because the thought-bubble words were from our texts. Which Sadie knew and didn't care.

I think Sadie only noticed the sparkle in her cartoon eyes. I guess it makes you feel good when someone sees you that way.

Which inspired me just now to look at Leo's IG and he liked a bunch of BLGirl shots. And added a smile. Bc maybe I have cute cartoon eyes too, full of truth and love, to him! Like Sunday!

Heart expanding, forgiving Deva, no need to worry. If she doubts me, she probably just needs a hug, like she says—*if you point your finger at someone else, you should be pointing at yourself.* Cartoon eyes spinning with sparkler love for friends and Leo! Am now able to write back to Hector. Also, gotta pee.

Back.

Me/Sadie to Hector re his question: *Rain is comfort, safe, cozy. Washes away doubts. Frees imagination to go wild with new ideas and hope. You?*

He wrote back a few minutes later: *Love rain in bits and spurts to freshen up world. As long as it doesn't put a damper on sunshine. I'm a sun man! Concerned going to school in Portland next year but will find good umbrella. Sweet precipitous dreams, Sweet Sadie.*

Gah.

Sent Sadie the abbreviated version. She laughed and now is getting him an umbrella!

Me drenched with stupid wingperson sadness but also happy with Leo hope!

Wednesday, February 20

My room, 10:30 p.m. Someone once said the definition of boredom is that you don't feel connected to anything.

Felt bored today at work so went by car mural I saw on Hector's IG and took photos. Not for him but for me. It's downtown and a really cool image of a girl in an old light-blue Ford pickup. Took lots of angles. One selfie, which I promptly deleted. Felt good.

Then, I put on Adele and Dad's old cowboy boots and sang and pretended to tap dance and filmed my feet and, like an idiot, posted.

It's my truth. Keep thinking about Aw Heck's drawing of Sadie with the "truth" bubble. Am inspired. Feel like if I do my truth, good things will happen. Somehow. Magic enforce.

Also, adjusted Jena's pink-cardboard-cutout horserace bc she now likes Screening Zeke best, who she met at a screening. Moved him ahead of Bumble Will, who apparently flaked. UP says he's betting on Bumble Will to redeem himself at Sunday brunch/museum date. Mike's betting on Screening Zeke bc he's taking her to see Dudamel, whom she loves. Everyone loves the horserace. Feels good to make them laugh. Plus, I have nothing much to do anyway.

Now going to write up script for BookishLens—*The Teenager's Liberation Handbook.* Feeling rebellious toward organized society even tho I know we need it to function. Optimism from Aw Heck cartoon bubbles makes me realize it's okay that I haven't found path yet, even w/freedom. It's good I have freedom. Now need to use it. I'm the one imprisoning myself. Need to be my truth.

What is my truth?

Attraction beacon for love!

Thursday, February 21

Cutting room, 10:30 a.m. Went to other building to rinse coffee pot and make more brew for Mike and saw Leo's comment on IG on my cowboy-boot dance! LL: *Hey. You. BookishGirl. Come by and give me your number so we can do this!*

OMG!!! It's happening!

12:20 p.m. Went by. Melanie not there. Door shut. Knocked. Entered. He was so happy to see me!!! "Finally. She visits me."

Cute. Flirty. I laughed, v. cutely flirty back.

"I want to show you something," he said and showed me the changes. That I suggested! At least what he could do, like keeping it so the boy doesn't help the girl and she always wins (like me with Jake!) until the end. "You were right!" he said, with the best smile ever.

I melted. And smiled back. Dr. Who tunnel of love. And cinematic wonder. Like I actually contributed to *something.* Beautiful.

Then I got nervous, realizing this something was real.

And he was okay with that—like maybe I had cartoon-cinematic-love eyes!—bc then he opened a blank contact screen on his phone and said, "Now, we can do this." I put my number in. He said, "Can I pick you up at 4:30?" And when I looked up, he was checking out my shoes. Or was it my ankles? Or legs? Which made my heart spin.

"The phone?" he said, with cute, funny smile bc I forgot to hand it back.

I handed it back, not even worried I was an idiot for not handing it back. And now he has my number.

And we're on for Sunday.

And my truth is happening. With normal happy love!

My room, 11:40 p.m. Normal happy love exchange on IG not so good re Hector. OMG!!! Apparently he saw what Leo wrote to BLGirl and called just now because of it. Called!!! Because he was jealous of Sadie. Thinking Leo wrote Sadie!

Nooooo!!!!

Luckily, I got away with it, like with my voice, like with this bizarre Wizard of Oz skill.

Which makes me feel terrible. Like will bad-karma Cyrano ruin the normal love I have w/Leo?

No! It's fine. It is not bad karma. Bc it's THEIR FAULT! Sadie and Heck! Their fault. Go away with your stupid Cyrano love.

Let's recap to see how THEY put ME in this awful position:

First, there I was, cozy, snuggling w/duvet and cute Leo love, trying to sleep, but also like an idiot when the phone rang, blinded by cinematic-beauty and ankle-admiring excitement, thinking the call was Leo, grabbing the phone off the nightstand without looking, answering! Ahhhh! "Hello?"

"Hey."

OMG. *What?*

I looked at the phone: "Sadie's Aw Heck." *Noooo!* "Oh, hi."

"Hey, I hope you weren't asleep."

"No, yeah, totally asleep," I said, which was good bc he thought I sounded sleepy, so I told him I was and sat up.

Then he said he just called to mix things up, add a little Sadie cheer to his day, or night. Which was sweet. And annoying. And

NOT MY FAULT!

"Hope that's okay. Or maybe I should call another time?"

"No, yeah, now is great too! I couldn't sleep anyway," I said, like an idiot. But I didn't know what else to say. Bc Sadie needs to GIVE HIM HER NUMBER! Stop being such a chicken, Sadie!

Which I didn't have the liberty of being then, no bawk-bawk here. I had to be brave eagle. Which was fine at first, like when he said he saw the boot-dance post. And I told him about taking photos of the Ford-girl mural because he inspired me. And he said he'd love to see them. And I said, of course, I'd send them.

But then the convo launched into weirdness and the pressure was on bc he asked if I worked on the lot too, bc it seems like I'm over there all the time, what with blue aliens and "snazzy directors inviting you to visit."

No!!!!

Which is when brave eagle (me) pulled out all the stops bc Heck's voice was super weird and I was thinking, *Oh my god, what if he knows I'm Sadie?!*

And I blurted out, "Saoirse!"

"What?"

And made stuff up on the fly. "That's her. For her. He wanted to talk to her, Saoirse. And for some reason, lord knows why, he couldn't just walk down the hall, so he wrote on Insta, and she saw it, because she obsessively looks at it all the time." Heh, heh, nervous laugh, cute laugh, heart racing.

All true.

And he said, "Oh," like that was a total possibility. *Thank god!*

And I said, "Yeah, yeah, it's kind of funny and weird, right? And I *am* over there a lot, to see my dad, and cousin, and mom too, though she's not always there, but usually it's only weekends, because of traffic, going east, on the 405, and school and all, but sometimes I go during lunch," with happy-cheerful voice, "And hence the blue alien, and also I just post at weird times, like at school, but with older photos." Ending on a high, chirpy note.

All fake. Lie, lie. Their fault, their fault.

And it worked! Bc he's blinded by love of Sadie.

So I continued, telling him Leo's the guy Saoirse (me!) is into and hence the whole Tarantino thing at Hummus Bar, which made him laugh. Hooray! And he said, "Is he into her?" meaning is Leo into me (Saoirse), and I said, "yes," and he was so relieved.

And jealous (of Sadie)! And complicated!

Which is the only good thing that came of this bc he noticed LEO WAS FLIRTING WITH ME!

Ah. Exhaling now. Relief. That is my truth. Leo love = real.

And Heck said, "Okay, well, I'll let you get back to sleep. And I'll look out for those shots. And see you manyana."

And I said, "Good night, Aw Heck."

"Good night, Sweet Sadie."

And we hung up and I sent him the Ford-truck mural photos and sent them to Sadie and told her about the call. She texted back: *Thank you for making it work! You're amazing. And glad he approves of you and Leo! Told you!* ☺ *xox*

Huh. Yeah, somehow it still doesn't feel as good as it should.

But thank you, Diary, for listening. And I'm glad we didn't get caught.

Friday, February 22

My room, 7 p.m. My excitement about Sunday is unbridled. My heart constantly pounding. I dyed my hair pink. Then saw Leo's face. Dyed it back. Borrowed Sadie's lime-green-and-pink dress with orange trim. I feel a need to be bright and colorful and noticeable. Yet classy. The dress is classy in cut. Just loud. It's different from Isla's style. Hers is a more nuanced, elegant, posh-type glam, while I am more…traditional and artsy? I feel good about it. Will wear hair up in bun to offset bright colors and bought cute platforms to be sexy yet casual. Or may wear sneaks. So can stand for long periods if needed, in case Oscar party is standing-around party rather than actual watching party.

Usually, we go to Sadie's for Academy Awards. Mom and Stupid

Jake are still going. We eat popcorn and take bets. One year, we went to Dad's director's house and it was more socializing than watching, and Mom said her feet were killing her after. So, yeah, not that I want to be Mom, but I want happy feet.

Nervous. Excited. Cute.

Later.

Night, my room, 9:30 p.m. Sadie came by after date w/Hector, so excited she had to tell someone. They got coconut chicken at Cha Cha Chicken and walked down to the beach. He held her hand. Sweet and real. Innocent. Like he didn't kiss her and seems shy and careful. Or maybe hesitant, like testing the waters or thinking she is (which she said she is). It's like courting, and he talks a lot. And is fun to tease. Like when she called him Aw Heck. And he called her Sweet Sadie back.

V. gross.

She said it feels like a grade-school crush.

Trying to be happy for her.

Also, she found a great green umbrella. It should get here next week.

And she gave me a necklace from her jewelry-making friend and said, "Thank you for helping me." It's a pounded-silver heart on a big, thick chain, like a rapper chain or dog leash. It's weird and gaudy but looks great with the dress for Sunday. I tried it on to show her and it makes everything pop. Sadie has great style! And is generous sharing it with me. We're a good team.

She also likes the cherry dress on me. And the green one with pears. She thinks they all look good. We couldn't decide. Ugh.

She thinks I should go with my gut Sunday. Not sure but at least I have three solids.

"I'm glad you're going to the party with Leo Landis," she said.

Me too. I was relieved by that statement and her in general. Finally again. She beamed the smile that shoots energy bolts and it felt like a hug.

She really does have it.

"And now, for some *Teenage Liberation*!!" I pulled out the book.

"Really?" She was so excited.

"Your favorite." She's read this book fully and I haven't. Prolly bc she didn't have freedom bc of AL and I did bc of Mom.

She threw a fist in the air. "Freedom for all."

"Great, and I say we film on the Metro. And all over L.A., free and learning in life."

She loves it, and we posted a teaser. With her in cowboy boots! Finally. W/a tap dance. Ha!

All in all great, though she didn't want to go home bc apparently her mom is still insane. Her dad keeps meeting w/J Boone and stopped telling AL completely. Sadie's worried bc AL and UP love each other so much and are also like an explosion. Which I know but she can't stop talking about it.

"It's exhausting," she said, "and Hector's the opposite. He makes me feel calm." A relief.

Which was a relief, standing at the top of the stairs to my little above-the-garage room watching her go across the lawn, reminding me that the whole stupid Hector thing is good and I can just friggin' relax.

I'm so glad I have her.

Saturday night, February 23

Eve of Oscars, Oscar Eve, day of Indies.   Stone stomach. Excitement. Dread. Both at once. Okay, so I watched the streaming Indies that happened this afternoon in Santa Monica, and guess who was there? Leo Landis. With...ISLA!!! Sitting with people in suits. Smiley and chatty. Not touching. I watched the video a gazillion times.

Also. LL texted flirty twice and asked for address. I checked it a gazillion times and sent. He replied: *Cool. See ya at 3.*

I am beside myself with excitement and confusion. What is up /Isla? I scanned social media for a clue. Nothing.

Am going to text LL. Can't stand it.

Later. Done. Better. Texted Leo: *Hey, saw you at the Indies!*
He must've known.
LL: *Yeah! Was cool. Our DP from my first film was nominated.
He invited me and the ex. Had to be there to support him. Luckily, he
won!*
Yeah. He got "ex" in there I'd say.
Wasn't sure. Called group-text pow-wow with Deva and River
despite ego. Just couldn't stand it. Had to get their take. Sent them vid
and said: *No negativity! Just tell me what you see!*
Deva called and screamed anyway, "I told you not to let him get
to you!!!" But then teased, "That said, they're definitely done. They
didn't touch once and he kept glancing at her, and she scooted her
chair away once, though you'd never know if you didn't look closely.
They're good. They're gonna be super successful in this business."
As if Deva has any clue at all. But is prolly right.
So I feel better. Tho now, Deva knows I'm going. River texted
separately that he's glad I'm going but "don't tell Deva." He's being
selfish. LL is hot. He wants the gossip.
So. Now. I. Can. Live. In. Bliss. And. Nerves.
Blair Witch Project—highest-earning low-budget indie. Or close.
Cost $60K, earned $240M+! Also *Reservoir Dogs. Napoleon
Dynamite.* Because of good marketing. *El Mariachi* made for only
$7K! Got $200K to finish, earned $2M. Amazing! Gonna do another
To Be Watched for BLGirl instead of TBR. I love movies.
Also got new shoes.
Multiple pairs.
Me tomorrow: Sassy dress. Sexy platform sandals w/strappy
ballet ties up ankle. Or maybe shiny silver sneaks w/heel. Or pointy
pink low-heel slingbacks. Still not sure. But will be hottest chicklet at
party. Am on marketing game, a la *Saoirse Dynamite!* Text w/Leo
good. *See!* Am putting it out there. Feel insane.

Later. Ran in and unplugged Stupid Jake's computer when he went
to bathroom. He screamed that his computer was broken. Mom
crazed. Then they saw it. Plug off. Hee hee. Not yet caught. This

might have been worth it.

Tho breaking 18 Hoorays. But I had to do something to get rid of this anxiety about tomorrow.

Also took a gazillion photos of me in dresses and shoes in standing mirror. Not helping. Can't focus. Going to try to sleep even though it's only 9:30.

9:50 p.m. Texted top photos to Sadie: *Still can't decide! Intuition wavering. What think you?*

9:55 p.m. Hector to me/Sadie: *?*
Crap. Crap, crap. Sent photos to Hector. Why? Why? Bc I have him under "Sadie's Aw Heck" to remind me why I'm even writing to him!!! Ever! I don't want to write to him! Ever! It's not my fault!!!
Me to Heck: *Sorry, wrong number.* As if that would solve it.
It will! Go to sleep!
Five seconds later, Hector to me/Sadie: *The green one.*
What?
And now he's calling on the stupid phone: *Sadie's Aw Heck*
Gah!

10:40 pm. I answered. Like idiot. Again, not my fault, but bc I just want this to be over with! Go away, Heck! But he didn't and immediately said, "Definitely the green one." Why? Why?

And it was funny somehow so I said, "With the pink and orange or the pears?" stupidly compelled.

"Pink and orange," he said and asked what was up with the dress, totally valid question, so I clarified with altruistic panicked lie..."Henry!" because that was the first stupid H name that popped into my head. "The text was supposed to go to Henry."

"Henry?" he said, as if that was weird too, which it was, and who is Henry, so I rallied with "Henrietta from school," also a lie, there is no Henrietta, but I said she's helping with the dress for "Seersh" for her big Oscar date tomorrow, "We needed another opinion, so thank you."

He was much obliged and nice and felt so weirdly safe, so I asked him why he picked the pink and orange, and he said because "she likes it the best, clearly," meaning I like it best, which was true, and amazing that he could see that, though also SO ANNOYING!!! Why does he have to be the one to see this about me? Like a stupid fashion HeckSheeran!

So I asked him how he knew, and he said it was my smile, a small smile but there and "she's relaxed and confident compared to the other two. She'll have a better date in that one cuz she feels good and like herself in it."

Poo.

Hate him even more.

He also likes the necklace from Sadie so I told him it was from her ("me") and he said the heart necklace suits "her" (me) and that Sadie knows me well, "A good cousin." So confusing!

Then it got silent and weird with blushy embarrassment on my end bc I felt emo weirdness about the attention and good observations of *me*, so I asked him if he likes the photos I sent of the Ford-truck mural to divert the convo flow.

And he said, "I told you I did," meaning he already told Sadie (oops!).

So I rallied with, "I know but what did you like about them?"

And he said, "I told you that too," which I guess he had.

So I told him to tell me again, bc what else was I supposed to do?

And he said it was "the angles."

Which I thought was cool.

And he said, "So *now* you're excited?" like Sadie must not have been.

So I played along, "Instead of?" And he said "coy?" And I said, "That's how it is, coy in person, gushing on the phone," as if that's how Sadie is, but really it's me, which was too weird and I had to try hard to not laugh.

And he said, "Okay..."

And I guess I was kind of having fun and asked if he wanted to know more of what I think about the Ford-truck mural and the photo angles and he said, "yes," in a funny, dramatic, low voice. Which was really kind of sexy, or at least it would be if it weren't him.

Which made me laugh, "Good," and I told him all about what I thought, like how I think things look different from different angles, like how colors change, and the feeling, even though it's all the same image, and how light changes things, and your mood, and how life is kind of like that if you can look at it from different possible angles, like people and drama and stuff that happens, and that everything would be better and happier if people saw the various angles, and that I wish I could do that and look at all things in my life like that, like my family, especially when they drive me crazy.

He laughed a big-happy laugh, like he agreed, "Yup, this is true." And I felt so happy!

And then, his voice cracked or something, and he got weird too and said, "Yeah, no, it's cool that you can see that. And express it."

And I was bizarrely bold for me and said, "Why does your voice sound so weird all of a sudden?"

"Because you're so direct on the phone?"

So I told him it was a good angle for me, "and our relationship," which felt way too personal bc maybe I was getting carried away.

But he laughed so I kept going with the weird bravery and said, "Why did that make you so…whatever that was. That emotion."

And he didn't know but agreed about the angles of life and said maybe the weird voice had something to do with that and how he wishes everyone could see the world like that and how that'd make it a better place, especially in his stupid family too.

And then it got quiet, like awkward, maybe because we were thinking the same exact thing, and I heard a car go by and asked where he was, and he said, "On the curb."

"What?!" I said, imagining him sitting on Sadie's curb! Which is ridiculous.

He laughed and said, "Not your curb," (thank god!) like he knew what I was thinking, but only partially, because he doesn't know I'm me and the panic was about getting caught not him stalking Sadie on her curb, but in a good, sweet way like he just wants to see her.

So I asked him what he was doing on the curb.

He made a weird motor-rumble-grrr sound and said it was a boring topic. So I said, "Oh, c'mon, I want to know," and he said he was fighting with Jose like usual and had to get out of the house, but that it wasn't that bad really, and like all fights, everything simmers down and you go back to watching *Family Guy* together.

I said I was sorry that was happening and asked, "Who's Jose?" And he said it's his dad.

Which is so funny, so I said, "You call your dad Jose?" and he said, "I do," and laughed, but it was sad too, like you can tell he loves his dad but his dad, apparently, is this "tragic" guy, "big soul, big heart, big talent, but nowhere to put it all. Jose has no wall," which meant to paint on, bc it turns out he's a painter too. But doesn't paint bc "he can't see the stupid angles anymore," bc Jose's dad (Heck's gramps) told Jose that painting wasn't a career *unless you're Rivera!* Or something like that bc they're Mexicans and lived in Arizona and *who the heck paints in Tucson? Especially when your dad's a friggin' cattle manager!* Whatever that is.

That's what Heck's grandpa told Heck's dad and Heck's dad took it on and gave up his dreams and studied history at ASU instead of art at RISDI and is now a school teacher and a ball of resentment, which he somehow paints on the wall that is Hector, the resentment that is, or some such metaphor. Heck was on a roll.

It sounded so sad and upsetting, so I told him I was sorry, and he said it's okay, and maybe my voice sounded kind, like a hug or something, and made him feel safe bc he started being funny again and said at least the tough love got his parents together long enough to have him and his bro, bc apparently Jose and Ofelia met at a Diego Rivera exhibit or mural bc Jose was still into Rivera after he quit painting bc Rivera's work is so passionate and represented the people, workers, painters, artists, like if Jose wasn't going to paint, he'd get behind something, and to Ofelia (Heck's mom, from the Yucatan) Rivera meant freedom.

Heck thought it was cool (and me too) that his parents got together from different Rivera angles bc of stupid passion and love, until Jose got way too into Fred Engels ideology (bc Rivera was into it too) while his mom was a hippy bookkeeper/healer (which I knew) and they split and now his dad won't let up with the ideology, which is what he fights with Heck about bc Jose wants Heck in the club.

"What club? Who's Fred Engels?" I had no idea what he was talking about.

"More boring," he said and didn't want to talk about it.

I looked it up. "Friedrich? The communist?"

Which was hilarious bc his dad's a communist, like Diego Rivera! And Heck was so happy I found it hilarious and I told him it was also weird.

He explained it's not that weird, which is where more angles come in, because, like with any ideology or party, everyone means well, humanity trying its best, doing good stuff for people, like what his dad does, but it gets distorted in the bigger sense, a grey area (interesting!). And he says he hates it, but not bc of the ideology but bc his dad shoves it down his throat and only sees Heck through that lens and won't talk about Heck's art bc it's all too painful on the inside, and on the outside he tells Hector, *You've gotta be good like Rivera to be an artist,* like what Jose's dad told Jose, "so don't go fooling yourself." Jose doesn't even comment on the drums.

Oh. My. God.

"Not your typical Mexicans, eh?" Heck said, then told me about his Aba (gran, Josefina) who's the ball-breaking silver lining bc she gets between Heck and his dad and puts Jose in his place or stealthy maneuvers so things work out in his and Mateo's favor, like secretly taking Ofelia's side with their weird schooling and always having Heck's back, which is so cool!

Then he went into full detail about his dad hating private school on principle and his mom always trying to find the best thing for them. Then he said Aba's the reason he's graduating a year early and going to Lewis & Clark.

"A year early?"

"Yup, just like your cousin. Aba's on it."

What?!!!!

Yeah, normally he'd be a junior but took a bunch of classes at SMC, "also just like your cousin."

OMG.

"So, you're 17?!"

"Yup."

I couldn't believe it and called him a younger man.

And he said I was the older woman, meaning Sadie, but still.

And I/Sadie found that hilarious.

Then he said he feels like sometimes he's the only one that can see all the sides. And if both his parents could, life would be a heck of a lot different...for Heck. I added that.

So I told him I could see that.

And he said, "So, there you have it. When you said the thing about the angles, I guess I felt all that and hence the weird voice."

Aw, sweet, interesting Heck!

And my heart expanded. And then sucked into that black hole thing like at stupid Hummus Bar.

Bc we have so much in common! Even how our parents met. Like Dad loving Mom's burnt-orange-robin-egg-blue sofa on the film they met on. But I couldn't even say that bc I wasn't me.

Which made me end the convo immediately but only after confirming the details of their stupid Oscar date tomorrow with adultish civility even tho I wanted to scream.

I really hate this stupid guy. And like him too.

"You're cool Sadie Svensson," he said.

"Thank you, Aw Heck. G'nite."

"G'nite."

Then I texted Sadie in complete annoyance: *On for tomorrow. He talked more about photos, angles and how it behooves people to look at things from all angles for a better life. World would be better if everyone did. And annoying when people don't. His dad's a communist and tries to make him be one. Mom got him scholarship to Wildroads. Dad thinks it's bourgeois. He didn't go to please dad but is graduating early. He's 17! His bro's going to Wildroads bc mom got him a scholarship w/AL's help. He likes you and thinks you're cool. Also, he helped you help me pick my dress. He likes green-orange-pink one w/necklace from you. He likes necklace. You have good taste and know me well. It's true! Love you! xox*

Glad am in love with Leo instead. Way too complicated.
Sadie didn't write back.

11:42. Sadie to me: *Did you have to say that much?*
Now, me not writing back.
Yes, yes, I did!
Now me writing in fake adultness: *Sorry, yes, my bad.*
Super annoyed.

Sunday, February 24

Oscar day!!! My room, 2:48 p.m. Went to Promenade. Tried on more shoes. A gazillion times. Going w/platforms I already have and cute mid-calf socks for street look to tone down dress in spite of AwHeck-approved confidence. Eyebrows a mess. Tried to even left to match right. Now left higher and I still look like I'm in constant state of inquisitive-mockingness. Oh, lord.

He'll be here in 12 minutes. Repeating Sheeran mantra over and over. If Ed Sheeran were going out with Leo Landis, he'd be so relaxed. He'd just go and have a blast. Blasting music. Dancing. Laughing. Meeting people at party. Relaxed. Happy. Channeling. I CAN BE ED SHEERAN ON THIS DATE!

My room, post Oscar-party date, 11:20 p.m. Am like rock goddess. Embodied female version of Sheeran and HAD SO MUCH FUN!

Leo Landis is so sexy. And okay, I will say it straight out: He kissed me!!!!!!!!!!!!!!!!!!!!!!!!! This is real. HE. IS. INTO. ME.

I feel sexy. And hot. And smart. And adult-esque and human-like. It's SO WEIRD.

But I digress. Let me back up and get the facts down.

He picked me up at 3 o'clock, promptly. Knocked. Stupid Jake yelled, "Someone's here!" even though his desk of gaming pathology is right by the door. Normally, I would've yelled, *Can you just friggin' get it?! What is wrong with you?* and stormed over and opened it. Unless mom is here. She does the same but says, *You're spoiled rotten, Jake; but I don't doubt you'll know how to open the door when you need to.* God, her logic and normalcy are insane.

This time, I yelled, "Okay, got it," and ran to the door. The change in behavior alerted Mr. Griffin, and he arose from his permanent gaming station to see who was there.

I opened the door as sexy as possible and tried to lift my right eyebrow to be even with the left as I smiled and said, "Hey," then blushed like a peach in the sun.

"Hey," Leo said and checked me out, smiling warmly, then peering in and waving at Stupid Jake, "Hey."

"Hi," Stupid Jake said all weird, then disappeared back to his station.

"That's my brother, Jake. Come in. I'll just grab my jacket. Want something to drink?"

"No, I'm good."

He looked around, honestly intrigued. Looked at Dad's Emmy and other awards and said, "Oh, yeah, great show," then mosied over to the superstation. "What're you playing?"

Normally, I would've been annoyed that he was even talking to Jake, but it was super cute bc he somehow got through to him, and Jake unbelievably showed him what he was doing and LL was honestly interested and asking questions.

My heart expanded. Dork. *And wow, he's great with kids! We could have a baby together!*

My heart leapt.

I reigned it in.

We walked out to his Range Rover. He held the door. Shut it. Went around. We drove. He commented that it seems like I have a nice family. I nodded, "I do." It was true and nice that he noticed!

Then he told me the party was at Alice Ackerman's in Topanga. Which was very exciting! She's an indie filmmaker and I knew they were friends from some article I read.

"Oh, cool!"

"Totally casual. Potluck. I got chicken from Versailles. So we all smell like garlic."

I laughed. He was so normal.

"Yeah, I don't know. I don't think Tarantino's coming after all, but I'm sure we'll have fun."

He looked at me. I was nervous. I felt so grown up.

Then it was my turn to talk and I didn't know what to say and felt utterly stupid. Why was I so stupid?

He turned on the radio. I felt more stupid. I searched my brain for something to say. So I said, "Oh, yeah, good song." I squeezed my earring and it broke. I hid it in my purse. I only had one on.

He nodded. So awkward. What would Sheeran do?????

So, I sang along, like literally just belted out a line. Which he found hilarious. So I did it again. Then, he joined, and within seconds we were both singing along at the top of our lungs. And I knew this was happening. I felt free. All chains off. SAOIRSE-DELPHINE-ED-SHEERAN-BERGER FREE AND HAPPY IN LOVE!

We parked up the canyon and walked down to the house. There was awkward silence and the peach cheeks happened again. He must've noticed bc he said, "You look great. Thank you for coming with me," and put his hand on my back. The other hand held the bag from Versailles.

We walked up to the door.

Alice answered. V. cool w/blond Rasta hair, jeans and a Berlin crop tee. V. urban earthy. "Leo!" She was happy to see him and cheek-kissed him and then hugged him tight.

"I brought Versailles," he said.

"Ah!!! You know me so well."

"This is Seer. Saoirse Berger. She's on Peter Svensson's film next door. Also a YouTube star."

Alice lifted her eyebrows. "Yes??? Come here." She hugged me too and made me feel welcome.

"Actually, Sadie Svensson, my cousin, is the star," I said. "I'm kind of behind the scenes."

"Oh, yes, that's the place to be. C'mon in."

There were people all over the house and in the yard and kids and dogs. V. casual. I was probably closer in age to the toddlers and dogs than most of the people. But Leo was more on my end of the spectrum so it seemed okay and like no one cared.

Alice told us, "Drinks and food over there. Help yourself. Red carpet on soon over here. All chill."

Leo was gracious, charming and did a little head bow, "Thank you."

Alice got pulled into another conversation and a big guy in a Clippers hat yelled, "Landis!" and did some hand-homey thing.

"Dude," Leo replied, then explained that it was his old crew. "C'mon, let's get a drink and bring the garlic over."

A girl in a short flowy red dress and butt-length curly hair took the bag. "Here, I got that for you, Honey. Drinks right over there. Oh, Sweetie, I love that dress. And those shoes. You are a blooming flower."

V. embarrassing.

Leo was amused and grabbed us two beers. "Cheers. To you blooming." He checked me out. "Wait, how old are you again?"

I blushed. "Eighteen."

He looked at my beer w/pretend shock. "Uh, oh." Then grinned. "C'mon, until it starts. Let's go talk to these homies over here." He put his hand on my back again. I felt so good! Tall! Strong!

We cruised and talked to people. Most probably thought I was his assistant but it was fine bc I knew I wasn't and felt v. grown up. And part of. Finally. I was so in love with him!!! He made me feel welcome. So did Alice and everyone. A miracle!

Also, every person I talked to mentioned my dress, which is dumb. And everyone noticed my lone earring and said nothing.

Then, QT walked by. I guess he'd been there all along and was leaving. He has a giant head and talked loud and incessantly, like rapid-fire. Alice introduced him to Leo. QT knew who Leo was and said they should get together. LL was thrilled but in a cool way bc QT seemed thrilled about meeting him back. A mutual-admiration society. So weird. I wish I belonged to that society.

Then QT left bc he was supposed to be elsewhere. And Leo was on a high from then on. I thought it was rather anticlimactic but somehow he was buzzing, which made me feel that way too. I still feel it!

While we were on a QT high, everyone else was buzzing from drinks and gummies. We watched the Oscars and bizarrely played charades. I got a song and whistled it out. My team got it right away. Everyone was impressed. I was embarrassed. Also, it broke the rules so we lost the point. Leo found that hilarious. More fun and flowing without overthinking.

I'm an excellent whistler. Maybe I need to own that more.

The flow ended when we left. Like that weird silence again after so much noise.

Leo asked if I had fun and I said I did.

Then more awkwardness as we walked uphill to the car, him exhaling, me thinking, *Why? Why?* And *now what? What to say? SHEERAN, help!*

So I sang, "I did! I had fun." And whistled.

He sang back, "Goooood," and laughed but wasn't as enthusiastic as in the car before. Distracted. He let me in and walked round and stood outside the car looking at his phone before he got in. Upset. He texted, shook his head, got in, threw his phone on the dash. I saw the next text come in: *Isla*. He looked then threw it in back. "The ex. She wants me to send our dog out."

"Where?"

"Connecticut. Where she goes to school."

"Oh. You have a dog?"

He seemed distracted and didn't answer and I felt stupid. He exhaled, big and strong, shook his head, then looked directly into my eyes, intense, flirty gaze. "Can I see you again?"

What?! My heart pounded. I blushed. "Yeah, sure." Dumb. Stupid. Idiotic.

Though it didn't seem like that to him.

"Great," he said. Smiled. Nodded. Almost relieved, like he was letting something go and finding hope and positivity, and it made him vulnerable but stronger, and I had a part in it.

Then, he leaned in and KISSED ME! ON THE LIPS! Strong yet soft. Exciting yet grounding. Optimistic yet real. Closed-lipped and a little bit open.

He looked at my eyebrows. And me. Smiling. "I like how your eyebrows are two different shapes."

I laughed. He seemed happy for making me laugh. Like it was a reward and confirmation that this was working. Like he needed that. Then, he drove me home and told me about his day tomorrow and what he thought about the Oscars and talked nonstop all the way home.

He really is a normal, rational person, and it feels super real, like I'm in the moment now and grounded thanks to his optimism and solidness bringing me down from my overthinking brain.

And now, I am in love. Happy ever after. Belonging. Finally. A. Part. Of. A. Couple!

Sunday wee hours of morn, February 25

1:02 a.m. Just was brushing goddess-princess Edwina's pearly whites as doth a text appear.

Aw Heck: *Thanks for a great night.*

Staring. Sort of ironic. Wish it were from LL.

Me/Sadie: *It was! Thanks, Aw Heck* ☺ *xo*

I took off the xo. Then put it back. Then sent it to Sadie. Tomorrow I'll get the skinny.

Saturday, March 2

Midnight, my room—a week later. Whirling. Whirlwind. Whirlybird of excitement. Have not written pages in days! Have been so busy. And happy. And in love.

All week filming BookishLens. Editing AT LEO'S!! And kissing. Holding hands. With boyfriend. I have a boyfriend!!!!!

Love.

It is love.

I hope it is love.

Is it love?

Holding breath. Have been holding breath all week actually. A paralysis of hope. Which has kept me from writing so as not to be taken down by details and overthinking in process of description. Holding breath to steel self in strength to forge through to now, tonight, when happiness has occurred. Now can force self to write, while still holding breath, but in hopes of spewing details of past week, as in exhaling them here on the page, so can purge self of analytical mind and make space to inhale only joy and never analyze again or grip so tightly onto hope.

Exhaling now but also still holding breath.

Oh, fubblegunk. Must get this out. Here it goes. A summary of the week as short as possible:

Leo was friendly at work all week, probably bc Melanie was gone. Assistant Dave filled in. Dave is older, 30s, really into Phish. Nice. Steady. Welcoming. Funny. Gets the job done. Leo loves him. But also, he loves Melanie. He says he knows she's not the friendliest but she's a great editor and smoothes out his cuts and gives him great notes.

Whatever.

Tuesday: He invited me TO HIS HOUSE! He texted midday: *Hey, wanna come over after work? Watch the Clippers? Eat my mighty-mean guac?*

YES!!!!!!!!!!!!!!!!!!! I replied in sentence case, even tho not doing that here.

I was so excited I don't even know what happened the rest of the day.

Then, I followed him home after work. It's a duplex in Los Feliz. A schlep. Airbnb. OMG! My heart was racing nonstop.

But then, he was so welcoming. I calmed down.

He made burritos and his awesome guac. He talked about movies and people and cutting-room and studio gossip. More like stories than gossip. He always finds the sweet or funny spot in everyone's behavior so it's more amusing than mean. Kind of like Unc Unc and Mike. I think he really likes people and is curious about them. Ultimately, though, he seemed more interested in making me laugh than anything.

That was in the kitchen. Then, we moved to the couch to watch the Clippers game and eat. This is when the stupid part occurred, starting with him dipping a chip and getting a heap of guac and then, before he took a bite, changing directions and flying it over to me like a stupid-but-cute tortilla-chip-guacamole airplane. Silly. Nice. Ahhhh!

Me: "Mmm."

Him eating the rest of the bite and agreeing: "Mmm."

We mmm'd in sync. Funny. Then he kissed me. And in reaction to the kiss: "Mmm."

Nice. Little kiss. Embarrassed to write about it. But still, I am! Chillax, Diary!

Then, he went back to watching the game until the ref called a timeout. We repeated the whole guac/mmm sequence. This time, he kissed me twice. Sweet. Playful. Then we kissed more. Longer. It was mmmm. Nice again. It kept going. Mmm in every cell of my being like a magnet from my heart to his. He touched my leg, above the knee. We kept kissing. I couldn't believe this was happening.

Was it happening?

The game came back on. Everyone cheered. They scored. Leo cheered and was completely engrossed in the game again, which was normal and nice and would've been perfect.

Except I started to think, which = deathnell of being in the moment, of being in love, of spontaneity, of kissing and more. All while he watched and ate guac and finished his burrito.

Why? Why did I start thinking? Because, well, kissing was happening. And he touched my leg! It was real! I started to think about what would happen next, like at the next Clippers timeout. What was *he* thinking? Did he want to do more? I mean, that's what people do, right? Who feel this way about each other? And are in a couple? And love each other? And want to be together? And share love? And more?!

I started imagining us kissing again and how we looked, as if watching from above. I imagined his hand on my leg again, moving northward, which was probably westward the way the couch was angled and how we were about forty-five degrees from horizontal. We looked weird.

Again, I started to think about what would happen next. Was this it? Was I going to do it? Finally? With a real guy? THE guy I wanted most in the world to do it with? And be with? And have a relationship with? In love, personally, and in my career, like work together and make amazing beautiful things together, like cinema?

Yes! My heart expanded.

Meanwhile, back in reality, there was a break in the Clippers game and Leo kissed me again. It was nice. He looked at me and smiled. We kissed more. His hand touched my leg again. Then, I was above us watching. Thinking. Heart racing. Thinking. Oh. My. God. This was happening. *Is this what I want?*

I stopped feeling. Thinking. Heart racing. Thinking.

He stopped. "You okay?"

Me: "Uh...yeah."

Him: "You sure?"

Why? How? How did he know I was nervous and feeling like I was out of my body? And in my head? At the same time!

I tried to be normal. I sat up. Somehow that seemed to help. "No, yeah, I mean..." Flustered. Him looking at me, honestly just waiting for me to...I don't know!...say something. Anything. Panic. "I mean, as long as you have protection."

No! No! No! Why did I say that? Cringe. Cringe. No!

Me again: "Right?"

He laughed. Like, actually laughed.

Oh. God. Isn't that what people say?

No! No, it wasn't.

Him: "Well, um." Chuckle. Nodding. Sitting up. Taking it in. "I wasn't. I mean..."

Like he wasn't even thinking that. We weren't even going to do it! I'm an idiot!

Him: "Why don't we go play pool? Okay?" Shutting off TV. Standing up.

Me: "No, wait, I'm totally fine with this." Bigger idiot. Embarrassment. Horror. Still feel it now.

He put his hand out. "C'mon, it'll be fun."

He pulled me up. Sweet. We were nose to nose. He smiled but didn't kiss me. I felt stupid. More than ever probably. I blushed too, which made it v. much worse.

We went and played pool at the Hollywood Athletic Club.

He got a beer and snuck me little sips. He was good and taught me what to do. He knew people there and said hi to everyone. He's t. chatty and social. He's like a guys' guy but also understands girls and everyone. People love him. I loved being with him in that moment and wasn't even jealous bc he was happy to be there with me. Like he's loved by all but isn't doing it to be loved but bc he likes people, just like in the kitchen. He's curious about everything. I felt so good. They loved him. He loved me. He was flirting even after my stupid thing that I can't repeat. He was present.

But then, we left. I got anxious and sad bc the night was over and maybe the whole thing was over bc I ruined it with my total and complete inexperience.

We drove back to his place. He walked me to my car and kissed me on my forehead. Ugh.

Then, somehow, he managed to ask if I'd ever had sex before. More like he assumed it. Like actually used the word "'assume," like: "So, is it safe to assume...I'm thinking it's safe to assume, yes. That you've never...right?" Clearly, this was awkward for him too but he's adult enough to have a conversation about it even though it wasn't excellent diction. Unlike me who just stutters and says idiotic things about protection, like wedging a metaphorical and actual shield between us when not at all necessary and totally uncalled for.

I scrunched my lips into a weird, sheepish, caving-in Halloween-pumpkin smile and shrugged, unable to hide how embarrassed and young I was and how I needed some kind of approval and wanted to ask if we were still okay. I exhaled.

He laughed.

"That's not too weird?" I managed.

He laughed again and shook his head. "No. Not too weird." He checked out my hair. Like maybe this was good that I was so weird. And funny. He was finding the sweet and funny POV of me, maybe, like he does for everyone else, even the people at the studio or in the cutting room. Or maybe that was my imagination. In reality, he said, "I'm just...you know...It's probably good for me. I could use this. Something new. And slow. Perfect."

Ugh. This didn't seem perfect.

I nodded. Paralyzed kind of. Not sure what to do next.

"Keys?" he said and held out his hand.

More embarrassment, like not only do I not know how to make out realistically or read the room properly or him, for that matter, but I also don't know how to open my car door.

"Oh, right!" I got my keys out.

He unlocked the car for me and held the door open with a charming, playful knightly head bow. I curtsied like a pumpkin princess and got in. He closed the door and waved through the window.

I watched him in my rearview mirror as I drove away. His smile turned contemplative as he watched me go, hands in pockets, like he was thinking, *Wow, she's young*, or, *Wow, I really want Isla back.* I was sure it was over. Even though he said it wasn't.

Is this what dating is?

I felt terrible.

That was Tuesday. Also that night, the Hector/Sadie thing was happening, which I couldn't really deal with but did anyway. The main points are, in brevity:

1. Hector called and wanted to hang with Sadie the next day. I told him I/Sadie had to call back. I asked Sadie what she wanted to do then set the date by text. Me to Hector: *Tomorrow is great! C u then. G'nite, Aw Heck.*

He replied: *G'nite, Sweet Sadie.*

No question of the day. I was relieved.

2. On phone, Sadie filled me in about Oscar night. Mostly good. They went to loft downtown. V. cool, artsy, mostly artists, kind of boho wild. There was even a naked guy walking around. I asked why. She didn't know but probably he just needed attention disguised as being artsy. Hector was chill bc he had to bring his little bro, Mateo. Sadie was happy bc it took pressure off her to talk so much, since Heck likes to talk nonstop. The only weirdness was when he asked her about some art in the loft—an enormous red heart over a giant tulip—and wanted to look at it from all angles. "So? What do you think?" Sadie didn't know, which confused him and he asked if she was okay. She played it off by trying to sound like me, making a joke about her *varied analysis patterns* being just one of her angles, which is great! She suggested I don't get so artsy on the phone again, even though she knows that'll be hard for me.

Ugh. I don't have time for this. At least I don't walk around naked!

3. She also said she's glad Hector is confused about her bc she's confused about Paulie still and going slow is helpful. Which is probably how Leo feels re Isla and me. Though overthinking this = deathnell to Leo love so ending this here.

And focusing on positivity and reality in love!!!! As in, Thursday...

But first, Wednesday: I didn't talk to Leo. Door shut. Just saw him while running errand on lot. He was on sidewalk in serious conversation with two suits. Felt like peon not good enough for hot, nearing-genius, A-list wunderkind director talking about important things with suits re making world-renowned cinema, who has already led globe-trotting life with renaissance younger-woman gf Isla with cute airplane kisses and romance in posh and unique destinations around the planet, with stellar architecture and weird and intriguing names, like perhaps Moab and Cesky Krumlov and Hvar.

Felt v. much less than. Held breath. Tried not to think. Moved forward.

Then, choir of angels Thursday!!! Walking in early morning from peon parking lot, noticed Leo walking in from his prestige spot. Forced self to be normal and say hi. His energy was low, contemplative, inward. But he brightened when he saw me, "Saoirse! Hey." He looked relieved, like I was something happy and normal as opposed to what was in his head. "How you doing?"

We toasted coffee mugs.

Me feigning normal: "Good." My spirits lifted quickly. We walked in together from his fancy parking spot.

Him: "Still shooting today?"

Me: "Yeah."

Because he remembered! From Tuesday night! About the BLGirl shoot today. With Sadie. That I told him about when we were standing in the kitchen. At his house. Bc I was desperate to sound interesting and SO HAPPY to have something to say!

Luckily, I calmed down in that moment.

And he said, "Still leaving at four?!" teasing me about getting to leave early and REMEMBERING THE EXACT TIME! Maybe not so weird bc on Tuesday he called me "spoiled" bc no one in editing ever leaves early, like actually sleeping under desks and pulling all-nighters and falling asleep in standstill traffic.

Which is true. Except Mike goes home on time so we usually leave by seven.

But I was leaving early bc Jena said I could. I told him Jena may seem serious on the outside, enforcing cutting-room rules and etiquette, but has an undercover-creative side. He likes my observations. Like his cinematic kitchen-character analysis. Hooray! We have that in common!

He said he couldn't wait to see it and toasted coffee mugs again, "Funny Bookish Girl."

My heart raced. Stupid half-pumpkin-smile-nod. "Thanks."

We parted ways, my heart aflutter. And I never, ever could've predicted what happened next.

Let's recap in brief:

I met Sadie, Deva, and River on the lot at four. We got on the Metro and went to The Broad to film Sadie/BLGirl about town. I invited Deva and River bc they always make it more fun and up the energy.

Then Leo FaceTimed. About 20 minutes in. OMG!!! Heart raced. Panic. What did he want? Should I answer? What if I sounded weird? Nervous? River looked at my phone. Ringing. Heart racing. Thinking. Deathnell to any chance at love sounding. River: "What are you doing? It's Leo Landis. Answer it!" I didn't. So he did! Crap.

Leo's bright, happy face appeared onscreen, all of us looking down. He laughed: "Well, hello."

We laughed back. My heart leapt. And expanded. It was so sweet!!!

Leo: "What are you doing?" Even though he knew exactly.

Me: "Going downtown."

River yelled, "We're filming BookishLens!"

Me: "Ow!" He was right in my ear.

Leo: "And you didn't invite me?"

WHAT??? River made a *WHAT? OMG!* face back at me.

Me to Leo playful: "You're working!"

Leo: "Dave's kicking me out." He showed us Dave in the BG funny-waving and yelling, "Get out of here!" and said that "Dave says if I don't leave and let him work, we won't be ready for tomorrow." They had a screening and Dave had to do his assistant stuff.

Sadie to Leo: "Come meet us!"

And he did!!!!

Oh. My. God. I still can't believe it. Heart racing thinking about how wonderful it was. Too good to be true. But it is!

He met us downtown at Pershing Square. I texted him beforehand bc I suddenly got nervous about my rules w/Sadie: *As far as you know, BookishLens is all Sadie and I'm just camera. I'm not supposed to tell anyone it's me. Per me. And I never told you. Pls?*

He agreed: *No problem, stealth BookishLensGirl!*

Hooray!

And it ended up being the best time ever. We rode the Metro, and I filmed, and Leo filmed, and I filmed him too, and he made a cameo, which is super fun, and even talked about the book and how he wished he'd read it in high school.

Also, he impressed Deva. Amazing!

We went up around Disney Concert Hall. And to The Broad. And had pizza. And Boba. And he told his funny stories, and we ended up at the Hollywood sign in the dark and Griffith Observatory. It was kind of crazy and fun, and by the end of the night, everyone loved him. And he loved them. And he loves me!

The only weird thing that happened was when Hector annoyingly called and I declined and Leo noticed and I told him it was "Sadie's boyfriend," which was weird and suspicious, so he asked why I didn't answer and I didn't have an answer, so Sadie chimed in with her funny smile and hugged me and said, "It's complicated. And my cousin has my back." Which Leo loved. And Sadie said, "Plus, Seer's helping him take photos of a mural for his channel about street art. So she has his back too." And he gave me the cutest, sexiest *I-love-that* smile. And even the weirdness ended up amazing!

It really was the best day ever. Like he's part of my life and my favorite people. Like it was such an important moment, meshing together as if it could last forever. Like meaningful on a bigger level.

And a small level too. Just real. Friends. Being creative. Laughing. Enjoying life. A tiny love-filled intersection of creativity and a turning point.

At the end, he did an awkward, shy wave to me, and Sadie said, "He likes you." And River agreed. We all looked at Deva. She said, "Okay, fine. He does, and I like him too. He's empirical. A realist."

Then to me: "Just make sure you know what you really want."

Which was the other weird part.

That I ignored.

Am ignoring.

Should I ignore it?

Yes! Because what I want is Leo. I know that. It's a fact. And this proved he feels the same. In a real way! He even likes my friends and what I do. And me. It's all so normal and comfortable and easy!!!!

That night Leo texted: *Was fun today, BookishGirl. You got a good crew there.* ;)

I texted back: *Thanks for coming!*

He replied: *Come over Saturday night? I gotta work but we can edit together. And get some dinner.*

YES! I have a boyfriend.

Which brings us to tonight, Saturday. Let me recap the wonder with quick analytics...

Actually, first, I should also mention I got my UCLA acceptance. And feel nothing about it, except maybe emptiness in stomach. Like mega-anxiety. Like I really don't want to go there.

But ignoring to focus on magnificence of tonight, in brevity, so don't get carried away:

First, went over to Leo's house in cute blue-jay dress and silver-heeled sneaks w/lemon barrette in hair. Was v. excited but exuded hot calm.

Leo was working, on couch, listening to score sample from composer. I started editing BLGirl Metro shoot on laptop next to him. Showed him cuts. Asked his opinion. He helped. He loves what we shot. The edits. The writing. The whole vibe. It felt so good to know that, and it was so much fun!!!

Then, we ordered takeout from Papilles and stood in the kitchen again and talked, and he gave me sips of his wine and fed me olives and kissed me. Once. A tiny kiss. It was different than Tuesday. Because it was light. And just on the lips. Then, he did it again and again, and we kept kissing with nothing but our lips touching. It was amazing. The lighter and shorter the kisses, the more I wanted to kiss him. Like a light-touch magnet. Is this what sexy feels like? I think so. I know so!

Then, he stopped and said, "I do like this going slow. And you. I like you." He nodded matter of factly, and then we took the dog, Amos, for a walk. He has to send Amos on a plane next week. He got quiet and shook his head after telling me the details. I felt awkward. I knew it was about Isla.

Then he said, "Things change. Life is funny like that," and that was over.

Until at some point he got a text, a group text. I knew bc a bunch came one after the other. Which also made him quiet. I couldn't see who it was. He exhaled and turned off his phone and explained that his friends are going to Big Bear in a couple weeks. Getting a house. Last year he went with Isla. The friends think he should go again, even without her. This sounded painful to him, and he said, "Wanna go to Big Bear?" But it was more of a pained joke. He didn't wait for my answer or seem to want one. It was like he was hurting too much and couldn't go there yet. But not like he didn't want to go with me, more like could he do it without thinking about her?

Then, he suggested we go back and watch a movie, something from our western vid!! On the walk back, he told me a funny story about a producer of his on a plane who obliviously annoyed another passenger and the whole plane had to turn around and the Air Marshalls got called in. And then Leo's Big Bear pain was over too.

The food was there when we got back (yum! French), and we watched *Once Upon a Time in the West*. Yay! Bc he was inspired by me. A miracle bc I'm inspired by him. Win win! He wanted to see how the movie inspired QT. I didn't tell him I haven't watched the other movies yet, except the ones with Dad, which was a long time ago and I don't remember. But I'm on the right track!

He also noticed a text from "Lorraine" when he put his phone on the table, which made him laugh. "Our exec liked your notes. I showed her the scene." I instantly got jealous. I don't know why. Maybe bc now the scene wasn't just mine and Leo's. Now, the exec was part of the excitement. And why was he so friendly with her? On a Saturday night? And what did she say that was so funny? He's so cute when he laughs.

I forced myself to remember filmmaking is a team effort, as UP always says. And at least his exec likes his movie. For him, that's good. That's what I was thinking. Still am. Must not let self be jealous and uncomfortable by goodness. Must be bigger than that. Older. Wiser.

Embracing goodness!

...like what happened next, which is that he told me about his DP's filmmaking/camera class at UCLA Extension and suggested I take it. See if it's really what I want. "Maybe it'll help you decide where to go. Sounds like you have a lot of great choices." Oh my god! He thinks it'll help me see if I want to be a DP. And help me decide on college! Yes! In addition to having hot, romantic, solid, going-slow boyfriend, also have boyfriend that hears me and thinks I can be a part of filmmaking. He takes my craft seriously! HE THINKS I SHOULD CHECK OUT CAMERA AND FILMMAKING! BECAUSE HE LIKED MY NOTES! And more.

This was amazing and the rest of the night perfect. We watched the movie, ate the food and had another long, lips-only-touching kiss at the door when I left, which was nice. And sexy. Feel sexy and like actual real adult! With boyfriend who is logical, solid human who gives good advice and doesn't get weirded out by emotions. May feel out of control bc he's so above me when it comes to normal life stuff but I can rise to his level.

And now, must stop THINKING. Because the truth is he really likes me!!!!

Action item: Go to bed. And have sweet dreams about your BOYFRIEND!

Sunday wee hours, March 3

1:00 a.m. Can't sleep. Must get adult-real about my future so signed up for Leo's DP's camera class just now and must do full adult eval of higher ed next week re what I want, where I'm going, etc. Even though I don't yet know. At least Leo helping.

Later. Went on IG bc still couldn't sleep. Liked the piece Hector posted from the Oscar party. It's beautiful. It's a giant pink-and-red Venetian glass/epoxy-resin tulip. Also, he got a photo of the naked guy from the waste up which made me laugh. And wrote: *Forthcoming.* Feel relaxed now. Art + humor = elixir of chill. Going to sleep. No worries at all.

Sunday daytime, my room, 4:30 p.m. Lorraine Goodwin is the exec. Found her on LinkedIn, couldn't resist. Went to Boston U, communications major, 27. Pretty, speaks French and does charity thing helping kids write scripts. Also, boring. How does she even know my notes were any good? Does she know? No! She has no clue. Whatsoever.

Finishing edit for BLGirl. Just sent to Sadie. She likes it too so am posting.

Keep looking at Leo's IG. Nothing happening. Now what? Don't know what to do with self. How am I supposed to just wait and do nothing?

Must focus on self. Camera class will be great but doesn't start till next month. Rest of college acceptances come in before and will have to decide by May. Must do realistic eval! Don't want to. Don't have enough info. Don't see clear path! Rrrrrrrrrrrrrrrr.

Also, don't want to help Sadie with stupid Heck's photoshoot of Nia's stupid mural. I don't have time!

4:45 p.m. Okay. Calming down now. Not judging Lorraine. Not judging Sadie/Heck.

Instead, remembering Leo's smile on Metro when he found out I'm helping Sadie/Hector with mural, me rising to Isla-Gordon-Ferraro-amazing level, like creative, unique, helpful eagle soaring high. Like goddess. Wizard-of-Oz/Heck weirdness making me interesting. The reward for goodness bc Leo adores my mad kindness and photography, wingperson and deception skills, even tho he only knows about BLGirl deception not Sadie/Heck. Am like perpetual Secret Santa, the deception and gifts that never stop giving.

Which is why I've decided to help with the mural.

Posting BLGIrl shoot now.

8:30 p.m. BLGirl vid = 1K+ likes so far, including from Leo plus comment: *Looks great!*

Hooray! Heart singing. Feels so much better.

Also, texted Sadie about doing Heck's mural next Sunday. Feel good about bringing in excellent karma.

But what about self? How do I stand independently while waiting for Leo? How do I not glom on? How do I have own life? V. depressing. Terrified about college. Going to get pie or other treat to forget.

Or perhaps to gather courage.

To think about self.

And what I'm doing with my life.

In fall.

By self.

At lonely college.

With no plan.

10:15 p.m. Feeling better now thanks to Mom. Silly, sweet, cheesy mom.

Went to get some of Gran's special apple cake and sat next to Mom at table. She's learning about making cheese, even tho she might import it. I leaned on her shoulder and ate strudel and read along.

Then, Mr. Griffin came over and gave Mom a hug from behind, wrapping his arms around her neck and looking at her screen, cheek to cheek. As if he wanted to be part of our coziness. For five seconds.

Then, he walked toward the kitchen and tickled me on the way. I chased him. Took him down. Pinned him to the ground. Chin-tickled him until he couldn't stand it, and Mom yelled, "Saoirse, stop!" and I kept going until he finally cried *Uncle*.

Mom was amused. I went back and sat next to her. She asked me how it was going. I said *fine*. She didn't press. Her usual. But clearly, she knew something was up, like Dad always does, with magical parental-mind-reading abilities. Or maybe she just wanted to know what I thought about getting into UCLA.

So she pried in her Mom way that gets to the heart of the matter without hitting it over the head. Which is probably why she asked about Deva instead of me.

"So, what's up with Deva?"

I told her the usual—*graduating in summer, amazing, only 20, going to med school*—which we've already discussed a million times.

"And Gus is transferring to UCLA still?"

"Yup."

See, UCLA! *Tricky, Mom. I see what you're doing here.*

"And River?"

She already knew this too—*Loyola, approved year off, econ/business classes in Paris, second gap year, Hot Steve going.*

"Oh!" she said, stopping with the cheese, eyes lighting up. "I saw Hot Steve at Home Depot last week. He thinks the English daisies'll look good in front too."

OMG.

"Very nice. Helped me carry them out. And very excited about Paris. And New Zealand!" Then she went back to scrolling through Camemberts.

You're so transparent, Mom! And you know I don't know where I'm going next year!

Then, she asked about Deva's graduation party. "Still doing the Alpine theme?"

I nodded. "In July. I think her dad's more into it than her."

"Oh, but it'll be fun. I love that fondue he does."

I agreed that it's good and also hilarious that her Indian dad is obsessed with Bavarian wurst and Dolomite crème brulee.

"I was thinking a nice fern as a gift, for her room. Or maybe succulents. But she does seem more like a plant girl, don't you think?"

"What?"

"I know, I'm a little obsessed with flora right now. But there're so many options. To go with cheese. And we'll find something nice for her, right?"

I don't know why but tears started rising. "Mmmhmm."

She saw my face. "You're not having a fight with her are you?" And the tears flowed. "No!'

Why? Why was I crying?

She smiled softly, like Brie, lovely, sweet mommy. "And you sent that nice RSVP."

I nodded, now full-on crying. "Yes, I RSVP'd."

"Which I'm sure she loves," she said and pulled me close, "Oh, honey, come here," hugging me, warm, in a little mom cocoon, like a croissant-cocoon full of cheesy us, or chocolate us, or chocolate-cheesecake us. "See, everything's going to be okay. Your friends are here. Or away, but here. We're here. Wherever you go. And it always works out, even when the path isn't straight...right?"

I nodded. *Sneaky Mom, luring me to truth with loving, cheesecake tangents.*

"Oh! And I have an idea. For a card." She pulled up a photo of me, Deva and River when we met in middle school. Malibu Canyon swimming hole, dripping wet, arms around each other, me in the middle, Deva standing tall, beaming, proud, confident, like always, and River with a funny face. It was hiker's class at Think Creative learning center and there we were just belonging to each other, like weirdos in weird education thanks to weird parents trying to help weird kids, and I was only in 6th and they were in 8th and liked me anyway. *I guess they still do.*

"We can print it, and make something nice," Mom said, somehow knowing all I needed was to remember I still belong to this sweet Deva/River friendship of weirdos.

I suggested I take a selfie of us now and put the photos together. Or make a slideshow!

"Excellent," she cheered with a little smile that said, *See, I'm not insane for giving you no guidance and letting you make your own roadmap with weird education path. As long as you're free and doing what you love, you'll be fine—just like it said in all those progressive education journals, documentaries and blogs I told you about ad nauseam.*

Oh, cute, silly Mom.

I laughed and told her I'd figure out the card. There's still time. And told her about the camera class. I was bizarrely nervous about that. I don't know why because it made her even more happy.

Sillier, cuter Mommy!

Tho still wishing I had future-path roadmap that someone else made, like her.

Also thinking this freedom thing she loves is about her, like she wishes she'd had it too. Like living vicariously through me. Though now she has cheese. I'm happy she has cheese. She looks so happy. And that makes me happy and free not to worry about her.

And Stupid Jake is happy. And I kind of love our cozy family.

I kissed her on the cheek and came back here.

Where I'm now flowing freely in adultish way, in my own little boat on river, not latching on to other boats, like HMS Leo's, rather floating freely down beautiful tributaries or exciting rapids, knowing I will end up with Leo's boat again. In peaceful pool. Or sea. Or ocean. In future. Always.

Like maybe I'll end up at a college by Leo's next shoot as previously imagined.

BTW, I just looked up Lewis & Clark (where Hector's going) and it looks super cool.

Ugh. I am not super cool tho. All I have are hopes about love and misdirected college apps and silly-girl humor, like cowboy-boot dances and writing secret fake essay about Aunt Lauren for Columbia—*Why I'm Only Applying Here Because My Aunt Is Obsessed, Controlling, and Forcing Me, and Ed Sheeran Would Tell Me to Ignore Her and Laugh It Off But I'm Not That Evolved*—which is hilarious. And pathetic. And also mean. Stop being so mean, Saoirse! I didn't send it of course. And wrote it pre Hoorays 18. Now, it wouldn't fly.

Trying to find positives re self: funny, smart, adult who will get in somewhere with un-snarky well-written essays and grades and will put colleges in hat and pull out winner. And go there. That college gets me!

Ugh. Too weird even for me.

Action item: Watch movie or anything to take mind off. Look up top DPs, watch and learn.

10:30 p.m. Hector just called and I idiotically engaged. Bc he wheedled his way into my stupid head. I blame him.

First, I didn't answer. Which was good.

Then, he texted: *Hey, you up? Wanna talk?* As if I hadn't just *not* answered bc I didn't want to talk!

So I called back, bc I was so irritated and hung up when he said "hello?" More idiotic. And had to call back again, because what else was I gonna do? He saw my stupid number!

"Sadie?" he said.

"Hi," I said, in curt, agro way and then, "I saw you called?" in weird, pompous Duke-of-Earl-in-the-English-countryside tone.

Which made him laugh. "Uh...yes?"

Gah! "Nevermind, sorry, long day."

And he said, "That's okay," like a normal nice guy trying to have a normal conversation.

So I tried to be normal. And idiotically told him what I thought about the art in the loft. How it's so neo-pop and needing love and attention but worth it bc it's bright and makes the room happy for everyone.

He agreed that the bright pop-red-and-pink Venetian-glass tulip is v. cool. Then asked, "So why didn't you say that Sunday?" Meaning, Sadie. And I thought: *Because she's not me! And didn't we already go over this? Coy! She's coy! C'mon, Aw Heck!*

Instead, I just said, "A girl likes to be mysterious sometimes."

Which he found funny, like I was feeding him bullshit, which I was. And he called me on it, even using the word *bullshit*, which is a word I like, come to think of it, for when you're feeling raspy.

So I said, "Sometimes I like bullshit," in a playful way, meaning the action of spewing bullshit not the word itself at that point.

He said that was a "little one-sided and unfair," though also in a playful way bc he wants to understand Sadie more.

Which made me mad because their relationship is none of my business but I said, "Fine, you want to know?" instead of staying out of it.

He wanted to know. So I panicked, like *Now what? What to say?* So I thought about me: Why don't I like to talk face to face? Why do I get stupidly nervous when someone's looking at me, listening?

So I yelled, "I don't know!" exasperated. "It's just hard to talk. And think. And if I care, it's harder."

"You care? I'll take that."

Gah! And then I was so mad I said *care*, which isn't even in the ballpark of *bullshit* as a satisfying word.

And I pulled my duvet around my head like a papoose bc it was cozy and it's kind of chilly tonight. "Great."

And he said, "I like this side of Sadie, very honest and bold."

And I said, "We gotta stop meeting like this, Aw Heck."

Which made him laugh his big-happy laugh.

Which made my heart leap. And I said, "Well, I'll try to keep this side of her out more, in person," like an idiot.

He liked that idea. And I told him next time *he* has to reveal something. "Fine, Sweet Sadie. I'm up next."

Gah! Not telling Sweet Sadie about this conversation. Bc this is SO NOT MY FAULT.

Closing eyes and breathing in happiness of bright, happy-tulip love like before. I am creative, fun, funny and self-analytical human being. That's who I am, winning heart of prince charming, while Sadie wins hers, and we all live happily ever after.

Though really not ever even talking to Heck again! Just don't answer, Seer-shuh!

G'nite, night pages. That are also morning pages. And all-day pages. You really come in all angles don't you?

Monday, March 4

Night, my room. Melanie back. Leo distant. Why are my moods determined by his presence? Or absence?

Tuesday, March 5

Cutting room, 3:40 p.m. Random girl in Leo's cutting room. Who is it? Walked by several times. She looks older. Wearing a suit. Maybe it's his exec. He's showing her scenes. They didn't see me.

My room, 10 p.m. Random girl is exec Lorraine. Saw on Leo's IG. Selfie of him and exec "Lorraine" w/same hair and producer Chris at microbrewery. They look happy. Assuming it's work drinks. Liked. Not thinking more about it.

Why has Leo not texted?

Aw Heck has, a million times. And liked the new stupid cowboy-boot dancing of just my feet that I posted earlier. Am ignoring. Can't deal now. Keeps talking about details for photo shoot of Nia mural Sunday. Ignoring that too.

Will have to show Sadie boot dance and get her to do more. Could be good excuse to get Leo to help!

10:07 p.m. Unliked Leo selfie with Lorraine and Chris.

10:10 p.m. Liked.
Unliked.
Liked.
Stop!

10:40 p.m. Followed Lorraine's IG. Nice. Normal. Boring. Mostly just friends and some work events.

10:45 p.m. Unfollowed.
Can she see?

Refollowed.

Unfollowed!!! I don't want to be her stupid friend!

10:47 p.m. Refollowed. If she sees, at least now following so thinks I want to be friends. Better for Leo. It's a work thing. More professional.

11:50 p.m. Disaster. Fake essay made it into Columbia app. At end. After actual essay, which is so short it fit.

Went into Columbia dashboard in attempt to determine if essays good enough as was thinking how Columbia is significantly more impressive than Lorraine's BU degree and I should be more selective rather than hat-pull decision-making technique for deciding future so can catapult self into high esteem in Leo friend circle. Clearly forgot to delete fake mean-to-Aunt-Lauren essay in rush as didn't care then but maybe do now.

Crap. Heart pounding. Does AL know? Did they show her? Crap. Tried to redo submission. Can't. Crap. I deserve this. Do I? No! It's her fault for pushing me! Ahhhhh! What would Sheeran do? Come clean. Unapply. I don't know what Sheeran would do. Reading fake essay on Columbia college app now pretending to be Ed Sheeran to determine what I/Seer should do:

Why I'm Only Applying to Columbia Because My Aunt Is Obsessed, Controlling, and Forcing Me and Ed Sheeran Would Tell Me to Ignore Her and Laugh It Off But I'm Not That Evolved

The reason I'm applying: I'm a chicken, bawk, bawk. In Polish, that'd be koo-keroo, hence the resto name. In German, that'd be keekeree-kee. In Spain, birds say peeu peeu, by the way, instead of cheep cheep. Birds speak different languages too. I'm a chicken because I'm afraid to trust my instinct, afraid it's off and AL's is on. Not yet evolved like ES, rock-god hero. Plenty to learn about instinct. Also, how do you say bawk in Russian?

Oh my god. How is it possible that I submitted this as an essay?

How did I even write that weirdness?
　Maybe they'll think it's a poem.
　That's what Sheeran would assume.
　Poem.
　Crap.
　Crap poem.
　Peeu.

Wednesday, March 6

Cutting room, 4:30 p.m. Things have gotten worse with Aunt Lauren. I don't know if she knows about Columbia essay. It's v. uncomfortable. But I don't think she does. I think she's just falling apart and it's making me v. uneasy. Like I've been holding my breath all day since this morning when she came by and was t. weirdo around UP, and then we went to lunch and she had a meltdown in front of EVERYONE, like TR's fans. And then was normal. And I don't know how to process this. Just want to make it go away so I can be normal and have a chance at normal love. As if she has that power over me.

I mean, I can't even tell if she's falling apart or not. And if I should worry. Or just let it go!

Please, please, I just want her to be okay and happy. And me too.

Okay, exhaling, recapping, reviewing what happened:

First, everything was fine, all week. Me answering phones, following advice of YodaSheeran, not worrying about outcomes, telling AL when UP's busy: "He's working and has asked not to be disturbed. I'm sorry. I know you get that." And she got it! All was good. I set boundaries. She respected them. Total adulting!

Then she fell apart. Today. But first it was like usual. She came in, nervous about seeing UP, said to Jena, "Mind if I poke my nose in?" Jena checked. More nerves. UP said of course and she went in. Then they came out, Jena took notes and everyone was happy. Like always, AL brilliant w/great notes.

NO NEED TO WORRY!

Then, it continued. Unc gave her a kiss in the hall—happy—but as soon as he left, her stupid shoulders slumped. Why? Why?

I rushed to my chair so she wouldn't see me seeing her weirdness, thinking *Please don't see me.*

She walked by. "See ya later."

And like an idiot I said, "Bye," with stupid nervy-chirpy voice. Which alerted her and she came back. "You okay?"

Noooo! "Hh-yeah?"

She saw right through that. "Okaaay."

I shifted uncomfortably and tried to maintain happy-pumpkin grin.

"Hey, wanna go to lunch?" she said like normal aunt, which made me think I was insane.

The Sheeran inside my head said: *Learn, Seerwalker, learn!*

GAH!

"You don't have to," she said re lunch.

"No, no, I…"

"I just never get to see you much, but seriously, we can do it another time." She smiled, like normal but maybe also a little hurt. Was she hurt? I don't know!

And YodaSheeran said: *It's not about you!*

Jena butted in, "That's fine, go, I got it," clearly wishing I'd leave.

So I went, and it continued, walking to her car with no escape, holding my breath in case she wanted something from me, like to talk about the essay. Or UP!!!

She was oddly quiet. For her. Then said, "Taylor Rae's gonna meet us. I hope that's okay."

Thank god! Like everything was fine again. And I said, "Sure."

And she said, "How are you, anyway?" as we reached her car and her great spot that says "Producer," right outside the cutting room, next to Leo's Range Rover. *Why didn't he come say hi?*

"Good!" I replied.

"Sadie said you guys are helping Hector out," she said, throwing her laptop and papers off the passenger seat so I could sit.

"Yeah, yes. I like his work. And Nia's."

"It's good, right? And he's a good kid."

Then we drove and she got weird again until the stoplight, when she noticed me again. "You okay?" she asked, as if I was the one being weird.

"Uh, yeah?"

"You have to stop doubting yourself Saoirse."

GAH!

"It's not a guy is it? You're too smart for that. Sadie, on the other hand, gets distracted with boys. You're focused. I love that. You need to own it."

She smiled like a proud mentor aunt, and I smiled back like a fake-pumpkin-smiling mentee niece. And we were back to our normal normal.

"So...what is it? College? Waiting?"

"Yeah, it's a little nerve-racking," I said, deflecting, bc there was no way I was telling her about LL or anything!

"Well, I'm sure you'll have some amazing options. If not all. And if you're still unsure where to go, we'll figure it out." As if we were a *we*, when I just want to be a *we* with LEO! And not even go to school!

"Personally, when I feel uncertain, I like to just make a choice. Try it. If I don't like it, I change," she said, drifting off into weirdness for a sec, then back. "I do that professionally at least. There's room to change. Personally it's a little more difficult. But still, you try things. Flexibility is an asset. And trusting things will work out. I believe in you, Seer. I hope you trust me on that."

She smiled, and I smiled back. Gross.

"And I'm helping you, but only because I think Columbia will be a win-win. They'll definitely benefit from having you. So I'm glad you did that interview with Brad. Shows you're serious. And know I'm not pulling strings for you. I'm just telling you what to do and you'll get in on your own merit. Nothing to do with me. Just that I told you they like the interviews. That's fair."

"Two weeks and we'll know."

"I'm so proud of you."

And she smiled like she actually loves me. Which made me tense and love her and hate her all at once. The usual.

What is wrong with her?!

"I'd love to read your essays. Just to see. I'm curious."

No!

"Sure. I mean, I really appreciate you helping me." *Never!*

Feeling sick to stomach. Sheeran says: *Proceed.*

Fine!

Then we pulled up to the cafe. Taylor Rae was already there, and everybody looked to see who she was meeting. It's kind of fun hanging with her and having people stare and wonder if you're famous too. But you're not. But you pretend to be. Also, TR's super chill and out there in the world, talking to everyone. I love that about her.

So TR stood up when she saw us, beaming, and opened her arms to hug AL. But then AL's face got distorted and TR hugged her. And AL started crying and shaking, like have a seizure, trying to hold it in, all over TR's neck. Like maybe this is where Sadie gets it from.

And I'm thinking, *Why? Why do I have to be here to see all this????*

And YodaSheeran repeated: *Learn, Seerwalker, learn.*

And AL snuffled, and TR shuffled her behind a ficus, hiding her from gawking fans, making a funny face at people at the next table, like—*Don't mind her, she'll be fine*—until AL calmed down. They were so excited to see TR I don't think they even noticed AL.

Then TR patted AL's face with a tissue, hugged her and got her to sit. And diffused the whole thing with humor (bc TR is all that!), saying it was my fault and Sadie's that AL was crying because we're leaving the nest. "And when little birds leave the nest, the mama birds have to figure out who the heck they are again, what they want to do with their life, reconnect to other relationships, start being more secure and confident again." Blah, blah, until she had AL feeling better and laughing.

"Thank you," AL said.

Taylor Rae hugged her. "Of course." Two bff peas in a pod. I was so relieved. Also grateful they didn't talk about UP.

Then TR spun solutions until AL's shield came down, like about a movie they're making together! What?!!! TR said she "talked to Hank, and he thinks it's a great idea," and on and on. TR asked me what I think but I had no idea. AL said she hadn't told me yet so TR filled me in. Basically, AL's writing a movie and TR's acting and directing. "And we're starting a production company!"

Wow!

"Because we don't play that game. We go out and make our own schitt, right Lauren?" TR said, which clearly is in reaction to UP "movie cheating" with J Boone, like AL/TR movie-cheating-empowerment revenge.

Exhausting. Then they ignored me and talked about the usual—friends, schools, work—until they asked if I could take a Lyft back bc they were staying. AL hugged me tight when I left. Which I have to remember.

Just the hug.

Not her freaking out.

That's all that matters.

Bc Leo's door is closed, and I'm sitting here. And AL needs to be the grownup in the room. And the world. My world. And Sadie and Nick's world!

And I have to figure out what Sheeran would do.

What would Sheeran do?

Text Leo.

My room, 10:30 p.m. Me to Leo: *Hi.*

Leo: *Hey! How are you?*

Me: *Fine. You?*

Leo: *That's it?*

Me: *Pondering college-app snafu. Not sure what to do.*

Him: *Sounds intriguing.*

Me: *You?*

Him: *Just back from dinner with Big Bear friends.*

Me, nonchalantly hiding how much I want to go to Big Bear if he ends up going: *Cool.*

Him: *Lunch tomorrow?*

Oh my god.

Me: *Great!*

Him: *Great! See you then.*

And that's it. Remarkable.

All thinking and worrying a waste.

Sheeran knows.

Plus, resisted signing off with "ciao" or "ta" or "peace out" or anything fun which I contemplated while doing boring peon tasks. Also let Leo get in last text so as to not look overeager, as if trying to appear worldly or mature.

I am chill girlfriend.

OMG!!!!!

Thursday, March 7

My room, eve. Just back from work. Leo lunch amazing. Tho now feel empty, hanging. Maybe this is what being chill gf is. Never knowing what's next or what it means. Do I wait for the future?

Or is the future now?

Or is the past now?

Or is now whatever I want it to be?

Let's recap and decide:

Went to Larchmont for lunch and took walk around Hancock Park on way back. Leo told Hollywood history and studio stories.

We held hands. We lightly lip-kissed on street. V. sweet and fun.

I told him about essay, actually read it to him. He laughed. Kept making Spanish *peeu* sounds. Also suggested I call Columbia and find out what's up. Truth is always best. Also, I should find out if AL knows or doesn't. See if they can delete it. Then, once I've done what I can, let chips fall where they may. That's his take.

Rational.

Also, he mentioned Hollywood Forever cemetery, right behind the lot, and summer movies in June and that we should go! He loves going. He wants to go with me!

Then, he *un*held my hand when we got back on the lot.

And didn't invite me to his house when I strategically (and hopefully) told him I'm shooting another boot dance w/Sadie and suggested, "maybe we can edit again," with super-confident, cute, sexy, stargirl-goddess smile.

Instead, he said, "Yeah, great, let's do it," without any commitment to this weekend or any other distinct future time.

He did, however, say, "Hey, maybe Hollywood Forever for lunch next week," at his cutting-room door when I was having a hard time leaving and he must've sensed it. I replied enthusiastically and hiding all disappointment, "Yeah, awesome," like an idiot, so now, for sure, I'm not seeing him this weekend bc I sounded like I'm busy and not waiting around for boyfriend to invite me over again. Why did I ever agree to go slow????!!!!

Did I agree to go slow?

Or make it sound like I want to?

Yes, Saoirse. There is recorded data in previous diary entries that describe your stupid go-slow behavior.

Calling Sadie to set up boot-dance shoot so can at least text Leo when ready to edit.

Why do I feel so desperate?

Later. Sadie can't do boot-dance shoot till next week. Super annoyed. Esp bc am helping her with stupid mural shoot Sunday for Hector and now won't have raw footage to poss. edit at Leo's.

Texted Hector per Sadie's request: *Let's meet Sunday at my house. K?*

Hector: *Sounds good!*

Me/Sadie: *Great. Thx. Ta!*

Stupid that I can say *ta* to Heck but not Leo. Whatever. Somehow freeing.

Going to bed.

Oh, now he replied with stupid question of the day.

Heck: *What say you to "The Phantom of the Opera is here...inside your mind"? A tweet by SpaceX man.*

I don't even know what he's talking about. Too weird for even me.

Ignoring completely.

Good night.

Friday, March 8

Work, noon. Leo door shut.

Called Columbia. Asked about essay error. Admin had no idea what I was talking about. Why am I so confusing? Sounds like only admissions reads essays. Nothing more to say. I have to wait and see now.

Getting practice at waiting.

Saturday, March 9

Night. Waited too long.

Lorraine at Hollywood Athletic Club with Leo. She posted selfie.

Liked.

Producer Chris is there too so I need not worry. They are simply cute, happy, work fam. Friends working together. Someday I will be their friend and family too.

Unliked.

Could've invited me!

Unfollowed.

Heart squeezing, crying inside. AHHHH!

Followed.

Going to bed. Under covers so never have to show face again.

Sad bird. Peeu. Peeu.

Sunday, March 10

Metro station waiting for train, 1:40 p.m. This Cyrano bonanza with Hector has to end. Once again, he and Sadie are fine and I'm not.

I really should never be in the same location as him.

I knew this but did it anyway.

Idiot.

Let's recap quickly and get it over with:

First, went to Sadie's. Felt good just to be there and see her after Lorraine downer last night. She was flitty getting ready and my mood picked up instantly. Aunt Lauren and Unc Unc were reading the paper. They seemed happy. No trace of AL weirdness or insecurity. Except when she put tea glass in sink too hard and it broke and her shoulders slumped and UP came to her rescue, hugging her and kissing her forehead, which helped and was nice in the end.

No sign of AL knowing about essay. Probably am off hook. Also, decided not to tell Sadie about essay. Ever. So as not to disturb the peace. At least, that's what I thought this morning.

I teased her when I realized it was family day. "Hey, you can't see Hector. It's family day!"

"That's why you're here," Sadie joked as we walked upstairs to her room.

Such a cheat. I told her love shouldn't be a free pass to cheating. She laughed and put on her favorite jeans and a tiny bit of makeup. She's so pretty. I put on her headphones. She was listening to Avenir (French house DJ). I like it. Singing by Phoebe Killdeer (just looked it up, will use for BLGirl). I put on Sadie's cowboy-boot mules that go to your ankles and danced and sang along. She found it amusing.

Then we went downstairs and danced for AL and UP. No boots but still pretty fun and funny. We did a thing we made up from *Pulp Fiction*, the batman-eyes thing.

Then Hector came to pick us up. I stopped dancing as soon as he saw us. V. uncomfortable. My voice even cracked when I said, "Hi," and I blushed. Ugh. V. strange. Not liking the attention.

Luckily, AL distracted him. Plus, he was looking at Sadie and didn't notice. Though UP saw me trip on the way to the bathroom and said, "You okay, Berger?" Like he could tell something was up.

I said, "Yup," with funny fake voice.

We got into Hector's old red beemer (must admit it's v. coolsy) and headed downtown. He put on his music, Avenir.

Sadie told him she's been listening to it and loves it. He shot her a sexy look. I could see from the back seat. Gross. I looked out window.

"What do you think?" he asked, looking in rearview mirror, probably just including me to impress Sadie.

"It's fine?" I said as if I couldn't be bothered.

Then he ignored me, like no "thanks for coming with us" or "gosh, it's awesome you did this on family day so Sadie could come with me" or anything to show his appreciation. He was oblivious.

We drove downtown and he showed us a bunch of art. Murals. On doors. And walls. Really cool stuff. His aim was clearly to impress Sadie, which annoyed me enough that I couldn't enjoy any of it.

Until we got to the mural he wanted me/her to shoot. It's beautiful. Nia made it. It's a young woman hugging her mom. They're at the beach. Santa Monica. The tide is low. It's flat and calm. Ferris wheel in BG. The mom looks island-y, like Caribbean or African. With colorful, mostly blues, flowy dress. Wise. Serious. Earth mom. Heck said it's Nia's mom from Bermuda. The girl looks hipster-ish, sweet, sassy, urbanite. It's so warm. My heart melted when I saw it.

But I kept that inside and said, "Cool," and handed Sadie the camera. She was awkward even holding it and took a few shots, which was worse. We should've practiced. Or not! Bc I didn't even want to be there.

I did listen closely though as Heck explained the story of the mural (it's Nia w/her mom). He also filmed Sadie looking at the mural, taking awkward shots. He's making a vid of her photographing murals and making art of the art and showing it from various angles. Gah! Inspired by "her"/BLGirl! Bawk!

I did everything to hide how irritated I was.

Then Heck told Sadie to take her time bc he could tell she was hesitant.

And she looked at me, *Help! What do I do?*

And I was like, *I don't know! You figure it out!*

So she did, lemonade from lemons, like the star that she is. Switching on the charm, making it about the mural, like she's in love w/it and distracted by how sweet Nia and her mom are. Then she made it funny, with cute flashing eyes, saying she and AL could learn from Nia/mom sweetness, and closed her eyes and overdramatically breathed in mural love vibes.

Heck laughed, totally charmed.

Sadie added that it might be better to take photos "with different light," beautifully played, and I, idiot, added, "You know, from my humble experience, Sadie works better alone," and took the camera back, "Like total biaaatch if you ever go with her while she's shooting."

Which Sadie, adorably, found funny. "Yeah, I think I should come back. But this'll give me an idea. And you got what you need for your video?" Like she knew what she was talking about!

He said he did and was so in love she could've said anything. "Great, today we just look."

And I come back to do all the work!

Then we stopped at a food truck and sat on the curb, Son of a Bun, super yum avo-egg burger. Fries yum too! Heck ate his fries inside his burger, which Sadie tried, and it looked scrumptch, so I got a bite too, yummy. Also, he used a ton of napkins, which was funny and weird and he made fun of himself about it.

So I laughed, which made him notice me again. "So, tell me about this graduating early thing," he said, way more relaxed talking to me, like *Sure, talk to the ugly chick then swoon over the beauty.*

Blood rushed to my face. "I, uh, well, there's not much to say. I got kicked out of third grade." Which made no sense.

Go away!

"What?" he laughed.

"It's true," Sadie said proudly about me, circus-seal cousin.

I added that actually my mom pulled me out because I kept getting in trouble and that was the start of it. He asked why and I didn't reply so Sadie happily told him I got bored and stopped listening and doing homework. "And took her third-grade bathroom partner on adventures during bathroom break and stole a pencil case because it was so shiny she couldn't focus on anything else."

Which made no sense unless you know the whole story.

But he was amused bc she's so stupidly charming, even with incomplete stories. "So you were a hellraiser."

"Not really."

Then he told us about how he *actually* got kicked out of second grade, all charming and badboy cute, like in a fun second-grader way, not really bad but hoping to sound cute and sexy for Sadie.

Which worked, and Sadie said, "What?!"

"My English wasn't good enough," he said, smiling, cute, playful with her.

"No way," she said, all charmed and flirty back.

"Yeah, *actually* kicked out. Well, asked to leave. I didn't tell you that part."

Throwing up.

He said he was at this Mandarin-immersion school in Venice, which he thought was the coolest thing, this Mexican kid learning Chinese, and how his English wasn't good enough to get good test scores, which is all the school cared about (maybe bc his mom isn't a native speaker, even tho it sounds fine now!), and the school didn't have time to help him learn. Bass-turds! "Luckily, my mom figured that out and told me I was too smart for them so I didn't feel bad. Or get discouraged."

"Like Thomas Edison!" I chimed in, bc I love that story. And told them about Edison's teacher who thought Edison was "addled" and kicked him out of school, and his mom told Edison it was bc he was a genius—the school wasn't good enough for HIM! Not bc he couldn't sit still and was bored and they couldn't handle him.

Just like Heck! (and me?) His eyes flashed w/magnetic connectors and my heart spun round like an electric-lightbulb sparkler—and he said, "Exactly," then turned to Sadie and said, "I think Ofelia stole that from her," with cute, flashy, SEXY SMILE meant for ME!

I WANTED TO SCREAM! And LEAVE! And started cramming my yummy burger in my face. While Heck continued charming Sadie about how he then got stuck in ESL at the next school and his warrior mom saved his butt there too—bc there was no science for ESL kids, lots of teasing, the principal not letting him out of ESL bc the school wanted the money, Ofelia raising heck (terrible pun!)—blah, blah. And Sadie said, "Bass-turd," in a cute sweary way that only sounds cute on her. And I tried not to throw up even tho I LOVE how awesome his mom is bc then she pulled him out again and homeschooled like Edison!

"My mom's the hellraiser in the family," Heck said.

Then Sadie did silly cute punches like a boxer, but a cute girly boxer, like imitating Ofelia, *fight, fight, fight*, like Meg Ryan in *You've Got Mail*, which Mom loves and Dad makes fun of—and maybe I actually threw up a little in my mouth.

And Heck said, "So are you happy now?"—to me about the gap year. AGAIN!

And all I could see was Sadie's cute punches and him loving her more and me invisible, bc who wouldn't love her more? And who cares about my gap year and being happy? Not him!

So I said, "What do you mean, like with my hellraiser status?"— trying to be funny but sounding jerky with clenched, irritated pumpkin smile after.

And he said, "Yeah, exactly, and in general, like with graduating early," sincere, just wanting to know.

So I said, "I don't know. It's a boring story," and stood up bc I couldn't stand it anymore.

And he smiled cutely at Sadie. "Sounds like me,"—like on the curb! About Jose! Which she had no clue about. With a smile MEANT FOR ME!

She laughed all sweetly and coyly (ahhh!), like it was actually meant for her.

And this stupid lava-hot fury rose inside, like I had to get out of there so I didn't do anything stupid.

I breathed in the lava-fury, barricading it in, and said, "Actually, it's not all it's cracked up to be," as if graduating early was cracked up to be anything, like *Ha, ha, you're graduating early and it's not going to work out for you either!* Terrible. Why was I being so petty?

Because I was SAWDUST AGAIN! And I couldn't help it.

"I mean, probably neither is college. What's the use if you don't know what you want? Or maybe even if you do. Waste of money. So, yeah, kind of lost really." And I nailed it home with, "All thanks to graduating early," with smug, sarcastic, jerky mean-pumpkin smile. Which felt good for five seconds. And then it didn't be it never feels good to be smug and mean and confuse someone instead of encouraging them, like saying, *Hey! I did this awesome gap year and fell in love and found out I want to be a DP!*

"Right," Heck said, confused, and maybe hurt, exactly like I wanted, and it just made me feel WORSE!!

The lava spiked in my chest again. I couldn't keep having this conversation. And not be myself. Perpetuating this stupid lie. I yelled, "It's all because I can't be me! And maybe I don't even know who me is!"

I grabbed my bag and camera off the ground. "I gotta go." And started to go.

Sadie, panicked, "Wait! Saoirse! What's going on?"

Which made me more angry, and I lost it and incoherently yelled, "It's not working!" and stormed off, leaving her alone with her desperate, stupid look.

And Hector yelled, "Hey, Saoirse, come back!"

But I didn't.

My room, 5:30 p.m. I rode the Metro for two hours. Hole inside heart. No news from Leo. No posts. No likes. No way to know if he's with Loraine. Or Chris. Or Big Bear friends. Or other friends. Or no one!

Don't know what to do with this feeling.

Sadie was here when I got back. On my steps. Sitting. On her phone. Waiting for me.

Sadie: "Hi."

Me: "Hi."

Both of us staring, miserable.

Me: "I'm sorry."

Her: "Me too."

I sat next to her.

Sadie: "Where's your car?"

Me: "Your house."

Sadie: "Why?"

Me: "I didn't want to run into any of you."

She nodded, understanding, not judging.

Me: "So what happened?"

Sadie: "I left. I mean, I don't know. I told him you were upset with me. And it was between us and it'd be okay. And I made it sound like I was upset about the mural because of my mom."

I nodded.

Sadie: "Are we okay?"

I nodded again.

Me: "I'm sorry."

Sadie: "It's okay." I could feel her reigning in tears, then breathing them out. She nodded again. "Are you?"

Me: "It's, um...fine." Then I felt like I was about to cry and shook my head that I wasn't okay. "I'm just really insecure..."

She hugged me.

I whispered into the side of her hair, "About Leo."

She whispered back near my ear, "You're amazing." And kissed my ear.

It was nice that she just got it.

We both felt the heaviness and laughed a little and shook our heads at ourselves.

I looked down at my phone and exhaled. "Also, I wrote a mean essay about your mom and submitted it to Columbia by accident."

Sadie panicked subtly under her cool exterior, for five seconds. Then it was all over her face. Even though she kept trying to hide it. She asked me if AL knows and what it said.

I read it to her.

Sadie: "Oh. My. God." She looked away, like half laughing, half crying.

I exhaled, slowly. "Exactly."

Sadie: "Please don't tell her."

Me: "I won't."

Then we both felt bad. And nodded. And were holding our breath but managed to exhale a few times. Then stood up.

She said she's seeing Hector tomorrow after school. She didn't look excited, rather v. serious, and said, "He's the only good thing in my life. I'm gonna try to make it work." She smiled like she was trying to convince even herself, then: "And you. I love you, Cous." She hugged me, full-on, and left. Going to bed. Under covers. Need to not think. Need to make clutching heart of discord stop!

Under covers, my room, 7:20 p.m. Hector just called. It stopped ringing after one ring. Go away! Leave me alone!

Still under covers, 7:40 p.m. He called again. I fumed. Watched it ring. Ring. Ring. Ring. Fuming. Finally just answered: "What?"
Idiot.
Hector: "Uh...hi?"
Heat. Tears. Holding it in. "Yes. Sorry."
Ahhh!
I sat up under covers. Duvet slid off head. Oh my god. What was happening? I exhaled. Had to stop emotions. Pulled duvet back over head.
Hector: "Uh...It's okay. I just...wanted to make sure you meant the French cafe tomorrow. And meeting there. I'll let you go."
Me, not knowing, not caring: "Yes."
Him, exhaling: "Great. Okay. Sorry. Hope you feel better. I'll see you then."
Me: "Yes."
Silence. Awkward. Breathing.
Him: "You okay, Sadie?" Honest. Nice. Caring.
Me, tears rising, reigning them in, barely audible: "Yes."
Him, clown voice, reaching: "Ohhh no!"
Me, squeezing eyes shut, scrunching face and clutching fists in balls, screaming inside throat inaudibly, beating bed, then barely audible speedy-whisper-croak: "It's fine."
Silence. Awkward. Breathing.
Me, flopping over, pulling duvet all the way over self, curling into

ball in duvet tent, looking at phone and "Sadie's Aw Heck" screen, not knowing how to make this better, then just trying to say it directly like an adult version of me/Sadie that didn't exist yet and came out in monotone whisper-like thing: "I'm having a hard time. I want it to work. With you. I like you. But..." Reigning in emotions, trying to express logical answer. "My mom is having a hard time too. And...my cousin. Her boyfriend..." Barely audible whisper: "She's very insecure."

Him: "Um..."

Me squeezing eyes shut, screaming silently and flailing like a tantrum in duvet, then pulling duvet tight around head like babushka doll: "I should go."

Him, exhaling, in relief maybe, because his voice sounded fatter again and kind of monotone-happy: "Yes. And thank you. For being honest. I, um, get it. Kaleidoscope family. Right?"

I forced a laugh: "Heh heh."

Him, probably noticing: "You're gonna be okay, Sadie. So is your mom. And the two of you, you and Saoirse. As long as everyone's got good intentions, everything usually works out for the best. In a good way."

I didn't know if he was talking about him and Sadie or me and Sadie or Sadie and her mom, but it made me feel better. I believed him.

Me: "Thank you."

Him: "You're welcome. See you tomorrow."

Me: "Yes. Ciao."

Him, laughing: "Ciao? What're you a French hipster now?"

Me, laughing: "Italian."

Him: "Aha! Well, Buona Notte then."

Me: "Ta."

I hung up. Not worried about getting the last word in, no matter how stupid.

I texted Sadie: *You're meeting Heck there. At the French place.*

Sadie to me: *TY. Love you.*

Me to Sadie: *Love you too. Ta.*

Sadie to me: *Ta.*

Monday, March 11

Cutting room, 5:10 p.m. I went before work and shot Hector's/Nia's mural. I couldn't sleep so I just got up super early and did it. Plus, it was nice because the light was at a morning angle and everyone was just starting their day.

I got a bunch of angles and a few with Dad's boots, foot up high on the mural. I wish I could've taken a photo of Nia hugging the wall. Or even Sadie. But what happened was good too. People walking by. Talking together. An old lady stopping, adjusting her shoe then looking at it. A couple standing nearby talking with coffee. Some girls in high school walking by, one noticing it. That was the best shot. They had on uniforms. I love that shot!

And the whole thing felt good, like all my worries melted away, like a hug of being in the space of the colors and angles and creating something new.

A day of splendor. And generous intent of heart. And like everything from yesterday is gone. I feel strong. Like I did last week. Like Leo will love me even if I have to wait.

And Sadie and Heck will be together. And everything will be okay.

I posted the boot shot and saved the best for Heck.

Leo liked it pretty much right away.

So did Heck.

Leo wrote: *Great shot!*

Heck wrote: *Yes!* And respectfully didn't ask about the rest that he's so impatiently waiting for, which forced me to do this in the first place. Which is annoying. Even though something good came of it.

I walked by Leo's closed door thrice and told myself I have good intentions. It will work out for me if I'm honest and patient and make positivity and calmness and hope hit a homerun. I have this!

Then Leo came by at lunch. And peeked in, and said, "Hey."

And somehow I hit a homerun. With chillness. And said, "Hi," back, calmly, emotions close.

And he said, "What's up?" with cute flirty smile.

And I shrugged, bc I was so calm.

And he said, "Great shot today," flirting more, stepping closer.

And I said, "Thanks," and asked if he wanted to see the rest. So he came in and I showed him.

Which is when Mike, UP and Jena came out and noticed the homerun too, stopping, like: *Interesting. Wow. Looks like they're more than just friends. Like he likes her.*

And I thought: *Yeah, he likes me, you stupid cows! Like that day at lunch!*

And Leo walked over to UP, breaking the trance of confusion, and said "Hey!" And UP asked if he wanted to go to lunch. And Leo said he couldn't bc this week's too busy. And he and Unc Unc shared an overworking-director-bro moment and then UP and Mike left.

And Leo asked if I wanted to grab something at the commissary. "I'm gonna grab something here. Wanna walk over?" with the sexiest smile, as if my calm mojo made me more alluring than ever. OMG.

So we walked to the commissary and he turned, playfully walking backwards, and said this week is busy but "I'd love to do Hollywood Forever next week."

What was going on?!

Also, he said Big Bear is probably on, the weekend after next. And if he goes "I'd love you to come. If you're free." And he smiled, so CUTE! Like he really wants me to go!

CALMNESS ON FIRE!

I teased, "You sure?" Like is he sure he can handle it without Isla? OMG, SO BOLD!

He laughed and said, "We'll see." Funny, cute, and teased back, "If I go. I'm still not sure."

"I guess we'll see," I said, more teasing.

"Yes, we will."

Then we got lunch and at the end, he said, "Alright, Bookish, I'll see you very soon." And flashed another sexy smile.

And maybe I did too.

OMG, am I insane? Am I that different? Or did I just never notice how much he likes me???

Maybe this is what being in a relationship is.

And calm.

Wish I knew for sure.

Dropboxed the rest of the photos to Hector.

10:40 p.m. Sadie texted and said I dropboxed while she was with Hector. I told her there was no way I could know that bc no one told me the time they were meeting and sorry. She told Hector we switched phones so I could organize stuff and upload photos for her. He bought it. She also suggested they play tic-tac-toe on napkins to further distract him, which they did, and she got him to ride scooters. And was totally in her element, keeping it light and cute w/playfulness. Which worked for her. She said it was fun and she really likes him again bc she's being herself more.

And that works for me. Especially if I don't have to be part of it.

I suggested again that we segue onto her phone but she said she still needs time to ease in, being herself, till next week, to be sure she knows what she wants.

How does she not know what she wants? She just said she likes him!

Whatever. She's happy. And I'm happy. Because I HAVE A BOYFRIEND!

And something to look forward to.

I think this is the most chill day I've ever had.

OMG, I might be going to Big Bear!

No text from LL tonight. Letting it lie. Goodnight.

Wednesday, March 13

Cutting room, 11:10 a.m. Leo out of town for week. He didn't tell me (weird!). Melanie did. Something with his family and work.

I texted: *Hey! Heard you're in Texas and work. Everything okay?*

Everything okay? Ugh. Stupid. But then...

Him: *Bookish Berger! Mom's birthday. Then New York. All good!*

Short. Sweet. To the point. All good!

Is it all good?

V. hard to wait.

Saturday, March 16

My room, post boot-dance *Breakfast At Tiffany's* shoot (book & movie), 9:20 p.m. Tonight was great. It's been really hard to keep good intentions and not obsess about Leo or get too excited about Big Bear or scheme with uncut editing footage to get him to invite me over. So it was the perfect distraction.

Sadie came over and we walked down to the beach and shot her boot dancing and talking about *Breakfast at Tiffany's* for what BLGirl is supposedly reading. Boots don't really go with *BAT* but she wore a pink boa and sunglasses and it was fun and I don't care! I love this whole TBR&W thing! Though, I do want to read the book to see how they changed it in the film. Am doing a full-on series of fun movies from books I decided!

We shot at the lifeguard station, Pier, benches and boardwalk. We played the Avenir song bc it's so great to dance to. Sadie was funny and irreverent and in her element, perfect for the telling of how the movie "took Capote's dark book and made it sweet and dreamy."

We didn't talk about anything serious. Like old times. Then, we went to the market on 4th for snacks. Ice cream, almond butter and English chocolate and sat on a bench at Hotchkiss Park and ate it all at once while staring at the sky and having sporadic conversation and pigging out.

It was great. We decided several things:

1. We're both tense about college and don't want to go and are both scared. All acceptances are out in two weeks and we'll have to decide.
2. Sadie's v. worried about her mom but Heck makes it better. Tension's high w/UP, and AL's going away w/Taylor Rae this weekend to Santa Barbara. Sadie looked like a little kid when she

talked about it. She said her mom's insane and she's worried about where that leaves her dad.

3. Sadie's finally letting go of Paulie and Heck is helping. She still misses Paulie but knows he's not The One. Paulie was safe. "And he liked me for me. Not you. And I'm never going to be you. And I don't want to be you. I mean, not in a bad way. But because I'm me." Which made it sound like Hector's a project. I didn't say that, but said, "You are totally you. And me as you. And yet, it is you." We laughed. Bc it's so stupid.

4. I told her about kissing/going slow w/Leo and did it in a funny way and we decided humor makes everything better. She esp. liked the deathnell thinking and watching us kiss in out-of-body experience, like I was drinking an iced-mocha and smoking a cigarette.

"You smoke now?"

"No. It was just an image."

She said her mind doesn't work that way. But sometimes she imagines Paulie kissing his stupid new girlfriend. We agreed both of us have to stop thinking and imagining and instead focus on the real and positive. Which there's so much of, including the amazing cookie-dough ice cream we were devouring.

Then, we played Words With Friends on her phone against people we don't know and the cousinship kicked their anonymous butts, both of us forgetting all the other stupid stuff.

Relief. In moment. Love.

And chill. Like sitting on Italian Riviera, sipping Prosecco. Eating pasta. Ciao.

Wednesday, March 20

My room, night. Has been hard to remain adultish gf all week but Leo finally back tomorrow. Only texted two hellos. He replied short and sweet immediately. He posted one shot of him with fam at mom's birthday and one in Central Park, no people. I liked both. Also have been editing boot dance to stay out of head. It's good.

Thursday, March 21

On bench outside cutting room, lunch. He's back! And excellent behavior from me at parking lot this morn. Wearing cute pear dress, calmly welcomed him with flirty smile. Said nothing about editing. Exuded chill confidence instead. End result excellent.

Leo, magnanimous hugging and awkward kiss on hair: "Hey! How's it going?"

Me: "Great." Smile, happy, cute.

We toasted coffee mugs.

Him: "What's new?"

Me: "Nothing. Just, you know, the same."

I shrugged and cutely indicated how happy, confident and okay I am with my life as is, in spite of having impatiently waited all week, holding breath, which propelled me forward to further alluring confidence.

"Great," he said, intrigued, checking out my hair.

"You?"

"Uh, the same too. *And*! I am going to Big Bear..." He looked at me all sexy and bright-eyed.

I held my breath inside.

"Maybe a mistake. And I gotta bring work. But I'd love it if you came along. If you want to. And have time. And there's space. I have to double check since I waited so long to tell them I'm going."

Me, screaming w/excitement under breath-held smile then inhaling through nose, shrugging w/demure, calm confidence: "Great. I'd love to. Just let me know."

Then, cheerfully, nonchalantly toasting good-bye w/coffee, then turning to go, but stopping cutely: "By the way, I signed up for that class. So thanks for that. And I find out about Columbia tomorrow. I think it's all good." I cheered again and went in.

Holding breath. Excited. Hoping it works out with Big Bear! I think it will!!!!

Friday, March 22

Noon, cutting room. Spent last night editing and posted cowboy tap with Avenir. Once again, Sadie knocked it out of the park. 4K likes in two hours. Missed Leo's IG post from last night bc of editing. Just saw now. Selfie of him w/stupid exec Lorraine, now dressed t. cute/sexy pants, a la Isla, but not as good, at Kings game. Producer Chris there too. Checked Chris's IG. Looks like a group again. And I need to chill. Leo has friends! Work friends and not work friends. And he's not going to bring me, the gf, to everything. He has a life without me too, esp. for work. And he'll bring me soon enough!

Breathing calmly to attract goodness and Leo positivity in spite of momentary emo insanity.

Liked the post.

Cutting room, 2:20 p.m. And it worked! I was right! Intuition intact. Intentions good. Leo has confirmed Big Bear.

He came by just now. His friends want me to go. They think it'll be good for him. Some met me at Oscars. "I think they're happy I'm dating and met someone new after, you know who." Funny, cute, humble.

I smiled. "Great." And screamed inside, YESSSSSSSSSSSSS!!!!!

He seems relieved I can still go. "Awesome. Gotta leave early though."

"Like how early?"

"Eight a.m.?"

"Great." Crap, that's early.

"Great." He did a funny thumbs-up, cutely and kind of awkwardly. Like he likes me!

And left.

I did a happy dance. So happy, happy...

Until I noticed Jena looking. And stopped.

She laughed. "Nice." And I smiled and she went back to her work.

Maybe she thinks I'm insane but also sees through my crazy and is rooting for me for love.

Am in love. It is happening.

His friends like me!

Sweet, sexy, loving boyfriend.

Sunday, March 24

My room, 10 p.m. Horror. Confusion. Need to regain faith and trust. Am no longer invisible but am insane. Need disappearing cloak.

Let me recap simply as am not ready for full analysis as am utterly fragile bird. Fallen from nest. Need to get back to branch.

Saturday morning. Leo picked me up. Mom was so happy to meet him. Especially bc Stupid Jake was so happy to see him. He knocked. Jake answered. Mom surprised. Jake awkward and shy. Bizarre. I suddenly imagined Stupid Jake in a wig of my hair. Is that how stupid I look around Leo? Because clearly Stupid Jake has a bro crush on him that is enormous. Don't go there, Saoirse, just don't.

Mom offered to make coffee but Leo said we should get on the road. He smiled at Mom. She got all weird too. Gross. What is he doing to our family? What is this pull he has on them?

But then, Jake said, "Hey, check it out, I made a new mod." And Leo looked at the mod and winked at me, checking me out, and Mom finally GOT IT, laughing at herself, and left. Yeah, what the EFF was that, MOM?

Then it turned back into the best moment ever again bc Leo was in our living room, hot and charming, even in the vicinity of Mom and the Grand Permanent Gaming Station, bc he was there for ME.

Then, we got in the car, and Leo asked if I'd watch his movie. He feels guilty about leaving town and said it'd help if we talked through the changes and he could do them "tomorrow night" (which is now— he must be doing them now as I write in torture, all the amazing notes we discovered in creative bliss, fulfilling fate of his wonderful characters, making sure every last frame is honest, which I will never see as it may be over between he and I).

He gave me his iPad and headphones. I watched as we drove (three hours) on freeways and gorgeous, curvy, pine-lined mountain roads, which I didn't notice, but got a tad carsick, and cried at the movie. It's that good.

We addressed his issues. Stuff like: Does *she need to enter? It makes her seem eager. Cut now.*

How does he notice this stuff? Does he see me as clearly as he sees his characters? I think so.

Also, he likes my red Chucks. Which I love too. He had on black Vans rather than his usual brown lace-ups which he wears most of the time w/jacket and bolo tie.

Then we arrived at the giant house across from the lake (movie notes done) and were off and running. With four other couples and four singles. All Leo and Isla's friends: Gen & TJ, Ali & Zach, Fiona & Dax, Surabhi (syrup-ee) & Joe, plus Maeve, Sean, Tucker, Rick.

They rent the same house every year. Five rooms plus an alcove where Maeve slept. Isla would've been there if they were still together. Apparently, they all know her really well. Apparently, they are super happy he met someone new. Apparently, she dumped him. Apparently, he's taking it really hard. Apparently, he was about to propose when it happened.

I got all this over the course of the day as we hiked and I tried water skiing (rocked it) and we drank mojitos. It was a day of firsts. I got really buzzed. And felt so good and relaxed. And cozied up to Leo. Even tho he's a bit PDA-shy. Fiona and Surabhi kept smiling at me and including me, like they like me and were happy I was there.

Later, Sean and Joe barbequed steak, red peppers and vegan burgers and we talked about all kinds of stuff. Then, at some point, people got tired and went to their rooms. By the time we went, TJ was passed out and Ali, Surabhi, Maeve, Joe and Rick were playing poker.

Okay. Blech. Quick recap:

In our room. Both pretty buzzed. Leo said he'd sleep on the couch (in room). I said okay. We brushed our teeth. I bumped into him accidentally. He kissed me. It was gentle. And it kept going. My back against wall by door. He looked me in eye like we were doing tango because also we seemed to be swaying bc of mojitos. I was in the moment in my body rather than watching from overhead. Then we were on the couch. Somehow our clothes coming off. Pretty buzzed, like maybe I was v. drunk. We continued. Almost doing it. He had protection (of course, me idiot reminder of past episode). Then we were doing it. Or maybe doing it. Like, literally, I'm not actually sure. It hurt. But just a little. Like it was okay. But maybe it wasn't. But still I think I said "ow" or some other stupidness. He stopped. "You okay?"

Me, frozen, reentering head, initiating deathnell to love. Looked at him looking at me, waiting for me to say something. Still frozen. Waiting, waiting.

Finally, I exhaled. All sexiness gone. Heart sinking. Embarrassment. I sat up. "I just...I don't... Uhuraoh..."

Him frozen still, except brow furrowing, studying me. Unsure what to do. Or say. Finally: "It's fine."

It didn't sound fine.

Me: "I don't know what's wrong with me."

Him: "Nothing's wrong with you. It's just not the right time. It's okay."

He smiled. Disappointed, probably thinking, *Wow, she's really young, younger than I thought*, and *Wow, last year, Isla was here and it was great and relaxed and normal and we were happy and I wanted to spend the rest of my life with her because it was so fun and easy and I really want her back because she's an actual adult even though only 20.*

I couldn't stand it. I side-rolled like I was getting out of a fire. *Stop, drop, roll.* Grabbed my clothes and ran into the bathroom. OMG. Idiot on fire. I looked. A tiny bit of blood. Did that mean we had sex? It was only a teeny drop. Maybe I imagined it. Maybe it was my period. Maybe it was something else. I don't know what, but something. Crap. Did we actually have sex? I DON"T KNOW!!!

He knocked on the door. "Saoirse?"

"I'm fine. I'm just. You're right. It's not the right time. I'm sorry. And embarrassed."

I heard him exhale. Then his voice changed and he said, "It's okay. Everything's perfect. You come out when you're ready. I'm just gonna cozy up on the couch or maybe one side of the bed and we are all good. Just drink some water. Your head'll appreciate it in the morning. I'm pretty sure we drank way too much. I'm sorry."

My head would appreciate it if I would stop thinking about him thinking and wishing he had Isla back.

I heard him walk away. I waited then peeked out. He was snoring on the bed all the way over on one side.

I went downstairs. TJ asleep on sofa. I went outside. There was Ali sitting on the stairs smoking.

Ali: "Hi."

Me: "Hi."

Ali: "Have a seat."

I sat next to her.

Ali: "You okay?"

Me: "Yeah, just can't sleep."

Ali: "Is Leo asleep?"

Me: "Yeah, yeah, definitely."

Ali: "Well, that's amazing because that is a man that never stops."

Then she told me that's why Isla left him. He's too into work (just like AL said). And he didn't see it coming. And was devastated. But then Ali reassured me Leo was over it and that they were all super happy he's moving on and how much everyone likes me. She also DIDN'T say HE likes me.

Which made me think about how, once again, I blew it and BOTCHED SEX WITH LEO LANDIS! The man I love. Who would surely love me if I'd only give him a chance. Who I want to be close to. Who invited me. Who I swore I'd be open with. Let it flow. Be in the moment. Be adultish. And now I don't even know if we had sex or not.

And I really just wanted to.

I went back. Leo was asleep. I lay down next to him in my

clothes. Jeans on. But Chucks off.

He said, "Come here." And hugged me and laughed. "You're wearing your jeans." And didn't seem to care about how we maybe only had a little sex or no sex at all, and the fact that I was a virgin and way too young for him, even if not in age but bc I'm inexperienced with life and relationships in comparison to Isla and stupid for not being mature enough to have sex with a guy I'm totally over the moon about and love. Unless we did have sex. And that counted. Did it?

He didn't seem to care either way.

At least that's how it seemed when he hugged me and kept teasing me over and over in his cute tipsy/maybe v. drunk way about the jeans and how he loves that I'm such a serious girl and how that reminds him of another stupid serious girl but that was a good thing and then stuck his right hand in the left back pocket of my Levis and started snoring.

The next day, I, the partial virgin, and us, the group, played baseball and Leo hit the ball and it hit me in the head by my eye and I was bleeding, like actually. Maybe that counted as sex more than last night! He tended to my wound and felt bad and kissed it and said, "At least you'll have something to remember me by," about the possible scar.

Am crying. Was crying. Will remember LL for ball scar on head rather than amazing first-time experience and first boyfriend. Heart breaking. Do not want to analyze but from a literal and logical stance that means he does not see us together in the future.

Half-virgin sadness.

One-tenth virgin sadness.

Make that's one-one-hundredth billionth.

Tried to be Ed Sheeran but that was complicated and weird as could not imagine Sheeran having one-one hundredth sex with anyone. Then just pretended to be amazing actress Sadie Svensson and feigned happiness and relaxation to self. That was worse. And confusing. I'm confusing even to myself.

And devastated.

Will reflect later.

Almost midnight. Okay, have been doing nothing for two hours but lying in bed reflecting. Then text from Hector came in: *Hey, fun day. Thx. G'nite, Sweet Sadie with the sexy smile.*
Oh, no. No. No. Nooooo!!!!
Throwing up in mouth.
Turned off phone. Because I just have to get away from it. Them. The proverbial *we*.

Monday, March 25

Morning, my room, before work. Okay, this is where I stand after logical, non-emo analysis. Here are the facts: Leo has had heart broken. But we are amazingly compatible, and I am in love. He does not seem at all phased by half-sex (or maybe even quarter-sex or probably one-tenth or billionth or less) experience. On the contrary, seems continuously flirtatious and engaging on creative and playful level. He needs time to heal. Like I need time to move into full relationship sex. (dork!) We are both understanding adult humans. We like to spend time together. Comment on scar, while could portend end of relationship, could also mean his heart has hardened and he is convincing self that he should not let heart get broken again and is protecting self, which I know he does not have to worry about as am sure I would never break his heart. Must go slow with him. Be gentle. Be gentle with self. Give it time. Time heals. Time tells truth. Time lets loving, normal relationships grow between loving, creative, nice, normal individuals, which Leo and I both are. Must have patience with him and self.

Later, cutting room. Walked by Leo's cutting room. Exec in cutting room again. Leo noticed me walk by. He waved with friendly politician face as she looked at me for a sec then back at screen.

Tuesday, March 26

Cutting room, 4 p.m. Leo and executive selfie on IG last night. He has not liked any of my posts. I walked by. Exec there again. He texts: *Thanks for the notes. The changes were great. Studio happy again thx to your awesome eye!*

Wednesday, March 27

Cutting room, 10:20 a.m. I go by again. He waves. I run. I go by and don't look. Passive aggressive? Maybe.

Afternoon. I do this three more times. The last time I look. Both Leo and Melanie are looking, horrified.

10 p.m. Leo texted: *Lunch tomorrow?*
Yes!!!!
Another shot of him and exec at bar with Big Bear friends. Do they like her too?

Thursday, March 28

Night. This may be last entry ever. Want to die. At lunch, Leo tells me it's not me but him. He's not over Isla. I knew that! His therapist says he shouldn't date me. I am too young. What???? He didn't know what to say but has to be honest. He also told me he locked picture.
Heartbroken.
Also, Sadie got into Sarah Lawrence and Harvard.
I got into Columbia. Feel numb. Texted AL. Weirdly she didn't ask about it first. She texted back: *Congratulations.*
Period. Ending with a period. And said nothing more.
What's going on?
Heart v. broken. May not recover.

Sunday, March 31

Night, my room. And now, absolutely humiliated. Went by Leo's Airbnb this morning to bring him friend flowers to congratulate him for locking picture. Wanted to let him know am okay and understand that he needs to heal from previous relationship. Wanted to offer friendship yellow. So he knows he can talk to me if needed as friend since, as he said, he is so comfortable being honest and open with me. Knocked. No answer. Hear music. See his car. Knock again. Decide to go around back. Perhaps he's working out to music as I hear random singing. Go in back door. Thinking this is fun. Music in living room. Sneak in. Jump in. Yell: "Surprise."

He and the exec are doing it on rug.

I run. He runs after me. Grabbing dishtowel as he passes through kitchen and we run in back. "What're you doing here, Bookish?"

I'm holding yellow carnations. "I. I just wanted to give you friendship flowers."

"Friendship flowers?" He looks like he's going to burst out laughing. At this point, the exec is in the door in his shirt.

Exec: "Everything okay?"

Yes! Yes, it's okay!!! I'm only just a stupid idiot who had HALF-ONEHUNDREDTH SEX with your…HOOK-UP! Because you can't possibly be dating him because he's NOT OVER HIS EX! HE IS NOT READY! THIS IS GOING TO END BADLY FOR YOU!

And I'm going to be here to be his friend as he works through this.

Me: "Yeah, I just, thought, because your cut came out so good." I swallowed hard and sang, "So good, so good, so good," expertly invoking Sheeran and Sadie all at once. Then whistling.

He laughed. "Not bad. Why thank you." He came out in his towel and took the flowers which made the towel flop off. "Whoops." So he pulled it back up and held the yellow friendship carnations over what seemed to be six inches. And we stood there awkwardly. And it means I only had negative-tenth-sex, at best.

"Okay, then, I'd better go." I waved to the exec. "Nice to meet you."

"Oh, sorry, this is Lorraine Goodwin. She works at the studio. In development. On the film."

She smiled at me warmly.

And I ran out the side gate.

Friday, April 5

My room, night. Devastated. Embarrassed. Unbearable. Trying to find hope after yellow-carnation-friend debacle and one-trillionth-tenth-virgin humiliation. Spent five days paralyzed under covers. During this time:

1. Responded to Hector: *Have new number.* Gave him Sadie's. Completely done with all deception and self-humiliation to help others. Only self-respecting behavior and honesty going forward.
2. Called in sick.
3. Dad came back. Shoot done and now working on first cut out of office space near director's office on Santa Monica Boulevard and 7th. Boots more worn in so look less dorky. Found new punk band obsession while in Vancouver and bought us tickets for Palladium in July. Tiny light as amused by weird-but-enthusiastic-teen-like dad and that he's taking just me to concert and not Stupid Jake.
4. Fended off Mom meddling and caretaking attempts but failed to pull wool over eyes. Mom sensed mood down while taking temperature. Also, normal temp did not get past her. She asked about Leo. I told her we're just friends. She knew it wasn't so but didn't push. Her usual. Appreciating that about her right now. Though then heard her whispering to Dad outside door so suspect he knows about broken heart too. They've completely left me alone. Will have difficulty looking them in eye when emerge from nursing broken-heart wounds.
5. Continued missing Leo Landis and still cannot help thinking about him. I cannot hate him. I can only hate self for putting unrealistic expectations on him when he's not over ex. Crying inside. And out.

6. Sadie freaked out in calm perfect-Sadie fashion. Texted. Called. Came over to try to see me. She can't handle that I gave Hector her number and that I'm no longer making her sound like how she thinks Hector wants her to sound. Deal with it! Blocked all contact and told fam not to let her in. Am furious that she thinks it's my responsibility to keep her relationship w/Hector going. Even if she hasn't said that directly, that's what's happening. Never ever want to speak to her again.

7. Also have not responded to text from Deva. Sure she'd soothe wounded soul. But need to be wounded a while longer.

8. Cancelled UCLA film/camera class.

9. Escaped Svensson Friday night thanks to Mom being so undemanding and not controlling. Though am guessing she broke mom-daughter confidence to tell AL about broken heart. Mom said Hector was there w/Sadie. She thought that'd make me feel better, but obviously, it didn't. They did usual talent show and Sadie boot-tapped the rap I wrote for BLGirl. Mom showed me on phone. Saw Dad laugh in BG and Hector too. Happy Dad got the humor and hate Hector more than ever. In other activity, Aunt Lauren was apparently completely silent during entire evening for undisclosed reason, which is v. strange and unlike her. Taylor Rae stepped up her game and hosted. Mom said re AL: "Your father thinks she's having a breakdown."

Ugh. No light there. Going back under covers.

Also, never doing BLGirl again.

Also got into all schools.

Terror.

One month to decide.

Too sad.

Peepoo.

Sunday, April 7

My room, 4 p.m. Jena messaged me that if I don't come back tomorrow she has to get someone else to fill in. I don't think they'd fire me but must consider.

Pros: If I'm doing this, I may as well face the pain now. As per Hoorays 18, I should continue job so as to behave like responsible adult, show up for people that like me for me, earn $ and help career and finding of path in some unbeknownst way.

Cons: Will face utter humiliation when passing Leo in hall. Am so sad.

Must be strong. Will go back tomorrow. Will be harrowing to see LL but will embrace good behavior and show him (and his therapist) that I am an adult and worthy of him. I can do this!

Monday, April 8

Cutting room, 11:20 a.m. Worse than expected. Completely avoided going by Leo's cutting room but somehow he saw me and poked head in to say hi. "Glad to see you're back, Bookish. Everything alright?"

"A-okay," I said, as if it was. Gave him thumbs-up and a smile and pretended to be super cheerful.

"Glad to see it, and nice sneaks again," he winked and left. Acting on fleek but then broke down. Crying incessantly. I like him so much. No one makes my heart open like that. Like his creative soul is touching mine even when I'm trying to push him away. Even when bleeding inside protective armor.

Then Jena asked if I'd mind cleaning the coffee pot so one of us (me) could make more. I tried to hide that I was crying but that somehow made it worse.

"You okay?"

My whole body shook as I tried to hold it in. I nodded. Waved her off. But stupidly she came over to see what was happening, which made it unbearable. The tears and pain grew inside until I couldn't hold them in and it all exploded out like a weird naval foghorn. A blob of snot landed on the bottom of Jena's pants, just above her shoe, and she was right there near my sobbing, blotched face, tears and snot.

A look of horror and fear came over her as if she'd never seen so much emotion on anyone, let alone in the work place. And I was just crying more in her direction and shaking my head to assure her I was okay. And not telling her about the snot-blob on her pants.

Then, Mike came in. "So I hear there's fresh brew from our fabulous barista." Followed by UP. They froze in horror too.

"You know what? I got it," Jena said, in likely attempt to protect Mike and UP from further barrage of emotional discomfort, and headed to the coffee pot.

I jumped to get in ahead of her. "No, no," I insisted. I wasn't going to let this sadness make them think I wasn't a stellar and responsible worker or ruin their coffee. I barreled through and took the pot over the bridge to the bathroom in the next building where I could clean it and cry in peace.

I cried until I thought I was done but somehow have been unable to stop. The tears keep coming. And Jena keeps trying to talk or tell me to go home. She doesn't really know what to do. And I'm not going. Can't she see me waving her away? I'm sure she wishes she just got a replacement for me.

My room, 6:30 p.m. Sadie just made everything worse. She was waiting when I got home. UP must've tipped her off that I was no longer "sick." I saw her and made a beeline for the back door. She chased me into the backyard.

"Saoirse!" she yelled.

I ran up the stairs on the side of the garage to my door and slammed it in her face.

She banged. "Why are you doing this?!"

Wow, that was a lot for Sadie.

I threw the door open, and it banged against my wall, denting the plaster. "Because I'm always covering for you, and I'm sick of it!"

"That's what we do. We cover each other. And now you just don't?"

I slammed the door in her face. How could she not know how I felt?!!!!!!!

"What is wrong with you?!" She grabbed the doorknob to open it before I could lock it. I grabbed on, fighting to keep it shut. She was strong.

Me, yelling: "You have everything! And now you have this too! *My* friend!" I let go and she fell in, like literally forward onto the ground.

She struggled up. I didn't help.

"What the hell?" she said.

Which just made me more angry, like she really doesn't get it!

"It's not fair!" I yelled, unable to hold it in anymore even though I felt bad for not helping her up. "And you can't even see how much it hurts me! Or maybe you just don't care! Because all you care about is you! And apparently, I did too! But not anymore! Now I just care about me!"

It felt like daggers shooting into me and her at the same time. But maybe it hurt her more because I was so angry and felt the heat rather than sharpness. Or maybe she hurt her knee. Tears started filling her eyes, and she turned and left.

Wednesday, April 10

Cutting room, lunch. Everything keeps getting worse and worse. All I feel is anger and hurt. Anger. Tears. Explosion inside. Tears. I may never speak to Sadie again. And she may never speak to me. And that makes me feel terrible. And the only one that makes me feel better makes me cry because he doesn't love me. Broken heart crying for Leo still. How will I get over this?

How will I move forward?

Also, tension between UP and AL everywhere. He's making changes and told her she can't see them until the screening. She is beyond livid. Out of control. Why can't she let it go? Unc knows what he's doing. And like any good artist is unsure. And she's outrageously critical. This is why artists need *yes*-people—because they're insecure and need help believing in themselves. Believing in what's coming out of them. Believing in their work by *yes*-people reflecting back positivity. AL makes him lose trust in his instinct, and somehow, she's lost trust in her own instinct that UP loves her, which he does, I'm sure. Why can't she see this? Separate it out. He's doing it because it's about him being insecure, and it's not about her.

Also, I'm insecure and can't stop crying, randomly and a lot. Everyone is uncomfortable around me and avoiding me.

Then, Leo came into Jena and Mike's part of the room and asked if we wanted to go to lunch. I stayed turned, back to them, and don't know if he looked or even saw me. Then I heard Leo whispering, and Jena asked if I wanted to go. I didn't. I'm sure they were relieved. Though, Leo stuck his head in and said, "C'mon, Bookish, let's go."

"Can't. Got a thing," I said, as if I did.

My heart broke inside as I kept the smile plastered on my face as he smiled and shut the door. Then, now, I see Aunt Lauren sneaking into Mike's room. Oh. My. God. I refuse to be the gatekeeper. Just because I'm not at lunch. Am leaving before she sees me. Feeling anger growing. Why can't she get it together and hold onto her self-respect?! Why is she giving UP all her power? When she's perfectly fine as is?!!!!!!

Planter outside cutting room, 1:30 p.m. Drove over to Mom's cheese shop. The one where she works as a cheese-sommelier apprentice to learn before she opens her own shop. I don't know why I did it. Maybe to balance out after seeing Aunt Lauren. Maybe because I was at wits end and even if Mom never gives me advice, I know she still loves me.

Mom was so happy to see me. "Saoirse! You're here! I don't believe it! Come in. Have a seat. I'll give you a taste."

She gave me some Petit Munster, Cotswold blue, creamy Caerfili, Norwegian Gjetost, Brie from Provence, Camembert de Normandie and grape juice. I liked the blue.

"Everything okay?" she asked, even though it was obvious it wasn't.

I nodded. She smiled and refilled my grape juice.

"I just, didn't want to go to lunch with everyone today," I said.

"It's good to change things up sometimes."

For a moment, I felt better. I watched her doing stuff with cheese. And taking so much care. And watched her with the customers. She was honestly so happy. I took photos of the cheese and her hands. And of her working with joy, like from her POV. It reminded me of something I liked about her when I was a kid, how she used to make avocado sandwiches for my lunch and arrange them in the container like works of art. And how she made French toast out of cinnamon bread and built it into a house w/strawberries for trees and powdered sugar for snow and bananas as a walkway. Then I'd say it was a house, and she'd say, *No, it's a castle!* Even when I was in high school. Or how she hand-trimmed the French window coverings in the kitchen. She pays attention to the details.

Afterwards, she walked me outside with a goodie-bag with way too much cheese. It was bizarrely comforting. She hugged me too, and I let her. For a change. Even though the cheese bag got smooshed between us.

Then, I drove back to the lot and walked the long way around from the parking structure. Everyone was doing their thing, working on different sets, driving around in golf carts, making deliveries, strolling, chit-chatting. I noticed them more than usual. Maybe I never really pay attention. Everyone in their own little moments, doing life from so many angles, different points of view, and loving every bit of it.

I pulled out my camera and took shots of people in some of the sound stages, like the guy taking his time, carefully spackling the set wall. And the woman placing the tree in the giant soundstage set of a jungle, gently adjusting the leaves just so. It looked so real! Like magic! And the teamster proudly cleaning the chrome on his vehicle. All artists in a way.

All engaged and happy.

Then, I walked back toward the cutting room and saw they were filling the Big Sky Tank. OMG! I've never seen it full. The set painters were busy on the giant backdrop, making it look like a skyline of mountains on the edge of a shore, maybe Hawaii!

Can't wait to see what it is. Maybe we'll know tomorrow. Just looked it up and it takes a day to fill the tank. Maybe it'll be a lake or the ocean, instead of a parking lot! It's a parking lot when they're not using the tank as a set. The one right in front of the cutting room where the alien parks!

It really is exciting. It says the tank's been in *Truman Show* and *Star Trek* and the *Ten Commandments* for the parting of the Red Sea!

I took shots of the painters then sat down on the planter by our building and looked at the photos.

I thought about uploading them to BLGirl, especially the one of Mom's hands with the Camembert, placing it on the plate like art. And her writing on the chalkboard on the sidewalk outside w/cheese specials of the day—a new kind of street art! And the set designer making trees in the jungle set. I love that one!

But then I thought about BLGirl and how it isn't even me anymore. But these photos are. And they remind me how much I love the lot. And working here.

I thought about my first day on UP's movie and how I parked in the Big Sky lot because I didn't know about the peon parking structure in back. I stepped of my car like the alien and saw the Big Sky screen stretching above me. I could feel the magic. How all these worlds are created here and magical filmmakers make stories come alive. Like from books! All those books I've loved and read forever.

It felt so special to be a part of it and maybe still does if I look at it in the right way, the right angle. Even though really all I do is make coffee and answer phones and say hi to people in halls that actually do the cool stuff.

But these photos bring me back in. Creating my own magic. Out of theirs.

Me, Saoirse D. Berger. Not hiding behind Sadie. Or being the Wizard of Oz.

But shining, like a flare.

So, I started a new IG account just now with my actual name: SaoirseDBerger. To protect my heart. And soar high! Like a proud eagle. Or a peregrine falcon. Yes! I love those!

I uploaded my shots. All of them.

And for a moment, right now, I feel relief. Beauty and angles of love healing wounded heart.

Also, hashtagged the chalkboard and sea-set ones with #lastreetart. Maybe secretly want Hector to see. Ugh. Confused about that.

Should I delete hashtag? No. Breathing. Empowered. KEEP IT REAL SAOIRSE.

Later, my room. New IG account of real self helping! Even though college decision worry exploding and getting harder to ignore. Ignoring!

Came up with new design plan for living room. French! To go with Mom's cheese! 18 Hoorays #12 on fire! Found affordable upholstery maker online and post-modern French-farm coffee table. Presented design to Mom and she loves it. Will have cute blue-and-white-check window covers w/white shutters. Also, French Moroccan rug w/spatterings of bright green and red-polka-dot throw pillows on creamy sofa. Also, found cute periwinkle milk can for vase in garage and cool chandelier in Mom's old set stuff.

Have also decided to attend film class at UCLA Extension after all. Will have missed one class but that's okay. Will catch up. Feeling reenergized and like creative awesomeness blooming inside.

Perhaps patience and easing into adulthood, nurturing and watering seeds of passion and creativity and love, slowly allowing self to bloom outward, as well as in beautiful garden where Leo roots and plays like tall elk. And tall oak. Oh, so metaphorical but concept in realm of realistic expectations for love w/thriving object of affection and soul connection that is like strong protective oak, playful fun-loving woodsprite and proud elk foraging for love and offering protection and inspiration and partnership. Do elks mate for life?

That's irrelevant at this juncture. Must focus on self, nurturing hopeful-elk self growing into strong, creative force that can stand alone and embody powerful, loving and playful qualities that want in partner in self. Perhaps we will meet said partner on exciting elk-grazing lawn in stunning college garden.

Snuck peek at LL's IG. His oak branches round exec in selfie. Elk tears flowing as walk alone through own garden.

Thursday, April 11

Cutting room after lunch. Bought new dress. For hope. It has pineapples on it and pockets. Also green (again!) and pink and orange. It's like a tropical fruit basket. I guess I like those colors, esp. green, more than I knew.

After class, my room, 10:50 p.m. Hope has surfaced.

Went to class. A-MAZE-ing. Have found calling and that all possibility is possible and turned around in life. Miraculous miracle? Maybe. Insanity and kismet all at once? Yes. Also, perhaps dress is lucky.

I am SO HAPPY. Full of joy and bliss. How is this possible? How can things switch so fast? First, I was loser aubergine-nosed lost person. And now, I am found winner, ready to take on world.

Perhaps that's a bit much, but honestly, after hitting depths of despair, this was like skinny dipping in fresh, cold spring water flowing off snow-capped mountains, like when you wake up and go, *Wow, it can be really gorgeous here, why was I slumbering in cave feeling sorry for self when there are active elks foraging and playing outside?*

Should take with grain of salt, but Leo's BSC-award-winning DP, teacher-friend Richard was great. He's a director too, apparently, which is why he's not shooting Leo's next film. The class is focused on camera as tool for storytelling. Lots of talk about angles and filling the screen plus importance of lighting and establishing mood through lens. Wow. Actually YES, it IS a miraculous miracle of inspiration and purpose fulfillment attuned with my natural elk-angle instinct.

There's also a woman named Eloise, some kind of documentarian/professor, to mentor us as we develop individual projects and fill in if Richard has to be away for work and miss class.

Would rather have Richard as mentor. Also, he needs a TA. Could be way to ensure getting him as mentor. I asked if I could be his TA. He said UCLA Extension handling it. I'll check it before next class.

The class is on UCLA campus. It felt empty, probably because it's at night. The old buildings with ivy are beautiful, but it doesn't inspire me to want to go there next year. Ignoring. Am excited about the class and doing the project. What will it be? Maybe something about street art. Or cheese. From the artist's POV. *YES!*

Also, class is spectacular for courage and realistic self-esteem building. May have set out to be amazing for Leo, showing him I am a flourishing, and perhaps foraging, adult creative type, but now am amazing for self too. Win win.

Also, finally texted Deva back. Didn't tell all but she gently insisted I hang with her and River Saturday. Hoping wounded heart is ready for snarky kindness and true-friend love and consoling.

Friday, April 12

My room after work. Saw Leo in same spot from coffee-pot bridge. Def. his spot to make calls. Yelled out in friendly tone wanting to show newfound, actualized, creative self, thanks to class, "Hey, Leo!"

He waved and looked up, so happy and surprised to see me. Bright-eyed with anticipation.

"I went to Richard's class! It's awesome! I'm making a movie!"

He waved and turned back to his call. Like he didn't even hear. Like my words didn't matter. Like he didn't care.

Wounded soul hurting again. Hoping snarky Deva friend-love will help.

Droopy elk antlers tussling through daisies, yearning for happiness and love.

Saturday, April 13

My room after day with Deva and River, 9:30 p.m. River decided
we should go downtown and do a photoshoot of them. He made it
sound impromptu, but it was probably a well-thought-out master plan
by Deva to move in quickly to soothe my bruised spirit. She's now
leaning towards Jungian analyst rather than orthopedic surgeon. How
is she 20 and about to go to med school? Probably will end up
youngest-ever analyst-surgeon hyphenate. Oh, and also opinionated
control freak, constitutional law judge, and wearer of vests. She's
really into these ski vests now and wears them all the time. Like, a
new one every time. Today's was burnt orange with a purple zipper
and lime-green tassel. I do like the color combo.

We met at the Metro at Bundy. The flood of tears started as soon
as she looked at me and I tried to talk. She hugged me and it got
worse. When it subsided slightly, she said, "Okay, we're moving onto
the Metro now," like I was five and unable to contain myself or
"integrate emotions with logic," using both sides of my brain, as
would be "more ideal."

The relentless tears continued. We sat down. She held me while I
cried until finally I said, "He doesn't love me," and told them
everything. She kept signaling to River sitting across from us,
probably to get him to stop laughing.

River also interjected once that I should try really hard to
remember through Big-Bear-cabin-mojito fog some measurement
details to determine true virgin-or-no-virgin or partial-virgin status,
but Deva shut that down too.

Then, when I got to the yellow carnations, River burst out in
hysterics, like bent over clutching his stomach, and had to turn away.

Which somehow made me laugh and say, "I'm so embarrassed."

"Everybody has that," Deva said.

"Not really," River said. "That one pretty much takes the cake."

"Not helping," Deva said, shooting him a look then turning to me.
"And you gotta just stop. Linear platitudes—half-sex or one-tenth or
billionth—are not what sex is. For godsakes, it's supposed to be good
and it doesn't even matter. It's the relationship that matters. Everyone

should try so everyone has a good time at sex and love and just being together."

"He tried!" I said, WAY too defensively.

They stared.

More embarrassment. I hung my head.

"Look, okay, you're right," River said, probably due to intense eye-prodding from Deva. "There's always weirdness. Like, until you find the right person, and then, you're like, *Hey, hey, I like you, me too, let's go.* And then, there's no more weirdness."

My heart sank further. "I was hoping Leo would be the right person."

"Still not helping," Deva said to River. And then to me for damage control, "But it's okay. That's what happens. Which I think is what River's getting at." She shot him another dagger or maybe a crossbow thing to *cool it* and said to me, "It's like your heart is right, but for some reason or timing, they're a dick at a particular moment or point-plane in the universe, and it gets surprisingly weird. But you have to think of it like training wheels. We all use them."

"As if you ever had to do that or even know what that's like," River said to Deva.

"It was like that with Wayne Finn," she said.

"Who?"

"Wayne Finn, at camp, the guy who lost half an index finger roping cattle."

"Oh, right," he said, clearly remembering Wayne Finn. Why did I not know about Wayne Finn? And roping cattle? Is that still a thing?

"We almost did it, and it was awkward, to say the least," Deva continued.

"Oh, yeah, yeah," River said, chuckling, remembering Wayne Finn with the half index finger.

"Because the relationship wasn't right or honest. Nothing to do with Wayne Finn or his character."

"Wait, is Finn his last name or part of his first name? Or middle name?" I had to ask.

"Last name," River said, as if it was a valid question.

"And why do I not know about this?" I felt left out, but the fact that Deva had weird almost-sex with Wayne Finn and it wasn't a big deal made me instantly feel better.

"It was when you were in Bulgaria with your dad on location," Deva replied as if I shouldn't worry.

"Oh, right," I said, still feeling like I miss out on everything important. I drooped again.

"It's not important," Deva continued. "That's the point. If it were, I would've told you. But I forgot about it. Why? Because when it's weird, you have to think from a scientific-slash-biology perspective. Like, you know, how male pigeons are always dancing and spinning for the females? And the females are like—*Yeah, no*—most of the time? But then, there's one male that does it for her, and they try it out. But maybe then their little pigeon bodies are like—*Yeah, no*— again. And it's just nature trying out what we're biologically meant to do. So, you chalk those bad ones up to misdirected biology, and then, when you find the right person, it works."

This was v. confusing but seemed to be going in a good direction.

Deva went on, "Look, you didn't have sex, okay? You did this other trial thing that was incredibly awkward and uncomfortable emotionally, and he's not a bad person and neither are you, but it's done. It's like I said before: training wheels. You don't need to feel bad or disappointed that your training wheels might hold you back from riding fast and free on beautiful paths. You want to be grateful for your training wheels, whether beautiful and making you feel proud to be learning or embarrassing and making you feel horrified at the awkwardness and that you're not perfect the first time. Either way, you don't want to keep your training wheels on. Leo and Trey (with the boob touch) were your training wheels. Let them go."

This made some sense. Like there's a free and happy path in my future. I may still be in the starting gate but I can see that if I take off the training wheels and get them out of my headspace, I could finally get my life started. Also, maybe I keep regressing to a tricycle. Not thinking about that now though. That's just paranoia.

I nodded. And felt some relief.

"Great," said Deva.

"Alright, are we done now, so we can focus on me?" River said with an over-the-top *ta-da.* "C'mon, I thought this was gonna be a photoshoot."

I finally could laugh and wiped my tears and took out my camera. And we had the best day ever.

We shot in the Metro and at a few spots downtown, and then after half an hour, Deva decided we needed nature so I can clear the crap away. I suggested Surfrider Beach because of the light. No matter where you stand, every photo is amazing. Like magic hour all day. So, we took a Lyft to get River's car and drove up PCH to Malibu.

The tide was low so I shot them walking through tide pools with the pier and longboarders in the background. It was gorgeous. Afterwards, we had fish and chips at Malibu Seafood.

It was the perfect time. Spontaneous. Easy. In the moment. And I didn't think once about how it's confirmed that I didn't have one-trillionth-bajillionth or any sex with Leo. Or how I really wanted him to be my first. Even though I really was just focused on the romantic parts and how my heart felt so open and happy around him.

River dropped us and I sat on the stairs and uploaded my photos to my new SDB IG and sent the others to Deva and River. Who knows what they'll do with them, but if the doctor and entrepreneur ever need good live-action shots, they're set.

Then, I texted Sadie because I couldn't stop thinking about her and feeling bad: *I'm sorry I was a jerk. Leo dumped me, and I've been very sad. But it's not your fault, so apologies for the asshole move.*

I wanted to say I hoped it was okay with Hector, but my heart hurt. Really, I just want her to be okay.

So I added: *I hope you're okay. xox*

Bizarrely honest. It felt good.

She didn't reply.

Later. Hector/CDB followed SaoirseDBerger.

My room, a week later, night. It's been strange, to say the least, and I'm not sure what to do or think and am admitting I know nothing about anything. Like, how *aporia* of me! (Aporia = Ancient Greek concept of knowing you don't know + name of my old school). It may sound stupid as a concept, but it's quite wise bc it means if you can admit you don't know stuff, you can ask questions and get to new truths. New angles!

Art-poria! For my short? Title? That's it! Asking artists their POV instead of just seeing it from your own angle. Bingo! Art-poria sucks as name tho. Maybe Kaleidoscope POV? Not sure.

Also, am v. confused about everything and pretending to be clever and aporia-like could be a crutch.

Bc I have TEN DAYS to decide on college! And Sadie is ruining everything! And I don't know!

Ignoring now again.

Here are relevant things that happened:

Saturday, yesterday, good. Had sushi with Dad at new hotspot. Calm. Nice. Love.

He's a foodie. So is Mom (read: cheese love). Me, not so much. I love good food but don't think about it all day or plan around it or make it. They also love good wine and are in a wine club (read: bookcrate for fermented grapes). They've taken me/Mr. Griffin to amazing restaurants and secret hole-in-the-walls all over the world, like on location with Dad. I admit there are some awesome places, like schnitzel in Budapest and ice-cream dumplings in Vienna, and I'd definitely go again. Also would love to show Leo Prague. Pfff. I love Charles Bridge. Also, that weird cowboy rodeo in Poland. Random.

But taking Leo is stupid FANTASY. Stop!

So, yeah, Dad's favorite boot-inspiring director told him about this place. The director he loves. As in, maybe Dad wants to be this guy. Mind you, he's pretty awesome. Australian, funny, we all love him. The movie Dad cut for him won the main Academy Award and Dad got nominated for editing. They filmed in Scotland. We got to be there for part of it. Best time ever for Dad, hence the boots.

And maybe I can relate, like holding onto things that make you happy and inspired and empowered. What's wrong with that?

Unless you have nothing to hold onto.

Like me.

At college.

In fall.

Stop!

So, yeah, Dad took just me today bc Mom's busy and Mr. Griffin's attached to his gaming station and didn't want to go. Which I LOVE, bc honestly (shhh, don't tell), I think Dad's my favorite. And I may be his. Which is mean. Bc you're not supposed to have a family fave, but maybe I do and everyone does and doesn't admit it. Do they? It's probably that you have certain people you'd be friends with even if they weren't family. And for me, that's Dad.

So, yeah, I told him about my class and film and he LOVES the art-poria idea. Hooray! So we brainstormed and he agreed to be in it. Like interviewing him about his POV. And maybe his director too. And we decided I should do Mom and the tree-building set designer, and a street artist. And maybe our heater-guy Emilio who creates art in a "beautiful" clean flame. So cool! And hot! Which Dad loved best bc it's weird and he knows how HVAC-passionate Emilio is.

I wasn't sure about the street artist, so Dad said, "Why not Sadie's boyfriend?"

Which made me cringe. "Or the girls?" Also blerg. So he said, "Well, I'm sure you'll figure it out," not pressing my weirdness and added that he's going to love doing it and surely Giorgi (his director) will too, "because he's a big part of my POV."

Which made me SO HAPPY!

Then he nonchalantly popped some soy beans and said, "So? And? College?...And getting into every place you applied to?" with PROUD, BEAMING eyes.

No! Don't be so proud my cute, little cowboy-booted-n-bald Dad!

I shrugged.

He laughed, "This is a good problem to have."

No, it isn't! I only have ten days. "And..." And I didn't know what else to say bc...I don't know! "There's just nothing. Nothing." Empty heart.

And he said, "Oh, Buddy...," like he so wanted to help but knows I have to figure it out myself.

And I said, "Even Aunt Lauren can't help," kind of funny, kind of not.

Which made him laugh. "Well, that's good. Because it's not about her. It's about you. And ultimately, you pick where you go. It's your life."

I don't want it to be my life. I want someone else to tell me where to go!

"And she'll handle whatever you decide. And so will you."

Exhaling. This was getting real. Schitt! The inside of my stomach spun. But I pretended it was fine, "You're right, I'll be fine."

Which he saw through and said, "Ask Sadie to ask her boyfriend to recommend someone for your film," wisely, "I know you guys had a fight, but I'm guessing it'll resolve?" Prying, gently.

Everything is failing!

Then awesome spicy tuna sashimi arrived while Dad waited for my answer. I ignored him, dipping sashimi in soy, shoving whole piece in mouth, then smiling, desperate-sushi smile w/funny, silly, full mouth. "Mmmhmm."

We laughed.

He shook his head. "Well, I'm sure you'll figure that out too." Funny now-believing-in-me eyes. "And after we eat, how about we go see the new Marvel?"

Awesome Dad knew exactly what to say.

And my heart melted. And everything was okay again.

Maybe this is what I can hang onto.

Next year.

At lonely college.

Lonely girl.

Bc Dad has funny cowboy boots and will catch me if I fall.

We ate the yummy sashimi, and I got tempura too, and then the boot-inspiring director randomly, serendipitously showed up with his assistant and sat with us and Dad was so happy!

Which made me happy.

And we had fun, and the director told stories, like all directors do (they have the best stories!), and I got distracted from my life. Then we went to the movies. Without Stupid Jake. And I felt bad bc he'd be so jealous. But Dad said we'll go again. Our secret. And Mr. Griffin will feel the love too.

Now today, Sunday. Awful. Tho trying to find the good and hold onto DadAwesomeness. And resolving.

So yeah, I went to Sadie's house bc I still felt bad and she hadn't replied. I texted from the car so I didn't have to deal with anyone else.

She came out. I rolled down the passenger window. We looked at each other, tense, awkward, for like seconds or minutes.

Finally, she said, "I'm sorry too." Which was good. I felt better and nodded.

She continued, "And I know it was never fair to you, and you were doing it for me. I just wanted it to work. And I appreciate you." She smiled like she meant it.

I felt relief and also wondered why she was talking about Hector in the past tense. I let it go. "Thanks."

She looked at her hands and blushed, a little wry smile appearing on her lips. "And I've been hanging out with a guy in my acting class."

What?!

She looked up. "I just don't want to lie anymore. And he's nice. And easy to be around. And I feel safe."

Safe?!

She smiled, like I should understand. "Like my feelings are safe. Or maybe it's just because he likes me and I don't have to say much." She laughed, a tiny twinkle in her eye.

I was supposed to be happy for her? Now?! When I ruined the best friend thing I ever had for her, and now she has a new boyfriend already and I couldn't even hold onto Leo's love for five seconds?!

I felt tears. Hot tears. And anger. All rising at once. I looked away and grabbed the steering wheel as tight as I could to keep it down. "Great," I said in a really weird voice.

Then, she got in the car and touched my arm. "I'm sorry about Leo."

The longer her hand stayed on my arm, the more the anger grew, until it exploded out. "I have to go!"

She looked at me like she had absolutely no idea what was going on. Again!

I yelled, "Please! Please, get out."

She got out, slammed the door, confused.

Tears everywhere. I started the car. So embarrassed.

"Saoirse, wait," she said.

"For what? To ask your permission if it's okay to talk to Hector? For my project? To ask permission if it's okay that I still have feelings for Leo even though he doesn't love me back and I'm a loser? Like a normal human being! You know, because you don't get to have everything!" And I peeled out and it was like we were back to square one.

Now I feel terrible all over. And too weird. Like I'll never fit in anywhere.

And like I don't want to lie anymore either. Did she think I *LIKED* the lie?!!!

Friday, April 26

Cutting room, 11:24 a.m. Am in armor of anger and pain and sadness. At everyone!!! And self. Keep crying. And punching pillows. Even took giant empty New Zealand water bottle from T. Joe's out back and bang, bang, slammed it on concrete porch. V. satisfying. Loud. Bouncing back with anger-releasing reverberation. Neighbor looked over fence. Told her it was science experiment.

Otherwise, kept head down at work all week and home and just did what's in front of me, mostly cleaning coffee pot and answering phone in angry robot voice. Also eating all donuts and cookies and going out to replace them over and over. Hating everyone. Everyone! With hot heart on fire!

And three days to college D-Day!

Also, texted Sadie 20 minutes ago bc couldn't stand it. This feeling needs to go away. Text said: *Sorry!!!!!!!!!!!!!!!*

Now feel more angry.

11:55 p.m. Sadie texted back: *It's okay. You're upset. I love you, and you're amazing.*

Yes, I'm upset!!!!!!!!!

Tho it does help that she called it out.

Oh no, here comes Mike and UP, leaving for lunch, separately. UP on phone: "I'll meet you there in five."

Putting up anger shield so no one talks to me. No one wants to talk to the angry girl anyway, as long as she makes coffee. Jena's constantly pissed and doesn't want to deal with me now at all. She hates the anger more than the crying. Ha! Anger shield!

Though now heart hurting and softening thinking about Sadie not being mad. And saying nice things bc she really does love me. And Jena is nice too. Tears coming. Damn.

And now Aunt Lauren in hall. OMG. What is she doing? Now in Mike's room.

Jena lurking to see but AL closed door in her face. Jena pissed. Am turning away so don't have to comment. Now Jena leaving, "I'm going to lunch!" Gone.

Crap. What the hell is going on? Now AL coming out. Am bracing self, looking at screen and you, Diary, pretending not to see her, hoping she'll just leave.

Peeking.

She's right there. Looks weird, looking at phone. Now slamming it down at her side.

Looking away.

"Hey, Saoirse."

Crap.

"You're not going to lunch?"

No!

Here she comes, hand on desk, leaning in, inspecting me. I put elbow on you, Diary.

"Oh, wow, you look upset."

Damn.

"You look like how I feel."

Go away!

"I think we should go to lunch. It'll do us both some good."

I declined.

She insisted, "As your boss, I insist," trying to be funny, and then nice, "And as your aunt, my treat, and maybe we can sneak in a quick pedicure after?"

Deceptive. Controlling.

I hung my head.

"Great," she said, as if I'd capitulated.

I stormed to her car ahead of her so she couldn't see my face.

Got in.

Now writing in car in you (Diary). Bc she's not even noticing me! Obsessed with phone! Map. What is going on?

Cutting room, 2:40 p.m. It got worse. We drove down Melrose. She was obsessed. With the map. Like I wasn't there. Then, she swerved into the middle of the road, broken yellow lines. In front of this Italian restaurant. Cars honking. Her staring at restaurant on right.

Then, she did random illegal U-turn. More honking. Swerved into valet. Across street from Italian resto she kept looking at.

Then, we went in. She said she wanted to sit at the window and kept looking at the restaurant across the street, not talking to or even acknowledging me. Until the waiter came.

He asked if we wanted something to drink. Then, she noticed I was there. And suddenly wanted to talk.

Blerg.

She leaned forward on elbows. "So, you did it, Columbia. What's going on there?" Her voice had an edge. She glanced at her phone. It made me think she knew about the essay.

But that wasn't it.

"I, uh, just, I can't talk about this right now," I managed, heat in chest, hot tears behind eyes. I felt defenseless and knew if I got into it with her about college, I'd get annihilated, even if she didn't know about the essay.

"Okay...," she said, uncertain by my reaction, maybe hurt, kind of pissed, "I understand..."

No she didn't.

"What else is going on then that's clearly more important?" Snarky, but then, trying to be a good aunt, "which is fine," and smiling and still glancing across the street.

I told her I started a class, trying to downplay it.

"Oh, really?"

"Camera work, at UCLA Extension, Richard Vadinsky's the teacher."

"Oh! Well, that's impressive."

"Yeah," I nodded, slight smile, not wanting to say more.

"That's it? What's it like?"

Ugh.

"We're doing a project."

"Yeah?"

"We have to do a short."

"What's it about?"

Damn. Couldn't she lay off?

"C'mon, I'm curious."

No, she couldn't.

I told her the basics. I'm interviewing artists to show them working from their POVs. "Or something like that. I'm just starting. I'm gonna film my dad on his movie and my mom's cheese and a street artist and maybe something else. Like maybe our HVAC guy who looks at the heater flame like a piece of art."

I thought she'd like that

"Interesting," she said, but then, "And you can always do me. Screenwriter. Lots of angles," smiling, funny face, trying to be funny. And cute?

No!!! "I, uh...," mouth dropping, *what is wrong with her?*

She got it...embarrassed. And rallied. "No, no, you already got your mom and dad," glancing across the street, "but you can do one of the girls! And our mural! For your street artist! They're starting tomorrow. Or Hector!" She grabbed her phone, shared their contacts. "Go get 'em, Saoirse."

She smiled, warmly, and it felt like she was squeezing my heart— and maybe hers too—and my voice, until it hurt and I was suffocating and wanted to scream again.

But I didn't, and said, "Thank you," with really weird raspy voice, and smiled.

Which is when it got truly bizarro bc suddenly she noticed something across the street and stood up. And there was Unc P coming out of the restaurant. OMG! Was she spying on him? Yes, she was!

He was with J Boone and a woman...Armistice! His girlfriend! I know bc of all the J Boone google stalking I did. What the hell was happening? Why was AL following UP?

"You know what? I gotta go," she said and fished in her wallet and threw her credit card on the table. "Enjoy the Caesar. It looks great." And she ran out.

I watched her crouch down and hide behind the valet sign so UP wouldn't see her, which he didn't bc why would he think AL was following him? As if he had something to hide? What could he possibly have to hide?

The paparazzi, however, noticed UP and entourage, probably bc of J and Armistice. Then they noticed AL. Super uh-oh.

My room, night. Still trying to block Aunt Lauren out of my mind. Also trying to learn from her paranoia and jealousy like true adult. While forgetting bc it's too much. Didn't go to Svenssons'. I have no excuse.

Maybe I don't care.

Is that adult too? Occasionally not caring? And eating entire box of chocolate-chip ice cream sandwiches to forget you ever cared? For a few hours, then going back to caring and trying?

They're SO GOOD!

Must replace tomorrow before anyone notices.

Also, deleted Heck contact from AL (already have) but kept Nia and Ellie. Not for film tho. Don't want AL to have anything to do with film. And glom on and control me and suck the air out of my world.

Will instead go by and see what's up with mural tomorrow to keep options open. On own. See what happens. No expectations. Nervous re Hector but sucking up fear and moving w/courage to put project first, which AL should do and leave UP alone. So what if he's making a movie with J Boone?!!!

Will see if fam wants to play cards or Dad wants to do crossword when they get back from Svenssons. Need to get away from AL thoughts.

And college thoughts.

1 a.m. Dad and I finished Friday NY Times crossword! We're amaze-balls!!! No one noticed the missing ice cream sandwiches.

For five seconds I thought I could go to college in NY.

Columbia or NYU.

But then I didn't.

Dumb.

Afraid again.

Forgetting.

Saturday, April 27

My room, 4:50 p.m. Sparkle of hope happening on one of most interesting and courage-provoking days of life. I know that sounds absolute but I may have used something I never used before: *patience*. Actually, maybe more like *trust*—that things will work out and there's a bigger plan for me. Like to actually make my film.

Or maybe I just did what DadSheeran always says: *Put the project first.* Which he does when annoyed with people at work: *Just focus on making the movie the best it can be.* That's his guidepost. His north.

Aunt Lauren says it too—*put the project first*—but doesn't walk the talk, esp. w/UP! And their movie! C'mon, Aunt Lauren, walk the talk!

In addition to patience and trust, I also used *resilience*. Mom likes that term. It means something like forcing yourself to do something.

So, yeah, I forced myself to walk through the forest of my fear-trees and went to see what Hector, Nia and Ellie were painting for Aunt Lauren's Street Art Collective-sponsored mural. It's the surrounding wall at Wildroads on Olympic in West L.A., facing an alley. I drove past. And there they were making stupid 12-ounce-art magic (paint can size). Other people were there too, so I parked down the block and watched from afar, like behind-a-bush-on-the-other-side-of-Olympic-Boulevard afar.

AL and Sadie were there too. Nick was taking photos and filming. Clyde was following him around. Which made me feel left out bc AL asked Nick to take photos instead of me. Even tho I really don't even want to help her and her nonprofit! So why should I care?

Let it go, Seer!

Which I did, invoking trust that everything'll be okay for me and my project. It wasn't easy. I also invoked resilience and told myself: *You're doing this no matter what!*

But I kept fuming. It wasn't fair! And all bc stupid AL and Sadie are out of control re me.

Hot tears rose and I yelled inside my head, "No!" and stormed across the street to get a better look from a closer bush. Aunt Lauren looked completely insane—tense, agro, pacing, looking at her phone, huffing, pacing, then waving and smiling at everyone as if she was fine and perfectly normal.

No one else noticed her. Instead, they laughed and were having a good time. My heart squeezed. I sat back. Felt sorry for myself, left out again. I did that for a while, maybe ten minutes, until finally all the heat left and I relaxed. Like I felt nothing. Emotional flatlining.

Silence. Quiet. Breathing. Safe.

Until bam! Someone, something, jumped out from behind the wall—rustling, barking, big dog nose snuffling—and scared the heck out of me.

I screamed. Hector laughed. Clyde barked and slobber-kissed me because I was sitting on the ground. "What the hell are you doing here, Berger?" happy eyes laughing. "This is a bush."

I fell over bc of Clyde jumping on me. Embarrassed elk caught and rolling on ground, Clyde kissing. Heart racing. Me wrestling him, "I don't know!" trying to get him off.

Hector laughed and pulled Clyde back.

I sat up, "Jeez," brushed dirt off, trying to hide embarrassment.

"Sorry," he said, charmed, amused by me. "Want to go to lunch?"

"What?"

"Lunch. You know...pleasant eating, light, maybe juice?"

"I know what lunch is."

"How long have you been out here anyway?"

"What?" More embarrassment, now blushing, trying to hide it.

He put out his hand, "C'mon, I'm starving. You should come with us."

Me?

"You'll have plenty of time for whatever it is you're doing here when we get back. To the bush."

What *was* I doing in the bush? Idiot. *Fine!*

I gave him my hand. He pulled me up. Nose to nose in cramped bush space. Funny smile. Me searching eyes. Exhale. He took my shoulders, turned me around and pushed me forward out of the bush. "There we go...now, to the car. March!"

Funny man. Unexpected.

We marched to his car, figuratively not literally. The silly old red Beemer. Luckily, it was round the corner so AL and Sadie couldn't see me. He cleared crap off the seat so I could sit. Clyde jumped in and scrambled in back to his spot—middle seat. Hector went round, got in, started the car. "So, yeah, where to? 'Cuz otherwise it's gonna be McD's or some crap."

"Sawtelle is good."

I showed him the Japanese market. He got sushi. I got green tea Boba across the street. My favorite lunch spot from when I went to Aporia, which is right around the corner. A definite perk of that place. Even though I'm not a foodie, I do love good atmosphere and Boba.

We drove out from the underground parking and parked on a side street in front of a random house and sat in the car while he ate until a woman came out of the house and looked at us, like what were we doing? And she was annoying, so we pulled forward a few houses more.

Clyde barked out the window at her as we drove past, and she squinted in suspicion. Hilarious.

Heck parked in front of another house, then leaned back on his door and looked right at me. "So what's the deal, Dawg? Who're you hiding from?" he said as he repositioned his sushi roll pack on his lap so he could keep eating.

Crap.

"I mean, I hope it's not me. Are you hiding from me?" Funny, laughing eyes. Playful. Teasing.

I blushed, damn. "No." God, what was I supposed to say? Heart racing.

"Well, thank god." Totally amused.

Why couldn't I be amused?

"Berger! What were you doing in the bushes?" Still playful.

I don't know!

I had to say something. I looked at my Boba straw, clutching. Moving it up and down. Screeching it. Screech, screech, screech, like squeaky mailbox doors opening and closing. Clyde barking.

"Well?" He waited, still amused.

"I don't know! I need an artist. For my film. Aunt Lauren told me to come by!" Exasperated.

Him, raised-eyebrow surprise at my outburst, plus held-in chuckles and amusement.

I screeched my straw more. Slurped. Loud. Long. Momentary escape, SLURRRRP. Exhale, also loud. More exasperation. "I don't know!...she's just...something." I looked at him, like I just wanted him to know without me saying it.

"Your aunt?"

He knew.

"Yes." God, why was this happening? So painful. And I really didn't want to say anything bad about Aunt Lauren because she's helping him so much.

"Well, I'm sure she'll be okay," he said, like it really wasn't a big

deal. "I mean, everybody has to have a breakdown sometime, right?"
Funny eyes, seeing the humor.

Damn. I had to relax. He already knew about AL from Sadie. *Let it go!*

I screeched my straw again, slurped Boba, regrouping. It *really* isn't a big deal.

"I mean, at least we're here, right? Free from the bush," he said and took a bite of spicy tuna, sushi smile, dripping sauce on pants. "Damn."

I watched as he wiped it up. Thick eyebrows. Long lashes. The weird Mexican bird tattoo.

He threw the napkin in the bag. "Right?" Warm, happy eyes.

Me, happy-pumpkin smile, nodding, grateful.

"So, what's up with the film?" he asked and leaned back again to listen.

And finally, everything normalized. The bush-hiding ridiculousness went away. And I told him about the film. And it was easy. And he likes the idea. And was curious about my mom's cheese. He said his mom likes cheese too. And the heater guy idea—totally original, and cool to see regular people get creative, seeing beauty in what they do, like heater flames. "Yeah, I like it."

He gets it!

Little Ferris-wheel sparklers danced around on my arms, wrapping up my little arm hairs so they twinkled with joy, like Ferris-wheel chills.

I told him I needed a street artist.

He said he has the perfect guy, this Argentinean dude Lalo, with a food truck. "Him and his cousin and brother have the truck, and he does this too, the street art. Amazing! You have to see it. He's gonna be huge. Much bigger than us." And he showed me Lalo's stuff. And it was good.

And I felt so happy he was helping me.

Then he asked for my number so he could hook me up. Like, why wouldn't he? Because that's what you do when you connect people, right? You get their deets.

But my number is Sadie's number to him!!!!!
I panicked. "Uh..."
He waited, holding his phone. "Or I give you mine?"
More panic.
"Also, fine," he said, "for me to give you mine, right...?"
Elk in headlights.
Him confused, "Or...?" searching.
"I get it from Sadie!" Big smile. Great answer. "Perfect."
"Perfect?"
"Yeah."
He looked at me like, *Wow, what the hell just happened?*
I felt insane, like a super weird person, but beaming to cover.
"Thank you."
He still had no clue what just happened. "Sure?"
I shrugged in cuteness as if totally normal, grabbed the trash bag
and threw the Boba cup in. Beaming again. "Great."
"You are one silly duck," he said and laughed.
Blue jay. I'm a blue jay. Or peregrine falcon. Yes!
I smiled as big as possible again. Like a cute falcon, speedily
using cuteness angle to make this go away.
"Well, as long as you're not blowing me off," he said, funny,
teasing.
"What?"
"Because you know, you can't just blow off a guy who listens to
your sob story then hooks you up with a super-interesting new-edge
street poet that's gonna rock your film's world, right?"
Funny Ferris-wheel sparklers spinning again through peregrine
falcon wings, now with humor and relief, as he started the car and
drove me back to the bush.
I looked at him before getting out, so happy and cute, and said,
"Thank you, Aw Heck."
Me smiling.
His facing falling.
Me realizing.
Crap.
Why did I say that? *Why did I call him Aw Heck?!!!*

I froze. Breath held. Ferris wheels clutching.

Silence.

Stillness.

Squeaky Ferris-wheel seats swinging.

"I mean, I..."

Him looking like, *crap, more stabbing to the heart*, but then with total resilience, like *you gotta be bigger than this, dude*. MomSheeran would be proud. And he said, "It's okay. You can call me Aw Heck too," funny, awkward, holding in broken-hearted pumpkin smile, like this really sucks but—another exhale—*get over it, dude*. "It's not like she really cares anymore, if you know what I mean."

Me, frozen, "Mmm," with nod. So awkward. Sad.

Him heart hurting. But also like adult. "Who the frig knows anything anyway, right?" he said and laughed.

Me exhaling, nervous laugh, nodding, smiling, awkward.

"But you better not blow me off," he teased. "That's still a thing." Thank god.

I shook my head, like I wouldn't. "You got it, Aw Heck," I said, teasing back, and got out, which made him laugh, like he was glad I can live in the world of teasing and making fun rather than the other sad-romantic-heart one.

I looked back in the car and saw happy eyes. Warm. Happy-dancing sparklers inside me. Heart melting.

Lonely girl melting.

Into sparkler-filled puddle of light.

Friend light.

Swirling into his.

Magic-sparkler heart all around us.

Together okay.

I felt okay.

And maybe I gave him the power to feel okay too.

7:30 p.m. Went and got a new phone with a number just for Aw Heck. Dumb. But what else am I gonna do?

I texted him: *Hey, it's me, Saoirse, not blowing you off.*

He texted me: *Good thing! Talked to Lalo. He's in! Sending contact.* He sent it.

I texted: *Wow! Awesome! Thank you!*

He texted: *What are you doing tomorrow?*

What did he mean 'what am I doing tomorrow?'

I texted: *What do you mean?*

He texted: *I mean, are you busy? Wanna hang? I need a break from my life. Something new. I don't know what. Any ideas?*

Why is all this goodness happening?

Sunday, April 28

My room, 10:15 p.m. Today I went to Escondido Beach with Hector. His secret beach. He picked me up. Honked from outside. And the whole day was nice. Plain and simple.

I told him I'd take him to Surfrider for newness and the light, but we had Clyde and you can't have dogs there. Hence, Escondido.

It's a public beach past Pepperdine, right before Paradise Cove, by Geoffrey's, through a tiny gate, hidden, that looks like it's private, part of a giant Spanish-style mansion. Then a tunnel of trees. Then the top of a staircase that goes down a cliff. Like Greece! Amazing. Ocean. Gorgeous! He found out about it from his English DJ-skateboarder friend who goes there every 4th for fireworks.

We hiked down with Clyde. It's v. isolated, big houses along entire stretch. He said that's why he loves it, plus the beauty and you can bring your dog and not get caught since it's so hidden and hard to get to.

Sneaky Heck!

Hee hee.

Ho ho.

I loved it. And I loved the beach.

We sat down on our towels in the sand, leaning back on elbows, watching the water, people swimming, kids splashing in waves, Clyde running up and down.

We talked and it was so easy. Like normal people.

He asked about my job. I told him everything, like I didn't need to impress him or anything, like how I'm a glorified, well-paid peon who makes coffee and answers phones but I'm learning about filmmaking too. I told him it's frustrating to watch everyone do cool creative jobs while I do mindless work and am mostly bored and have to entertain myself. But it's nice that Mike and Jena like me and hired me because I'm a good fit, which makes me feel wanted and part of.

I told him I'm kind of lost though, like I don't know what to do next and don't really want to go to college without knowing, but that I love my filmmaking class. Finally something. And that I'm doing it to help me better decide about college.

Which is tomorrow. I have to decide by tomorrow.

He laughed. And I was so honest! Why is it so easy with him?

"So, I guess the gap year thing and graduating early is working out after all?" he teased.

I laughed. "Yeah, I guess I was a little upset that day." So embarrassing!

"Yeah, c'mon, Berger, get it together."

So cute. Sunshine eyes.

My friend has sunshine eyes. V. weird thought. What does that mean?

Then he asked what I'm going to do. Tomorrow. About the colleges. And I didn't know. And my heart started racing. And I said, "I'm not sure."

Which is when Clyde barked and ran off down the beach after a bird and Heck chased him and brought him back and made him sit with us next to the towel, not on it, to keep the sand off. Until Clyde rolled on his side getting sand everywhere.

Heck laughed and leaned back on his elbows again, looking at the water. So chill.

I was sure he'd want to talk more about tomorrow and my college decision but instead he told me about his stuff, like knowing I was nervous and it might help. He told me he doesn't know about anything either, like graduating early. And he loves art and photography and comedy. And of course drumming. And he's just gonna go to college and see what happens. V. optimistic. Like it's all gonna work out because it's an adventure and there's so much to experience. And he just wants to learn and build stuff and invent new things and ideas.

So positive! And calm. Sunshine sparklers spinning in heart. Bc it helped.

Then he said he wasn't always that way, "But this guy, definitely helps," meaning Clyde, and he wrestle-hugged Clyde's head. Which was v. cute.

Then, he told me stuff I knew. Like about his parents disagreeing and how his dad's controlling and how this college thing in Portland is perfect—enough distance to be independent but close enough to come home. Like at Christmas. "And eat my mom's Christmas cookies and Stollen, which is German because she had German neighbors in the Yucatan. Go figure. And it's the best. Wouldn't miss that."

Coming home for something. He has an anchor.

I could come home for cheesecake and Brie.

I said I wish I could be as relaxed as him and told him about AL and Columbia and applying to all the wrong schools bc of romantic book fantasy and thinking I'd be a writer and everything about my life.

He said it sounds like I just need to be making stuff and go to a JC or film school or whatever supports that and get on with my life and stop thinking I have to do the exact right thing for me and everyone else. "No one knows exactly what they're doing. But you're better off than you think. You know when you like something. Like when you talk about your project, your eyes light up."

Little Ferris wheels of joy jumped up and down. For five seconds. Until I thought about leaving in fall and being alone.

He must've noticed bc he laughed. And I blushed. And he suggested I get up tomorrow morning and ask myself point-blank where I should go to college, without thinking! And do whatever my heart says. That's what he'd do. HeckSheeran.

Also, I should tell Aunt Lauren the truth. And everyone. "And yourself."

Which made me feel extra weird. Like it was so nice. And impossible.

Which made him laugh, like *it's all good*, and he said I shouldn't feel alone. He has my back. "And I'll send you this..." He handed me his phone w/earbuds. "It always helps."

Then he stared at the waves while I listened to his playlist that he maybe made for me, bc it had Avenir and other French DJ stuff plus QT film tracks. Everything I love. Even "Girl, You'll Be A Woman Soon."

How did he know?

Funny and sweet.

Then, he fell asleep. I did too. I felt so calm and relaxed. Safe and warm.

When I woke up, he was sitting up, arms on knees, watching the water, his hair wet so he must've gone in, lines of salt on his arms. Lean arms, but with definite strength. Like from inside. Like from certainty and confidence, even though he says he has no idea about life. Perhaps he's a true aporia master.

His arms glistened in the sun.

I wiped drool off my mouth and fell back to sleep. Until Clyde flopped down next to me and he said, "Drooling again, Berger," and went down to the water to draw in the wet sand.

I wiped off the drool and watched him for a bit, then went down too. He drew a face, a woman with wild hair. His mom maybe? And filled it in with seaweed.

I took photos and filmed him too.

"Ta da," he said when done. Then playfully grabbed my camera and turned it on me. "Say, hi, Saoirse. Time to come out from behind the lens."

I hid my face. He tried to get in there. So I ran.

All the way to Paradise Cove. Him chasing. Us laughing. Until I couldn't run anymore. I was laughing so hard. I yelled for him to stop.

"You really don't like to be in front of the camera do you?"

I shook my head.

"Invisible Girl. Invisibility is her superpower! She only reveals herself when needed."

I laughed. My heart expanded. Someone actually noticed. And made it sound like a superpower!

I grabbed my camera back. "There." And started filming him. "And here we have our sand artist of the day."

He posed and did funny over-the-top dance moves. "The artist who loves to be the center of attention. At least more than Berger."

Brat.

Then, we walked back and grabbed our stuff and drove to meet Lalo, who was nothing like I expected. We met him at the food truck. It has a graffiti-esque Gaucho cowboy on it, and they sell Argentinean food. Lalo smoked cigarettes while we talked. He was all edgy and agitated and short with his words.

Hector told Lalo about my project. Lalo said, "Yeah, sure, great. Just call me." And nodded to Hector, like, yeah, he approved and Heck should give me his number, and he flicked his cigarette into the street.

"So, I can film you working?" I yelled after him.

"Yeah," he yelled from the back door of the food truck and went in.

I went to the window. "Is there a good time? Or do you know when you're working next?"

"Just call me, okay?" he said and turned and started working, no niceties at all.

"I don't think he really wants to do it," I told Hector.

"That's just his way of saying yes," he said and told me not to worry. "He's sort of a dick but with a big heart."

We laughed. His eyes crinkled. Cute, funny guy. He told me he met Lalo bc he liked his art so much and would go watch him work. He said Lalo came here from Argentina for film school but dropped out and got into street art and food. "Now, he's gonna take off. With that Puma campaign. He'll be great for you."

It made me so happy that Heck was helping me and we had such a great day. And I just beamed, like all my little friend sparklers came out, and I said a simple, "Yeah, thank you," looking him right in the eye, smiling, honest, maybe too honest. Like with all that happiness and gratitude behind it.

And something about that made him weird, like reminding him of Sadie or something. Maybe it was my voice. And he said, "You don't have to pretend. I know she's done with me."

Ohhh noooo. And all the air got sucked away. And the friend sparklers stopped. "Oh."

"I mean, it was great as long as we weren't together, apparently, but then..." He shrugged, like an exaggerated Italian mime. "Who knows?" And he laughed to himself, shaking his head, then just walked back to the car without me. Leaving me standing there.

I felt terrible for him. He still loved her. Heart broken. And it's my fault.

I walked over. He was already in. I got in.

Both staring straight ahead.

He exhaled. "Sorry. That was...I dunno."

"That's okay."

Then we just sat there, more staring. No idea what to do. Both feeling miserable, hating selves.

So, I punched him in the arm. Randomly. Hard. But not that hard, more like a playful-punch hard. Like what the heck else was I supposed to do?

So weird.

He laughed.

I laughed.

I guess it was the right thing to do.

"Thank you," he said.

"You're welcome."

"I hope we can do this again, without the dramatic ending."

I laughed.

My friend.

"Sure."

His friend.

"Good," he said and started the car and blasted the music and drove me home.

He also said he'd come along to the shoot with Lalo, if I'll have him. Because it's "gonna be based." And he thinks I'm going to get just what I need.

Today, I did. I got what I need.

New friend. Old friend. Just friends.

Perfect.

Happy.

Inspired by life!

Ready for truth.

True self.

Always say truth.

What is my truth?

Whatever it wants to be!

Just looked at a shot Hector posted of me getting slobbery kisses from Clyde at beach. I didn't even know he took it. He tagged SaoirseDBerger.

My truth is a lie.

I hope he never finds out.

My room, D-Day, 6:30 p.m. Today I told Aunt Lauren the truth about Columbia. Thanks to Aw Heck and Dad's advice. Maybe I was also hoping it would make up for the other lie.

I also said yes to Columbia.

More lies.

Forever lies.

Getting worse.

Hate self.

Here's how it went down:

We were at work. I was nervous and waiting for the right time to tell AL I wasn't going to Columbia. Bc at that time I still wasn't.

This morning when I woke up I did exactly what Heck suggested—asked my heart: *Where should I go?* And my heart said: (nothing). Literal silence.

I'm sure Heck wasn't expecting silence when he suggested that. But that's what I got. HeartSheeran does not love the colleges. HeartSheeran sees no path.

So, I figured I'd tell AL in case the truth might motivate HeartSheeran to give me an answer. It didn't.

She was lurking in the hall. Pacing.

I psyched myself up, my inner 18 Hoorays like a drill sergeant: *Go out there and tell her now!*

I asked Aunt Lauren if I could talk to her for a second.

She said, "Sure," and stood there waiting for me to talk.

"I think we should go outside," I said, trying not to show discomfort.

Her eyebrows lifted, *Outside?*

I shrugged, *Yeah, why not?*

Her eyes squinted, suspicious, like was there an ulterior motive.

Like maybe UP was trying to get her to leave so they could sneakily recut the movie in five seconds. Paranoid!

She said, "Fine," and we went out of the building. I immediately turned to her and said, "I'm not going to Columbia. I'm sorry. But I appreciate everything you've done for me. Thank you." No fluff or defense. Just straight-up information. My heart raced. It was awkward.

I probably should have given her a reason why.

She tensed up like she was filling with rocket fuel and about to shoot off, as if the blond short hairs on top of her head were lifting off. She blinked three times. And went back in the building.

I definitely should've given her a reason. I didn't feel better either, even though it was the right thing to do. I stood there outside because my heart was still racing and I felt anxious. After about five minutes, AL burst out the door and stormed past me, as if she didn't see me, to her car and sped off, almost hitting UP's Prius.

10:20 p.m. I didn't have the heart or guts to tell you earlier. But now must.

I went and sat on the bench after AL left. Stared at the Big Sky tank parking lot. Asked HeartSheeran again, *Where should I go?*

I had one hour. Or so. Given EST. I think there's an extra day for acceptances at Columbia (more for England). But I had to decide and get it over with.

So I asked again, *Where should I go?*

HeartSheeran said: (nothing)

My stomach hijacked by panic. My entire future riding on this stupid decision.

All blood went...somewhere, my stomach, feet, which were sweating, and I said each college by name: UCLA, Berkeley, Exeter, etc. Columbia, NYU. Each time, nothing.

And I said, *Please, just tell me what to do so I can forget about it and pretend I'm never going away and just finish my sweet, cute little movie. That makes me happy. That I love. And makes everything okay.*

HeartSheeran was silent. Darn you, HeartSheeran.

I exhaled and stared at the stupid Big Sky screen. And all I could see was Aunt Lauren. And her rushing to her car. Pacing in the hall. On phone. Stressed. Paranoid. But then smiling at me. Like trying. Because she loves me. And her cheesecake. And taking me to Columbia. Showing me where she lived. The campus. Beautiful. Classrooms. So proud. Loving me. Caring. Hugging me. And kissing my hair.

And all I could see was how she's holding on so tight. Even to me.

And I said yes to Columbia. In that moment. And no everywhere else.

10:50 p.m. Also, I paid for the deposit with my savings bc I was too embarrassed to tell Dad.

Friday, May 3

My room after Svenssons', 9:40 p.m. Told Mom and Dad I didn't want to talk about college when they asked. They didn't press.

18 Hoorays.

Good or not good.

Nervous stomach.

Holding breath.

Focusing only on film. It will make everything okay. It always was going to make everything okay.

Somehow.

Will breathe again.

As adult.

Someday.

Moving forward.

Marching, literally not figuratively.

Also feeling better after Svenssons. Which was tense. And awful.

Because Hector was there. And I didn't want to tell him about college either.

Luckily, he didn't ask. Because it was too weird.

And Aunt Lauren was ignoring me.

And he was stiff, for reasons other than me, looking like Mr. Griffin, holding everything in so as not to be noticed or make a wrong move. Like wanting to be near Sadie. Which I hated. Why was he there?

And he made me feel so uncertain. Like quicksand. The opposite of at the beach.

And Aunt Lauren's face made my heart crumble. Paralyzed. Holding breath tighter so no thoughts could escape.

Thinking only of film, set designer, trees, leaves, cheese, looking down at floor, sitting on couch next to Nick playing on phone, trying not to move my head so nobody noticed me either, trying to invoke Invisibility Girl superpowers.

Which worked until Mr. Griffin wanted to play ping-pong and Dad didn't feel like it so he asked me to. We did. Then I came back in and met eyes with Hector talking to Aunt Lauren. AL turned and saw me and made a smirky face and excused herself and went down the hall and slammed a door.

Everyone looked at me. Hector uncomfortable, like he wanted to say something to Sadie but didn't know what. Sadie paralyzed.

I couldn't stand it. "Hey, Sadie, can I show you something at the car?"

"What car?" She knew I rode with Dad.

"I don't know. Any car. Please."

She got the message it wasn't about a car. We went out front and stood on the sidewalk.

"Why did you invite Hector?" I asked. "Are you with him again?"

She looked pained. "My mom?...I don't know. I didn't want to tell her. He makes her happy. She's so unhappy."

I exhaled super audibly. "Fine. It's fine. It's just weird. I should go."

"Please don't go."

I felt awful. Everything was a mess and it was worse for her. Her mom was losing it.

I wondered if she knew I told AL about Columbia, even if a lie. I wondered if Hector told her we hung out.

I rallied. "Look, you're gonna be fine. Your mom is just, well, she'll get over it. Whatever this is. And you'll be fine." I hugged her and meant it. She let me. I squeezed extra hard. She needed it. I did too. I felt relieved to have Sadie back. She seemed to feel the same about me.

"Okay," I said. "I'm just gonna tell my dad and get a Lyft."

She nodded.

"And...I don't know about Hector," I said. "I mean, it'll be fine. He told me...well, no, he didn't. He's helping me with my project. But he seems to get it about you, like he knows you're moving on, if that's what's happening, and he just...he's like...he has a good attitude." I thought about him inside, looking so uncomfortable. "But maybe he needs a little time. Like, be careful with his heart." And my heart ached, lord knows why. Like I cared, I mean, really, not fakely.

She smiled and hugged me tight. "I will." Like she'd be careful with my heart too.

It was exactly what I needed.

Thursday, May 9

A week later, almost, my room, 11:30 p.m. I hung out with Hector again today and one other time this week. I don't know if that's good or bad but it's what happened. And I like him.

First, we went to a music thing downtown with Lalo and his gf, Amy. She's from Sacramento. Old too. Like 22, I'm guessing, because she just finished Fresno State and got a job in advertising and has long wavy blond hair and drinks margueritas. They kept fighting but seem to love each other or maybe it's just that they have the same tense energy and seem perfect for each other. Hector thought it'd be good if me and Lalo got to know each other more. But we barely talked.

It was fun being with Hector though. He's easy and funny mostly, and I didn't worry about him and Sadie. Though if he ever figures out what happened and the lie, I'm sure this friendship is over.

Hopefully not. I really hope not. I think I'd crumble and have a broken heart. And maybe so would he.

His DJ friend Frank played a set, and we danced, which is bizarre because I never dance. But Heck does, weird and funny, like a blender. Like he bends his knees and keeps his upper body straight and his arms too and swishes his lower body back and forth with his arms going at his sides. Then he moves around and does circles, but always with his legs bent at 60 degrees. Like he must have strong quads or be sore. So, it made me feel normal and was fun and put me at ease.

Also, he must be in good shape. He said it's because of drumming—which is a workout and fun, so you don't notice you're getting a workout and end up drumming longer and more intensely than if you were, say, snowshoeing.

I was v. worried he'd ask about HeartSheeran and college, but he didn't, thank god. The only thing was when Amy mentioned Fresno State and he gave me a funny, raised-eyebrow—*And?*—like—*what did you decide?* And I quickly peregrine-falconed my eyes away, like slurping my soda and innocently implying, *I know not of what you speak. I didn't have a crazy panic deadline about my entire future and make a decision that had nothing to do with my true self.*

Which made him laugh, like, *Fine, but some day you're gonna tell me.*

And now it's just sitting out there.

Also, I started filming Dad in his cutting room and Mom doing cheese. Hooray!

And I got the set designer making trees in the jungle! More Hooray! She's an art department assistant working her way up to production designer. She's worked on a ton of big films and is starting to get tiny indies as actual set designer. The director's POV is always her inspirational north (like Dad). She also likes the realism angle, even for fantasy, so if she's making leaves in a magical world, she'll ask—*How would I see this as a real leaf if I lived in that world?*

So cool!

The second time I hung with Heck was to show him what I shot before I started cutting. He brought fries and we ate and watched. He likes what I got. And I like that he likes it and gets it, which made me blush bc we're on the exact same page. And he guy-punched me in the shoulder. Whatever.

Also, I got nervous when he looked at my books. Like what if he figures out I have every single book ever posted on BLGirl? But he didn't. It was easy hanging with him then too.

Also, I've been quite normal around Leo. He's on the stage so I barely see him, which makes it easier overall, but I saw him on the coffee-pot bridge and didn't even say hi. Then, at the commissary, he said, "Hey, Saoirse," and I said, "Hey, Leo," back, like a normal person.

Which is when I had a momentary fantasy lapse of me winning an Oscar for my short, him in the audience, me flirting during my acceptance speech, then him chasing me down after to say he was wrong and loves me, grabbing my face and kissing me.

Which I promptly nipped in the bud with: BACK OFF, HOPE WEAVER! Invite him to the screening when it's done, so he knows you're AWESOME and he was wrong, BUT STOP WITH THE ROMANTICS!

Yes, I've been secretly planning a screening since day-one of the assignment. On the lot, hopefully. Secret even from you, Diary. But now admitting. Hoping UP can help me get theater. And I can invite LEO!!!! And everyone. It'll be v. impressive to Leo!

But first, I have to make my movie!

Speaking of...

Eloise is my mentor now and I'm v. happy bc Richard is useless. First, I went to UCLA Extension office to say I'd be TA for Richard. The office lady was happy to check that off her list. Done. Assigned. Richard Verbinski has a TA. But then, this stupidness happened:

After class (second class), I told DP/teacher Richard I was his TA. I thought he'd be happy. I was happy! UCLA Extension was happy. I, overenthusiastic go-getter, did all the footwork and he had a TA. Everybody wins! But no, he panicked.

Me: "Hey, so I'm your TA now."

Richard, shocked: "What?"

Next to him was short, cute Lindsay (another student). Let's call her "hot *co-ed*" bc this is SO STUPID! Plus, I've always wanted to use that word, *co-ed*. I mean, when else can you?

Richard: "Lindsay was going to be my TA."

Me: "Oh. You said you didn't have a TA so I went to the office. They seemed happy. But..."

She smiled at me. Then him. OMG. She was flirting.

Richard: "You know what, why don't you both do it, okay?" Annoyed, putting stuff away.

She smiled again. "Great."

OMG, this was bc she's cute and flirty. And I'm me.

And is he really that much of a superficial idiot, caring more about looks than cinematography in his students? Maybe they're in love. Still, v. disappointing.

And I felt stupid and fat. But rose above. "No worries. I was too busy anyway. Just trying to help." Stabbing self in eye.

I left and asked Eloise to be my mentor. Which is the silver lining, bc when I pitched my idea in class, Richard said it's a bit "pedestrian as a concept," overdone, but Eloise sees how I can make it original, which is the point! She sees the fresh angle and says people tell similar stories over and over, it's human nature, and it's about embracing your true voice, which will always make it fresh!

Am v. impressed with her. Unexpectedly. She's sweet and regimented, and I misjudged her. She made a cool doc about educating girls in Uganda. She's stealthily fabulous as opposed to Richard who's all flashy, with his stupid cute co-ed TA.

Also, feel like rational adult not getting emo about TA thing. Esp since Richard's a friend of Leo's. Practicing diplomacy for future. Standing-tall elk with antlers in air in spite of getting moss tossed in elk face and maybe on antler too. Shook off. Now am big-nosed, proud filmmaking-elk with diplomacy.

Called Lalo and set a time. It was easy. It's clearly meant to be.

Unlike TA-ship.

But I really like awesome, secretly fabulous mentor Eloise.

Not thinking about Columbia at all.

Friday, May 10

My room, 10 p.m. No Hector at Svenssons' but schitt hitting fan due to break-down aunt. She sat on couch w/pouty face for entire talent show. Unc and Nick enacted *The Princess Bride*'s battle of wits. Sadie and I hosted sing-along w/rounds of B-I-N-G-O Was His Name-O, "RESPECT" and "Shout!" Everyone danced. Mr. Griffin told jokes. He's v. funny, I'll admit. So dry.

Everyone walked on eggshells around AL except Taylor Rae, who fed her cocktails and gave her hugs all night. I think AL's mad about Columbia (even tho it's a lie). Not sure what to do. Am I adding to her breakdown? Makes me anxious. Stop it, Aunt Lauren! Get back to judging talent show like usual. Why do you have this power over me?!

Dad noticed my discomfort and told me to wait out the storm.

He thinks I'm NOT going to Columbia. I think.

Maybe I just need a hug.

Wednesday, May 15

Cutting room, 3:40 p.m. Uncle Peter has not been at work for three days. No one knows why.

Thursday, May 16

Cutting room, 10 a.m. Mike agitated, nervous, making Jena annoyed. Studio wants to talk to UP. We keep making excuses. He keeps not answering his phone. Mike complains that UP is like a teenager. Jena mutters, "Look who's talking," under her breath. I go and make new coffee even though we have full pot so they don't ask me to get involved. They don't. They have good work boundaries. Noted: People, outside my family (read: AL and UP) have healthy boundaries.

4:30 p.m. I guess UP got the messages and finally called the studio and they gave him notes on the cut. He called and gave the notes to Mike and Jena. That was a bit after lunch. Mike was annoyed with the whole thing and said he's not doing notes today and left. Jena got annoyed with Mike for being so emo about it. Tension high. Then, she left.

Now, I'm holding down the fort.

My room, 9:30 p.m. Aunt Lauren is missing.

9:50 p.m. Schitt.

10:40 p.m. Dad called a family meeting and debriefed me and Jake. Mom served sweet cheese and bitter bespoke orange marmalade on mini French toastinis with a pot of ginger-turmeric tea with honey, the one from Trader Joe's that I like, to help calm the mood and settle the stomach. "The turmeric is great for inflammation," she informed us for the millionth time. "Very helpful in times of extreme stress, like right now."

Dad shot her a look.

"But it's all going to be okay," she said to diffuse her last comment. "I know it. And I really do love the blue checks on the window coverings in here, and the comfy white shutters, Saoirse."

Aunt Lauren was, apparently, gone when the Svenssons woke up Saturday morning. UP sent Dad a photo of the note she left: *I know you all want me out of your hair, so enjoy it. I love you. Be sure to drink the goat milk before midweek so it doesn't turn. L*

"That would be now. Midweek," Dad said. "Peter said they drank the milk. Also, she left her phone behind."

"That doesn't sound like Lauren," said Mom.

It didn't. But I knew she probably left the phone behind so they couldn't track her, like she did to UP on Melrose.

Then, Dad told us UP called the police Monday. They also got into her phone and email. Nothing abnormal except their neighbor,

Louise, sent 40 texts saying she was *sorry* and *understood*. They interrogated Louise. Apparently, Louise and AL talk outside every day on the sidewalk, and Louise declared her love for AL last week. AL didn't feel the same. Louise said that was the earlier part of last week and both of them were devastated. Louise is married too and surprised even herself with her feelings.

Wow, you really never know what's going on behind the scenes, do you? It's v. disconcerting IMHO.

Louise also said AL has been feeling v. jealous of UP and can't let it go. AL thinks UP is purposefully excluding her from his next project. That part I knew.

Louise said she's never been in love with a woman before Aunt Lauren. Aunt Lauren isn't in love with her though. Louise realizes now that she should've waited to tell AL, but Louise has her own issues with her own husband and self and needed to figure it out. This might've put AL over the edge, and Louise feels badly. That part I didn't know.

"Wow," Jake said and laughed. Mom and Dad looked at each other like they really didn't want to deal with any of this, especially around us, or know how. This is insane.

"So...now what?" I asked, as Mom gestured to the cheese and we all went for it.

Stupid Jake spit out the marmalade, "Gross," and dumped his plate and started over with just cheese and toastinis.

Mom poured him tea.

"Can you put that special sugar in?" Jake asked, with a sweet pouty face that gets Mom to do anything. Mom got the organic powdered sugar and spooned it in for Jake, which annoyed the hell out of Dad because he thinks Mom over-spoils Jake, which she does, and that Jake could've just gotten it himself. But Dad didn't say anything about Jake to Mom.

Instead, he said re Aunt Lauren's disappearance, "Nothing, we do nothing. We wait till she comes back."

"But where is she?" I asked.

"We don't know," he said.

"I hope she's okay," Mom said.

"She's not okay!" Dad snapped.

Mom let that go. Probably because she knows AL is the thing that triggers Dad most. Instead, she offered him cheese. Dad exhaled in annoyance but took the cheese, and it calmed him down.

"She's *gonna* be okay," he said, as if he had any clue at all. "Maybe she went to Cork. She always says she wants to go to Cork and ride a bicycle up the coast." He shook his head exasperated.

Mom took the empty plates into the kitchen. I could see her laugh to herself. She must think it'll all be fine.

After helping Mom clean up the cheese, I came back up here and called Sadie.

Me: "Hey."

Sadie: "Hey."

Me: "I heard."

She exhaled and then whispered, "I'm scared, Saoirse."

"I know. But my dad thinks it's gonna be okay. And probably my mom too. We just have to wait."

"Thank you."

"Are you gonna be okay? Should I come over?"

"Andy's here."

"Who?"

"From acting class."

Oh. My. God.

"Wow, cool," I said, as if that were the most normal thing ever. But WHAT THE HELL?!!!

"Yeah, it's nice," she said and exhaled. "It will be okay. Somehow."

OMG, how is this stupid guy there five seconds after she dumps Hector? Did she even officially dump Hector? It's like she's repeating what Paulie did to her! What a mess.

Friday, May 17

Work, 2:20 p.m. I went to Dad's cutting room and tried to film him cutting a scene. His director, Giorgi, was great and animated and teased me for being a very forward-thinking up-and-coming filmmaker. He likes me. Dad always works for great people. Probably bc Dad is great at his job. But Dad was super low-energy today, which is unusual, and everything I shot was crap. Dad says he's fine, but I think he's too worried about Aunt Lauren to function normally.

Usually, he's funny and happy to show off his yardstick ruler that he waves around like a conductor baton whenever he's not cutting, then blasts punk rock and cuts battles to it. Today, he just sat there distracted, looking out the window.

Giorgi said he's not "on good form," with British accent, even though he's also part Bosnian and Georgian, apparently. Though it's not clear if that's true. Giorgi has many layers of humor and storytelling abilities according to Dad.

There's also weird tension bc AL and UP are semi-famous, and Sadie and Nick too, so we have to keep everything on the DL. Giorgi clearly knows though, and when Dad was seriously "on bad form," he took me and my camera down the block to his office and we sat on his rooftop lounge and ate Neuhaus Belgian chocolates from his wife, Annabel, who was just in Antwerp for a shoot. He also showed me a cool fortress model for their movie, which I filmed, w/Giorgi narrating. Which'll be super fab to cut together w/interview of Dad and him creating emotions and rhythms of scenes!

I uploaded everything. And am going to edit since no one's here.

Also am v. excited about the stuff I got of Mom. And the HVAC guy! He took me to a job and said, "Look at that beautiful flame!" A true artist enjoying his work.

Also, just texted Hector: *Hey, wanna come visit on the lot? I got new footage and we can cruise around.*

Want his opinion about Giorgi. Plus, I'm sure he'd love to check out the lot. Everybody does. Even me. It never gets old.

He sounded excited. I told him to come at four and I'd call him a drive-on: *Just come to the Melrose gate. The one closest to Gower (west gate).*

Work, 5:40 p.m. Hector loved the stuff of Mom and Giorgi. He was esp. impressed about Giorgi. Love that he admits being movie-director starstruck. Like LL w/ QT. Dorkhood makes them all weirdly cute. And it's nice that famous people can be superfans too, not that Heck is famous but LL and QT sort of are.

It's v. easy to be around Heck. I feel like myself. None of the usual emo-crap glomming on.

The only odd thing that happened was when we went for a walk and saw Leo. He waved and I waved back. And Hector teased, "Leo Landis, your guy." But it was v. strange. Uncomfortable. His voice had an edge.

"Not anymore," I said, also strange and uncomfortable.

Then we walked without talking, and it was like Leo and Sadie were there too.

Then Heck did a weird exhale, like he was bored and done with it. And jumped up on a planter, tightrope-walked the edge, then jumped down, happy sparkly eyes again, like he was laughing it off and said, "This place is cool. Thanks for having me."

And we were good again.

Saturday, May 18

My room, 8 p.m. Am spinning. What to do?

UP just came over. I guess to see Dad. He cried. I've never seen him cry. Even though he wears every other emotion on his sleeve readily all the time. Dad hugged him. I don't think I was supposed to see. But it happened right in front of Stupid Jake's superstation, which is by the French windows next to the newly designed living room. Stupid Jake always has headphones on, and I don't think he noticed until they stopped hugging and he peeked over while taking a slice of pizza from the giant pizza box on his desk. Why did he get pizza and I didn't even hear about it?

UP noticed me and told me to come out. "Sorry about the...you know. How's it going with Mike?"

"Uh...," I managed, not sure what to say bc of everyone's rules down the chain of command of me answering and working for Jena who works for Mike who works for UP. I didn't want to betray Mike. UP didn't press luckily. "Don't worry. We talked earlier. He's fine. I know. We'll all be fine." He looked at Dad like he wasn't going to be fine at all and needed reassurance.

I lifted up the pizza-box lid.

And there it was, the strangest thing ever: "*OK RE C,*" written in pepperoni. No letters after C bc Jake ate that slice.

"What the heck?" I looked at Jake taking a bite of another slice. "Who wrote that?"

He shrugged, chewing. "It came like that."

"So the pizza people just wrote stuff in pepperoni?"

"I guess."

"Who ordered it?"

He shrugged. I looked at Dad. Dad shrugged. I yelled to Mom who was eavesdropping from the kitchen, "Mom, what's up with the pizza?"

She stepped out from her eavesdropping spot. "What pizza?"

I looked at Mr. Griffin.

Jake: "I don't know. It just got delivered. And this one came yesterday." He showed us on his phone—another pizza w/pepperoni writing: *"PLS FORGIVE ME."*

Me: "Oh my god, you took two pizzas that no one ordered. With pepperoni writing? I mean, did anyone order that one?"

Dad, UP and Mom came over to look.

Crickets. It was too strange, especially given the whole AL situation.

UP finally asked, "So what did the rest of this one say?"

Jake: "Col, C-O-L." He swiped to show today's photo: *"OK RE COL"*

UP: "That's weird. We got a couple wrong-house pizza deliveries too, I think yesterday and maybe the day before. We sent them back."

Mom: "Maybe it's a thing. Like the latest in pranks."

Dad: "Was there a receipt?"

Jake shrugged.

Dad: "And you said nothing? Like to see if we ordered it? Or it came to the wrong house and should send it back? Or if we wanted some?!"

Jake looked unfazed and said, "orry," with pizza-stuffed mouth.

That's when it all came together. The pizza box was from a place by Taylor Rae's. I know because she had a girls' facial thing once when her friend was selling beauty stuff and makeup and ordered pizza for the kids and Mitch (her husband) while we had tea and crumpets and champagne (what are crumpets anyway? I still don't know), which was cool bc they let me and Sadie sip bubbly and try all kinds of makeup. And the "COL" had to be Columbia! This was a message to me from Aunt Lauren! *OK RE COLUMBIA!* Or was I crazy?

No, in that moment, I knew: Aunt Lauren was at Taylor Rae's.

I said nothing. My heart raced. I could barely swallow or breathe. What was I going to do?

I stood there frozen for a long time maybe. Like, I don't even know what everyone else was doing. I just kept imagining AL at Taylor Rae's sending pizza messages like a crazy person. I wonder what the pizzas said that went to UP and Sadie and Nick.

Mr. Griffin was annoyed I was just standing there next to his gaming superstation. "Can you move?"

This snapped me back from my stupor. UP, Dad and Mom were by the couch looking perplexed.

He repeated, more annoyed, "Can you just...*move*?"

I gave him a quick tickle to annoy him further.

He yelled, "Stop!"

I moved closer to the adults. Their faces looked like they were smashed by bricks.

Mom to me: "It'll be okay."

I nodded. Did they know it was AL that sent the pizzas?

"Alright, I'm gonna go back," UP said. "Thank you." Dad clapped him on the back as he left.

Nope. They had no clue.

8:40 p.m. Going to Taylor Rae's. AL has to just stop this!

11:58 p.m. Back in my room after mega mess. Heart pounding. Still.

Snuck out and took Lyft to Taylor Rae's so no one would hear my car. Got out a block away on Almar. Stealthily crept up lawn to giant bay window at front. And there, on the sofa, sipping wine, was Aunt Lauren. TR, Mitch, Violet and Otis were playing some kind of board game. AL seemed to be zoning out but TR kept talking to her, like trying to include her, and AL forced a laugh and responded but then went back to staring off.

OMG! The whole world had stopped and there she was sipping wine on the sofa playing boardgames, or at least pretending to. I stormed over and banged on the door.

Mitch answered, "Saoirse! Fancy seeing you here on a Saturday night at almost bedtime." I like Mitch. He's a director too and has the best dry humor. All his movies are satire and me and Dad are superfans.

Me: "I'd like to talk to my aunt, please."

Mitch, as if he'd never heard of her: "Who?"

Me: "Aunt Lauren!"

Mitch: "She's not here. Why would she be here?"

Me: "Yes! She is! I just saw her on your sofa!"

Mitch: "Taylor?"...with slight desperation in his voice and looking over but only opening the door a crack so I couldn't see in, which was weird because they're super hospitable and there was no reason to keep me out.

Me: "Can I just come in?"

Taylor Rae came out, shutting the door behind her. "That's my sister, visiting from Michigan. She does look just like your aunt."

Surprisingly, they were really bad at lying and covering up. Surprising for people that are professionals at making stuff up for the screen and being super convincing at it. This was out of their league.

Me: "No it's not. I saw her. I know what my aunt looks like. And I know she's sending pizzas and she just has to go home." I felt desperate.

TR: "What pizzas?" I could tell she didn't know about the pizzas.

Which made me feel crazy. What if Aunt Lauren hadn't sent the pizzas?

Me: "I don't know! Just tell her she has to go home then when you see her, BECAUSE I KNOW SHE'S IN THERE!"

Taylor Rae stared. Frozen.

"I know you're in there Aunt Lauren, and it's not okay!" I screamed at the door and stormed off.

"Saoirse!" TR yelled but didn't try to stop me.

I kept walking north towards Sunset. Then, maybe two blocks up, I heard yelling, "Don't you dare tell them where I am!" It was Aunt Lauren, like a crazy person, walking towards me, then stopping. I ignored her and kept going, ready to explode with anger and anxiety, and stormed all the way up Almar to Sunset, then turned right as if walking to Santa Monica. I was too angry to stop or think. I had to keep moving to get rid of this terrible feeling. I stormed past Pali High until I got to Starbucks and called a Lyft. I still didn't know what to do.

When I got home, I stood outside our house in an angry and confused stupor until somehow Mr. Griffin noticed me. Maybe he came out front to pee in the garden. He does that sometimes if the bathroom downstairs is taken because he's too lazy to walk upstairs.

"Dad? Saoirse's standing outside!...I don't know!" he yelled from the door. Dad came into the doorway too and saw me.

"Saoirse?" Dad said.

I was frozen. Feet glued to the sidewalk, fists and teeth clenched. A neighbor walked by with her two shepherds. Dad said hello and came out, "What's going on?"

I exhaled, deliberated, knew I had to do it, "Aunt Lauren's at Taylor Rae's." As I said it, fear filled my stomach, like anxiety, because I felt bad, like I was betraying her and something bad could happen to her because of it, but it also seemed like the best thing to do for her and everybody. She needed to know everything was going to be okay, like Mom and Dad and UP kept saying. She needed to KNOW! And she needed them to HELP HER!

Dad nodded and took it in, clearly thinking what to do.

"I haven't told anyone else," I said, meaning UP or Sadie.

"You did the right thing. I'm sorry that happened." He kissed my head and didn't ask how I knew and said, "Thank you for telling me." Then, he took a deep breath. "And now, I guess I've gotta tell Uncle Peter," as if he knew this was going to be a nightmare. He nodded as if to convince himself it was the right thing to do and he had no choice. "And go get her back. I hope she comes. At least she's not in Cork." He laughed, sort of. It was almost a cry.

I think Aunt Lauren is going to hate me forever for telling though. The Columbia thing doesn't even compare.

Sunday, May 19

My room, 6:30 a.m. I went and curled up in my parents' bed after writing that last thing and fell asleep. I guess I needed to feel safe.

At some point in the middle of the night, Dad came in, fixed the duvet snuggly around me up to my chin and kissed my forehead like he did when I was a little girl.

I woke up just now and Mom was snoring.

Dad was downstairs sleeping on the couch. "Saoirse?"

"Hi. I'm going back to my room if you want your side of the bed back."

"No, I'm good here. Much quieter," he said, joking about Mom's snoring like always. A good sign.

"Is everything okay with Aunt Lauren?"

He said it would be.

I guess we'll see.

Friday, May 24

Work, 2:40 p.m. Uncle Peter and Aunt Lauren are away on a "retreat" on Vancouver Island. I don't know what that means, but the story we're telling everyone is that AL's family had an emergency Back East. Sadie and Nick are home and Mom keeps going by to check on them and bring cheese, which they like. Me and Dad went grocery shopping for them once too.

No one is talking about Aunt Lauren.

The cutting room is on hiatus. UP told the studio about the fake family emergency Back East. He's supposedly coming back next week. Mike is "working" from home and Jena leaves after lunch but I'm supposed to call her if anyone's looking and she'll come back.

It's all weird.

I keep trying to focus on editing my footage but it's hard to concentrate when I just want to know what's going on. Also, Sadie wants me to send BookishLens footage to Hector because he's helping her update her reel. Why? Why would he do that? Why would she do that if she's dating Andy and knows Hector is still into her? She said it's because he offered, but still. She told him I have the footage because my hard drive has more space and I always do the editing. Blech. This is not being gentle with his feelings like she said she would be. Or mine.

Can't deal. Going for walk.

4:10 p.m. I went and sat on my bench near the walkway to the commissary in the sun like a lizard whose blood was cold and needed warmth. Leo walked by on the phone and waved, engrossed in a call. He paced around. I watched him. My heart raced out of nowhere. No feelings attached. Then, he waved and shot me a smile.

I waved but didn't smile.

That must've alerted him, and he came and sat next to me. "What's up, Bookish?

I shrugged and shook my head.

"Yup, some days are like that," he said, leaning back, happy. "It's pretty fantastic working on the lot though, don't you think?" He was trying.

I nodded, heart racing more, hands sweating. I didn't want to say anything in case it came out wrong. Or what if I seemed crazy bc of AL and UP? By association? Did he know? I was paralyzed.

"We're reshooting the breakfast scene by the way. With the eggs!"

"Cool," I said in weird monotone.

"Your eggs! Which we can drop right in. You okay?"

My stomach turned. I was an insane elk, maddened by fear of an unknown variety. I clutched the bench, squeezed my toes, trying to regain control.

I nodded. My heart raced more. Panicking. Face sweating. It felt numb, like a facial. "Okay. Gotta go. See you later." I stood up and raced back here without looking at him.

Now he's in the doorway. God.

"What's going on?" he said.

"I don't want to talk."

5:20 p.m. Leo came in anyway and shut the door. He looked through to Mike's room. No one. Crickets.

"They're on a retreat!" I yelled out of nowhere, even though I swore I wouldn't say anything. Ever! And now I'm worried I sound insane AND he'll tell someone. Because I'm so confused about being honest!

"All of them?"

I said nothing. And just heard silence in my panicked-elk brain.

He could see things weren't normal with me.

"Saoirse, I'm sorry about what happened. I know you don't want to talk to me, but I really am in a confusing place. I shouldn't have even started anything with you. That wasn't fair. Even though you are fantastic."

He waited for a reaction. I had none. Then: "It's fine."

He studied me. Like he wanted to know what was going on. And could see I wasn't taking it well. Then he looked down and in a super low voice—like he knew it was going to make it worse, make me feel worse, but wanted to be honest because he's an actual adult, like he didn't want pity and would take my wrath—said, "Isla and I are giving it another try."

OMG. A thousand things raced through my head.

"And I've been dating Lorraine. Who is extremely even-keeled and didn't deserve this either."

Nooo!!! Even-keeled? Why is he telling me this? I can be even-keeled!!!

He stared, almost sheepish, waiting for a reaction, as if hoping I was more adult than I acted and could rise to the occasion and understand and maybe forgive him for hurting my feelings because he's just human and didn't mean to. Which is probably true, I think. And like I had that power. And he trusted me with his heart.

My elk self felt my heart open to receive his vulnerable heart, feeling sad for him, like empathy for my fellow elk, just wanting him to be happy in some altruistic bigger sense, even though I felt sad for me. Don't ask me why, except I probably really just love Leo. He puts his feelings on his sleeve and is so honest and raw. And he lives. He isn't at the starting gate. His tricycle is in the shed, or donated, as are his training wheels. He has love and drama and a movie in his life.

I nodded and smiled a little. It seemed to encourage him.

"Thank you," he said, in a sweet way that was also strangely attractive, like an elk mating call.

Which made me blush.

He looked at my hair like he used to. "Looks like you have someone too."

"What?"

He walked around the room, looked at notes on the wall and the horse race, like a weird detective, like MacGyver, like Deva, waiting for me to fill in the blanks, curious, like Mike and UP.

"Oh, you mean yesterday, the guy?" I said, wanting to make him jealous but then saying, "He's Sadie's boyfriend. Was. That one. He's helping me with something." Like an idiot.

"Oh, right, I remember. That's nice." He looked at me with that twinkle in his eye. "And what I love about you, Saoirse. Kind and always helping people and seeing the positive side."

Like a doormat. Did he think I was *just* nice?

Then he looked at my hair again, even though he's in love with Isla. And I thought maybe he knows he won't stay with her. That I'm the one. Maybe he knows I still adore him. Maybe he adores me too. Deep down. Even though now we're just friends.

Or maybe I'm insane and just trying to make myself feel better.

"Mixed with a lot of brains," he added. "And another new pair of sneaks. Good style, Bookish."

Thanks?

He left and my heart sank. I felt so empty, even tho when he revealed his heart, even if not for me, it felt so full.

Then, he stuck his head back in. "By the way, Verbinski says you're getting an A-plus in class. Nice work. Says you got a knack for photography. Keep it up, Seer. Maybe we'll work together some day."

OMG, a glimmer of hope. Me and Leo working together! But only for five seconds. Bc why did he call me kind? And nice? And why am I so honest?

And why is Lorraine so deserving and EVEN-KEELED?!!!

I went over to the table and shoved three of Mike's Milano cookies in my face to alleviate the misery. Mike isn't here anyway. Then, I shoveled a whole and partially eaten container of Magnolia Bakery banana pudding in. The half-eaten one was Classic vanilla. Everyone loves that one. Must replace Monday on way in.

Then, I looked at my phone.

Hector: *Hey. I know you're super busy but Sadie suggested I get her BookishLens stuff from you for her reel. Am looking to wrap it up tonight. Any chance I could come by and put it on a drive? Or maybe you can DropBox it? Tho may save time if I look at it quickly and just take what I need. TY*

Ahhh!!!! Why? Why is he helping her? Why is he being so nice?! And why am I so fat? And bloated with Magnolia pudding?

My room, 10:50 p.m. Went over to Hector's house after work with laptop and video files. He was so awesome, helping Sadie, and it was so hard to watch. Him being nice. And kind. Like a doormat! Like me. Stop being so nice and kind, Hector! Ahhh!

He was at his dad's house. A three-bedroom condo on Granville in West L.A. near Stoner Park. A bunch of kids were running in the courtyard, including his twin half-sister and brother, Hana and Che. It was loud. I think the stepmom is Swedish. I met her at the end when she got back from work.

Hector grinned when he opened the door. "Welcome to our loud and humble abode." His grandma was in a comfy chair in front of the TV nodding off. "Aba, this is..."

"Your girlfriend! Finally, I've been waiting to meet you and see your beautiful smile. The one I've heard about so much."

Hector shot me a "please go along with it" look.

"Nice to meet you...Aba?"

"You can call me Josefina."

"Josefina, what a beautiful name."

"Or Josie. Helen calls me that. I like it."

I laughed. I didn't know if I should call myself Sadie after that. But Heck said, "This is Saoirse, Aba."

"Saoirse! Ah, the other girlfriend."

What?!

"With the film."

She knew about me!

"With the *shuh, shuh* in your name that looks nothing like it's pronounced."

We laughed.

I told her it was seer-shuh, and she asked where it's from.

"Saoirse's Irish, but I was born here."

She asked if my parents are Irish, and I told her my mom just liked the name and my family's from Lithuania. "But that was a long time ago."

"Well, wherever you're from, you make Hector happy." She smiled over her glasses. "And you graduated early too."

Yup.

"Just like this one, smart cookie, too smart for his own good." She made a funny kissy-fish face at him. V. sweet! Then told me to lookout for Lalo. "You be careful of that Lalo. He has a fiery personality. But I do like his work."

Clearly, Heck told her everything.

"Aba, she'll be fine!"

"Come here," Aba said and squeezed his cheeks. "So fun. But that beard has to go."

"Alright, we're going to work," he said.

"Always with the work," she teased. "You'd better come back out and eat when it's ready."

Then, Jose the communist came out. He was surprisingly super nice too. He wore shorts and a Dodgers jersey and cap. Apparently, he's a superfan of not only Karl Marx but the Dodgers as well. He was yelling as he entered, "I'm going out!" Then saw us. "Oh, Hector." And shook my hand. "Jose Rojas."

"Saoirse Berger. Nice to meet you."

"Likewise." Kind smile. Sincere.

"She's helping me with a project," Heck said.

"Great, you two have fun. I'll be back after the game. And don't forget, tomorrow, 10:30." That last part had an edge.

So did Hector's reply. "Yup."

"Great." Jose looked pleased, kissed Aba. "Nice to meet you." And left.

Hector exhaled. Aba looked at the TV screen with a poker face, not pleased with that interaction. "Be patient. He will learn," she told Hector.

Then, we went down the hall to the first bedroom. Happy, yellow, bright. Josefina's room that she shares with Hector and Mateo when they're there. Three beds plus Mateo gaming with headphones on. Same superstation as Jake, same intensity, more compact.

Also a gorgeous painting of a hibiscus, deep red and charcoal, covering one entire wall. Beautiful!

"It's Jose's."

"Your dad painted that?"

"Yyyyup," Heck said, with a deep funny voice.

"And you call him Jose?" I pretended not to know.

"Sometimes." He grinned.

Which made me laugh.

"He's a painter. And a lot of other things, which makes him very complicated and hard to live with. Maybe Sadie told you."

I nodded, which seemed okay.

"And he plays handball at the park. Super intense dude. And tomorrow's a party workshop. Fred Engels' intro to the Manifesto. That's what that was about."

"Tomorrow?" Mateo said, with an over-the-top *mwa-ha-ha* laugh.

Heck batted Mateo with a sock. "Shut up, Squidfart."

"Stop!" Mateo yelled, without breaking gaming-stride.

"This guy gets off easy. No party indoctrination for him." Quick swat to the head. "Just wait though, mwa-ha-ha."

"In your dreams!" Mateo yelled. Clearly this was a thing.

I looked closer at the painting. Crimson. Gorgeous. "Wow. A true artist."

"Tell her about rizzz-dee," Mateo teased.

Heck smacked him again with the sock. "Nada. Nothing to tell."

"He could've gone, just like you!"

Heck shook his head. "It's an art school. Jose had a scholarship and didn't go." Then leaning in to Mateo. "And *Aba* applied *for* me. *And* to Lewis & Clark." And he blew on the back of Mateo's neck.

"Stoopppp!" Mateo yelled, brushing Heck away.

"Aba applied?" I said. This was strange. And funny.

"Yup," he said, then back at Mateo, "You hear that Squidfart? Aba applied. For me," and playfully tickled his chin.

Mateo batted him away. And the whole thing was hilarious. And Heck said, "Aba's got cajones. What're you gonna do?" And shrugged.

Which made me laugh.

Mateo yelled, "You said cajones!"

And we all laughed. And his eyes sparkled. And there was the sunshine smile like at the beach.

Remembering beach. Heart racing.

Sand.

Sun.

Happiness.

College talk.

Ohh...nooo!!!

And I just said it, "Columbia. It's Columbia. I said yes to Columbia."

OMG.

"What?!" He laughed. Out loud.

"I know," I said, heart racing, instant red-robin face.

"I thought you didn't want to go there."

Mateo stopped to look, sensing my panic. Two red robins, one on each cheek.

No air.

"I don't know why," I said, holding my breath.

Hector studied me then waved the sock in front of my face, back and forth, trying to make it better.

I tried to grab it. Missed. Again. Got it. Both of us clutching sock. Funny smiles. Mateo laughing.

"You'll just have to meet me back here for Stollen," Heck said finally.

And Mateo yelled, "You said Stollen!" and went back to his game.

And everything was better.

The phone rang from other room and Aba yelled, "Your mother's calling!"

Heck yelled, "I'll call her later!"

And Aba yelled, "Don't you leave your mother waiting!"

And Heck said, "See, brazen," then yelled to her, "I won't!" Then to me, "She'll be fine." Cute, sincere friend smile. "So will you."

And my heart melted.

And I believed him.

My friend.

Which is when the stupid part began.

Because then we had to look at Sadie's reel. And Heck pulled up a chair for me and said, "Let's see what we've got," and turned on his screen.

And there, frozen in super-cute close-up, was Sadie, looking down with a sweet and joyous smile.

On Hector's sweet unrequited love.

And I wanted to run.

But had to stay for my friend's heart.

So I opened my laptop and went along with the task at hand.

Which was adding BLGirl footage to Sadie's acting reel. First, he showed me what he'd done—new stuff from her film, smoothed-out pacing, changed-up music.

Everything had his heart all over it.

Which was depressing as hell. And amazing too. Because it was so good.

"Wow, it's so much better!" I said, with fake-emo-chirpy voice.

He asked what I thought about adding the BookishLens bit after the new footage to end on a light note.

I thought it was a good idea, as was the whole stupid reel to help Sadie get the audition next week. Trying to remain positive: I love Sadie. I support Sadie. She works harder than anyone I know, which is why she's so good and I love that about her. Like how she even gets Mr. Griffin to run lines with her. A miracle, and why I know he won't end up a cretin. I must remember all this.

So I found the BLGirl boot-tapping footage and Heck thought it was perfect. And I wondered how he can be so positive when he's stabbing himself in the eye with happy 4th-of-July love sparklers and burning off cornea, iris, eyelashes and heart all at once.

He has really nice eyelashes. Long. Really long. I hope he keeps them safe. And doesn't singe the ends.

No more tears, gorgeous, sweet, funny Hector.

We pressed on. Without tears. And he added, "Welcome to BookishLensGirl, I'm Sadie Svensson, and we're going to see what's happening in the world of cinema!" to the start of the reel. And "Sweet dreams, all. See you soon!" to the end. Corny. Cute. And the reason the BLGirl cousinship rocks and the fans love us. And her. Why he loves her.

And why this reel popped. My words. Her acting. His brilliant cutting. Stealth team effort.

Perfection.

...as I cried hidden Tarantino-blood-squib tears inside my eyeballs, eyelashes intact to display fakeness on outside. Hector heart betrayed by spear of desperate and vacillating cousinship loves.

Why did we ever do that?

"It's great," I said.

Hoping he never finds out our lie.

"It is," he said, followed by momentary longing for Sadie cuteness just sitting there onscreen. Then, "You hungry? Aba's the queen of dinner."

So I stayed. Even tho I thought maybe I should run. And we sat down to dinner with Aba and Mateo, the twins and Swedish Helen. It was nice. I forgot about Hector's heart and enjoyed him instead, funny guy, putting on show for twins and Aba, over the top. He loves to make them laugh. When I left, Aba gave me Air-Fryer chicken in foil. She's obsessed with the Air-Fryer. Says it makes everything taste better.

Tomorrow, Hector's giving the reel to Sadie in person after his Fred Engels indoctrination workshop, which is hilarious somehow. The workshop, not the stupid teamwork reel that he should JUST SEND!

Idiot.

I hope it goes well for him.

I hope his heart stays intact.

And mine too.

Saturday, May 25

My room, 12:55 p.m. Hector went to his Fred Engels indoctrination and then straight to Sadie's with the reel on a flashdrive. Andy was there. Hector left before she could watch it. I know this bc she called me, overflowing with excitement right after.

"It's so good!" Sadie screamed into the phone. "Thank you!"

But what about his heart? Which is when I asked her point blank if Hector knows about Andy. "What's the deal?"

She went in another room so Andy couldn't hear and told me she told Hector she's not ready bc of Paulie, her heart is elsewhere, and she wants to be just friends but thinks he's great and it has nothing to do with him. "He seems okay with it," she said. But she didn't tell him about Andy. Ugh.

Seconds later a text from Hector: *Wanna go for a drive? Go to Joshua Tree? Anything? Bring your camera? We can make something!*

My heart raced. Really?

This was strange. Unexpected. I didn't know what to do. Would I be crossing a line? With Sadie? Heck? Myself? *Anyone???!!!*

Should I make up an excuse, like that I have to study?

Insanity! No more lies!

Which meant truth.

Which meant going with Heck sounded fun and exactly like what I needed.

And an escape from overthinking brain.

Also, how does this person know what I need when he barely knows me?

Elk Saoirse tossing daisies back and forth in antlers with elk Heck. Happy daisy bundles. Happy elk friends playing all day long.

Moo.

Or whatever sound an elk makes for love. And friendship.

Sunday, May 26

My room, 10:22 p.m. Life is full of surprises. And happy daisy bundles.

Hector picked me up yesterday after he texted. We drove to Joshua Tree/Yucca Valley. We hiked. We laughed. We had a picnic. Clyde came along. Happy dog, back seat, middle back. Wind in face. Blown-back gums.

Look at those canines!

Later, we got chili fries and split a catfish sandwich at Pappy & Harriet's. OMG, this place! Pappy & Harriet's Pioneer Town Palace. Old movie western set town. Biker cantina. Famous musician hangout.

Clyde loved the fries. Us too.

Then, we went to Wal-Mart and tried on hats. We got matching blue skullcaps. Stupid! We sat on a rock and ate the leftover fries and gave some to Clyde and drank beers and a "hard kombucha." I liked that one. Fruity. Heck had them in his trunk. I don't know how he got them exactly, but it's something about a guy named Leaf that's a DJ that he and Frank play music with.

He spray-painted the sand. In green. And pomegranate. A cactus flower design with southwestern sun circle around. I filmed it. He showed me how to paint. I spray-painted too. I made his face. In gold. It looked dumb. And was hilarious. I got it all on my phone.

Clyde chased some animal into the brush. Heck chased him down. Brought him back. Luckily, no animal caught. He told me I might like some of the bushes over there. Terrible bush-joke callback, Heck! You teasy meany!

Then, he brought out his drum. One drum. Like the big one in a drum kit or a marching band, but on its side. Hilarious. He had sticks too. He put it in the middle of the painting and did a rock-jazz mashup. He's v. good. And weird. A guy on a drum on a street-sand painting in the dessert. Super bizarre. And funny. And laughing, like he was totally having fun.

We watched the sunset. I felt love and beauty all at once. But barely, because mostly I felt hard kombucha and joy. I wondered if Heck was thinking about Sadie. I think I wasn't thinking about Leo at all. Barely. Except in that moment when I was wondering what he was thinking and thinking about what I was thinking and not thinking.

I think we both were just thinking about the stars in the end. And the jackrabbit that ran by. And how Clyde didn't notice. How did he not notice? I think it was the fries. And all the excitement.

And there was *this* too. I mean, the moment. *This* moment. In time. And perfection. Of love. And it was now, as in then.

And my heart expanded. And maybe his did too, because surely my heart couldn't be expanding if his wasn't too. It was easy to forget the stupid other stuff right then.

And it really didn't matter. We were just two friends being. And it was the best thing ever. And he was so weird and funny and laughing all the time.

Then I had to pee. I went behind a bush. He shined the headlights of the car on me. And off. Then a flashlight. "You look like a chicken laying an egg," he yelled as I crouched to pee, and he rolled an old tire at me. "Bowling for chickens." Clyde barked and ran after it. Luckily, the tire didn't come close.

"What the hell?!" I yelled.

"You looked like a chicken!" he laughed..

And Clyde howled with all the excitement.

Him funny. Me funny. Hilarity that I'm even writing this.

We slept in the car. Me in back. Heck in front on the emergency break. It couldn't have been too comfy. But funny at least.

Clyde slept in back and in front, like between the two seats, and shifting up and back, both of us getting dog love and giant floofy-fluff-ball cuddles.

We lay there and talked about stupid stuff for a while, ten million questions of the day. That's an exaggeration, but he asked a bunch. The one I remember most is the one about the Phantom of the Opera that he asked Sadie/me before and I never answered.

"The Phantom of the Opera is here...inside your mind. What do you think about that?"

It sounded like a trick question that wasn't about thinking. Or the mind.

"I don't even know what that means," I said. "What does that mean?"

"That's the point. What do you think it means?" And he told me some guy who makes rockets and Teslas and owns a company called SpaceX tweeted it. Heck follows him bc the guy is weird and wildly smart and interesting and writes obscure cryptic stuff, apparently. Perfect for Heck. The spaceman also has a girlfriend that's like a Manga character and a kid named X. Even more perfect.

I told Heck I'd think about it. I mean, the Phantom just always seems like a real ghost in the story to me. "What do you think it means?" I asked. "I mean, clearly you think it's a metaphor. Or at least this space guy does."

He sat up w/funny, dramatic eyes. "A big, ugly, lonely monster in my head." Trying to keep a straight face.

Which made me laugh and he smiled sweetly, and it happened— eyes meeting, perfect connection, both perfectly, equally weird, perfect friends, perfect feeling, like everything I felt when we first met on IG and he messaged me and it always made everything okay, no matter what was happening, even when it was just *day weird*. I felt safe. Heck always feels safe. Then and now. And I knew it'd be okay, I'd be okay, and so would he.

He flopped back down. "But I don't think we're all monsters. Maybe the beauty is in the ugly. Or some such nonsense." I pondered and he started snoring, like a second later.

Still pondering.

On the way back, we stopped at his mom's for dinner. I felt anxious as we approached. Maybe bc she was at Sadie's when they met. And saw the love between them. And knew he was hurt. And it was my fault. And there was this other thing, friendship. And maybe she'd read between the lines. And would see whatever is there. What is there? Maybe it's just the Wizard of Oz. Or friends. Or something more.

Why did I feel that?

But the anxiousness went away as soon as we went in. Ofelia smiled so bright when she saw him. And me too, and she hugged me as if she's known me forever. And gave me sweet coffee that tastes like cinnamon and said it welcomes the warm spirits. I don't know what that means.

Heck brought the drum stuff in.

"He loves the drums; it's his passion," she said and gestured for me to follow him. Heck was setting the drum up with the kit in their room. Mateo was there. Same gaming station, different location.

"Aren't you gonna say hi?" Heck said to Mateo.

"Full concentration," Mateo said, ignoring us, bang, banging on keyboard.

This was familiar.

Heck grabbed drumsticks and made the biggest noise possible.

"Not now!" Mateo screamed, trying to concentrate.

Heck played louder.

Mateo yelled harder, "Stop! Mom, tell him to STOP!!!"

Then, bang, bang banging from the apartment below, broom to

ceiling. Heck's mom yelling to downstairs neighbor, "Deal with it! You live in an apartment! It's the way it is! You don't want noise, don't live in an apartment!" Clyde barking. Hector cracking up. Hee, hee. Me too.

Mateo bang, banging on keyboard.

OMG, hilarious! How could I ever feel bad about Mr. Griffin again?

Hector said this happens all the time. "My mom's an apartment warrior and defender of us."

God, I love these people.

Also, his mom is on a Greek food kick (and all healthy foods) and made amazing mousaka AND baklava. It was her second try, and everyone agreed both dishes came out better this time. There was also fresh goat cheese (Mom should check out!) and an assortment of olives, organic from TJ's. Ofelia confessed that's her secret place for great olives.

We told her about my film. She was excited for me and wants to see it when it's done. I blurted out that I'd invite her to the screening. Which was too soon. And Heck said, "Really? Am I invited too?" as if I wasn't ever going to tell him.

I said I wasn't sure it's even happening but I'm hoping and dreaming.

And Ofelia said, "Sometimes hopes and dreams are all we need to start with. Enough to make the unforeseen happen."

I want to believe her. She seems wise. Maybe she is.

Then we ate, and Hector filmed me and his mom talking. Which got super annoying. So we tried to bat him away and finally I just chased him down and wrestled the camera away. The downstairs neighbor bang, banging with the broom on her ceiling. It was pretty hilarious.

Heck said the neighbor's always pissed about us. "Talking. Laughing. Farting."

"Farting?"

"Farting!" Mateo yelled and cracked up.

"Drumming. Yelling. Yes, apparently, she can hear us fart."

"And then Mom defends us," Mateo chimed in.

"Your mom defends your farts?" I said.

"I do," Ofelia said. And we all laughed.

"And you're okay with that?"

Heck said it embarrasses him sometimes but Mateo is totally fine with it.

On the way home, Heck filled me in about how his mom is a ball breaker like Aba. Always defending the underdog. Especially against "the system." She thinks mostly the system helps no one. Whether it intends to or not. Especially kids. Like appropriate noise levels. No kid can follow that. It's unrealistic and whoever makes these rules is stupid. And that kids are the most downtrodden minority.

Hallelujah! I agreed.

He said that's the kind of stuff his parents fought about but he knows it's a grey area. Love is, and relationships. And that actually, his dad's the one that taught him about the grey area but then goes off on opinionated tangents and has a hard time expressing love or anything positive. Heck says his dad expresses love through Marxist indoctrination.

We laughed.

And also tough love about being an artist.

But is it true? Is there a grey area?

That became the question of the day. We laughed. Neither of us knew the answer. We literally have the same answer: I don't know.

Take aways:

1. Hector feels like an old sock. Easy. And comfy.
2. His mom is really really nice and it's really really nice and warm at their house.
3. I like both of his families. Including Clyde. Esp Clyde. And Aba.
4. They're kind and full of truth and honesty and humor.
5. They fight a lot. Like AL and UP. But my parents don't, except little digs covered up w/cheese and wine. Is that bad that they don't fight more?
6. When I'm around Hector, I feel like everything is okay and will be and I don't have to worry.

7. Our friendship is real.
8. I think there's a grey area. In the angles. Relationships and opinions and facts have a lot of angles.

I hope he never finds out about the Wizard of Oz. I think the happy sparkling Ferris wheel inside me would fall over on its side.

But now, not thinking about it. Focusing on putting project first above relationships anyway per seasoned filmmakers, like Dad, who does it well, and AL, who doesn't.

Set up to do BookishLens with Sadie tomorrow night. Staying in action instead of overthinking.

And Lalo is Tuesday, 2:00 p.m. I told Jena I have to leave after lunch. Woo! Then I have one week to finish and turn in my film.

Monday, May 27

My room, 10 p.m. BookishLens TBR & Watched in the can. One take. Sadie is on fire. Glad she convinced me to do it again. We did fun teen movies that come from books or plays that you can "read and watch or just do one or the other to get the story, depending on your mood," Sadie said with all her wise cuteness. We featured my favorites: *10 Things I Hate About You*/*Taming of the Shrew*; *Easy A*/*The Scarlett Letter*; and *Clueless*/*Emma*. And added in *Bridget Jones's Diary* but now am taking it out because it's not teen and we can do it next week instead.

Tomorrow is Lalo. Taking back control. We're meeting during the day so Hector can't be there, which is a bummer.

Tuesday, May 28

Cutting room, 2:20 p.m. It was the best of times. It was the worst of times. Great book. *A Tale of Two Cities*, Dickens. Posted it on BLGirl just now and did silent BookTube vid of just book on armrest of mini couch in cutting room. Got book from home at lunch. A v. emo thing but it helped.

Here's what happened.

Lalo flaked. Me and lighting crew there, ready. And not even a text. I had to track him down.

Lalo: "Oh, sorry, yeah, my girlfriend needed me to pick her up from work. And you know how that goes. I no show, she kick my ass."

T. demoralizing.

I asked when we could reschedule. He can't, at least not before my project is due.

Oh. My. GOD! Maybe I'm just not meant to be a DP/filmmaker after all. Once again delusional. Disillusioned.

Sad.

Nothing to hold onto.

3:50 p.m. Hector keeps texting to see how it went. Haven't responded. Don't want him to feel bad. He was so excited for me.

Going to see Leo. I DON'T CARE!!!!

4:30 p.m. Saw Leo. Went by and said hi. He's randomly here from stage looking at something.

It was normal. I was normal. He talked to me like normal. Like everything I always wanted.

Still feel bad but this was good.

No weirdness. I stuck my head in the door like a regular person-friend and said, "Hi."

"Hey, what's up?" he said.

Melanie glared.

I went in anyway. The door slammed behind me. "I was supposed to film someone for my project and he flaked." I let myself droop instead of pretending I was happy. "The main guy."

"Oh no," he said like a normal friend and peer-mentor filmmaker and gave me a hug. He was sorry that happened. It's happened to him, but it always works out he said. "You just hang in there and do the next thing and sometimes you end up with something better." The beauty comes when you trust the process.

I wanted to believe him. He could tell I didn't.

I told him I had to finish by Monday. He said to stay open and strong and a solution would arrive. "Sometimes you just don't know how."

Melanie groaned audibly.

He shot her a look like, *What the heck?*

While I thought, *Easy for you to say. Things like that only happen for people like you and Sadie.*

And he said, "Seriously, go back out there and find someone else."

OMG.

Tough love.

I wondered if he was always like this, liking me and thinking I can do it, with full respect. And I just imagined he wasn't?

My room, eve. Told Hector Lalo flaked. He feels bad and said he'll help me. I can film him and Nia and Ellie, assuming they agree, which he's sure they will. Or any one of them.

Feel sick to stomach as if loser sitting here alone in room. I don't know why.

Also, Aunt Lauren came back from Vancouver Island. Everything supposedly back to normal.

Wish Hector and the girls didn't have anything to do with her. Makes me feel like loser that couldn't figure this out on own without help. Contemplated not having street artist in film but that blows as it's built around street art and will lose impact.

Why can't I just let Hector help? It was fine before.

Lonely loser-elk trying so hard to fill heart with Leo-genius-filmmaker-friend encouragement.

Who cares where the help comes from?

Lifting antlers and letting nose glow.

Rudolph beacon.

Terrible metaphor.

Hate self.

Still trying.

Could everyone else please buck up?

Later. Maybe people do come through. Maybe I don't have to do it all myself.

And be perfect all the time.

Leo text to me just now: *Hey, Bookish. Idea. Going on location scout with new DP tomorrow for new film. Daytrip to Taos. Small plane. Am double dipping with other studio so don't tattle if they find out I'm playing hooky. Wanna come and film her in action? For your film? You might learn a thing or two as well. She already said yes. She's a rockstar. Almost as talented as you ;)*

Wednesday, May 29

My room, 8 p.m. Went with Leo and new DP Ramona. Filmed her testing camera angles and set-ups and location. I learned so much. Also got to interview her, and Leo chimed in but made it all about Ramona, like he kept making her the star. She talked about inspiration and how she gets her POV.

The silver lining of Lalo happened.

Leo rubbed it in: "Told you. You never know where it's gonna come from. The good that's lurking. Even for you."

Cute, funny, cinematic mentor and friend.

8:40 p.m. Also...

I texted Hector: *I'd love to film you and Nia and Ellie.*

He wrote back: *Good :) they said yes!*

Me: *Saturday?*

Him: *Great! I'll set it up! But it has to be early.*

Me: *TY*

Him: *NP. It's an honor to be in the film! Unless we end up on the cutting room floor :D Wanna see Gas Food Lodging and Mi Vida Loca at Aero Friday? Director might speak. She did Four Rooms with QT.*

Cute cinema friend.

But Svenssons' is Friday and we're watching Sadie's film.

Crap.

Don't want to hurt feelings. Hers or his.

Me: *Let me get back to you.*

Thursday, May 30

9:30 a.m. Heck figured it out: *Hold on now! Tomorrow is Svenssons'. Forgot! All good. See ya Saturday!*

Big heart.

Sunshine sparklers in heart.

Silly friend.

Weird and normal.

All at once. He comes in many sparkles.

And angles.

And he understands.

Friday, May 31

My room, 11:30 p.m. Bizarro night at Svenssons'.

First: Aunt Lauren normal to everyone but me. Completely ignored me. Couldn't even look at me. Awful.

Pissed.

Then: We watched screener of Sadie's movie. It's SO GOOD. She's SO GOOD.

Then it got weird again. UP told me and Sadie to get Nick and Jake for dessert. AL made cheesecake and fig tart (good sign). Mom brought a bespoke handmade Brie.

They were in Nick's room.

I followed Sadie down the hall. Door closed. Laughing inside. Sadie finger to lips, "shhh!" We burst in.

Screams. Giant image of Aunt Lauren on Nick's screen—behind valet on Melrose, crawling on ground, cops, J Boone, UP, Armistice and "DUI for J Boone's Secret Love?"

OMG!

Sadie lost it. "What the hell are you doing?! This isn't funny!" She shut it down. "You know this is bullshit! And it's just gonna make it worse!" Fuming red. Nick and Jake laughing, pretending not to care.

She stormed out.

Jake and I shared a rare bro-sis-bond moment, like *OMG, thank god our parents aren't famous!*

Then, I followed Sadie to her room. She paced, exhaled, like a storm, then, "It's terrible."

"Your mom got a DUI?"

"No! She barely even drinks! You know that." She was pissed at me for not knowing.

I apologized. She accepted.

Then filled me in:

Fake: Armistice dating other actor while J Boone filming in Mongolia—not true. J and Armistice splitting—not true. J Boone seeing someone on sly (like AL?!!!)—not true. The DUI—also not true.

Real: J and Armistice met UP bc they're making a movie together—true. J and UP writing movie, Armistice starring, all three producing (which I knew)—true. J and Armistice happy in love, no secret dates on side—true.

Sadie had no idea why her mom was on the ground at the valet but said AL made the illegal U-turn so they tested her for being drunk, which she wasn't.

And now Sadie's doing press for her movie and they keep asking her about her mom, like circling hawks.

"Vultures?"

"Yes."

The press even followed UP and AL to Vancouver Island. Which means Sadie keeps having to lie and say there was a family emergency with a fake aunt on the island. And then say that the fake 'Back East' story was to protect her mom bc she likes to keep her family private and "I can't talk about the aunt on the island, because she's private too." Even though there really is no aunt anywhere. "And no, my mom is not having an affair with J Boone! She loves my dad! And it's just silly."

I couldn't help but laugh. Sadie did too. Bc it's so absurd! Then she said J Boone's publicist had Aunt Lauren do an interview with a screenwriting magazine and made sure the journalist asked about the whole valet-DUI-supposed-affair debacle, which fixed everything. AL told the journalist she'd been overworking on her current film (UP's) and the one she's writing/producing with Taylor Rae, which is TR's directorial debut. And that UP is doing a film with J Boone, and that's great, and she was having lunch with her niece (me) on Melrose, talking about college, because UP and AL had a meeting after (lie), and she tripped outside by the valet because she had a migraine that messed with her vision (lie) and she did make the illegal U-turn (true) but definitely didn't drink before 7:00 p.m., which was a joke that the journalist pulled off perfectly to give her a sense of humor and charm because "I think the PR person is friends with the journalist" and gently encouraged her to write the piece to make AL look amazing. It was completely believable.

"So that's good," Sadie said. "But I don't know about my mom and dad. They're doing their next projects separate. So they can have space and spend time together not working. So, Mom'll go on location with Dad and vice-versa when she makes her movie." Sadie didn't look convinced this was good. "My mom still just doesn't trust my dad, and I wish she would."

I didn't tell her about the spying thing.

So many lies. But Sadie felt better telling me at least. And then we went back out and had yummy dessert and AL continued to ignore me.

Main takeaways from tonight:

It's amazing what people can make up and spin! It's also fun when people believe you. Sometimes.

Never trust what you see or read unless you know the whole shebang IRL.

When there's something happening, you can sense it but it's impossible to know what it is unless you're in it.

Sadie and I both loved the BLGirl spin until Hector. I feel guilty. I don't know if she does.

I feel better when Sadie and I are friends.

I wish AL would change her perspective so good things would happen for her too, or at least she could appreciate them instead of having to hide. And then me and Sadie would feel better too.

Saturday, June 1

My room, night. Today was a beautiful day, and I'm not sure how to process that.

Hector picked me up early, 7:00 a.m. early! He wanted to make sure we found a spot and didn't get stopped. He told me to sit shotgun and film him.

We picked up Ellie and Nia. They sat in back.

We drove up PCH. He talked about his art. Nia and Ellie talked about what they're doing. I filmed them too. I love my new camera. I'm so glad I bought it. Did I tell you I bought it?

Heck said he brought his drum. *What?* He laughed when he saw my face. Nia and Ellie teased him and he loved that. I felt v. judgey about his stupid drum. Bc he's so cute when he plays it. Kind of like when he dances. V. impassioned and funny and good too.

We went to Surfrider Beach bc he knows I love it and the light is good and parked on PCH. He told me to keep filming—just me, my camera and the natural light.

He grabbed his backpack of paint from the trunk. It was next to the drum that got left behind. Nia and Ellie had theirs. We found a wall. He painted a face. Instead of hair, the girls painted around it, girl warrior stuff.

He painted me. She was ugly. And beautiful. All at once. He said, "Masterpiece." It came out amazing.

I took photos. I am now looking at them, and it really is me.

I am speechless at how he sees me. I look beautiful. I don't know what to say. Or do.

He talked while he was making it. Explaining. Telling a story of a beautiful girl. He described me. It took my breath away. I really hope he didn't see me get teary.

He held up the video he took of me when we went to the secret beach when he chased me down to Paradise Cove. "This is my POV," he said and held it up for my lens as I filmed him.

Then, he talked about what street art means to him. Nia and Ellie did the same. To him, it's about telling a story. To Nia it's about love/relationships. To Ellie it's about voice and the city embracing her and hearing her. Heck said art is for people to enjoy. A way to beautify and connect. A voice for the community and city itself.

Then, he said to me: "What do you think of her?"

He took the camera and filmed me next to her, the painting of me, and said, "Ah, it looks like these are the same beauties."

My heart expanded.

I felt honesty and love and poetry.

And I felt like I belong.

To the city.

And this wall.

And a friendship.

Sunday, June 2

My room, 3 p.m. I went back again today and just sat in front of it, the painting of me. I shot it from a bunch of angles. And ate a Caesar wrap from California Chicken Cafe and grapes.

How did Hector see me in such a good light? It was so intense, and from different angles. My hair was making weird shapes, like hearts and flowers and a sword. The colors were orange and pink. It was stunning.

I feel loved.

7 p.m. Am cutting the new stuff in. It fits like a glove. Went quickly.

Still feel loved. By everybody in it. Heck and Leo too.

Hector also sent me the video he shot of me at Escondido running away and texted: *My POV. Add it to your film and you'll have a masterpiece.*

Does he know I know the warrior girl is me? Yes. I guess that's the point.

I didn't want to add the video of me. I didn't want to be in it. The mural was enough. But I cut it in. His POV, me running from the lens but being seen. I didn't watch it. I hope it's okay. Thursday night is our last class, and I'll be turning in my film tomorrow morning.

I dedicated it to my aunt. In the end credits, it says: *For my aunt, Lauren Berger*

Weirdo.

Thursday, June 6

My room, after UCLA class, 11:30 p.m. Everyone loves the film. Eloise gave me notes after I sent it Monday, and they made it better.

Now what?

The soufflé has popped.

Feel exposed. Embarrassed. Too much attention.

Hector texted: *How'd it go?*

Sadie texted: *And?*

Leo texted: *They loved it, right? Told you so, Camera Girl!*

I didn't respond to any of them.

Mom and Dad asked.

I just said it went "great." They want to see it.

Hector wants to see it.

I am frozen.

Friday, June 7

My room, night. Today I sent the film to Hector. I thanked him and told him everyone loves it. I didn't send it to anyone else, just told them it went well. And hid in the coffee-pot bathroom so no one could see my face.

After work, went to Deva's. I got there early so I sat in front of her house in my car. I really didn't want to go home. Her mom noticed when she came home and Deva came out.

I told her I was in a crisis: Everything great. My film. Leo talking to me. Sadie and I friends again. AL mad but fine. (Didn't mention Columbia. Everybody thinks I just don't want to talk about it and only Heck knows.)

"So what's the crisis?"

I told her about the film and that I feel embarrassed bc everyone wants to see it and I don't want to show them, besides Hector. Who I also didn't want to show but did.

She thought this was ridiculous.

I said the film was too personal. "And why did I let Heck convince me to put me in there?"

Really hate self now.

"I thought it was about other people," she said.

Gus opened the front door and looked out, listening.

God.

She suggested we go get something to eat and then I could show her. I said I didn't want to show her.

She said we should go anyway.

We went to the Promenade. Gus came too, annoying PDA all over her square, pre-med-student neck.

We got burgers and sat by the dinosaur fountain. I also got frozen yogurt with ten-gazillion-billion scoops of Oreo cookies and white yogurt chips. I felt SO BAD!

It didn't help. She wanted to see the film. "While we eat. C'mon, no biggie." As if it was going to be a blast for me to show her. She even shoulder-bumped me playfully,

I didn't want Gus to see so she told him sit on the other side of me so I was in the middle. "Stay there."

Then she watched on my phone. Two seconds in Gus was back next to her. I guess he doesn't know how to stay.

I let it go. What else was I supposed to do?!!!

I watched them watch. Felt sick. Devoured more gazillion-billion cookies and yogurt chips.

They finished. She said, "Wow, he's in love with you," meaning Hector.

Nooooo!

"Hector is in love with you."

I didn't know what to do with that.

"Does Sadie know this?" Deva asked. "She's got a new boyfriend right?"

I couldn't breathe. No air.

Gus replied for me, "Yeah, you said Andy."

Which is when Deva sent my movie to Sadie without me knowing. On MY phone!

And I said, "Probably," to Gus about Sadie being done with Hector and onto Andy.

"But *he* doesn't know you were her, right?" Deva said to me, meaning Heck doesn't know I was Sadie.

I clutched the paper on my hamburger. The yogurt was gone.

Deva said, "He'll be fine," as if she KNEW about Hector!

But I didn't think I would be fine. It was too much of a betrayal.

That's when she told me she sent the movie to Sadie and showed me what she wrote: *This is Deva. Pass it on. She did an amazing job.* "Is that too much of a betrayal?" she asked.

"What? No! Why did you do that?"

"Because sometimes the most awful thing is good for you. This is good for you. And probably Hector too. Maybe you never would've gotten to know each other if it weren't for the whole Cyrano lie."

I couldn't accept it. *It just...no!*

"Things change," she said. "People forgive."

"Not always."

Then she asked Gus if he thought Hector would forgive the lie if he found out. Gus said, "No," he's sure Hector would be pissed and that he (Gus) would be livid if that happened to him.

Nooooo!

Then Deva admitted maybe she was wrong.

And Gus said, "Definitely. The dude's gonna be pissed."

And my heart sank. And nothing was better. DevSheeran fail.

Sunday, June 9

My room, 4:20 p.m. Sadie loved my film and sent it to UP and AL who sent it to Mom and Dad.

Hector loved it and texted Friday: *It's great!*

I texted, feeling totally weird: *TY :)*

He texted this morning: *Beach surf day with Frank. County Line. Wanna go?*

I didn't want to go bc of—*TERROR!*—but I went. I boogieboarded. They surfed. We ate In-N-Out. It was fun. My heart leapt when Heck smiled.

What did that mean?

Did I want to be more than friends?

Did he?

I reigned it in and the day was easy in spite of the random happy nerves in my stomach.

I'm delusional. He'll find out about BLGirl and even this will be history.

Foraging on as happy elk friends.

Tuesday, June 11

My room, eve. This morning, Aunt Lauren texted me: *Lunch?*

I deliberated. Didn't answer. Then she just showed up in my doorway because, apparently, she was on the lot for a meeting with Taylor Rae and somebody about their new movie.

I didn't have a choice.

We drove downtown. She said she wanted to do something completely different. We went to MOCA. I suggested it. That's where Jena took me for my job interview. It's a good spot to talk about serious stuff without having to look each other in the face.

But the serious talk happened before we got into the museum, at the little cafe where we got sandwiches. There was v. awkward tension, and AL acted as if nothing had ever happened and I just went along in terror of what this could be about or if we had to discuss Columbia—and her thinking I wasn't going—after all the effort she made to help me get in when I didn't ever want to go and just went along with it for her and out of chickenhood, like in the Ed Sheeran bird-essay poem, even though then I idiotically said yes to the acceptance after telling her I said no. And I still don't really want to go but have been avoiding the topic all together as if my film could save the day.

Which maybe it can.

Because then, she looked at me and said, "I'm sorry. I was embarrassed. And I was wrong about pushing you to go to Columbia. I just want the best for you, but clearly, that wasn't it."

OMG! And wow, just wow, bc she meant it.

And I felt like an idiot bc of the lies.

And then she asked me if I got the pizza. And I said, "Yes."

She looked relieved. And smiled. "I'm really sorry, even though that's pretty embarrassing too." And she took a bite of her rosemary-chicken and soft-mozzarella sandwich. Yum!

"I kind of liked it," I said, honestly.

And some of the ice around her edges melted. "And that's how you figured it out." She smirked mischievously.

I nodded then felt embarrassed about the whole ordeal, even though I could tell she thought we were bonding. I guess we were. It was kind of funny and nice that I figured it out through the pizza. Like we had our own little secret mind-meld.

She smiled. "Thank you."

I couldn't believe it. As in, I did.

We stared. I said, "Okay."

She took a deep breath. "You're really good, Saoirse."

"What?"

"Your film."

My heart started racing.

"And, if you'd let me, I'd like to do something special for you."

Uh-oh.

"I'd like to organize a screening. Maybe on the lot."

What?

"Make it nice. Do a little reception. Your mom can bring cheese."

How did she know? "Really?" It's exactly what I wanted!

More mind-meld.

Then she got hesitant. "And I thought...if you're okay with it..." She studied me, sheepish, but not like a sheep following the herd, more like a prairie dog looking up after having been a naughty dog and not wanting to repeat that. "...maybe invite my friend from AFI, my personal mentor, who's on the board. Just in case you ever wanted to go there. After you do whatever it is you need to do and if you decide that would be good. And my friend who does the Sundance Lab."

Wow! "That would be incredible," I said.

She was surprised by my reaction.

"I mean, thank you."

And for the first time ever, it was easy with her. Moving in the same direction. Finally. Instead of butting heads. I felt like an adult. I felt love. Like a real elk. And she's the aunt elk.

Even tho now I have weird-elk Columbia-idiot acceptance lie.

She was so relieved. And happy. And we ate and talked about the film and walked around the museum.

Jena gave me the stink eye when I got back because it was a two-and-a-half hour lunch but then it was worth it. Also, I told Jena about the screening, and she's happy for me.

"I'll let you know when we can get it on the calendar and then we'll make some nice invitations," AL said as she mosied over to UP's shut door and knocked. He opened the door with a smile.

Everything is back to normal for real, even for them. Better than normal.

Except for my lies.

Monday, June 17

Work, 2:40 p.m. I picked the invitations up from the printer today. They're gorgeous. Aunt Lauren made sure of it. We designed them together in her office with UP's assistant Beth once we had a date, which is next Wednesday. It's so weird to see AL this way.

She's going to invite some of her friends and now I invite mine.

My heart is racing thinking of asking Leo. If he's around. I need to psych up even to find out. And I will!

The same goes for Hector. I don't even know what to make of it.

I could mail them. Old school. Add some class. Character.

My room, 7 p.m. Okay, so I drove to Hector's mom's house with the invitations. Old school. Like in an Oscar Wilde play. Like I'm the messenger on horseback (and author of letter!). I imagined bringing invitations to the door and putting them on a silver tray for Hector's butler.

IRL, butler/mom Ofelia answered the door, so happy to see me. She invited me in and I handed them each an invitation, sans silver tray. "It's next Wednesday at four."

Ofelia was so excited. "Congratulations. I heard it's fantastic. I can't wait to see it. "

I wondered if he showed her already but let that go and told her to bring someone. And Leo too. Hoping he'll bring Frank and not a date, which made me blush. I'd be jealous if he brought a date.

Then Ofelia followed me out to the car while Hector watched from the window, amused. Maybe she sensed something bc of the blushing or was in warrior-mom mode.

She touched my cheek. "I just wanted you to have these." And gave me three tiny, clear, very light lemon-yellow stones. "For good luck. And to nurture and empower your truth, the real Saoirse, to shine. They're sunstone. Very special and precious from Oregon. I got them when we went to look at Hector's school." She touched my cheek again. "You creative souls have tender hearts that need to be handled gently."

What did that mean? Was she talking about me? Hector? Did he think the film was terrible and was preparing me for mean non-friend critics?

I came home and sat in my car for a while. Hector was weird. And cute.

And the film is probably fine. Not worried about critics.

Now focusing on screening.

Tomorrow, I'll invite Leo. In person. He'll make me feel better if Hector brings a date. At least now he sees me as a friend. Leo is my ally. He makes the worry go away.

Why do I keep imagining Hector bringing a date?

Get over it.

Tuesday, June 18

Cutting room, 2:40 p.m. Success. Invited Leo. And Melanie (ech). He asked if Richard is going. I said I hoped so. He said, "Great! Can't wait." Most normal conversation ever.

I walked back to the cutting room and imagined me and Leo at dinner in Austin on location on his next film, where they're actually filming. We're a couple and talking about the dailies with DP Ramona and her partner, a French painter (I made that up). Sophisticated, funny and creative all at once.

You never know. Maybe, like Hector's mom says, if I can imagine it, it's the first step towards being true.

Then, I had a flash of me and Hector parasailing over the Loire Valley. Above everything. Happy. Together. Free. So weird. I don't even know what parasailing is or if that's the right word.

Also, we were elks. Which is funny.

Just looked up parasailing. It's the thing you do with a boat, so I guess we were hang gliding.

Huh.

Also looked up the Loire Valley. It's in France. Beautiful lavender fields.

Friday, June 21

My room, after Svenssons'. I met Andy. He's fine. Though Sadie is clearly not in love. But she shines around him so he's probably easy and makes her feel good about herself.

Everyone is excited about the screening. Two people from AFI are coming. And AL's agent Joe. AL said I'm not ready for an agent, or even close, but someday I might be and then people will know who I am and it's always good to start networking.

I'm so nervous about Columbia. Really don't want to go.

I sort of believe her that she's not trying to push me on anyone. That's how she networks. She honestly likes the people she works with so it comes together naturally. Like Leo for me, I guess.

Taylor Rae is coming too and Eloise and maybe Richard. Mike and Jena, of course. Mom, Dad and even Giorgi if he can! And Mom's bringing cheese friend Jean-Francois, bff Kate and my gran Lina. Sadie is doing lavender flowers.

I have chills. Maybe overkill. Bc it's just a silly short and means nothing. But am trying to embrace the attention for once. I need to do this like an adult who wants to be an adult. Who makes stuff.

Also, I called NYU to see if I could retract my "no" and defer. They said no. I'd have to reapply next year. I said I think I will.

Sunday, June 23

My room, night before screening. I FaceTimed Hector. I don't know why. I was insane. And nervous. And thought he could help. Now I'm not sure what to think.

First, I was blasting "Girl, You'll Be A Woman Soon" and dancing like Uma in *Pulp Fiction*. Psyching self up. Super excited. And then, bam. Just called. On FaceTime.

Woooooo!

And there was his cute face.

And he said hello, with extra deep voice, like this was weird and more intense than usual, and I said hi and he asked, "To what do I owe this honor?"

More intense! And cute!!!

Which made me nervous, and I told him I was super nervous, and he asked how he could help.

By loving me!!!!!!!!!!!!!!

Which made me happy and shrug and then stupidly say, "Hrhhhuph."

Which made him laugh and lean forward.

No, no. Close, different, smiling, sexy!

And he said, "It'll be great." With def sexy-flirting smile. This was new.

My stomach leapt. I didn't know how to handle it. Couldn't hold his stare. I had to look to the side, up at the air, inside my head. Then I exhale-laughed and with chirpy, nervous-cutesy-quirky-gross voice said, "You're right. It'll be fine. Thank you," as if the intensity and non-friendship hotness would go away, but he was still staring.

Criminy.

Then he laughed at my nervousness and said, "You'll do great."

Did his voice suddenly get lower again? But in a funny way?

My palms are sweating.

Okay. Deep breath. Film first.

V. much insane.

Monday, June 24

Screening Day, my car, studio peon parking lot, 6:10 p.m. Hideous horror worse than anything that could be possible. I just don't know what to do. My heart is broken and I want to disappear.

Here's what happened. Will try to recount as best as possible (good and bad) even though it will be like stabbing self in heart so expect staccato...

Everyone showed. It was beautiful. Loved by all. Then, after.

Me, Heck and Sadie talked to Sadie's agent, Joe, who is also AL's agent.

I wore the green dress from Sadie with orange and pink that Hector said I looked best in and flowery Blowfish sneaks, lemon pin in hair off to side. Amelie in full swing. Leo wore bolo tie. Hot, hip, solid and professional all at once. Gold star.

Hector wore light-green short-sleeved button-down shirt (tattooed arm out), fancy jeans, nerd glasses, desert boots I'd never seen before. Clearly, he dressed up. He looked smokin' hot too. My heart skipped a beat when I saw him. Esp. his smile.

The best was Mr. Griffin in his suit jacket, one size too small, that Mom made him wear. And, of course, Dad wore his boots. Everyone else looked like their normal selves.

We were outside by the cute little reception area Mom and Aunt Lauren made. Part French themed and part graffiti, which was pretty cool. And thoughtful.

Leo started making his way over, stopping to say hi to everyone, bc he's like that. Like a politician kissing babies, like UP but with good posture. Our callisthenic-loving exec walked by, Rude-y Dork. He saw the party. Leo waved him over. Shook his hand. They talked, Leo clearly telling him about the screening, gesturing to me.

They came over.

"Here's our star." Leo kissed my cheek. Our exec shook my hand as if I was the most important person in the room (outside) and like he'd never met me or exercised in front of me through an entire screening of UP's movie. Also, he acted as if he'd actually been in my screening today, which he hadn't.

Rude-y Exec: "Fabulous work."

Then, Leo and Exec fawned over Sadie and Agent Joe. Clearly, they all know each other. Leo nodded to Hector. "Nice work. Great eye. Keep it up, man."

Hector shook his hand. "Thanks, Dude. Very cool." It was obvious Hector admires Leo. This was a big deal for him. Hector told Leo, "The location stuff with your new DP was great too." I was Hector's Leo wingman.

Then, the disaster.

Leo to Rude-y Exec about me: "And she's a YouTube star, BookishLensGirl."

Oh, snap.

Exec: "Really?" Way too excited.

Leo laughed: "More subs than me."

Exec didn't get the self-deprecating joke.

Leo added: "Impressive."

Rude-y Exec to me impressed: "Nice."

Hector to Sadie: "Wait, what?"

"Uh," she said.

Hector to Leo: "Isn't it...? I mean...?" He gestured to Sadie. Sadie looked at me. So did Leo and Hector.

"Uh," I said.

"Yeah," confirmed Agent Joe about Sadie, not at all sure. "I've seen the boot dance. That was definitely all Sadie." He laughed. No one else did.

Me: "Yes, definitely her." I looked at Hector. His brow was furrowed. My heart raced. Me to everyone: "It's complicated."

Hector: "What's complicated?"

I looked at Sadie for help. I didn't know what to do. She inhaled and exhaled through her nose.

Leo laughed and said to Agent Joe and Rude-y Exec: "Complicated and brilliant. Seer runs the show and Sadie's the cover. Because she's an amazing actress."

Agent Joe, relieved: "Yes, she is."

Hector paled.

Leo about me: "And the rest is all this one, photos, witty bookish and movie-ish and oft-irreverent discussion," smiling at me. "Saoirse D. Berger. More..."

Sadie, turning a weird shade of pink: "Stop, Leo. Cut."

Leo, finishing his sentence: "...fans than me."

Rude-y Exec, finally looking up from phone: "Well, that *is* interesting."

I shot angry "be-quiet" eyes at Leo.

Leo not getting it: "What?"

Me: "Just stop."

Leo: "I don't get it. You guys are brilliant." To Rude-y Exec: "They'll pull the wool over anyone's eyes."

Hector got it.

Sadie to Leo: "She said stop."

Everyone stopped. This was out of character for Sadie, even though it came out super sweet.

Leo to Sadie, still not getting it: "Because...?"

Hector, pained, realizing he'd been hoodwinked: "Because I'm an idiot. And they're trying to be nice."

Leo stopped.

Hector to Sadie: "And because it was all a show? Or a game? Like, who was I even talking to?"

Sadie deflated.

Hector to me: "I mean, was I talking to you the whole time?"

And everything magical about all those talks and messages disappeared in that moment. My heart sank.

I didn't know what to say.

I blew it.

And he hated me.

I hated me.

Hector: "And you never mentioned it? Ever? Not in Joshua Tree? Or at the beach? Wow. I am...a fool."

Hector looked at Sadie. She exhaled and smile-frowned with furrowed brow. I don't know how else to describe it but she obviously felt awful and looked sorry, sweet and like it was all okay—all at once. Because it was her. That thing that Sadie has. That diffuses everything.

Hector exhaled as if he could accept that from her but that it was super frustrating at the same time. I think it's physically and emotionally impossible to be or stay mad at Sadie.

Andy to Sadie re Hector: "Wait, so...you and...you were dating?"

Hector: "No, apparently, I wasn't dating anyone. Or even just hanging out as friends. Which I guess is why it kind of sat there like an apple pie, with all that empty air between the apples and the top."

Leo, finally getting it: "Wow."

Hector: "Exactly."

Leo to Hector: "I'm sorry, Man."

Hector: "Thanks. Me too."

Leo: "Brutal."

Hector: "Yup."

Leo bro-slapped his shoulder: "You'll be fine."

Hector to Leo with funny jokester twinkle in eye: "Be careful, Dude." To us: "Brilliantly played, BookishLensGirls." The twinkle vanished, and he walked off.

No air.

Rude-y Exec: "I have no idea what just happened but it all sounds promising. I'll check back in." He shook Leo's hand, waved to us as if our world hadn't just collapsed, and bailed on his phone.

We all just stood there.

Andy to Sadie: "So, you...? We're good?"

Sadie to me in a whisper re Leo: "I can't believe you told him."

I was speechless. She looked like her heart was frozen or something. Like her emotions were fighting to get out but she couldn't access them. Some part of them wouldn't let her. She shook her head. Then in a weird voice, trying to hide possible tears without looking at anyone: "I gotta go. Bye. Thank you."

She walked off to her car in the lot in front of the big screen. Andy stood there for a second then followed. She yelled back at him: "Please, I'm fine." He kept following. She yelled again: "Go away. Please!" Even yelling she was polite.

Agent Joe joined another conversation.

Leo was still there next to me. We watched Sadie and Andy.

Sadie got to the car. Couldn't find her keys. Lifted her purse above her head. Slammed it to the ground. Her stuff scattered. She got on her knees to get the stuff that rolled under the car. Andy helped. Sadie beat the ground with both fists. Then she cradled one hand like she hurt it, grabbed her stuff with the other hand, got in, drove off.

Andy stood there. Like he probably rode with her and would have to call a Lyft.

Leo looked at me, like, wow, like astounded him. "I, uh, like...," like he was about to apologize but realized it wasn't his fault. And maybe I scared him a little, but in a funny way. "Uh, Bookish?"

I felt like a traitor.

"I'll have to think on this, but excellent work on the film." He smiled, warm, kind. "Just be careful with his heart. And respect your own." Then he chuckled, like—*wow, she just got away with that with someone's heart*—and bro-slapped my shoulder. "You're smarter than you think. And also have a lot to learn. But you'll be fine, Young Bookish. We all make mistakes. No doubt." And he waved to Agent Joe and Aunt Lauren and left.

Everyone hates me.

From behind me: "Saoirse?" It was Stupid Jake standing there patiently and looking actually kind of half stupid and half dapper in the suit jacket that was too small that Mom made him wear.

Jake: "Aunt Lauren wants you to go over there and talk to someone." He talked in a completely monotone voice so as not to show any emotion at all so as not to embarrass himself.

Aunt Lauren was talking to the guy from AFI. But her attention was on us. She smiled. Waved me over.

Jake and I walked over. He said, "That was awesome. Your film." Still monotone. No emotion. But clearly, he meant it.

I saw Hector's mom by the cheese. Her face was somber. My heart sank. I waved and smiled, trying to make it better. She nodded. Face still somber. She hates me too.

Aunt Lauren hugged me when we got there and whispered, "It's okay. Everything is okay." Then she wove her magic, holding me close with one arm, shoulder to shoulder, telling the AFI guy in a whisper, as if letting him in on family-drama secrets, that: "I think Saoirse spilled the beans on Sadie's good news a little too soon." Then she looked at me as if playfully scolding me: "I think Sadie really wanted to tell people about it herself."

I had no idea what she was talking about.

Then, she added in a lower whisper for AFI guy: "Sadie just got a fantastic role." Then back at normal level: "And it's a tough time. Off to college for these girls. Big changes. Hormones. You remember that." And AL and the AFI guy laughed. And everything was better. And she hugged me again like she understood and has my back. Like my crazy is her crazy and she's there for me. I felt better. For a few seconds.

Then I crumbled inside. And wanted to run after Hector and make it better. I really was AL's mini me.

My room, night. I went over to Hector's house. His mom let me in. Hector came out of the bedroom and stood in the archway to the living room. His mom held the front door.

"I'm sorry," I said. "I didn't mean for this to happen."

He stared. Shook his head. Looked away. Looked back. "Please just leave."

I exhaled. Thanked his mom. Left.

Ofelia didn't try to mom-warrior stop me this time.

Tuesday, June 25

My car, peon parking, after lunch. I went over to Sadie's. Stood on the lawn. One of them must've seen me so Sadie came out. Aunt Lauren stood in the doorway. Sadie had a cast. She broke her hand on the Big Sky parking-lot asphalt. A "boxer's fracture," apparently, a slight fracture just up from the pinky knuckle. Should take two months to heal. First, Sadie thought the asphalt-punch pain would go away, but her hand ballooned up and bruised, and Aunt Lauren said it had to be broken and took her to the doctor.

They told the doctor Sadie punched the sofa in anger bc Nick snooped through her texts and she didn't want to punch him but had to get steam out. They said she hit between cushions where the wooden frame is. The perfect fake story in case anyone inquired. Even though they figured no one would.

Aunt Lauren smiled and waved at me from the door as Sadie walked over.

She said her mom is proud of her for letting her anger out.

I didn't know how to react. I was still trying to read Sadie, and she didn't smile. I waved back to Aunt Lauren. She was back in her element, helping everyone else, the one with all the answers.

I told Sadie I was sorry.

She nodded and stared, just like Hector, then said, "Me too." But not like it was her fault too but like she was sorry I told Leo. "It feels like a betrayal."

It was. I nodded, stomach clenching, hot tears rising and pouring over. "Yes, a lot of betrayal," I said and just stood there and felt very small as tears streamed down my face.

"If you just wouldn't have told Leo, it would've been fine. We had a plan. But you put him first. What about us?"

We stared. Then she took a step forward, hugged me tight and went in. Like she'd forgive me in time. But not yet.

Her mom closed the door behind them. Inside, they were safe. Together as a family.

I feel so sad.

And alone.

Later, my room. I drove to the beach way up by Neptune's Net after I left Sadie's and curled up on the hot sand and slept for an hour. I called Jena and told her I was sick. She got it and was cool.

Then, I went by Mom's cheese shop and asked for help. I may never be a real adult or actually get my life to start and feel happy but I needed that hug now.

I got a hug. And I got cheese and my mom's warm smile and all the encouragement I always crave. Her friend/boss/cheese-sommelier of 30 years, Jean Francois, and Mom made me a spread. They were beyond happy to help.

Some of their cheese friends sat down and had wine too. It was like a salon, everyone chatting, and they made me feel comfortable and included without making me feel like it was about me and awkward and like my entire life had just fallen apart.

In the middle of them chatting away, Mom came and sat on the stool next to me and turned me to face her and took both my hands and said, "Life comes in cycles...up and down."

I think she meant round and round.

"When it's not working, things get wiped out. But then you grow from the ashes, like a Phoenix."

"Phoenix?"

"The bird. That's you. You're the Phoenix."

I laughed and snorted and sort of cried. She sounded ridiculous but I knew what she meant and it was nice. And she was finally giving me advice. Finally MomSheeran.

"You feel like a failure, and your life is over. But that just means it already started."

It wasn't really helping though. Even though I thought it was all I ever wanted.

"But most important of all is that we love you. Me and your dad completely love you just as you are. In fact, we adore you."

I felt myself crumble inside again. "But what am I supposed to do?" I cried. She held me.

"Be yourself. Completely and honestly you."

"I don't know how to do that."

JF the cheese guy leaned over and said, in his charming French accent, "Courage, ma petite, Courage."

It sounded like cou-raj. And that helped. More than anything.

Monday, July 1

My room. Eloise wrote me a letter. She told me how proud she was to have me as a student and that I have a lot of talent and hopes I pursue a career in film. She says I can use her as a reference and to come to her for advice or help any time.

Hector stopped following BookishLensGirl. He also unfollowed SaoirseDBerger.

And took down the mural of me on ClydeDogBoy. And us at the beach.

I feel sad again. Cou-raj waning.

Tuesday, July 2

My room, night. Still sad. My life is over and it hasn't begun. Actually, I guess it has per mom. It was short-lived.

Thursday, July 4

My room, 4 p.m. Freedom is love is a kaleidoscope of flying away. Alone. Misery.

Monday, July 8

Cutting room, 4:30 p.m. Leo moved to Sony to start his next movie while finishing up his mix/double dipping.

He texted to ask if he should set up a meeting w/Rude-y Exec bc Rude-y mentioned again that he might be able to do something with

BLGirl. Leo wasn't sure if that meant me or Sadie or both.

I texted back: *No, thank you.*

He replied: *I understand. Probably a good move, BookishG. You'll find your way.*

Also, Jena took me to green-corn tamales at El Cholo. Her favorite. I think she wanted to cheer me up. It felt good to get out of my usual space. V. yummy!

She also mentioned she has a friend doing a short and maybe they need a camera assistant. I told her I'd love it, maybe too enthusiastically, but it didn't seem to be a problem. She said she'll find out and was happy to help. I like Jena. Secretly enthusiastic, creative and supportive.

Friday, July 12

My room, night. Dad took me to that show at the Palladium. It was fun.

Jake is being nice to me. Maybe Mom and Dad are forcing him. I played Hearts of Iron IV with him, which is his thing and not my thing at all but it was a good distraction.

Saturday, July 13

My room, night. I went to Deva's college graduation party. It was at their house, with the Alpine theme. Mom came too and loved Deva's dad's fondue and flirted with Hot Steve and talked to him and River about Paris and how she's going to look them up when she goes there for a cheese thing in fall.

Deva's grad ceremony was actually in June but she was still finishing up a class, hence the party delay. She now has a BS in BioEngineering and BioPscyh, double major. Premed. And definitely pursuing psychiatry. Deva and River still like me. It's hard to face them tho and pretend I'm fine bc they see right through it. It makes me feel empty and lost.

Sunday, July 14

My room, night, Bastille Day. I went and lay on the beach again across from Neptune's Net. The sand makes me feel safe or something, like soaking up everything and giving me back goodness. I slept. Is this what grounding means? Maybe.

I was seeking courage. Or cou-raj. It only really helps when you say it in your head with a French accent.

I went down to the water and dug my feet in the wet sand. I stood as tall as I could and said cou-raj over and over until it powered me up.

Maybe I should move to Paris.

Monday, July 15

My room, 8 a.m. Today I begin my foray into honesty. The true Saoirse D. Berger. With courage. Pronounced cou-raj with a deep French accent with your mouth all pouty. So it has impact.

Ugh.

Wish me luck.

First step: See if Sadie will do a final BookishLensGirl episode. For the fans. It's weird that we just stopped. But this will give us a chance to say good-bye. That's my truth. And maybe our fans deserve it. And being nice to our fans is my truth too.

I didn't ask Sadie before because it felt inappropriate given everything that happened. But I think we need to do this. So...courage!

My room, 7 p.m. Sadie said no. She can't do it. She's done.

I asked her in person so as not to hide behind my phone. Same scenario. Me on lawn, except this time I texted in case no one happened to be looking out.

At least I tried I guess.

Tuesday, July 16

My room, night. Today, I texted Hector to ask if we could talk: *Hi, it's Saoirse. Please, can we talk?*

I wrote my name in case he deleted my number.

Or both of them.

He didn't reply. Maybe he blocked them.

Wednesday, July 17

Night. I tried Heck again. In hopes of being honest, which right now = desperation and insanity.

Thursday, July 18

Cutting room, 3:10 p.m. Crickets. How am I supposed to show him my true sorry colors and beg for forgiveness and cry about how bad I feel for hurting and deceiving him so that maybe he won't be mad and feel better and I can feel joy again...if he won't even see me?

Saturday, July 20

My car, 1:40 p.m. Today, I stalked the communist party meeting. Heck told me about it so I knew where it was. I guess they're having a series of classes on Fred Engels or something. It actually sounded interesting whenever Heck talked about it, back when he still talked to me, but he always just rolled his eyes.

I stood in the parking lot until they came out. Hector stopped when he saw me, but close enough for me to hear his dad say,

"What's she doing here?"

"I don't know."

My heart sank as the other communists exited the meeting chatting, friendly, like they would coming out of any fringe party meeting, Libertarian, Green Party, whatever, I guess. Or even a 12-step meeting, like River took me to once. It looked the same. It also looked like the class I had to take when I ran a stop sign so it wouldn't go on my insurance.

I told myself to have courage and shouted over to them, "I'm sorry, please, I didn't mean it to come out that way. I wish I could take it all back."

Heck stared then walked off to his dad's car. He leaned back on it, arms crossed, looking over. I needed to teach him the word "cou-raj" to give him power to push me away. Because it felt like he was pulling me towards him, closer. To him.

I stood there frozen. Jose had no idea what to do. Neither did I. Then he yelled, "Do you want to come inside? We have some nice tea."

I still couldn't move. He looked at Hector, then went inside and came out with a pamphlet. He handed it to me, put his hand on my back, led me to the tea and cookies. "C'mon, take a look at that. Talk to someone. Have a treat. Oh, look, this is Constance, say hello."

He left me with Constance and hurried to his car, happy to have someone to take me off his hands. He started yelling at Hector, waving back furiously, like I was Hector's fault. Hector frozen. Then they got in and drove off.

Hector look over as they turned out of the parking lot, slowly, responsibly.

I wonder what communists think about tattoos.

I wonder what I'm supposed to do now.

Sunday, July 21

My room, 2 p.m. Hangover. Second ever. Went to Deva's last night out of desperation. She called in the troops—River, Gus, Hot Steve.

We walked to Bowlmor with a secret Jaeger flask.

River is terrible at bowling. His feet hilariously flipped over his head when he forgot to let go of the ball. Ouch.

I'm pretty bad too but I remember to let go. Maybe only in bowling. Need to apply that to life.

I remember that moment about River and one part about the soul-searching conversations we had until 4:00 am. That's it. The rest is Jaeger fog. Here's what I remember:

Deva to me: "Amends is changing your behavior not saying sorry. What are you afraid of? What can't you change? Be honest."

Me: "I am! I'm honestly sorry and wish it never happened."

River: "No, she means *really* honest."

Me: "Eff you." As if he's so much better at this than me!

Deva pressed the issue: "What would be really honest?"

Me re Heck: "I want him to forgive me."

Deva: "Hm, yeah, you can't really force that one. What else?"

Me: "I don't know. It doesn't really matter then."

Deva: "Sometimes you gotta just do the right thing for the sake of it. So you know it for yourself. Have self-respect."

How did she know that? She didn't know that. As if she knew!

Hector seemed to know too. Respect. Ugh.

Courage, Saoirse, courage.

Am now looking at sunstones on ledge (from Ofelia). Looking through (they're pretty see-through) at light. Waiting for them and the light to tell me what to do. And how to get Heck to forgive me. Looking. Nothing. Dammit. The stones are pretty though. Like lemonade. Sweet and bright and happy.

Wednesday, July 24

My room, night. I looked through BookishLensGirl from start to finish, starting Sunday night. Three years of IG only and two w/BookTube and Sadie too. My entire being is in there. It's perfect. And funny. And poignant. So many books! I used to really love books. Disappearing into those worlds. I wish I still did.

But I don't. So now what?

Do I really need to tell *my* truth if I'm putting BookishLensGirl first? She is who she *is*, already. People love *her* as is—Sadie outside, me inside.

What would happen if I told them she's me too? Showed them what I look like on the outside?

Sunday, July 28

My room, night. I put on my favorite pineapple dress and flowery Blowfish sneakers. It's what I was wearing when Hector painted me. I let my curls go wild as if made of flowers and warrior-girl shields like the girls painted for me. I wore the lemon barrette too, on the side in front. And had the sunstones in the dress pocket for good luck and to illuminate and encourage my truth.

I was nervous.

I stood in front of my Polish *Blow Up* poster from the movie by Antonioni. It's old. Dad got it backpacking in Europe. Krakow. Making subversive movie posters gave the artists a voice during the Soviet era. I love the poster. It's full of dots, like when you blow up a film photo. If you look from the right angle or take a photo of it, you can see a girl's face in the dots. A beautiful woman. She's a fashion model in the movie, and some Italian detectives blow up a shot of her to solve their case. It's quite appropriate today for me. This girl has been hiding and finally shows herself. I'm this girl. At least, I don't get murdered, like in the movie. It's really good. The poster artist is Waldemar Swierzy. Maybe I should do a video about that. If I were to continue BLGirl. But I'm not.

I set up the camera. You can't see my cute sneakers but I know they're on, so cou-raj!

I turned on the camera and read what I wrote on paper. I tried to smile, but I was too nervous.

I read: *Hi. My name is Saoirse D. Berger. And I am BookishLensGirl.*

My heart raced so fast. I couldn't even look up from the page at the camera.

I've always loved reading. More than anything. This is my room. And my books. And five years ago, I started BookishLensGirl #bookstagram.

That made me laugh. I don't know why. But thank god.

My favorite book is Franny and Zooey by JD Salinger. Hence the recent repeat. I also discovered I love taking photos, hence the bookstagram appeal. I guess everyone liked what I was doing and asked me to do BookishLens on YouTube. But I don't like to show my face, as you maybe noticed, so my brilliant cousin Sadie Svensson agreed to be me.

I had to stop. Hands shaking. Cou-raj, cou-raj, imagining French JF toasting Brie. Deep breath.

Sadie's been amazing and so much more interesting than I could ever have been. But it seems I've become the Wizard of Oz, and you probably don't care, but maybe someone in real life does and it's not okay any more. The lie. That Sadie's the only beautiful Yellow Brick Road. And I'm not.

I took a quick breath and continued.

So I'm here to tell the truth. My truth. The rest of it, that is. Because I've always loved photos and books. And movies. Disappearing into magical worlds. And I hope I, we, brought that to you. I think we have.

And now, BookishLensGirl is changing. I'm not sure what she'll become. But today, she leaves you with this. Things I love that bring me joy, so you can get to know the real Saoirse D. Berger:

1. I love the word courage said with a deep French accent as taught to me by cheese-i-tarian Jean Francois. Cou-raj. It's the only thing that helps.

2. I love photos. Looking at them. Taking them. Showing things from all angles.

3. I love art and seeing people find joy in making it. Hence, I made a short doc about artists. And what inspires their POV. I'll link to it below. It's about unexpected artists and expected ones. And people I love. My mom, dad, a set designer, DP, Emilio and a good friend and street artist Hector Rojas. He's doing great stuff so follow him!

4. I love filmmaking. That's new. I hope to pursue that.

5. I love making Sadie laugh, especially on here. She's so happy and free. And I adore her and am grateful for her friendship.

6. I love hanging with my dad and playing cards and boardgames with my family.

7. I love it when my mom sits across from me in the morning with her coffee and watches me pick at my granola and asks what's happening and doesn't listen but just loves me instead.

8. I love watching movies, especially with my dad. Like Pulp Fiction and obscure movies, like old French and Italian and Czech films. Also, JoJo Rabbit and Amelie and Chocolat.

9. I love my opinionated friend Deva who tells it like it is. And River, especially when he tries to hide his true feelings but can't. He's the opposite of me and I love that he's so free.

10. I love going to my aunt and uncles' on Friday nights. They're welcoming and I always feel safe and have fun too. Plus they make delicious desserts and food.

10.5 My Aunt Lauren's raspberry cheesecake.

11. I love my life in La La Land. I know people say it's fake but it's full of people with dreams, creating magic. It's my home. And I'm terrified about leaving and going to college next year.

12. And lastly, I love annoying my brother Jake. Because I love him a lot. I love that he's wiser than he seems (he's 12) and for what he said yesterday that got me to do this.

Deep breath.

Yes, Jake made it obvious. He'd hate that I'm talking about him but he'll never see this so I guess it's okay.

It was yesterday, Saturday morning. My mom insisted my dad take us for a hike. My dad hates to hike. He's more of an inside guy and wears cowboy boots. You'll see in the video. But he took us anyway because he's a good dad, complaining all the way. At the top—we went to Temescal—we looked out at the bay, LA and saw Catalina. It was clear. I was anxious because of this lie and people being mad at me. My family knows the story. My dad asked if I was okay. I wasn't. My brother got annoyed and told me to stop complaining (even tho I didn't say anything). "If you don't like something, change it. You're free to choose what you want."

God.

So, here I am. Choosing to be me, Saoirse D. Berger, in front of the lens. Thank you for watching.

See 'ya.

I quickly turned the camera to the *Blow Up* poster bc I didn't know what else to do, and said, unscripted, "By the way, check out this cool poster. Can you see the girl's face in the dots? It's from the movie *Blow Up*. By Antonioni. Polish poster artists may be my next thing! Ciao!"

I stopped the camera. And posted it. Immediately. No editing.

Ten minutes later Jake burst in and yelled at me to take it down. I guess he does watch BookishLens.

I told him to eff off.

Monday, July 29

My room, before work, 8 a.m. I took it down. TMI. Going to work to hide.

8:30 a.m. Put it back up. C'mon Saoirse, you've gotta do this, like it or not!

Lunch, bench. Took it down.

After lunch, coffee-pot bathroom. Put it back up.

All afternoon, cutting room. Told myself repeatedly that I'm not allowed to touch it and must let the chips fall where they may. I really just want Hector to see it and forgive me.

My room, almost midnight. Sadie was standing on my doorstep when I got home. She hugged me and said, "That was very brave," with a big Sadie smile, "and why I admire and love you." My heart expanded and I felt like we'd get back to normal sooner than later.

"My mom asked if you want to get a pedicure with us after work tomorrow," she said.

I told her, "Sure. Thank you. That'd be great."

She hugged me again and said she was off to meet Andy and asked if I want to come. I didn't but it didn't bother me at all.

AUGUST

Hotchkiss Park, noonish. I told Columbia I'm not coming. Not sure about the down payment. Dad says he'll pay for the new NYU application. I told him and mom about stupid Columbia. They didn't seem to care. I'm not applying anywhere else besides NYU. If I don't get in, I'll see what to do then. Also, I signed up to finish my general ed at SMC this coming year so I'll be entering NYU as a junior film student next fall. Dad's paying for SMC, which costs less than Columbia so he's happy. What a nice, loving Dad with cowboy boots I have.

So I'm going to work and go to SMC and take film classes at UCLA Extension and maybe make some shorts.

I still have the sunstones in my pocket for good luck and keep wearing that dress.

I still am sad about Hector.

Friday, August 9

A week later, my room, 2:20 p.m. Fifty-two people unfollowed BookishLensGirl total on both IG and YouTube. One hundred twenty more followed.

Hector hasn't surfaced.

Sunstones on ledge. Beauty. Light. Lemonade. Hope. But no luck.

Wednesday, September 4

Kitchen table, 9:10 a.m. In Russia, sparrows say *chick-chirick*, and chickens say *pee pee*.

Wednesday, October 2

My car, Svenssons', 10:10 a.m. In Vilnius, ducks say *creck creck creck*, and parrots say *chick chick chick*.

Sunday, November 24

Big house table, noon. In Amsterdam, the little bird says *tjiep tjiep*, while in Istanbul, it's *jick-jick*. In Athens, *tsiou tsiou*.

Tuesday, December 24

Living room, fireplace, 5:40 p.m. A partridge in a pear tree in Paris says *cui cui*, and the rooster says *cocorico*.

Monday, January 27

My room, night. It's almost birthday 19. I haven't written in a long time. I've been recovering from year 18.

Things have gotten different. Sort of. I got early acceptance to NYU and will be going in fall.

I've been helping Mom and Aunt Lauren with marketing—Mom's cheese business, which is a cheese box so far and hoping to be a shop soon, and Aunt Lauren's street art nonprofit. I built websites for both and am doing all their social media, like making really cool videos. Me and mom even went to France for a cheese thing and I filmed her. Cou-raj! We saw River and Hot Steve too!

I don't like doing the writing but I like the photos and filming.

Also, I did a three-week ultra-indie camera assistant job (no pay). I loved it! Jena hooked me up. Amazing! The DP says he'll call me again! (Jena's dating Horserace Rob, who she met at the actual horseraces! When she went w/Assistant Dave.)

Aunt Lauren is taking credit for me going to film school, but I just let her think it's so. Sadie tells AL it's not her doing, and I tell Sadie to just leave it.

Sadie's at Sarah Lawrence but is taking next semester off because she's in a movie filming in Canada. Her other movie did amazing and she's nominated for a Spirit Award for best actress! Leo's going. He's back with exec Lorraine because it didn't last with Isla. I didn't talk to him for months till I texted him about NYU and he texted back: *Good work, Bookish.* It made me feel good.

Then he texted last week that he was going to be near the studio and asked if I wanted to have lunch. I told him I wasn't there any more. Duh. I'm on the Westside. He told me to come to lunch at Fox: *What are you waiting for?*

So we had lunch. On the lot. It was Friday so I had the seaweed salad, my favorite. We are def. just friends. We both seem to agree on that. He said a few things of note when my life came up and I admitted I still like Hector and wish he'd forgive me.

Main takeaways:

1. Leo and I are friends and that's awesome. For both of us. And real.
2. Leo says a relationship is two people, like with Heck. "You can tell him how you feel, which you should, but you can't control what he does with it."
3. He thinks I'm very yang, like yin-yang, but masquerade as yin (like w/him). He thinks I should take my time more and let things unfold before I react. Let good things happen instead of assuming they won't. "Do your best and know you can't control the outcomes. In everything. Life. Relationships." He thinks he's more yin even though he seems more yang on the outside. Like having a Tao rising sign I guess.
4. LeoSheeran thinks if I want to know how to make it better with Hector, I should ask him. I haven't.
5. At least me and Leo are friends. At least I was right about that.

I wore my pineapple dress with the sunstones in the pocket. They make me feel good. Luckily no one notices me still bc I keep wearing the same dress repeatedly. With stones. It's weird, but I don't care.

Unc Unc's movie came out and did fair. Now he's making his movie with J Boone and AL's making hers with Taylor Rae.

Dad's still wearing cowboy boots and Jake probably hasn't talked to me since he burst into my room and told me to take down the BLGirl video that mentions his awesomeness. I still occasionally tamper with his gaming station when he's not looking, just to bug him, and deal with Mom's after-wrath.

Hector hasn't surfaced and I don't feel better in any way about being honest on BLGirl. I know I did the right thing but I still miss him and his stupid questions of the day and just being around him and how silly and nice he is and how he always makes me feel better about myself and happy and like I want to do stuff and everything will be okay.

Why does he make me feel that way and no one else does? I don't know.

Why am I holding my breath, waiting for him to come back around? Paralyzed.

I stalk him on IG. He's at Lewis & Clark. He seems to love it. He's in a band. He plays drums. But they also do this DJ-electro thing where they mix music and play too. He and Frank (who still lives here) make cool vids and give shout outs to street artists in L.A. and Portland now too. He wants to do this for artists in other countries, like go there and film them. It's v. cool. Tons of people follow them.

Also, he does small editing jobs for money. And hangs out at various McMenamins'. I can't tell if he's doing art there but it looks cool. He says they have the best fries ever at Kennedy School (restaurant in renovated school). All McMs are in old renovated cool places.

I can see which dorm he's in from his photos and MacGyvering it on the school website.

WHY WON'T HE FORGIVE ME?????? I MISS HIM SO MUCH.

Part of me just wants to go up there and yell at him and tell him he should've known Sadie was me. It's his fault. The other part knows that trying to make things happen hasn't really worked out for me, especially when the doors don't open. I mean, at some point you kind of think you should try another door.

Doing nothing. Out of self-respect.

Looking at closed door with eyes open.

Not going up there.

Wednesday, January 29

My room, bright and early, 7 a.m. Looking at stones on window ledge again before they go in pocket. Light shining through. Beautiful lemonade kaleidoscope of joy. Still waiting to see shimmer of truth and direct instructions on how to be more me for year 19. Or how to breathe without Heck around.

All I see are shimmers of beauty. It's kind of peaceful though and makes me happy. I feel good about that. Like I'm not floating away but immersed in lemonade light and powered up by it.

Wish it would last all day. Sunstones back in pocket.

Friday, January 31

Under covers, wee hours of early morn, just before 2 a.m. Can't sleep. Lying here. Reminds me of lying in car in Joshua Tree. Except now holding breath. Wasn't holding breath then. Why can't I let go?!!! EXHALE!

Imagining Phantom of Opera inside head, running around, back and forth like AL on landing strip. Poor Phantom, afraid he'll lose love. Too ugly. Not worthy. Not lucky. Even with lucky sunstones, he is me with Sadie mask. Scaredy-cat running back and forth. Doing everything for love. But invisible. He's also on the friggin' landing strip so love can't land! I can see it's his fault. Jake wouldn't approve Phantom choosing stupid mask so no one can see his truth. Also, Phantom's in the friggin' way.

Now, imagining me as me inside head taking mask off Phantom. There he is. Scaredy-cat. But also loving. Without mask, can see sweet heart in Phantom. Love makes ugly beautiful. Beauty no longer hidden by fear. Brave.

Exhaling.

But also insane.

Must sleep.

And get grip on self.

Do not in any way convince yourself to do anything more to get Heck back. You've done it all. He does not want you, and you must stand to the side of the landing strip like a normal person now.

You must be brave.

You must stop clenching your toes.

You must inhale and exhale.

Go inside the little airport thing and get an ice cream or something!

My room, eve before birthday 19. Today I flew to Portland, rented a car and drove to Lewis & Clark.

After shining light on my stupid fear this morning again, like a sunstone in my mind illuminating the hiding Phantom, the ugly turned beautiful like a superhero and I became free to choose love. Which was beyond idiotic. But it happened and I got it in my head that I was going to stand outside his window, Hector's I mean, and say what I had to say. Do what Jake said—*Do what I want, not what I don't.* And like Leo said—*Tell him what I need.*

I got there early. I threw a tennis ball at the dorm window. His roommate looked out. I asked if Hector was there. He said, "No." I said, "Okay, thank you," and left. I waited by one of the entrances. While I waited, I thought about how Heck probably already has a girlfriend, because why wouldn't he, he's amazing. But I decided I just had to do this anyway. If I wanted my life to start (again), I had to make choices and take actions to get it to start (again), and saying my peace with Hector was key. Plus, I owed it to myself. I was going to tell him how bad it felt when he didn't know Sadie was me. I was me!

I was going to shine light on all my scaredy-cat fears and exude truth!

The roommate passed twice as I stood by the side door. I asked if he thought Hector used this door. He said he didn't know. I was embarrassed but kept standing there.

Finally, a little after 11:00 a.m., Hector showed up. He didn't notice me at all, and just before he went in, I said, "Hi."

He stopped. Shocked. "What the heck are you doing here?"

I froze.

I unfroze.

"I wanted to say a few things. In person. Face to face."

"And you came all the way up here?"

"Yes."

"Okay."

We stared.

Me: "I."

Oh god.

Me: "I really like you."

He stared more. It felt immense. My palms started to sweat.

I wanted him to say he liked me back. But he didn't.

He kept staring.

Me: "And, um."

I felt stupid. I panicked.

Me: "I'm sorry. None of what happened is okay. But I couldn't help it. I'm. Majorly flawed. I just. Wanted to talk to you. Then. On the phone. And whenever. All the time. After. Like when we hung out."

He stared still. Luckily, I didn't say anything about the Phantom. Even though I thought it. That would've been too weird, even though he brought it up in the first place.

Me: "It made me happy. When we hung out."

Still staring.

Me: "Say something. Please."

He didn't.

I felt tears coming.

Then he said, "It was a long time ago," like he didn't care and was over it.

That made it worse. My heart raced. My face flushed. I couldn't stand it. All I could feel was stupid for still caring and hating myself and him hating me for all this. I panicked again.

"Thank you," I said. And bowed. OMG, I bowed. What an idiot.

Then, I bolted. I don't even know how he reacted to the stupid bow.

Then, I stopped. It couldn't end this way. I was just there being an honest loving elk. With a broken elk heart. Like if my antlers could droop, they would. And I had to get it out. My elk truth.

I turned back. He was still there. Probably because it had only been seconds in reality, not years like in my elk head. Me: "I. You..."

Stupid elk tears and stammering. "You were my friend."

I sounded desperate. I could barely look at him. I was desperate. I had to get it out.

Me: "And then you liked Sadie. More. And you didn't even know it was me. How could you not know it was me?"

He exhale-half-laughed and shook his head, like he couldn't believe I was saying this.

I drooped.

Him: "Because there was no way to know! How could I *not* not know?" He was incredulous.

And he was right.

My heart raced. I nodded and eked out, "You're right." Nodded again. Panicked. "I'm sorry. I understand. It's a hard thing to forgive." Still nodding like a nervous fool. "Thank you for listening." Bowed again. Idiot. And turned to elk-gallop out of there again.

"You understand?!" he yelled after me.

I stopped.

Him, incredulous: "You came all the way up here and you understand and are okay if I just, like, let it go?!"

I stared.

Him, more incredulous: "I mean, am I even here to you? With you? At my dorm? Do you even care how I feel? Me? Aw Heck? Was that even real?"

Oh crap. I didn't know what to say. Was it real? Did I think it was real? Yes, now I do.

Him: "Yeah! Not cool. And I mean, I want to forgive you, Saoirse, but, like, what's going on?"

I didn't know what to say to that either. I didn't know how to do this.

Him: "Why didn't you just tell me the truth?"

Panic. What was the truth? What? What? Because of Sadie. Because...

I just said it: "Because you would have hated me." Tears. I tried to ignore them. "And I didn't want you to." Tears came out anyway. "Right?"

He looked at me crying. Pathetic.

Him: "Actually, no. Probably not. I probably would've still liked you. And maybe even thought it was funny."

I didn't know what to do with that information. All I could think was how I really blew it. My heart raced. I felt awful.

"I really messed up," I said, barely audibly. Maybe out loud. Maybe not. But probably.

"I really liked you, Saoirse. BookishLensGirl."

He stared, like it was over. *Liked.* In the past.

My elk heart drooped.

And I couldn't hold the tears back. I nodded. "Thank you. Thank you for listening. Maybe someday you'll give me another chance. Bye." One last bow. And: "Tomorrow's my birthday." I nodded. No idea why I said that. I faked a happy-elk smile. "Thank you."

And left.

Idiot.

I went downtown before my flight to shoot art. But I couldn't. I was too sad.

He texted: *Why do you keep running? Right when I said I liked you. Do you even want me to like you?*

I didn't answer. I didn't have the answer. I still don't. I think I'm still afraid he'll see how awful I am. How big my nose is. All the mistakes I make all the time. How afraid I am that I won't be enough. Or that he won't love me. Or that I'll lose him anyway for no reason at all.

So, yeah. Now, it's really over.

Just when it started. The night before 19.

Hoorays for 19? Maybe just: Elk be.

Saturday, February 1

19th birthday, morning, 7:30 a.m. Just woke up. In bed. Fantasy: Weird taps on windowpane wake me up. I go to window. Open it. Glimpse someone running, turning corner. Across yard in neighbor window, I see Mrs. Patterson staring at me in shock. I look and see entire side of garage room covered in paint. Oh, wow!

I run out. It says: *HAPPY BIRTHDAY, SAOIRSE D. BERGER*, in giant gorgeous letters. In corner: *SDB, I love you just the way you are. Love, Aw Heck*

I round corner. Hector smiles mischievously. I blush and, without thinking, throw my arms round his neck and kiss him. On the lips. He kisses me back.

My life begins.

I'm 19. And full of courage.

Like a smoking-hot, gorgeous-on-the-inside-and-out grownup elk, strolling through the urban woods of La La Land with no Phantom mask and birthday graffiti on the outside of my backyard garage-room wall from a super-hot elk that I love inside and out too.

Courage!

Ugh.

Because then what? If that happened IRL, what happens after the big storybook ending? I'd be dirt. Like now. He already made me a cool graffiti piece. And I fell apart, like I can't just have a normal relationship.

DadSheeran texted: *Happy Birthday! Breakfast is waiting!*

Me: *TY! There in 10!*

I have to let go. Exhale. Embrace my yin. Eat ice cream in the airport instead of on the field. Let things come to me and stop trying so hard.

Later, just now, after breakfast. Hector texted: *Happy Birthday,*

Saoirse!

Then: *What's your take on looking people in the eye? Do you think you could look me in the eye for a minute straight?*

What?! What the heck did that mean? Super weird. Also, he rarely sends a new question before I answer a previous one, like yesterday.

Me: *TY!*

Then: *What's my take on looking people in the eye? It's hard! It shows your truth. What's in your heart.*

Then me again: *A minute straight? IDK. That's a tall order. You mean without bolting? lol I hope so. You?*

OMG haha.

He replied: *Looking someone in the eye elicits a kaleidoscope of feelings emanating from your heart down to your fingertips and back, but it's like they're dancing with the feelings of the other person.*

Weirdo.

Then: *Yes, one minute. If you let me.*

Okay, then. Now what? Does he want to FaceTime?

Waiting.

Nothing.

Taking a nap or reading or something. Not thinking about this!

My room, birthday 19, night. Maybe it is possible for this elk to just elk be. And for good things to happen to me. Maybe this elk is enough. And worthy of love. Maybe this elk just had to sit still for a moment. And take an elk nap. Though not standing, as I assume actual elks actually sleep standing. Do they?

Here's what happened today:

I was taking a nap to make myself stop thinking and embrace yin.

There was a bang. And a "Damn." And a bark. It was almost two hours after the texting. In reality time.

I looked outside the window.

There was a tire and hot pink flowers everywhere. Carnations.

And Clyde.

Also, there was Hector walking towards the tire in his fancy green shirt and desert boots. This was important.

He set the tire on its side. Stuffed the flowers back in and got ready to roll. He saw me in the window. Waved. I opened the door.

Him: "That didn't really work as planned. Let's try it again." He rolled the tire full of flowers at the bottom stair, Clyde barking after it. It hit and flopped over, flowers spilling out again. Clyde nosing them. "Better," he said.

OMG.

We looked at each other. Awkward. I wondered if he was real. He was. I walked down to the stairs. He came over. Put hands in pocket. Almost shy. Weird for him. "Happy birthday."

"Thanks."

We stared.

It made me nervous.

I laughed and had to look away. Covered my face. He stepped closer. Like right in front of me. "Okay, shall we try?"

I laughed again. "What?" Nervous. Butterflies. I knew exactly what he meant. "Uh..."

"Okay." He set the timer on his phone. "Ready?"

I laughed at him. "Really?"

"Yeah. Ready, set, go."

I stepped up on the bottom stair so our eyes could meet. His were dark, intense, happy. A kaleidoscope of feelings exploded in my heart, his feelings in my heart. They danced. Just like he said they would. For a second. But then all I could see was him seeing me. I got nervous. Was he looking at my nose? Did it look giant? Did I have food on my face? I couldn't breathe. I panicked. Because worse than the big nose and possible gook on face was that he could tell I cared. My heart naked and vulnerable. I shook my head. Had to look away.

Nervous laugh.

Time: 17 seconds.

Him: "That's okay. Let's try again."

Perhaps impossible. But funny. "Okay."

We tried again. This time: overwhelm. His eyes. My embarrassment. Tears threatening.

Time: 5 seconds.

I exhaled. Shook my head. Tears pressing. Embarrassed to be seen.

Him: "Dude, stop. This is supposed to be fun!"

He tried to get me to look at him. Playful. Funny. A game. I laughed. Finally. Looked at him again. Tears retreating. He stared with bug-out eyes. Laughs.

Him: "Okay, good. Now again." He got into stare position. "Ready?"

Both of us stared with bug-out eyes. Both laughed. Both broke stare.

Him: "Excellent. Now..." He looked at me again. Happy eyes, smiling. I softened. He makes me so happy. I looked at him without trying. Kind, happy person. He relaxed too. Long lashes. Unsinged. Slightly smiling lips.

Phantom fears dissolved. Two hearts choosing love.

Which is when he took my face in his hands—KISMET!—right when I was elk-being all that. "Let's try this." He held my face, warm hands. Him right there in front of me. Me laughing. Heart pounding. Clyde barking.

Now kissing. Real. Magic. All at once. It lasted probably...who knows. Now is now.

Wow.

We stopped and he was right there still, looking. Gentle, kind eyes. Our noses almost touching because mine is so big. I moved and it bumped his. He laughed. Thank god. And said: "That works too. At least a minute right there. Or not, but better."

Sunshine eyes. My friend has sunshine eyes. And he's hilarious.

I turned red. And deflected: "So, um, tire?"

"Yeah, Frank helped me procure that."

"Sweet."

And then he got slightly nervous and asked if I was free today. At all. "Like, between birthday stuff? Or like, with you with other birthday stuff? That you may have already planned?"

Cute.

And I told him yes. "But, are you, like...here? Today?" Bc what the hell was he doing here?

He nodded. More embarrassment. And admitted his mom called him yesterday randomly and figured out something was up when he told her I appeared out of nowhere at his dorm then ran away. He said he had no clue what to do or what it meant, "like does she like me? Or not? And what does she want?"

And then he told me she got a ticket till tomorrow. And he made fun of himself for that. And telling his mom. So cute!

And I told him I like his mom. And he told me what she said: That I probably do like him and he should just come down here. And that perfection doesn't make a relationship. Mistakes do. And anyway, it's really just about if you like each other and want to hang out. Because if not, mistakes do matter. And the stupid stuff bugs you. Like how the person chews. Or their favorite music. But if you like each other, it's all based.

Then she told him to come down and see. Which is why he's here. He thinks she also bought the ticket because she wants to see him and we should probably go by and say hi.

So we did.

Then we came back here and went bowling at Bowlmor with my parents and his mom and Mr. Griffin and Sadie and Nick and AL and UP and Deva and Gus too. (River's in Europe w/Hot Steve still!).

Aunt Lauren made my favorite cheesecake and Mom did a cheese bonanza.

We played Pictionary, which was super fun!

And now, Aw Heck is sleeping on my couch in my room. Clyde in the orange beanbag. And I'm writing to you, dear Diary.

It was nice. Today. And perfect. Even with some mistakes.

Like how when we came back here and kissed again, my stupid nose bumped his again and I felt embarrassed. But then, he said, "Cute nose."

Cute.

I have a cute nose. And a cute boyfriend. With cute elk kisses.

Also, elk do not sleep standing up. Also, female elk don't have antlers. Also, male elk (bulls) have a harem of cows. Which is maybe why elk popped into my head randomly. Me and Sadie were the cows in Heck's harem. That's weird. But it does explain why I'd randomly think of elks. Elk. Also, though, elk remind me of when we went to Yellowstone—me, Mom, Dad, Mr. Griffin—and saw elk. It was nice. Happy family. And fun. Therefore, elk make me feel happy. And that's probably the real reason for elk randomly popping into my head.

Or maybe my mind is a bull with a harem of way too many thought cows!

Weirdo.

Heck snoring. V. cute. I guess I must really like him.

Love him.

Love.

ACKNOWLEDGEMENTS

Many, many thanks to:

The fabulous Noelle English, my friend and editor, whose encouragement and brilliant insight kept me on course to bring the detail of Saoirse's world and the joy of her voice to each page.

The friends and *Yes And-ers* who threw cheerleading lightning bolts that got me to write another book: Ami Clover, Elaine Chu, Toni Eyeler, Kate Mazur, Seth Nagel, Kathrin Nolan, Ginna Moran, Julie Rogers, Jenny Shutak, Tina Woods and the Areté Book Club, in no particular lightning-bolt order.

Illustrator Sandy Wu Nguyen for her beautiful work on the cover illustration and for being such a joy and inspiration. I first saw her gorgeous street art on Main Street in Santa Monica. It's wonderful. Check it out if you get a chance!

Everyone at Earnest Parc Press, especially Jacqui Worthing, for believing in me and this story and taking a chance on it. Also, the awesome creative team.

LHMS for patience while I was glued to my laptop and my mom, Elli, for her kind heart and believing in me always.

And last but not least, all my fabulous movie families and dear filmmaking friends. You inspired this world with all the blood, sweat, tears, joy and humor we experienced during those endlessly long days crammed together in little dark cutting rooms…it was mostly joy and humor! Some wonderful films were also made in the process. You're gems of light and inspiration!

Nicole Schubert is an award-winning author and screenwriter with a soft spot for comedy and romance. Her debut novel, *Blues Harp Green*, delved into coming-of-age and family issues as well and received Independent Publisher and Readers' Favorite Award nods. Nicole dabbles in other behind-the-scenes activities, like producing *Improv Diary Show* at Santa Monica's Westside Comedy Theater. She produced a music awards TV show and European-wide photo exhibition out of Brussels and enjoyed another side of storytelling working in the editing rooms of numerous Hollywood feature films. Nicole lives with her family—including The Kid—in Los Angeles, by way of Brussels and New Orleans, where she was born during a hurricane. Visit her at **nicoleschubertwrites.com**.

Made in the USA
Las Vegas, NV
29 March 2021